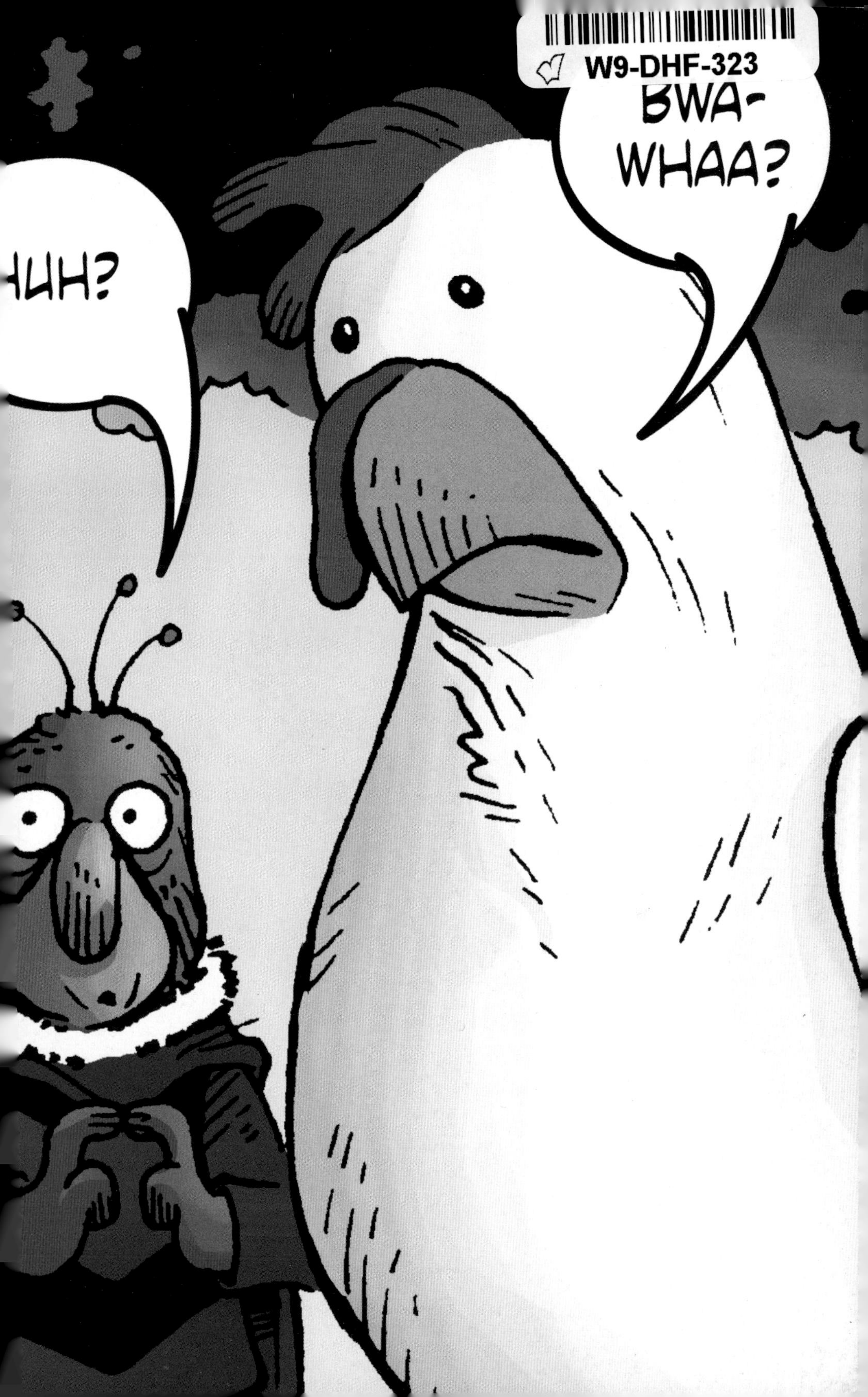
HUH?
BWA-
WHAA?

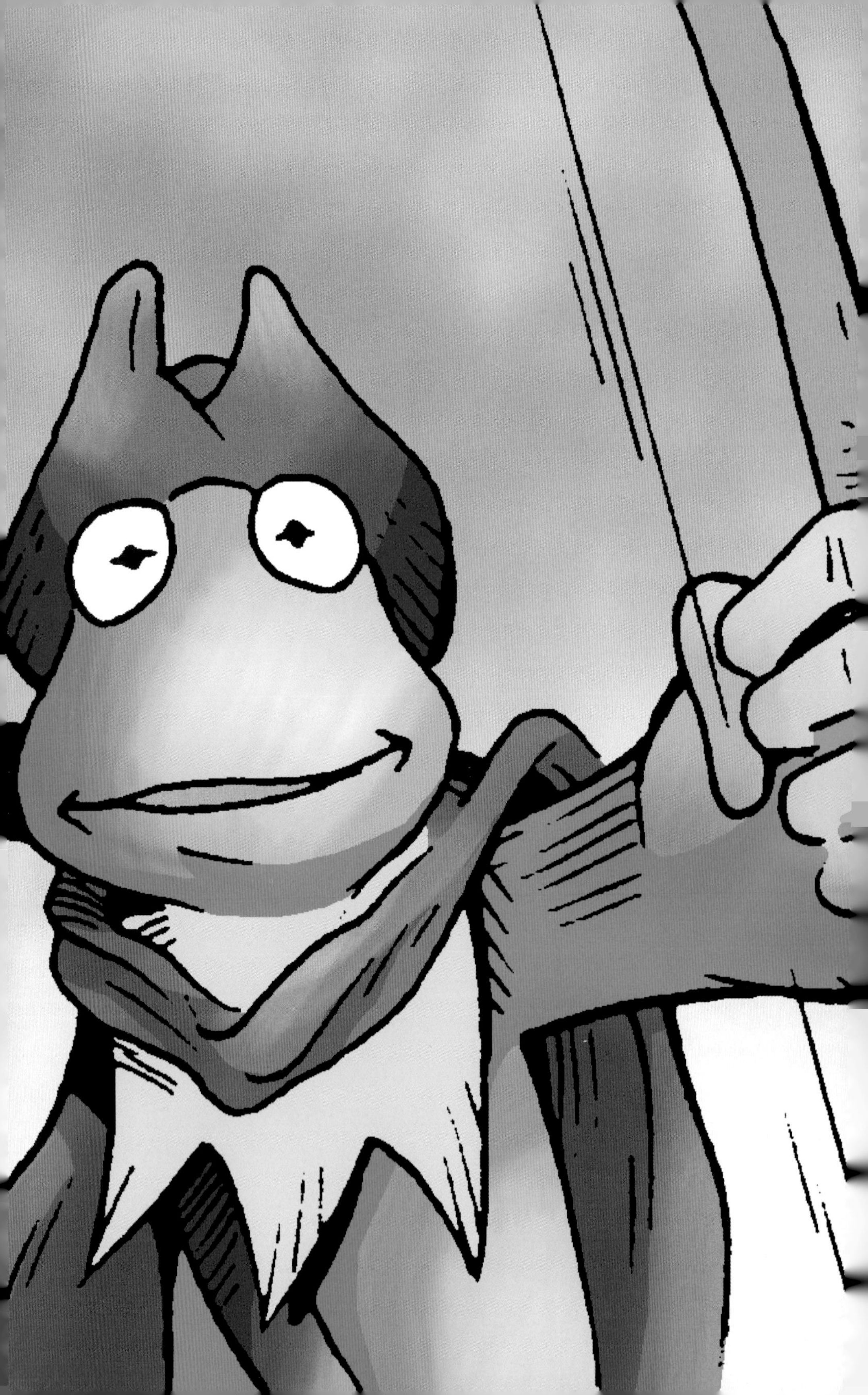

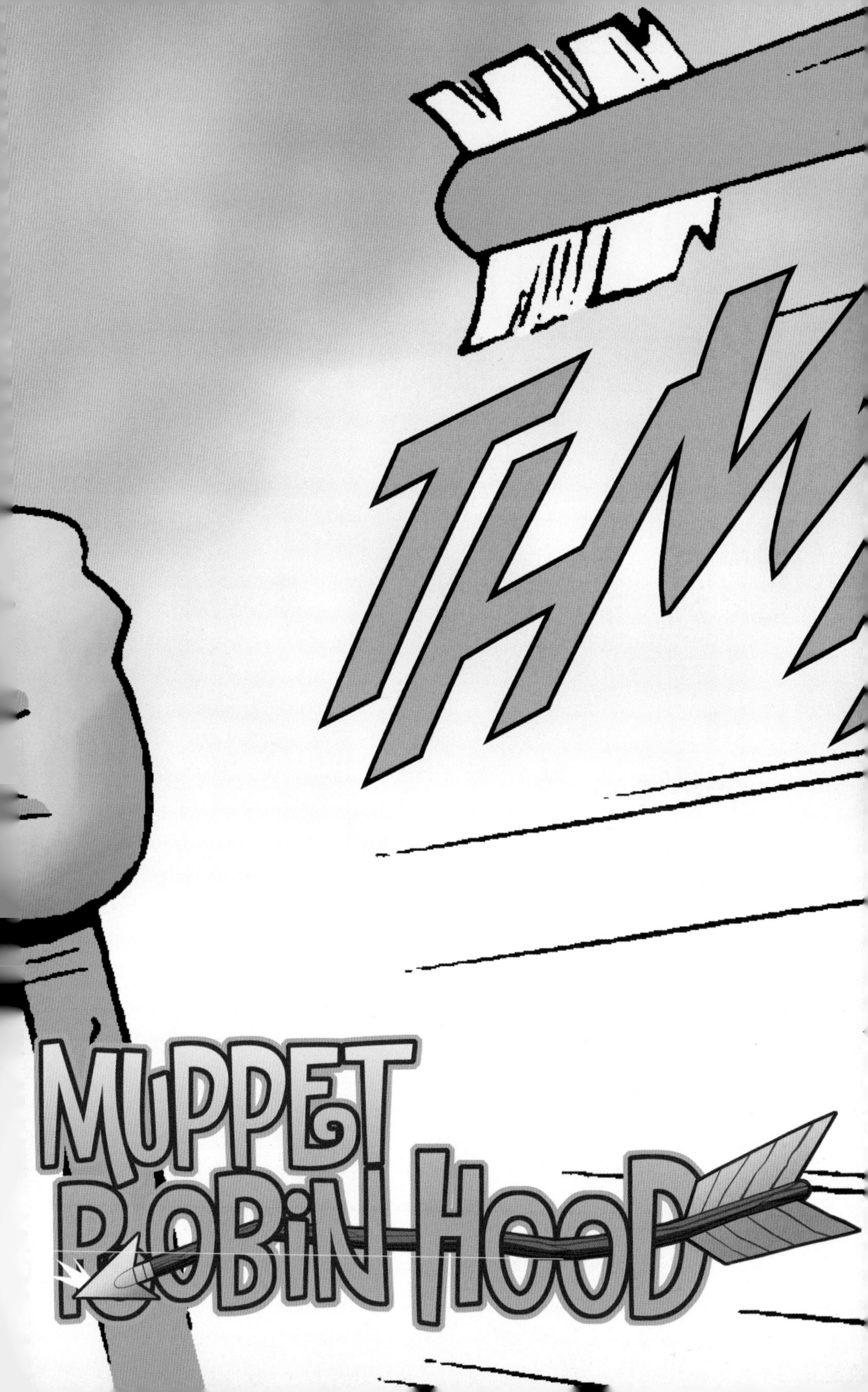
MUPPET
ROBIN HOOD

MUPPET ROBIN HOOD

ROSS RICHIE
chief executive officer

ANDREW COSBY
chief creative officer

MARK WAID
editor-in-chief

ADAM FORTIER
vice president, publishing

CHIP MOSHER
marketing director

MATT GAGNON
managing editor

FIRST EDITION: JULY 2009

10 9 8 7 6 5 4 3 2 1
"PRINTED BY WORLD COLOR PRESS, INC., ST-ROMUALD, QC., CANADA.

Office of publication: 6310 San Vicente Blvd Ste 404, Los Angeles, CA 90048.

Written by
Tim Beedle

Art by
Armand Villavert, Jr.

Colors
Mara Aum
Issues 1-2
Kat Valliant
Issues 3-4

Letters
Marshall Dillon

Editors
Paul Morrissey
& Aaron Sparrow

Cover
David Petersen

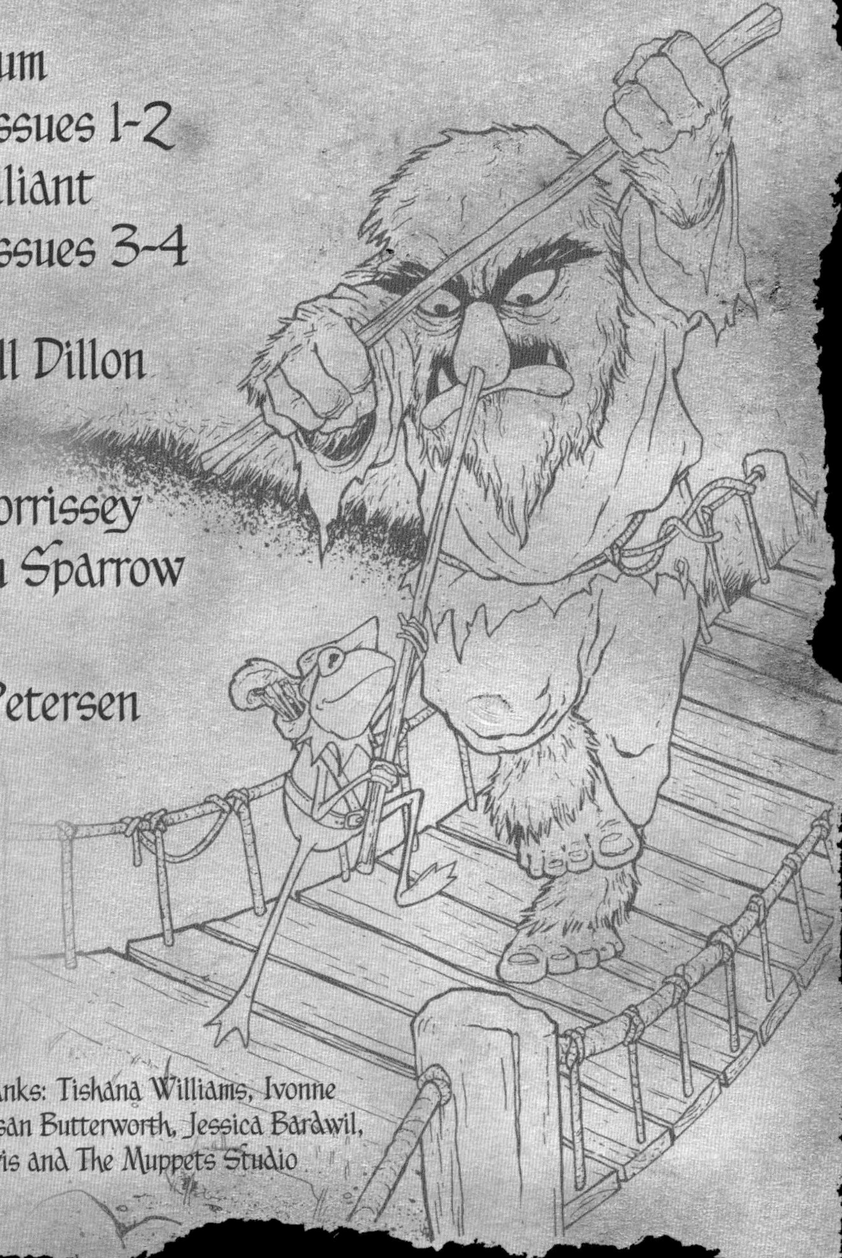

Special thanks: Tishana Williams, Ivonne Feliciano, Susan Butterworth, Jessica Bardwil, Jim Lewis and The Muppets Studio

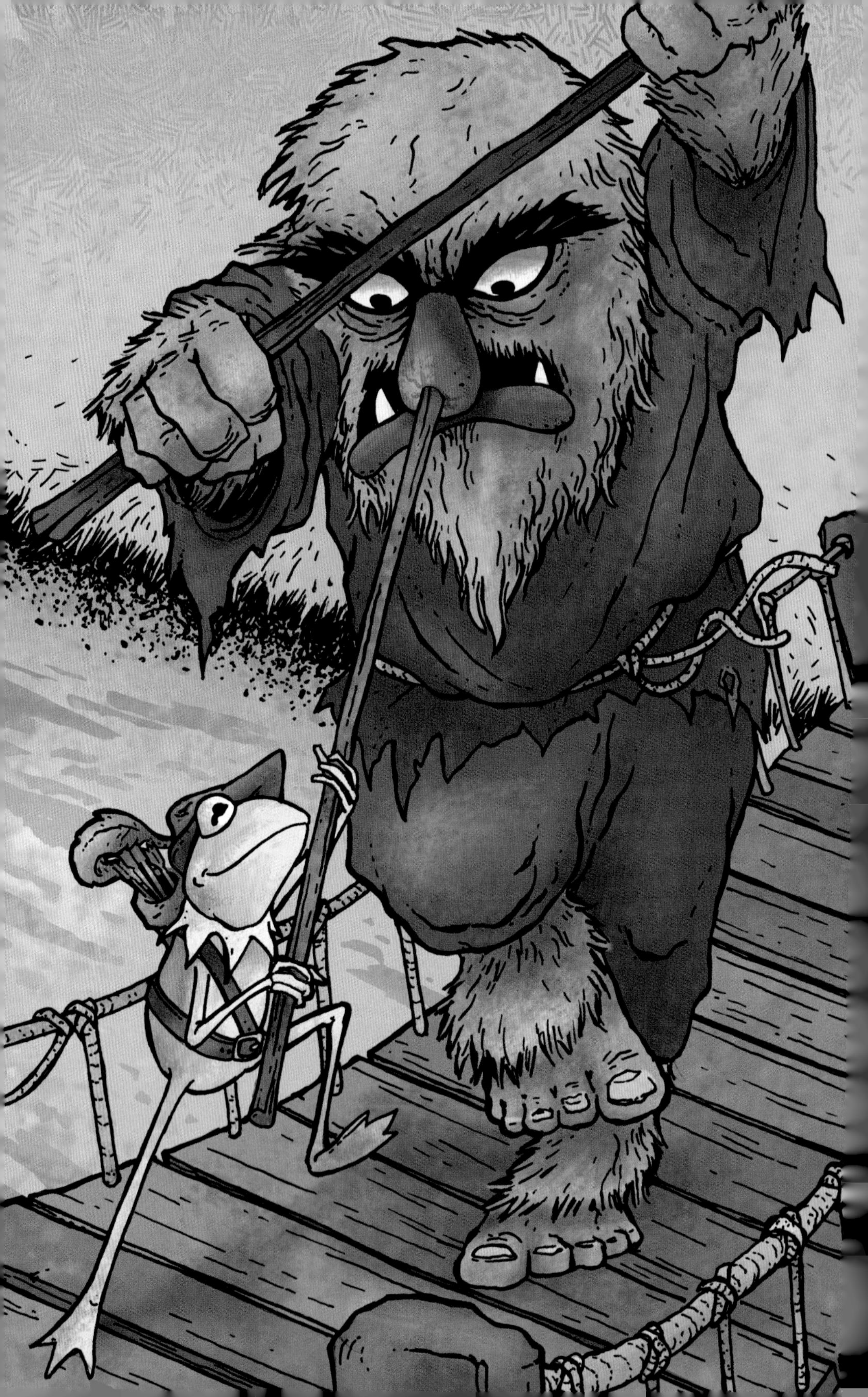

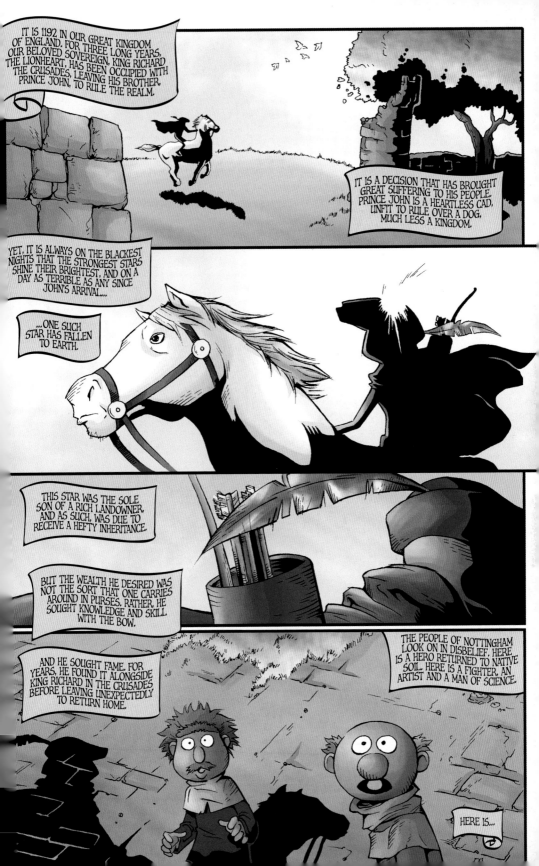

IT IS 1192 IN OUR GREAT KINGDOM OF ENGLAND. FOR THREE LONG YEARS, THE LIONHEART, OUR BELOVED SOVEREIGN, KING RICHARD THE CRUSADES, LEAVING HIS BROTHER, PRINCE JOHN, TO RULE THE REALM.

IT IS A DECISION THAT HAS BROUGHT GREAT SUFFERING TO HIS PEOPLE. PRINCE JOHN IS A HEARTLESS CAD, UNFIT TO RULE OVER A DOG, MUCH LESS A KINGDOM.

YET, IT IS ALWAYS ON THE BLACKEST NIGHTS THAT THE STRONGEST STARS SHINE THEIR BRIGHTEST, AND ON A DAY AS TERRIBLE AS ANY SINCE JOHN'S ARRIVAL...

...ONE SUCH STAR HAS FALLEN TO EARTH.

THIS STAR WAS THE SOLE SON OF A RICH LANDOWNER, AND AS SUCH, WAS DUE TO RECEIVE A HEFTY INHERITANCE.

BUT THE WEALTH HE DESIRED WAS NOT THE SORT THAT ONE CARRIES AROUND IN PURSES. RATHER, HE SOUGHT KNOWLEDGE AND SKILL WITH THE BOW.

AND HE SOUGHT FAME. FOR YEARS, HE FOUND IT ALONGSIDE KING RICHARD IN THE CRUSADES BEFORE LEAVING UNEXPECTEDLY TO RETURN HOME.

THE PEOPLE OF NOTTINGHAM LOOK ON IN DISBELIEF. HERE IS A HERO RETURNED TO NATIVE SOIL. HERE IS A FIGHTER, AN ARTIST AND A MAN OF SCIENCE.

HERE IS...

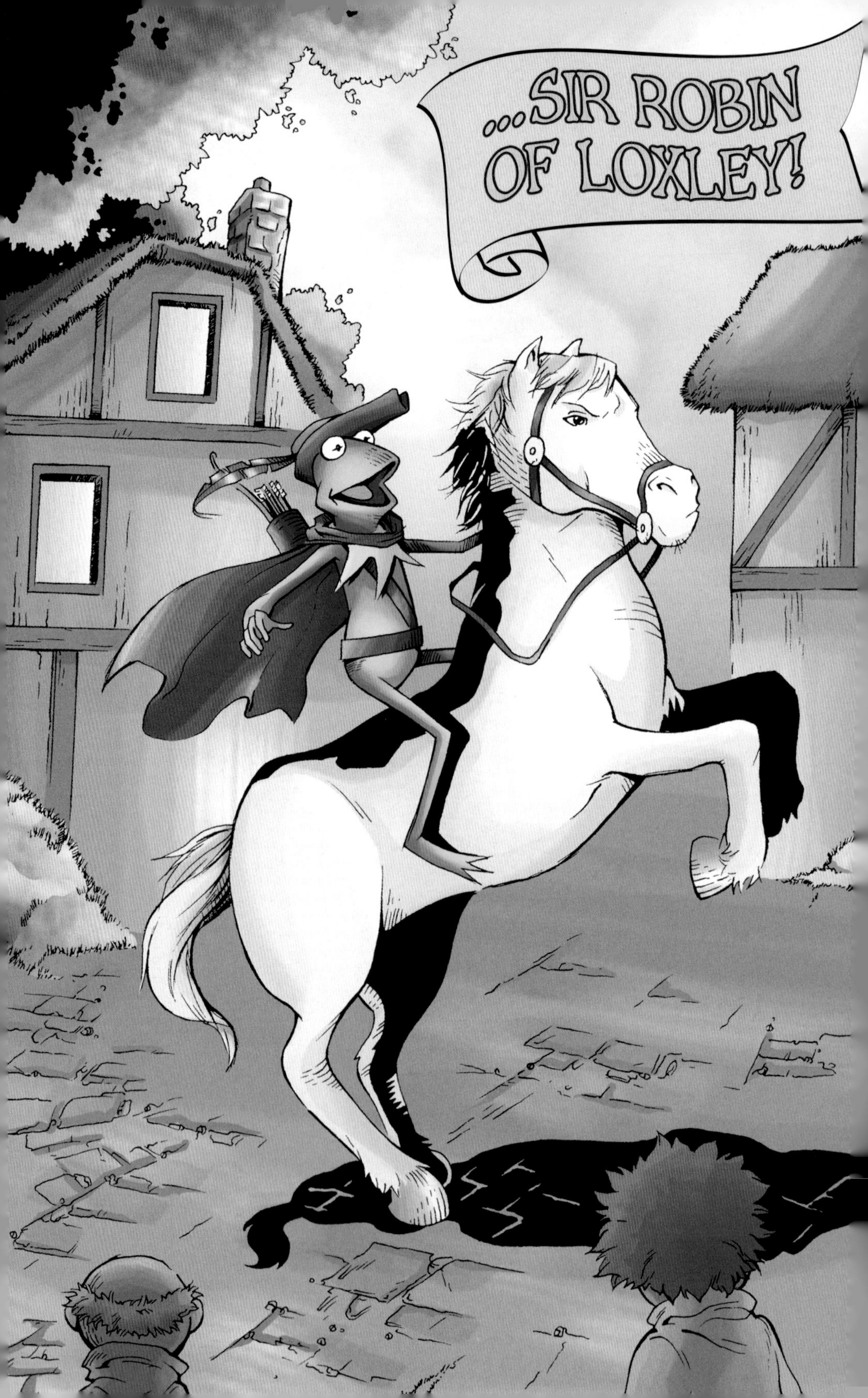
...SIR ROBIN OF LOXLEY!

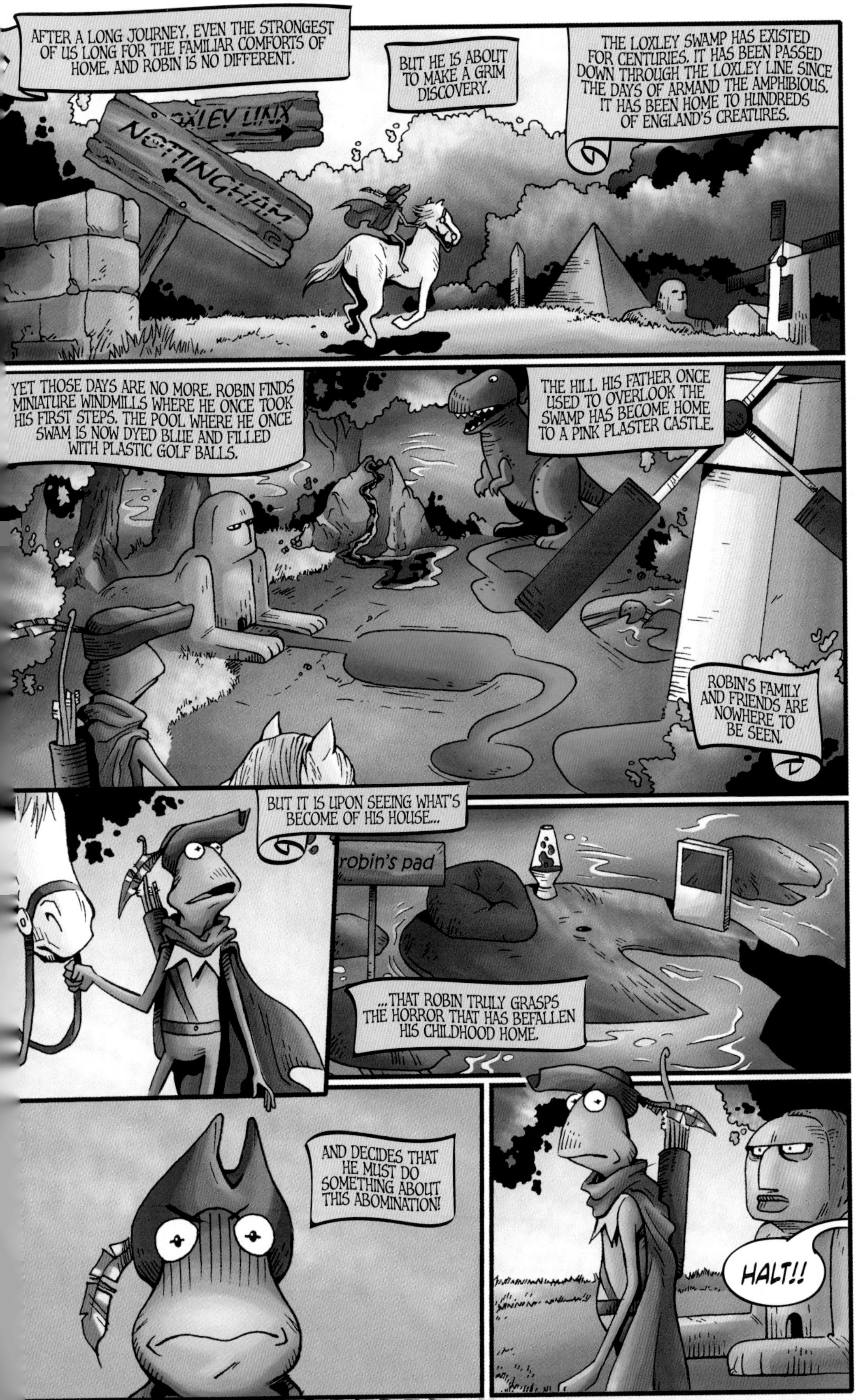

AFTER A LONG JOURNEY, EVEN THE STRONGEST OF US LONG FOR THE FAMILIAR COMFORTS OF HOME, AND ROBIN IS NO DIFFERENT.
BUT HE IS ABOUT TO MAKE A GRIM DISCOVERY.
THE LOXLEY SWAMP HAS EXISTED FOR CENTURIES. IT HAS BEEN PASSED DOWN THROUGH THE LOXLEY LINE SINCE THE DAYS OF ARMAND THE AMPHIBIOUS. IT HAS BEEN HOME TO HUNDREDS OF ENGLAND'S CREATURES.
NOTTINGHAM
YET THOSE DAYS ARE NO MORE. ROBIN FINDS MINIATURE WINDMILLS WHERE HE ONCE TOOK HIS FIRST STEPS. THE POOL WHERE HE ONCE SWAM IS NOW DYED BLUE AND FILLED WITH PLASTIC GOLF BALLS.
THE HILL HIS FATHER ONCE USED TO OVERLOOK THE SWAMP HAS BECOME HOME TO A PINK PLASTER CASTLE.
ROBIN'S FAMILY AND FRIENDS ARE NOWHERE TO BE SEEN.
BUT IT IS UPON SEEING WHAT'S BECOME OF HIS HOUSE...
robin's pad
...THAT ROBIN TRULY GRASPS THE HORROR THAT HAS BEFALLEN HIS CHILDHOOD HOME.
AND DECIDES THAT HE MUST DO SOMETHING ABOUT THIS ABOMINATION!
HALT!!

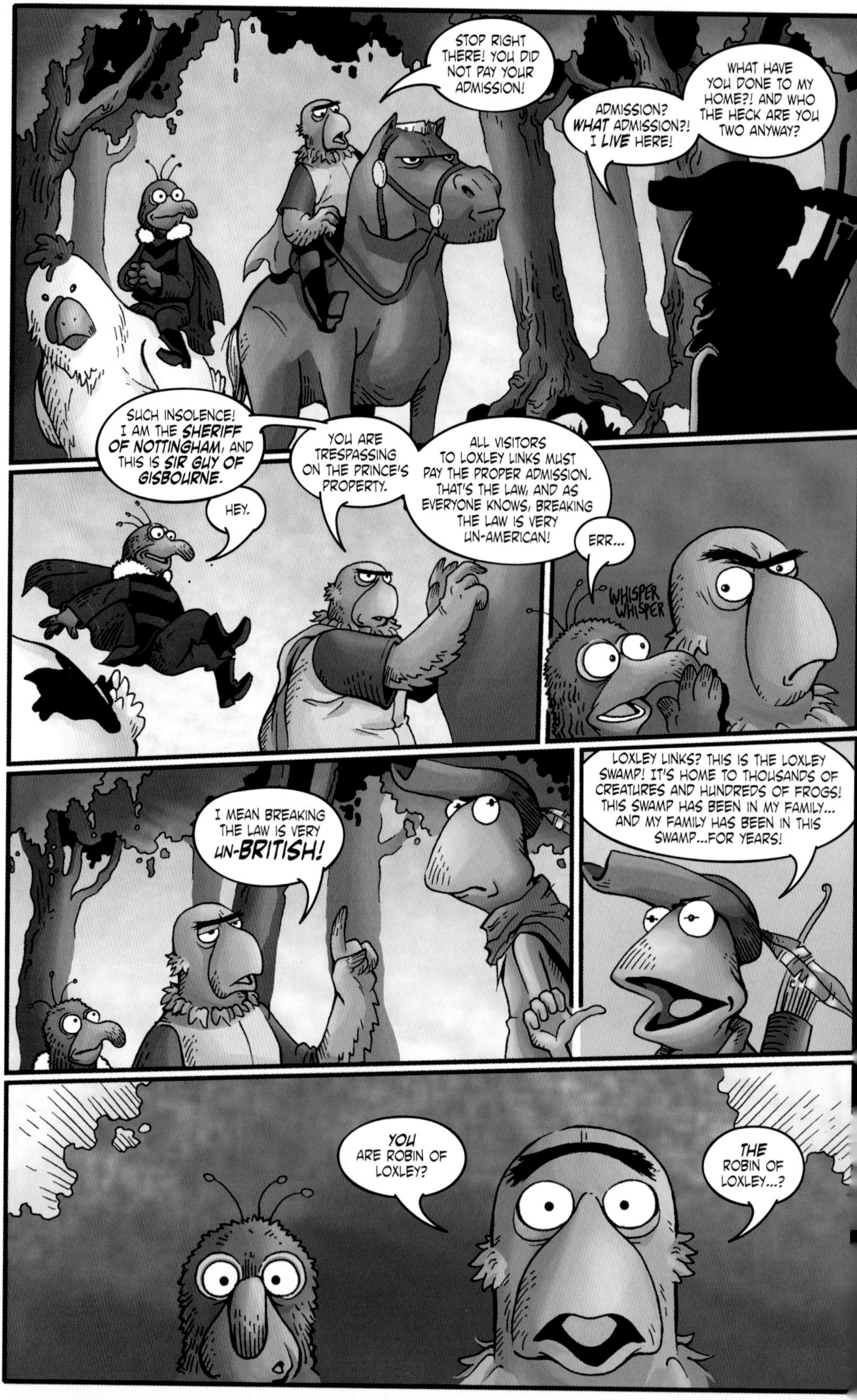
STOP RIGHT THERE! YOU DID NOT PAY YOUR ADMISSION!
ADMISSION? WHAT ADMISSION?! I LIVE HERE!
WHAT HAVE YOU DONE TO MY HOME?! AND WHO THE HECK ARE YOU TWO ANYWAY?
SUCH INSOLENCE! I AM THE SHERIFF OF NOTTINGHAM, AND THIS IS SIR GUY OF GISBOURNE.
HEY.
YOU ARE TRESPASSING ON THE PRINCE'S PROPERTY.
ALL VISITORS TO LOXLEY LINKS MUST PAY THE PROPER ADMISSION. THAT'S THE LAW, AND AS EVERYONE KNOWS, BREAKING THE LAW IS VERY UN-AMERICAN!
ERR...
WHISPER WHISPER
I MEAN BREAKING THE LAW IS VERY UN-BRITISH!
LOXLEY LINKS? THIS IS THE LOXLEY SWAMP! IT'S HOME TO THOUSANDS OF CREATURES AND HUNDREDS OF FROGS! THIS SWAMP HAS BEEN IN MY FAMILY... AND MY FAMILY HAS BEEN IN THIS SWAMP...FOR YEARS!
YOU ARE ROBIN OF LOXLEY?
THE ROBIN OF LOXLEY...?

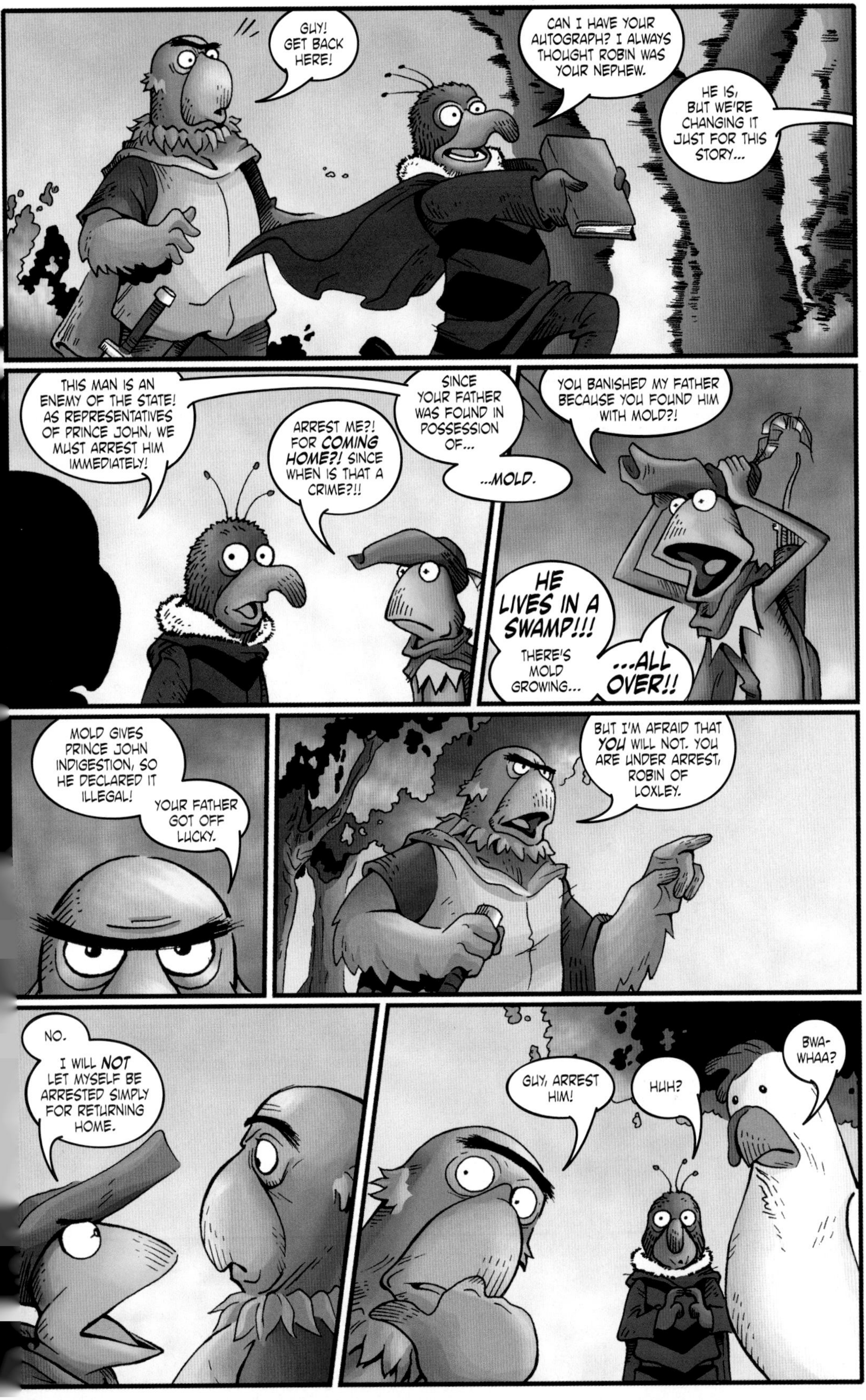
GUY! GET BACK HERE!
CAN I HAVE YOUR AUTOGRAPH? I ALWAYS THOUGHT ROBIN WAS YOUR NEPHEW.
HE IS, BUT WE'RE CHANGING IT JUST FOR THIS STORY...
THIS MAN IS AN ENEMY OF THE STATE! AS REPRESENTATIVES OF PRINCE JOHN, WE MUST ARREST HIM IMMEDIATELY!
ARREST ME?! FOR COMING HOME?! SINCE WHEN IS THAT A CRIME?!!
SINCE YOUR FATHER WAS FOUND IN POSSESSION OF...
...MOLD.
YOU BANISHED MY FATHER BECAUSE YOU FOUND HIM WITH MOLD?!
HE LIVES IN A SWAMP!!!
THERE'S MOLD GROWING...
...ALL OVER!!
MOLD GIVES PRINCE JOHN INDIGESTION, SO HE DECLARED IT ILLEGAL!
YOUR FATHER GOT OFF LUCKY.
BUT I'M AFRAID THAT YOU WILL NOT. YOU ARE UNDER ARREST, ROBIN OF LOXLEY.
NO.
I WILL NOT LET MYSELF BE ARRESTED SIMPLY FOR RETURNING HOME.
GUY, ARREST HIM!
HUH?
BWA-WHAA?

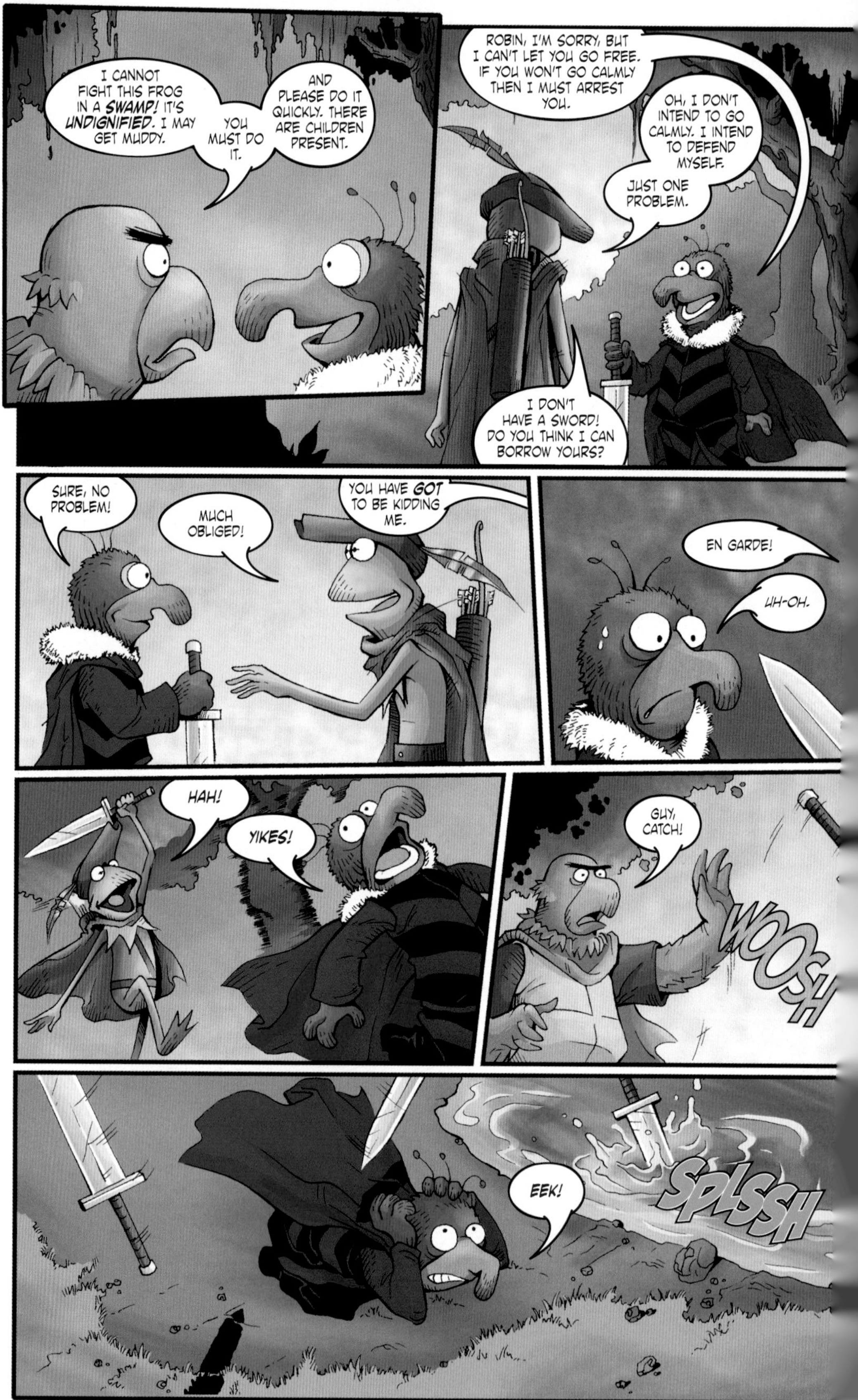
I CANNOT FIGHT THIS FROG IN A *SWAMP!* IT'S *UNDIGNIFIED.* I MAY GET MUDDY.
YOU MUST DO IT.
AND PLEASE DO IT QUICKLY. THERE ARE CHILDREN PRESENT.
ROBIN, I'M SORRY, BUT I CAN'T LET YOU GO FREE. IF YOU WON'T GO CALMLY THEN I MUST ARREST YOU.
OH, I DON'T INTEND TO GO CALMLY. I INTEND TO DEFEND MYSELF.
JUST ONE PROBLEM.
I DON'T HAVE A SWORD! DO YOU THINK I CAN BORROW YOURS?
SURE, NO PROBLEM!
MUCH OBLIGED!
YOU HAVE *GOT* TO BE KIDDING ME.
EN GARDE!
UH-OH.
HAH!
YIKES!
GUY, CATCH!
WOOSH
EEK!
SPLSSH

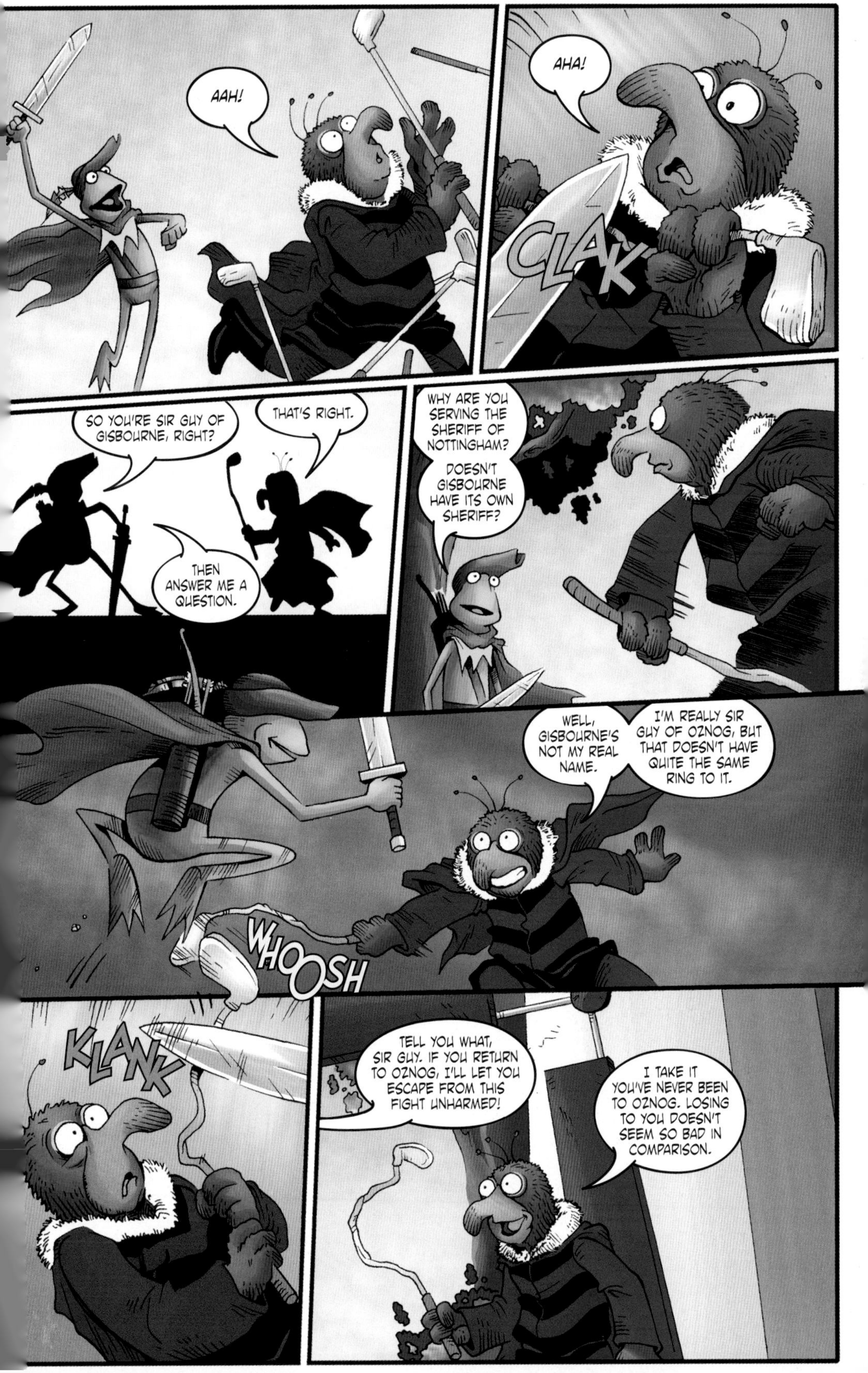
AAH!
AHA!
CLAK
SO YOU'RE SIR GUY OF GISBOURNE, RIGHT?
THAT'S RIGHT.
THEN ANSWER ME A QUESTION.
WHY ARE YOU SERVING THE SHERIFF OF NOTTINGHAM?
DOESN'T GISBOURNE HAVE ITS OWN SHERIFF?
WELL, GISBOURNE'S NOT MY REAL NAME.
I'M REALLY SIR GUY OF OZNOG, BUT THAT DOESN'T HAVE QUITE THE SAME RING TO IT.
WHOOSH
KLANK
TELL YOU WHAT, SIR GUY. IF YOU RETURN TO OZNOG, I'LL LET YOU ESCAPE FROM THIS FIGHT UNHARMED!
I TAKE IT YOU'VE NEVER BEEN TO OZNOG. LOSING TO YOU DOESN'T SEEM SO BAD IN COMPARISON.

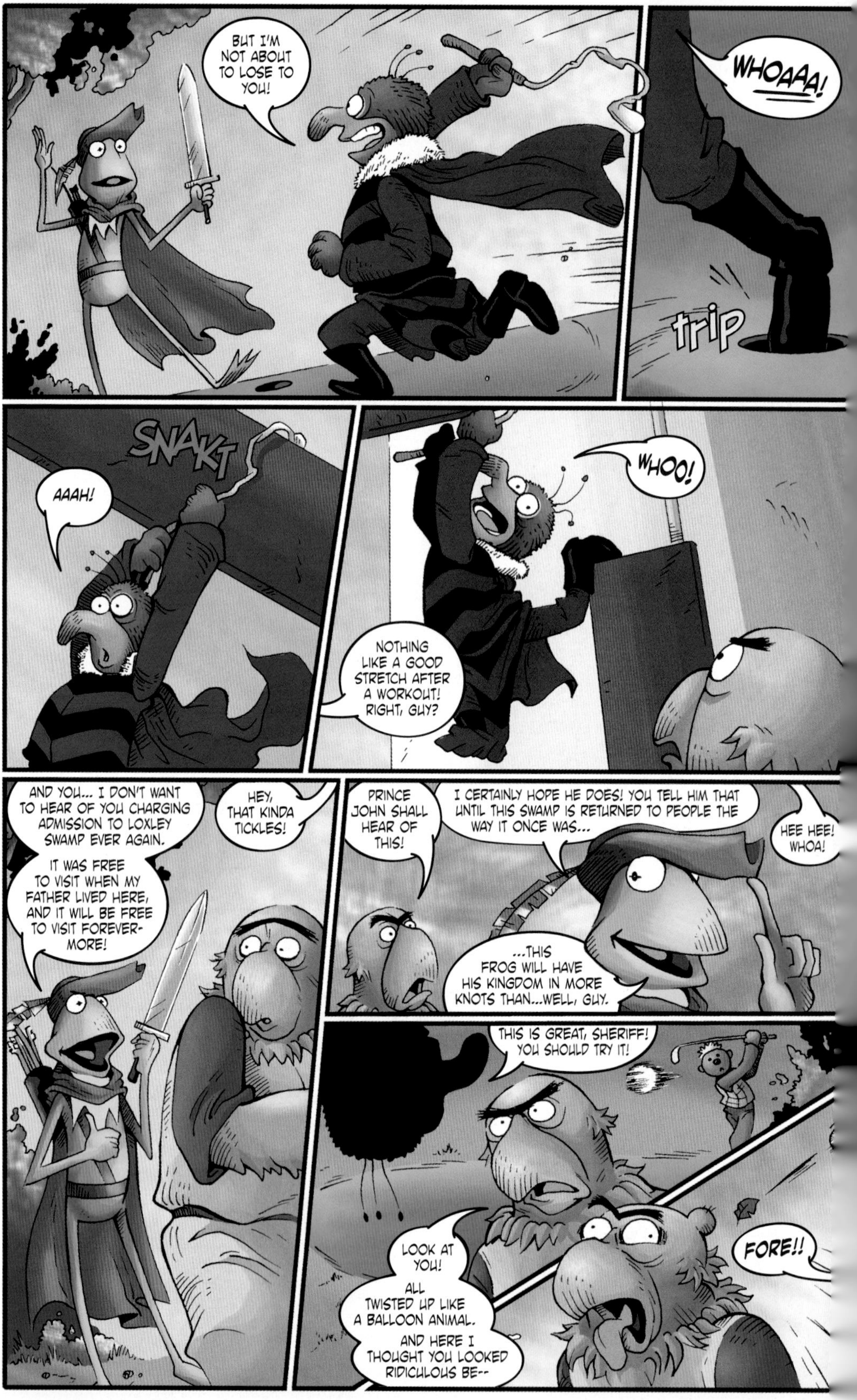
BUT I'M NOT ABOUT TO LOSE TO YOU!
WHOAAA!
trip
SNAKT
AAAH!
WHOO!
NOTHING LIKE A GOOD STRETCH AFTER A WORKOUT! RIGHT, GUY?
AND YOU... I DON'T WANT TO HEAR OF YOU CHARGING ADMISSION TO LOXLEY SWAMP EVER AGAIN.
IT WAS FREE TO VISIT WHEN MY FATHER LIVED HERE, AND IT WILL BE FREE TO VISIT FOREVER-MORE!
HEY, THAT KINDA TICKLES!
PRINCE JOHN SHALL HEAR OF THIS!
I CERTAINLY HOPE HE DOES! YOU TELL HIM THAT UNTIL THIS SWAMP IS RETURNED TO PEOPLE THE WAY IT ONCE WAS...
HEE HEE! WHOA!
...THIS FROG WILL HAVE HIS KINGDOM IN MORE KNOTS THAN...WELL, GUY.
THIS IS GREAT, SHERIFF! YOU SHOULD TRY IT!
LOOK AT YOU!
ALL TWISTED UP LIKE A BALLOON ANIMAL.
AND HERE I THOUGHT YOU LOOKED RIDICULOUS BE--
FORE!!

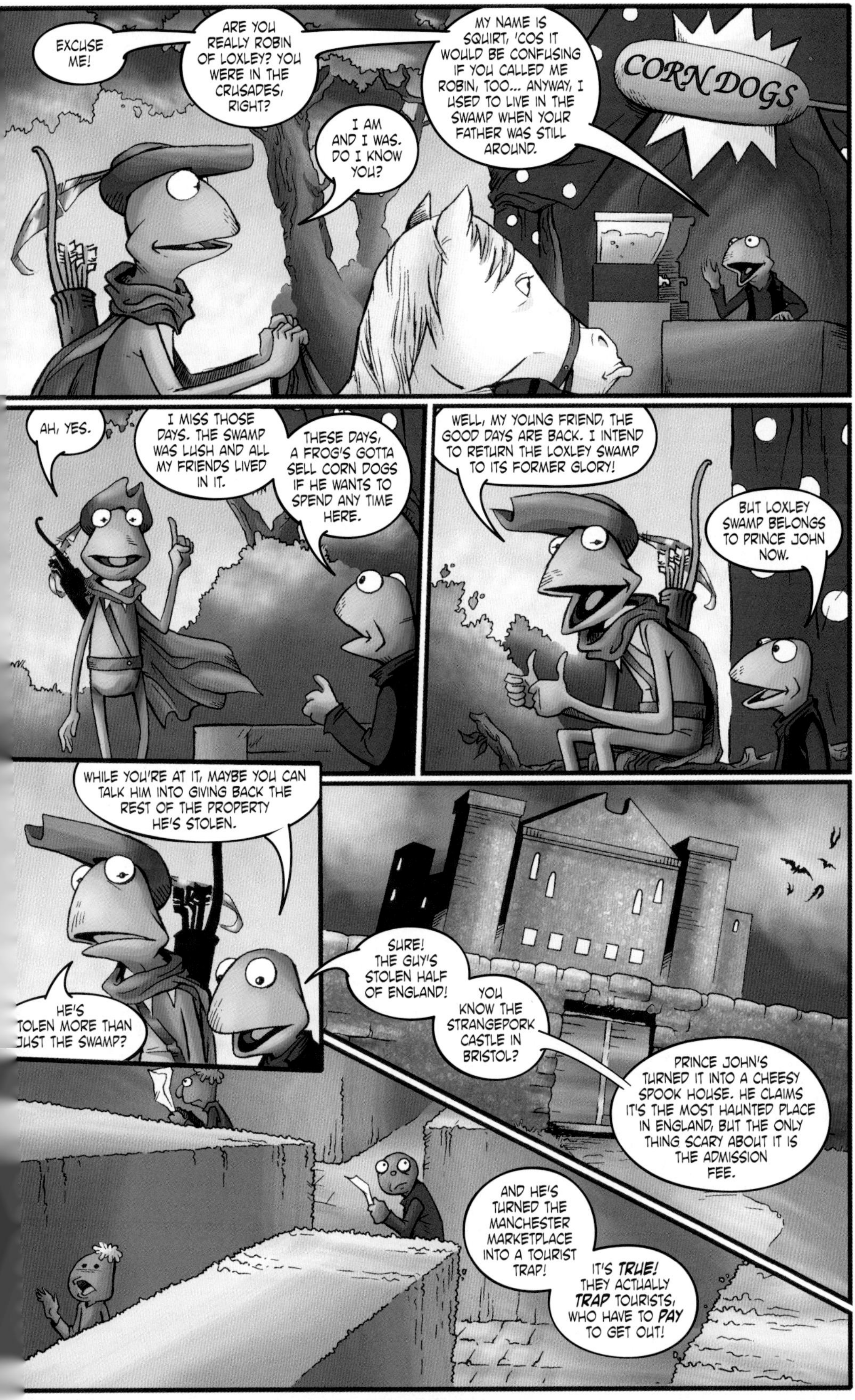

EXCUSE ME!
ARE YOU REALLY ROBIN OF LOXLEY? YOU WERE IN THE CRUSADES, RIGHT?
I AM AND I WAS. DO I KNOW YOU?
MY NAME IS SQUIRT, 'COS IT WOULD BE CONFUSING IF YOU CALLED ME ROBIN, TOO... ANYWAY, I USED TO LIVE IN THE SWAMP WHEN YOUR FATHER WAS STILL AROUND.
CORN DOGS
AH, YES.
I MISS THOSE DAYS. THE SWAMP WAS LUSH AND ALL MY FRIENDS LIVED IN IT.
THESE DAYS, A FROG'S GOTTA SELL CORN DOGS IF HE WANTS TO SPEND ANY TIME HERE.
WELL, MY YOUNG FRIEND, THE GOOD DAYS ARE BACK. I INTEND TO RETURN THE LOXLEY SWAMP TO ITS FORMER GLORY!
BUT LOXLEY SWAMP BELONGS TO PRINCE JOHN NOW.
WHILE YOU'RE AT IT, MAYBE YOU CAN TALK HIM INTO GIVING BACK THE REST OF THE PROPERTY HE'S STOLEN.
HE'S STOLEN MORE THAN JUST THE SWAMP?
SURE! THE GUY'S STOLEN HALF OF ENGLAND!
YOU KNOW THE STRANGEPORK CASTLE IN BRISTOL?
PRINCE JOHN'S TURNED IT INTO A CHEESY SPOOK HOUSE. HE CLAIMS IT'S THE MOST HAUNTED PLACE IN ENGLAND, BUT THE ONLY THING SCARY ABOUT IT IS THE ADMISSION FEE.
AND HE'S TURNED THE MANCHESTER MARKETPLACE INTO A TOURIST TRAP!
IT'S *TRUE!* THEY ACTUALLY *TRAP* TOURISTS, WHO HAVE TO *PAY* TO GET OUT!

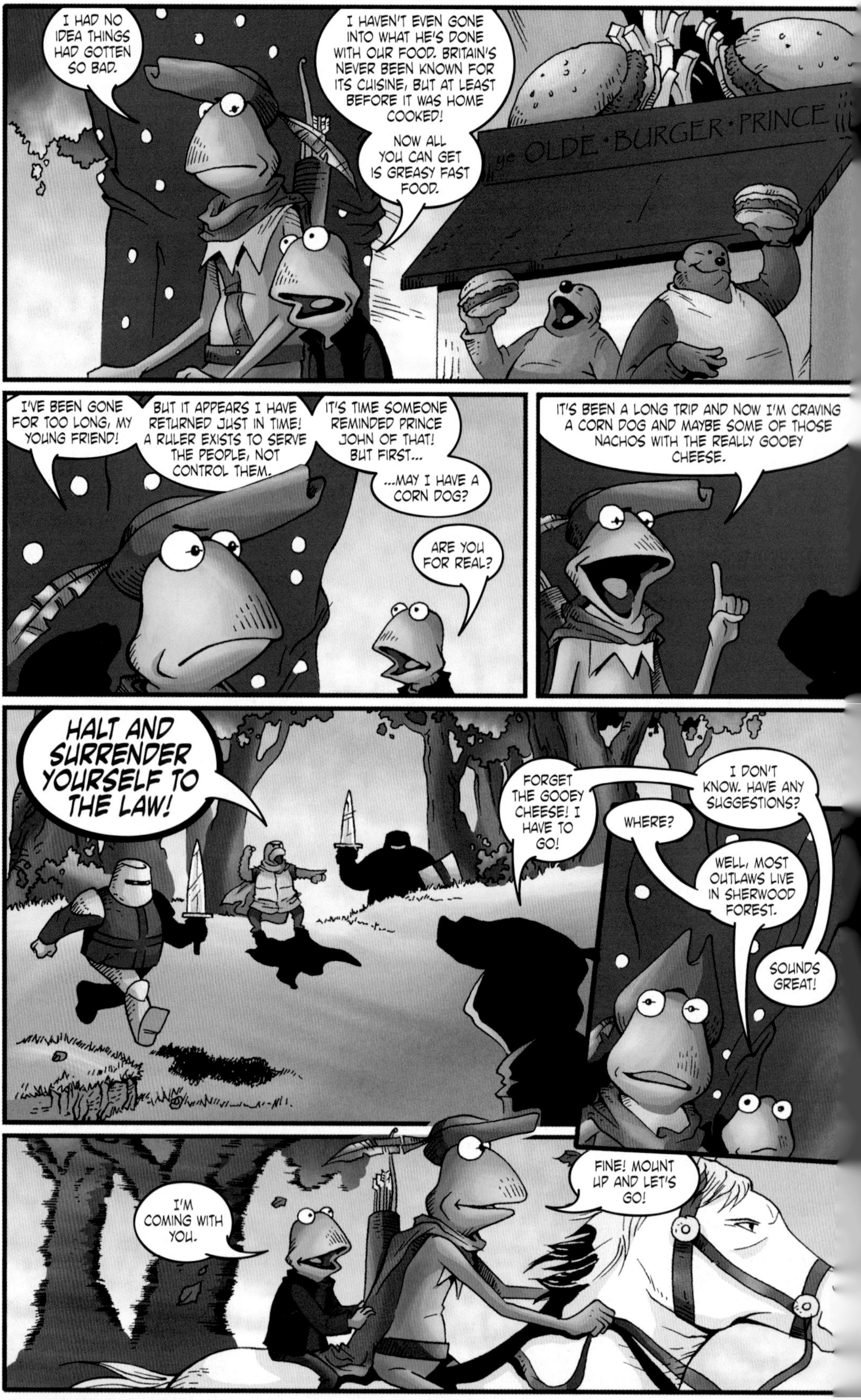
I HAD NO IDEA THINGS HAD GOTTEN SO BAD.
I HAVEN'T EVEN GONE INTO WHAT HE'S DONE WITH OUR FOOD. BRITAIN'S NEVER BEEN KNOWN FOR ITS CUISINE, BUT AT LEAST BEFORE IT WAS HOME COOKED!
NOW ALL YOU CAN GET IS GREASY FAST FOOD.
ye OLDE • BURGER • PRINCE
I'VE BEEN GONE FOR TOO LONG, MY YOUNG FRIEND!
BUT IT APPEARS I HAVE RETURNED JUST IN TIME! A RULER EXISTS TO SERVE THE PEOPLE, NOT CONTROL THEM.
IT'S TIME SOMEONE REMINDED PRINCE JOHN OF THAT! BUT FIRST...
...MAY I HAVE A CORN DOG?
ARE YOU FOR REAL?
IT'S BEEN A LONG TRIP AND NOW I'M CRAVING A CORN DOG AND MAYBE SOME OF THOSE NACHOS WITH THE REALLY GOOEY CHEESE.
HALT AND SURRENDER YOURSELF TO THE LAW!
FORGET THE GOOEY CHEESE! I HAVE TO GO!
WHERE?
I DON'T KNOW. HAVE ANY SUGGESTIONS?
WELL, MOST OUTLAWS LIVE IN SHERWOOD FOREST.
SOUNDS GREAT!
I'M COMING WITH YOU.
FINE! MOUNT UP AND LET'S GO!

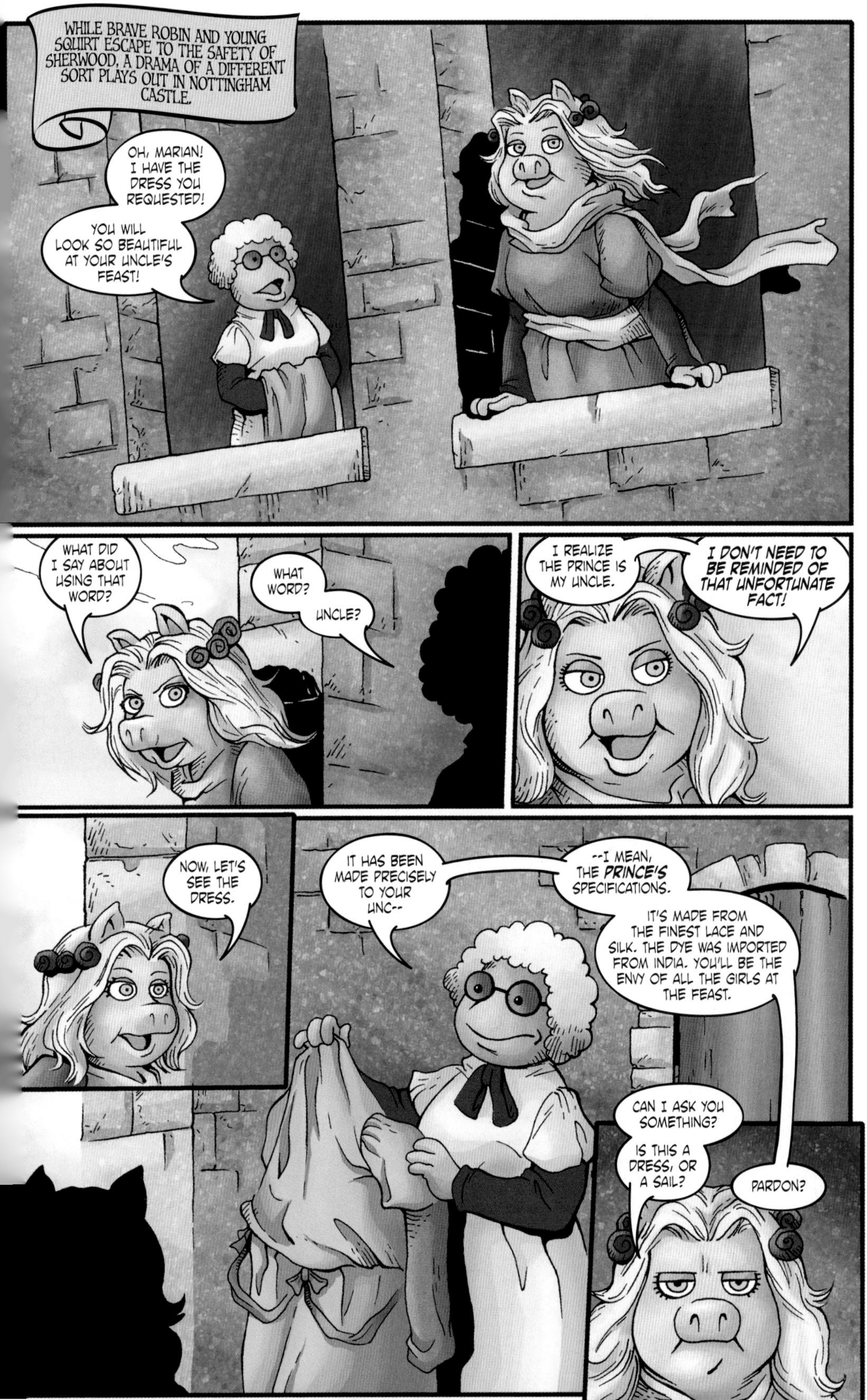

WHILE BRAVE ROBIN AND YOUNG SQUIRT ESCAPE TO THE SAFETY OF SHERWOOD, A DRAMA OF A DIFFERENT SORT PLAYS OUT IN NOTTINGHAM CASTLE.
OH, MARIAN! I HAVE THE DRESS YOU REQUESTED!
YOU WILL LOOK SO BEAUTIFUL AT YOUR UNCLE'S FEAST!
WHAT DID I SAY ABOUT USING THAT WORD?
WHAT WORD?
UNCLE?
I REALIZE THE PRINCE IS MY UNCLE.
I DON'T NEED TO BE REMINDED OF THAT UNFORTUNATE FACT!
NOW, LET'S SEE THE DRESS.
IT HAS BEEN MADE PRECISELY TO YOUR UNC--
--I MEAN, THE PRINCE'S SPECIFICATIONS.
IT'S MADE FROM THE FINEST LACE AND SILK. THE DYE WAS IMPORTED FROM INDIA. YOU'LL BE THE ENVY OF ALL THE GIRLS AT THE FEAST.
CAN I ASK YOU SOMETHING?
IS THIS A DRESS, OR A SAIL?
PARDON?

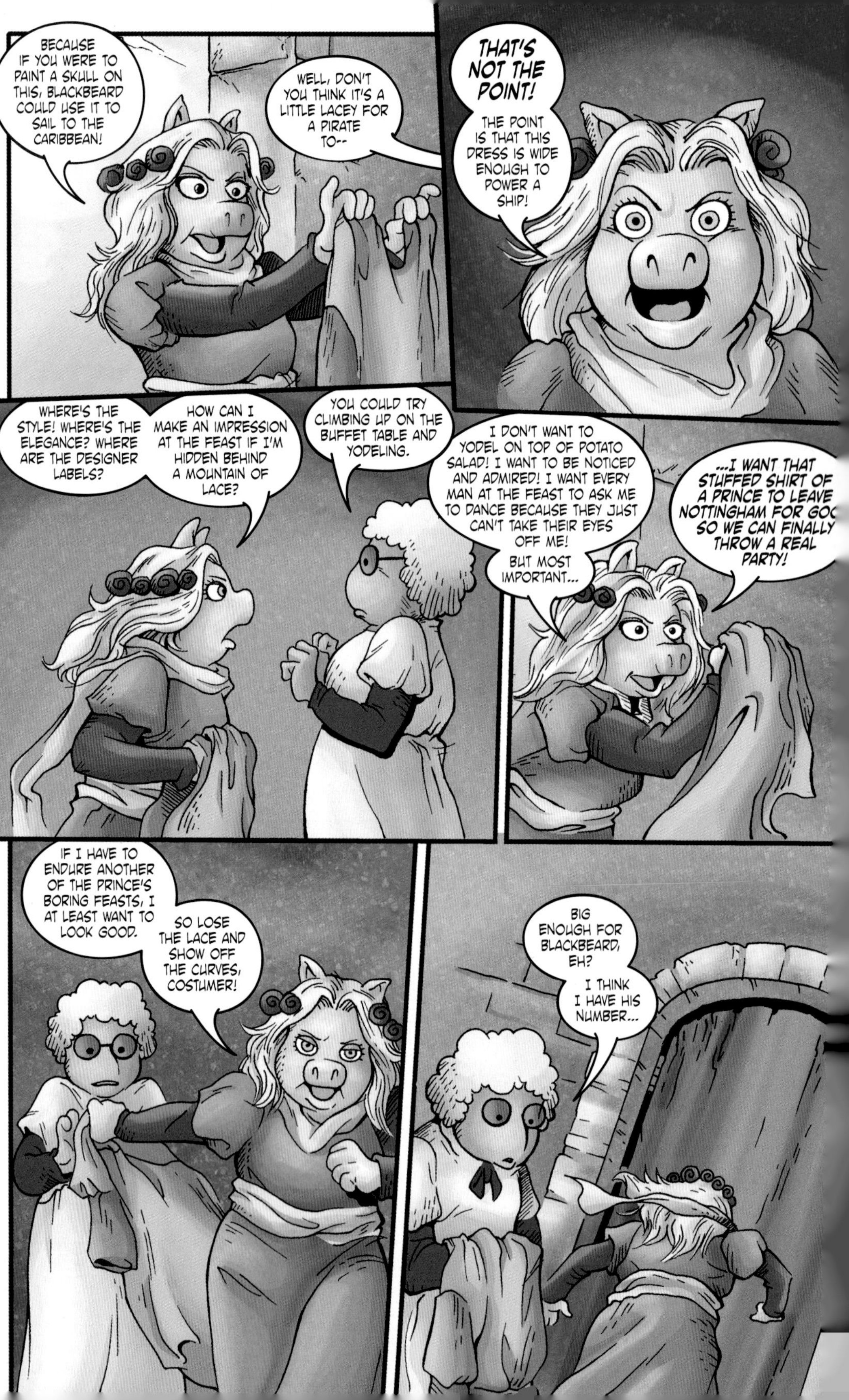
BECAUSE IF YOU WERE TO PAINT A SKULL ON THIS, BLACKBEARD COULD USE IT TO SAIL TO THE CARIBBEAN!
WELL, DON'T YOU THINK IT'S A LITTLE LACEY FOR A PIRATE TO--
THAT'S NOT THE POINT!
THE POINT IS THAT THIS DRESS IS WIDE ENOUGH TO POWER A SHIP!
WHERE'S THE STYLE! WHERE'S THE ELEGANCE? WHERE ARE THE DESIGNER LABELS?
HOW CAN I MAKE AN IMPRESSION AT THE FEAST IF I'M HIDDEN BEHIND A MOUNTAIN OF LACE?
YOU COULD TRY CLIMBING UP ON THE BUFFET TABLE AND YODELING.
I DON'T WANT TO YODEL ON TOP OF POTATO SALAD! I WANT TO BE NOTICED AND ADMIRED! I WANT EVERY MAN AT THE FEAST TO ASK ME TO DANCE BECAUSE THEY JUST CAN'T TAKE THEIR EYES OFF ME!
BUT MOST IMPORTANT...
...I WANT THAT STUFFED SHIRT OF A PRINCE TO LEAVE NOTTINGHAM FOR GOO SO WE CAN FINALLY THROW A REAL PARTY!
IF I HAVE TO ENDURE ANOTHER OF THE PRINCE'S BORING FEASTS, I AT LEAST WANT TO LOOK GOOD.
SO LOSE THE LACE AND SHOW OFF THE CURVES, COSTUMER!
BIG ENOUGH FOR BLACKBEARD, EH?
I THINK I HAVE HIS NUMBER...

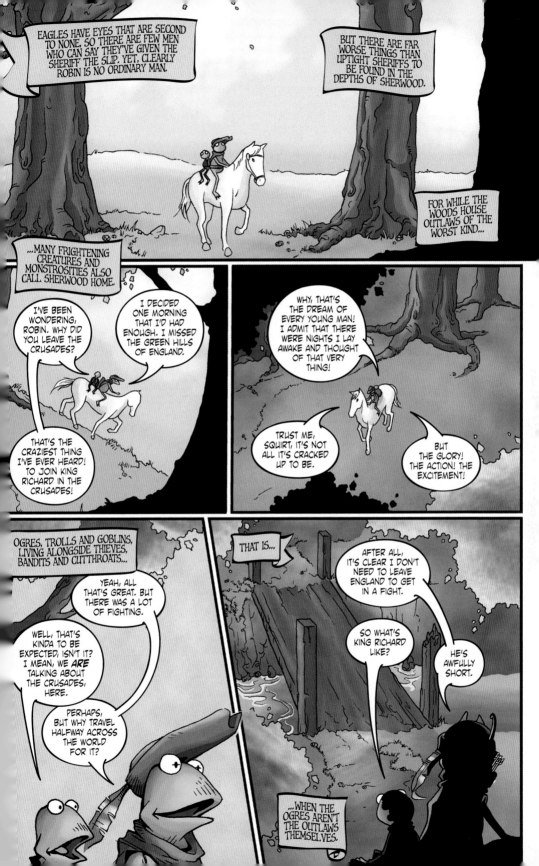

EAGLES HAVE EYES THAT ARE SECOND TO NONE, SO THERE ARE FEW MEN WHO CAN SAY THEY'VE GIVEN THE SHERIFF THE SLIP. YET, CLEARLY ROBIN IS NO ORDINARY MAN.

BUT THERE ARE FAR WORSE THINGS THAN UPTIGHT SHERIFFS TO BE FOUND IN THE DEPTHS OF SHERWOOD.

FOR WHILE THE WOODS HOUSE OUTLAWS OF THE WORST KIND...

...MANY FRIGHTENING CREATURES AND MONSTROSITIES ALSO CALL SHERWOOD HOME.

I'VE BEEN WONDERING, ROBIN. WHY DID YOU LEAVE THE CRUSADES?

I DECIDED ONE MORNING THAT I'D HAD ENOUGH. I MISSED THE GREEN HILLS OF ENGLAND.

THAT'S THE CRAZIEST THING I'VE EVER HEARD! TO JOIN KING RICHARD IN THE CRUSADES!

WHY, THAT'S THE DREAM OF EVERY YOUNG MAN! I ADMIT THAT THERE WERE NIGHTS I LAY AWAKE AND THOUGHT OF THAT VERY THING!

TRUST ME, SQUIRT, IT'S NOT ALL IT'S CRACKED UP TO BE.

BUT THE GLORY! THE ACTION! THE EXCITEMENT!

OGRES, TROLLS AND GOBLINS, LIVING ALONGSIDE THIEVES, BANDITS AND CUTTHROATS...

YEAH, ALL THAT'S GREAT. BUT THERE WAS A LOT OF FIGHTING.

WELL, THAT'S KINDA TO BE EXPECTED, ISN'T IT? I MEAN, WE *ARE* TALKING ABOUT THE CRUSADES, HERE.

PERHAPS, BUT WHY TRAVEL HALFWAY ACROSS THE WORLD FOR IT?

THAT IS...

AFTER ALL, IT'S CLEAR I DON'T NEED TO LEAVE ENGLAND TO GET IN A FIGHT.

SO WHAT'S KING RICHARD LIKE?

HE'S AWFULLY SHORT.

...WHEN THE OGRES AREN'T THE OUTLAWS THEMSELVES.

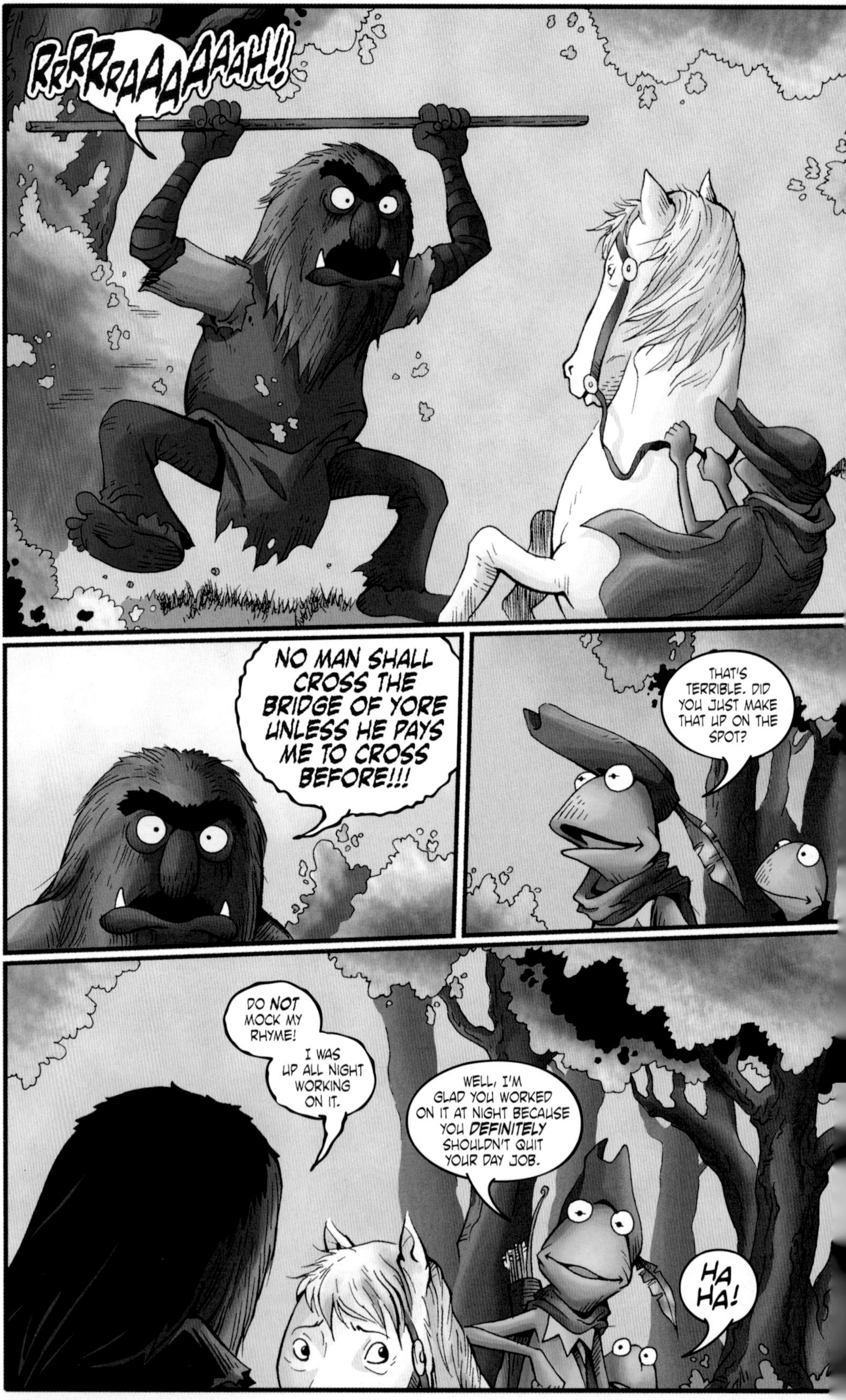
RRRRRAAAAAAAH!!
NO MAN SHALL CROSS THE BRIDGE OF YORE UNLESS HE PAYS ME TO CROSS BEFORE!!!
THAT'S TERRIBLE. DID YOU JUST MAKE THAT UP ON THE SPOT?
DO NOT MOCK MY RHYME!
I WAS UP ALL NIGHT WORKING ON IT.
WELL, I'M GLAD YOU WORKED ON IT AT NIGHT BECAUSE YOU DEFINITELY SHOULDN'T QUIT YOUR DAY JOB.
HA HA!

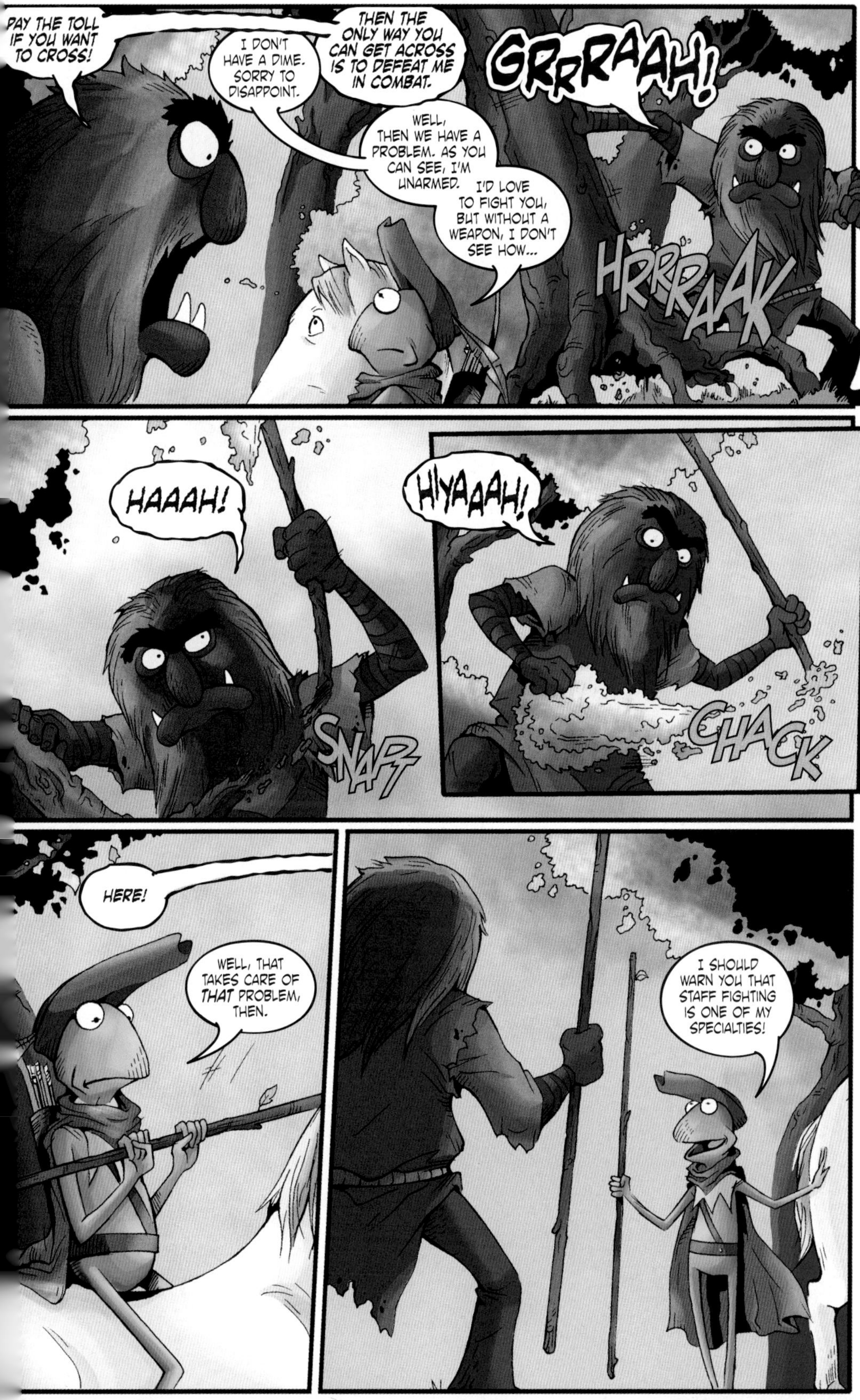

PAY THE TOLL IF YOU WANT TO CROSS!
I DON'T HAVE A DIME. SORRY TO DISAPPOINT.
THEN THE ONLY WAY YOU CAN GET ACROSS IS TO DEFEAT ME IN COMBAT.
WELL, THEN WE HAVE A PROBLEM. AS YOU CAN SEE, I'M UNARMED.
I'D LOVE TO FIGHT YOU, BUT WITHOUT A WEAPON, I DON'T SEE HOW...
GRRRAAH!
HRRRAAK
HAAAH!
SNAP
HIYAAAH!
CHACK
HERE!
WELL, THAT TAKES CARE OF THAT PROBLEM, THEN.
I SHOULD WARN YOU THAT STAFF FIGHTING IS ONE OF MY SPECIALTIES!

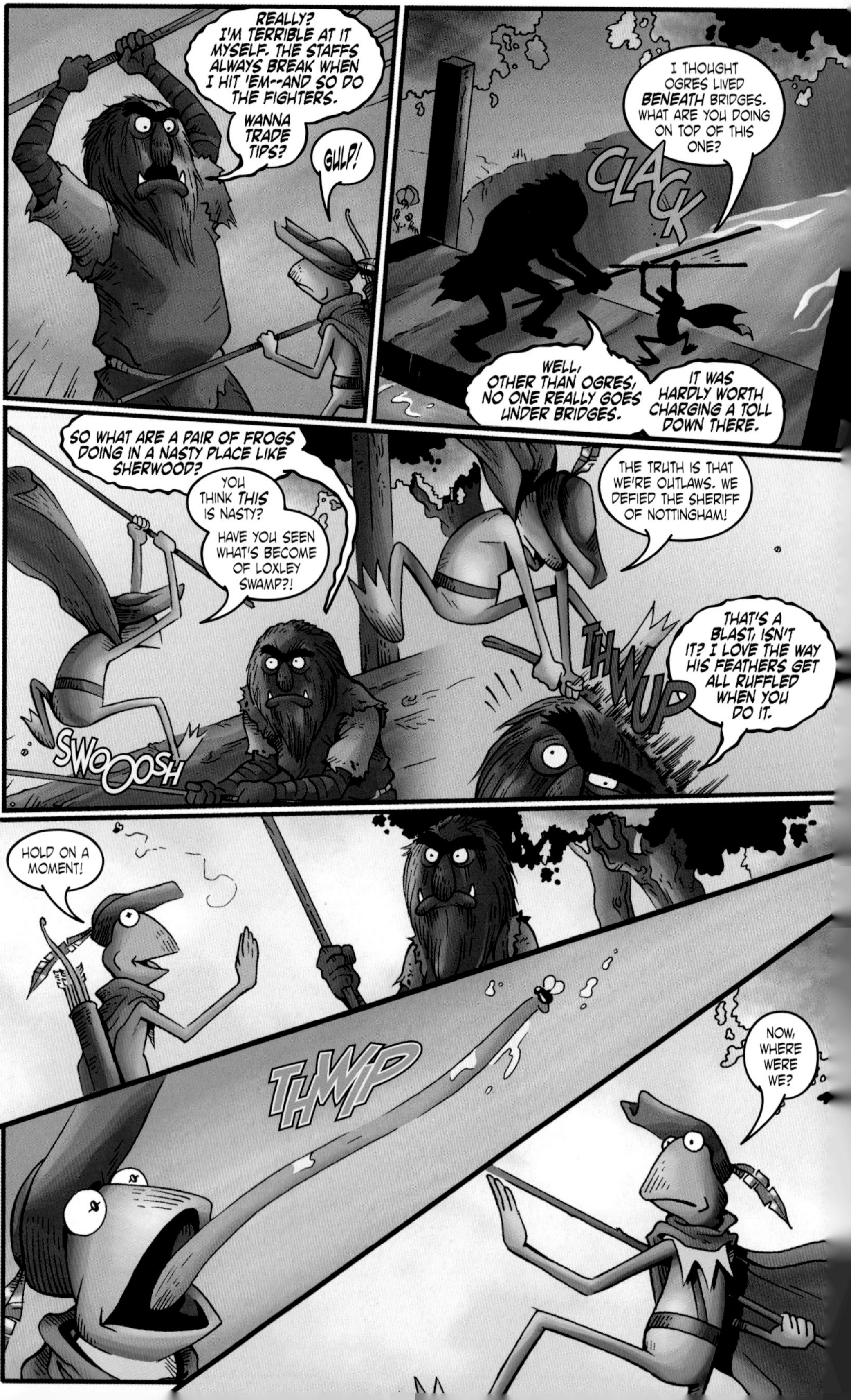
REALLY? I'M TERRIBLE AT IT MYSELF. THE STAFFS ALWAYS BREAK WHEN I HIT 'EM--AND SO DO THE FIGHTERS.
WANNA TRADE TIPS?
GULP!
CLACK
I THOUGHT OGRES LIVED BENEATH BRIDGES. WHAT ARE YOU DOING ON TOP OF THIS ONE?
WELL, OTHER THAN OGRES, NO ONE REALLY GOES UNDER BRIDGES.
IT WAS HARDLY WORTH CHARGING A TOLL DOWN THERE.
SO WHAT ARE A PAIR OF FROGS DOING IN A NASTY PLACE LIKE SHERWOOD?
YOU THINK THIS IS NASTY?
HAVE YOU SEEN WHAT'S BECOME OF LOXLEY SWAMP?!
THE TRUTH IS THAT WE'RE OUTLAWS. WE DEFIED THE SHERIFF OF NOTTINGHAM!
SWOOOSH
THWUP
THAT'S A BLAST, ISN'T IT? I LOVE THE WAY HIS FEATHERS GET ALL RUFFLED WHEN YOU DO IT.
HOLD ON A MOMENT!
THWIP
NOW, WHERE WERE WE?

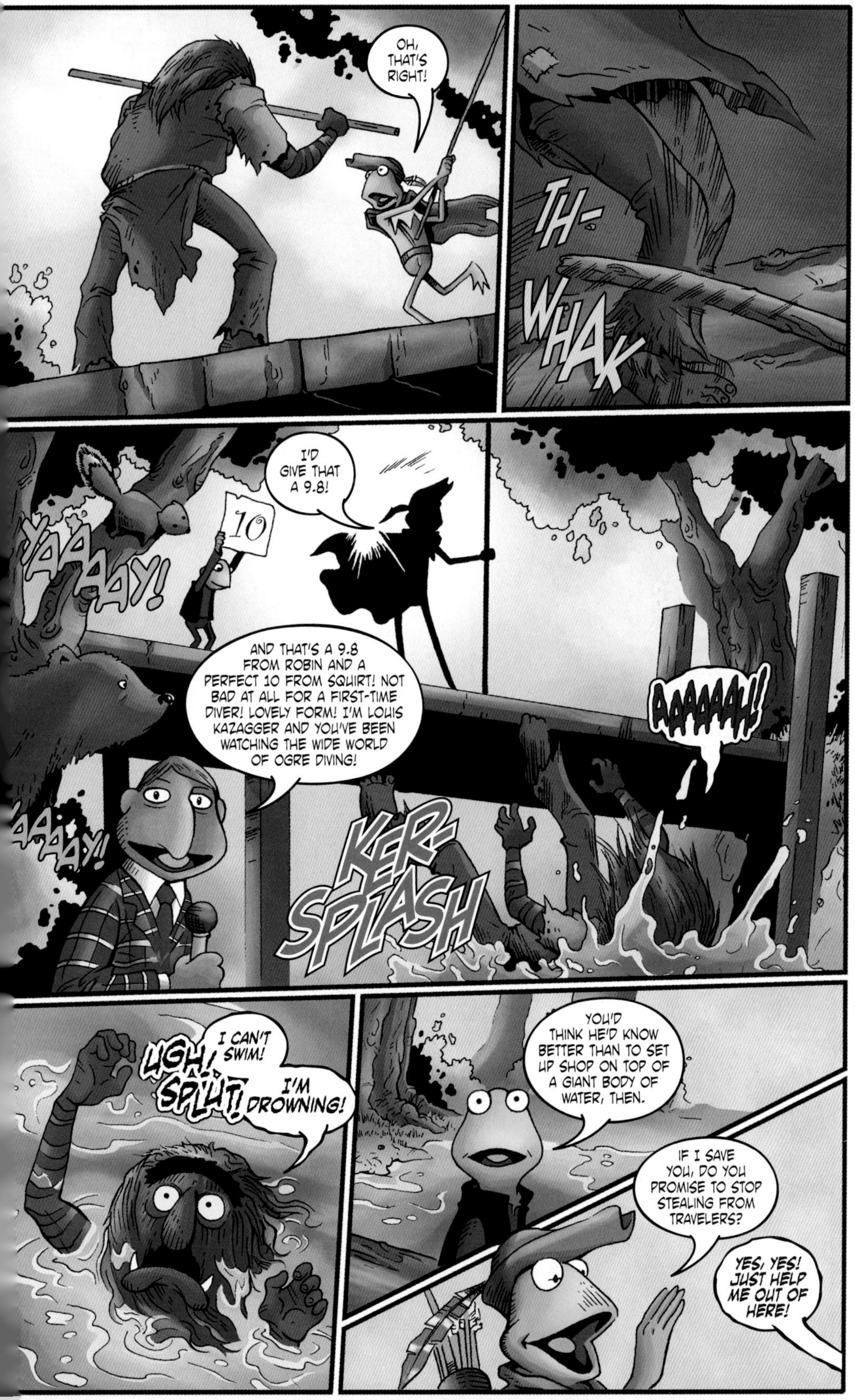
OH, THAT'S RIGHT!
TH-WHAK
I'D GIVE THAT A 9.8!
10
YAAAAAY!
AND THAT'S A 9.8 FROM ROBIN AND A PERFECT 10 FROM SQUIRT! NOT BAD AT ALL FOR A FIRST-TIME DIVER! LOVELY FORM! I'M LOUIS KAZAGGER AND YOU'VE BEEN WATCHING THE WIDE WORLD OF OGRE DIVING!
AAAAAAH!!
AAAAAY!
KER-SPLASH
UGH! SPLUT!
I CAN'T SWIM!
I'M DROWNING!
YOU'D THINK HE'D KNOW BETTER THAN TO SET UP SHOP ON TOP OF A GIANT BODY OF WATER, THEN.
IF I SAVE YOU, DO YOU PROMISE TO STOP STEALING FROM TRAVELERS?
YES, YES! JUST HELP ME OUT OF HERE!

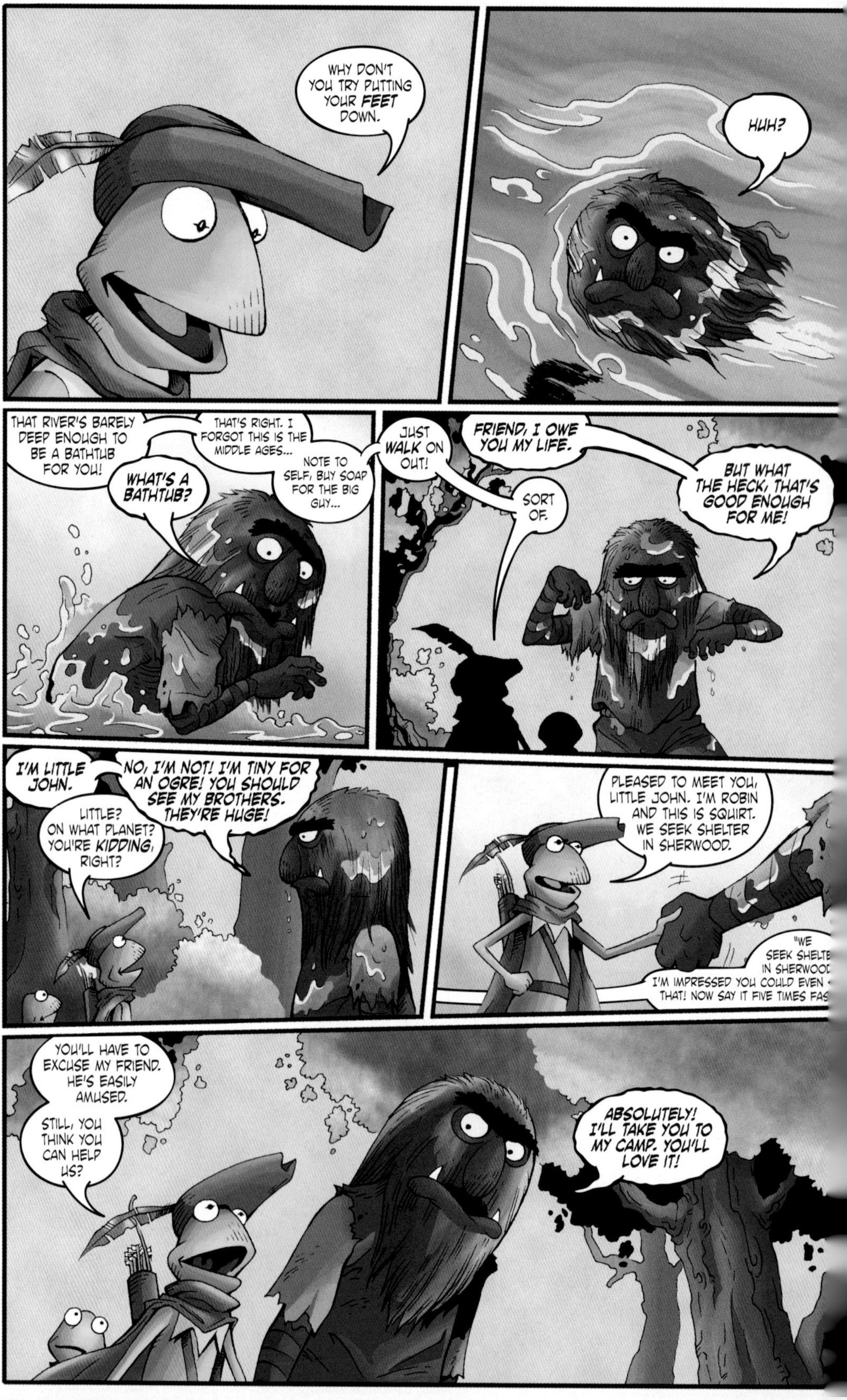

WHY DON'T YOU TRY PUTTING YOUR FEET DOWN.
HUH?
THAT RIVER'S BARELY DEEP ENOUGH TO BE A BATHTUB FOR YOU!
WHAT'S A BATHTUB?
THAT'S RIGHT. I FORGOT THIS IS THE MIDDLE AGES...
NOTE TO SELF, BUY SOAP FOR THE BIG GUY...
JUST WALK ON OUT!
FRIEND, I OWE YOU MY LIFE.
SORT OF.
BUT WHAT THE HECK, THAT'S GOOD ENOUGH FOR ME!
I'M LITTLE JOHN.
LITTLE? ON WHAT PLANET? YOU'RE KIDDING, RIGHT?
NO, I'M NOT! I'M TINY FOR AN OGRE! YOU SHOULD SEE MY BROTHERS. THEY'RE HUGE!
PLEASED TO MEET YOU, LITTLE JOHN. I'M ROBIN AND THIS IS SQUIRT. WE SEEK SHELTER IN SHERWOOD.
"WE SEEK SHELTE IN SHERWOOD
I'M IMPRESSED YOU COULD EVEN
THAT! NOW SAY IT FIVE TIMES FAS
YOU'LL HAVE TO EXCUSE MY FRIEND. HE'S EASILY AMUSED.
STILL, YOU THINK YOU CAN HELP US?
ABSOLUTELY! I'LL TAKE YOU TO MY CAMP. YOU'LL LOVE IT!

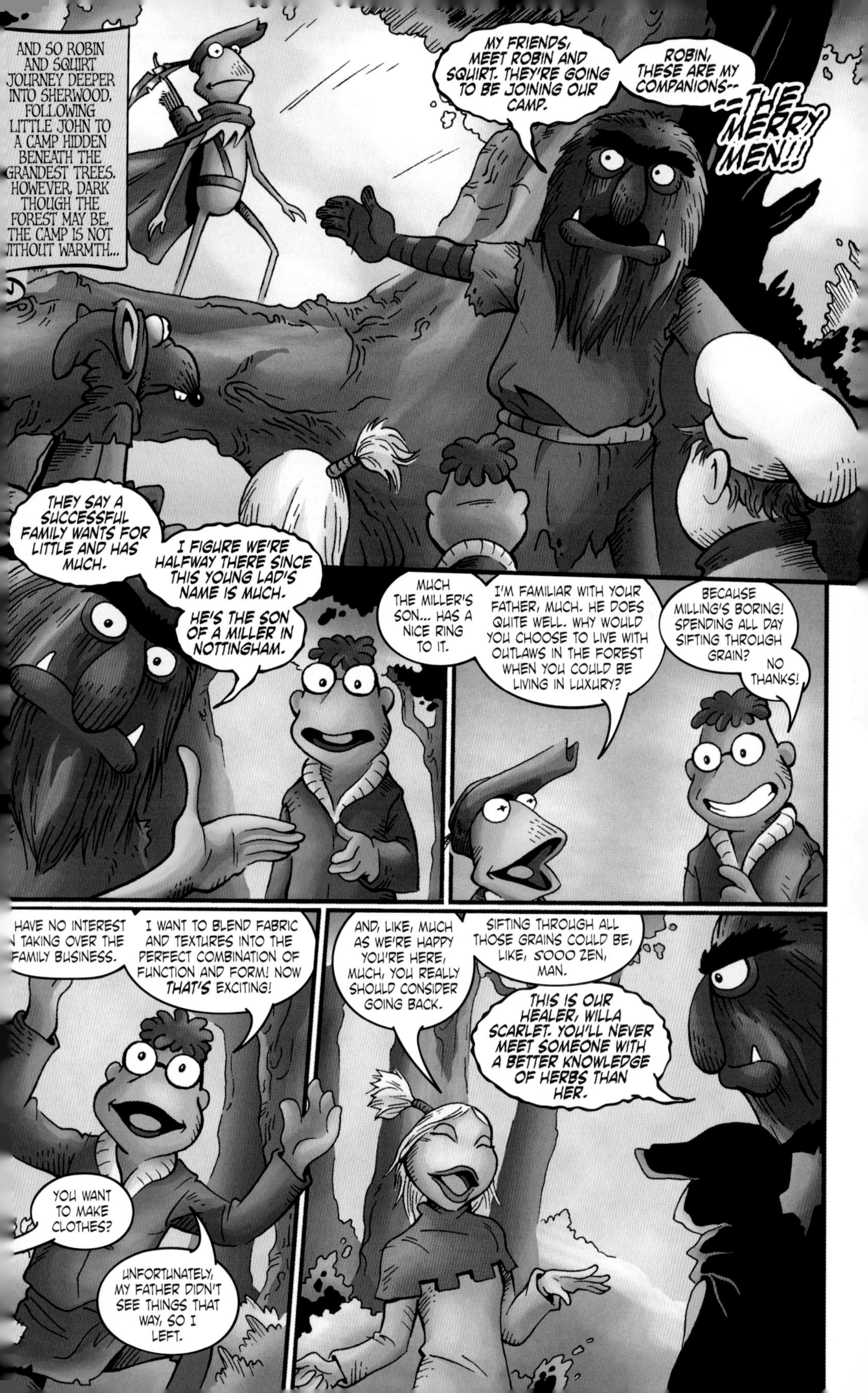
AND SO ROBIN AND SQUIRT JOURNEY DEEPER INTO SHERWOOD, FOLLOWING LITTLE JOHN TO A CAMP HIDDEN BENEATH THE GRANDEST TREES. HOWEVER, DARK THOUGH THE FOREST MAY BE, THE CAMP IS NOT WITHOUT WARMTH...
MY FRIENDS, MEET ROBIN AND SQUIRT. THEY'RE GOING TO BE JOINING OUR CAMP.
ROBIN, THESE ARE MY COMPANIONS--
--THE MERRY MEN!!
THEY SAY A SUCCESSFUL FAMILY WANTS FOR LITTLE AND HAS MUCH.
I FIGURE WE'RE HALFWAY THERE SINCE THIS YOUNG LAD'S NAME IS MUCH.
HE'S THE SON OF A MILLER IN NOTTINGHAM.
MUCH THE MILLER'S SON... HAS A NICE RING TO IT.
I'M FAMILIAR WITH YOUR FATHER, MUCH. HE DOES QUITE WELL. WHY WOULD YOU CHOOSE TO LIVE WITH OUTLAWS IN THE FOREST WHEN YOU COULD BE LIVING IN LUXURY?
BECAUSE MILLING'S BORING! SPENDING ALL DAY SIFTING THROUGH GRAIN?
NO THANKS!
HAVE NO INTEREST N TAKING OVER THE FAMILY BUSINESS.
I WANT TO BLEND FABRIC AND TEXTURES INTO THE PERFECT COMBINATION OF FUNCTION AND FORM! NOW THAT'S EXCITING!
YOU WANT TO MAKE CLOTHES?
UNFORTUNATELY, MY FATHER DIDN'T SEE THINGS THAT WAY, SO I LEFT.
AND, LIKE, MUCH AS WE'RE HAPPY YOU'RE HERE, MUCH, YOU REALLY SHOULD CONSIDER GOING BACK.
SIFTING THROUGH ALL THOSE GRAINS COULD BE, LIKE, SOOO ZEN, MAN.
THIS IS OUR HEALER, WILLA SCARLET. YOU'LL NEVER MEET SOMEONE WITH A BETTER KNOWLEDGE OF HERBS THAN HER.

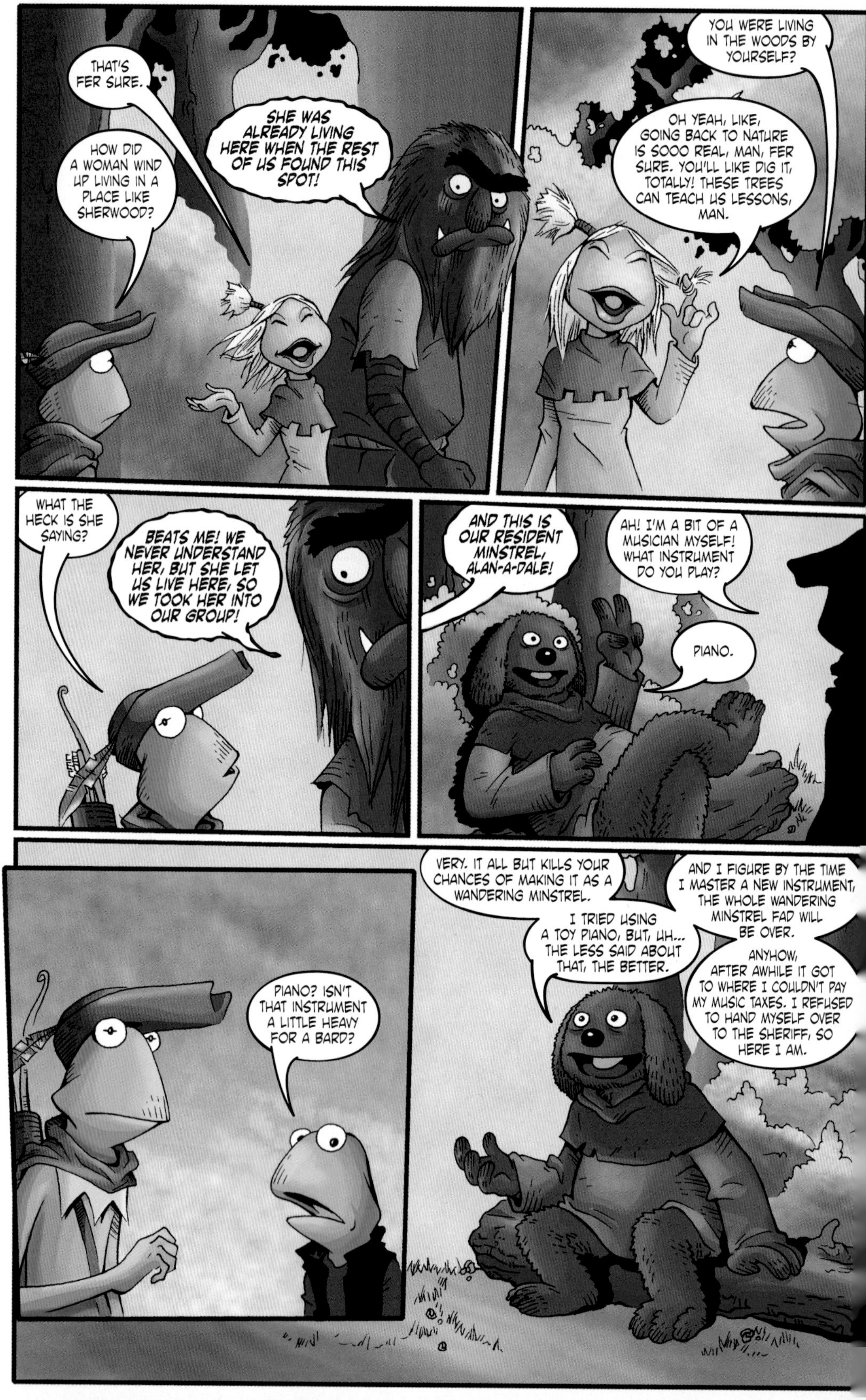
THAT'S FER SURE.
HOW DID A WOMAN WIND UP LIVING IN A PLACE LIKE SHERWOOD?
SHE WAS ALREADY LIVING HERE WHEN THE REST OF US FOUND THIS SPOT!
YOU WERE LIVING IN THE WOODS BY YOURSELF?
OH YEAH, LIKE, GOING BACK TO NATURE IS SOOO REAL, MAN, FER SURE. YOU'LL LIKE DIG IT, TOTALLY! THESE TREES CAN TEACH US LESSONS, MAN.
WHAT THE HECK IS SHE SAYING?
BEATS ME! WE NEVER UNDERSTAND HER, BUT SHE LET US LIVE HERE, SO WE TOOK HER INTO OUR GROUP!
AND THIS IS OUR RESIDENT MINSTREL, ALAN-A-DALE!
AH! I'M A BIT OF A MUSICIAN MYSELF! WHAT INSTRUMENT DO YOU PLAY?
PIANO.
PIANO? ISN'T THAT INSTRUMENT A LITTLE HEAVY FOR A BARD?
VERY. IT ALL BUT KILLS YOUR CHANCES OF MAKING IT AS A WANDERING MINSTREL.
I TRIED USING A TOY PIANO, BUT, UH... THE LESS SAID ABOUT THAT, THE BETTER.
AND I FIGURE BY THE TIME I MASTER A NEW INSTRUMENT, THE WHOLE WANDERING MINSTREL FAD WILL BE OVER.
ANYHOW, AFTER AWHILE IT GOT TO WHERE I COULDN'T PAY MY MUSIC TAXES. I REFUSED TO HAND MYSELF OVER TO THE SHERIFF, SO HERE I AM.

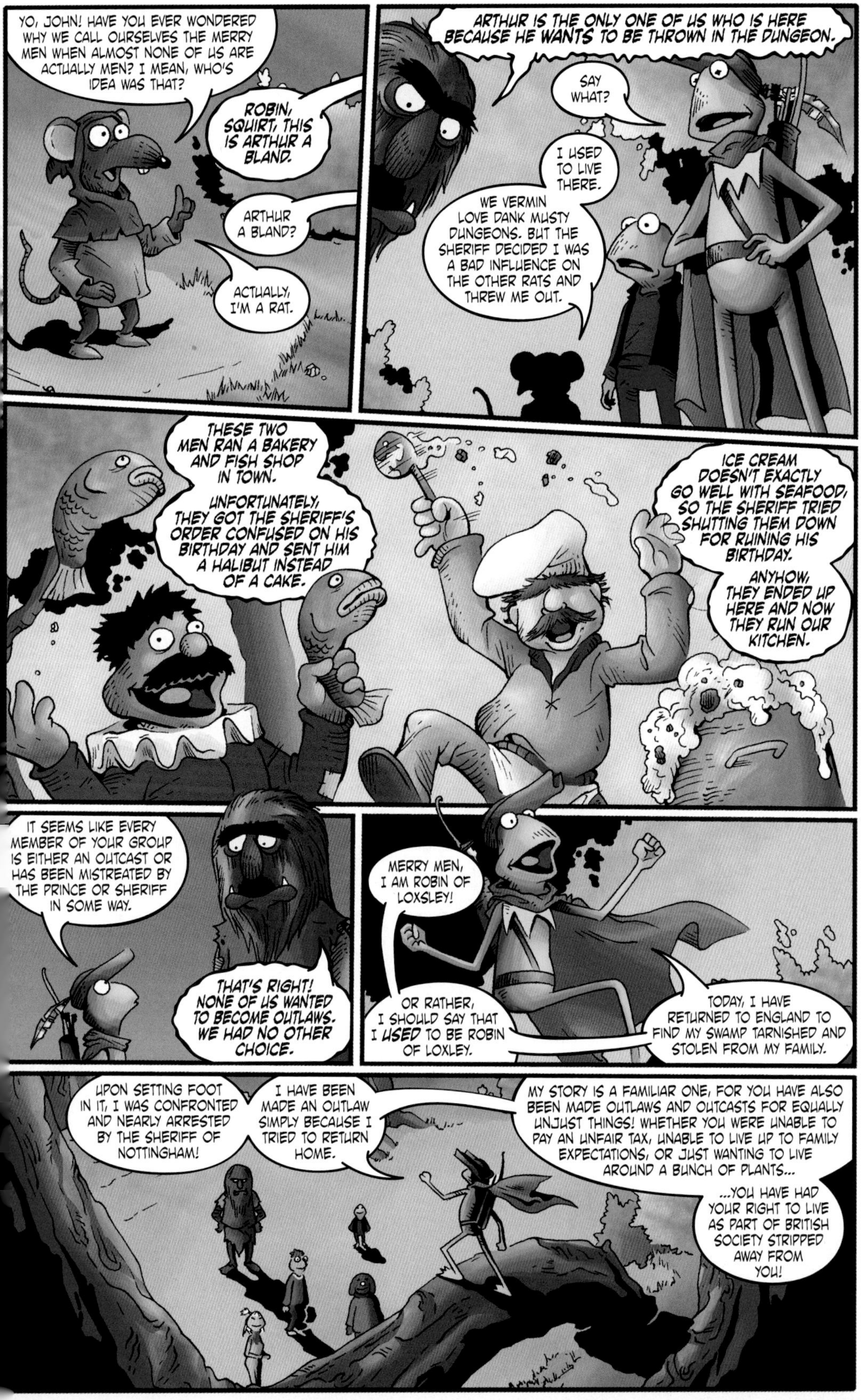
YO, JOHN! HAVE YOU EVER WONDERED WHY WE CALL OURSELVES THE MERRY MEN WHEN ALMOST NONE OF US ARE ACTUALLY MEN? I MEAN, WHO'S IDEA WAS THAT?
ROBIN, SQUIRT, THIS IS ARTHUR A BLAND.
ARTHUR A BLAND?
ACTUALLY, I'M A RAT.
ARTHUR IS THE ONLY ONE OF US WHO IS HERE BECAUSE HE WANTS TO BE THROWN IN THE DUNGEON.
SAY WHAT?
I USED TO LIVE THERE.
WE VERMIN LOVE DANK MUSTY DUNGEONS. BUT THE SHERIFF DECIDED I WAS A BAD INFLUENCE ON THE OTHER RATS AND THREW ME OUT.
THESE TWO MEN RAN A BAKERY AND FISH SHOP IN TOWN.
UNFORTUNATELY, THEY GOT THE SHERIFF'S ORDER CONFUSED ON HIS BIRTHDAY AND SENT HIM A HALIBUT INSTEAD OF A CAKE.
ICE CREAM DOESN'T EXACTLY GO WELL WITH SEAFOOD, SO THE SHERIFF TRIED SHUTTING THEM DOWN FOR RUINING HIS BIRTHDAY.
ANYHOW, THEY ENDED UP HERE AND NOW THEY RUN OUR KITCHEN.
IT SEEMS LIKE EVERY MEMBER OF YOUR GROUP IS EITHER AN OUTCAST OR HAS BEEN MISTREATED BY THE PRINCE OR SHERIFF IN SOME WAY.
THAT'S RIGHT! NONE OF US WANTED TO BECOME OUTLAWS. WE HAD NO OTHER CHOICE.
MERRY MEN, I AM ROBIN OF LOXSLEY!
OR RATHER, I SHOULD SAY THAT I USED TO BE ROBIN OF LOXLEY.
TODAY, I HAVE RETURNED TO ENGLAND TO FIND MY SWAMP TARNISHED AND STOLEN FROM MY FAMILY.
UPON SETTING FOOT IN IT, I WAS CONFRONTED AND NEARLY ARRESTED BY THE SHERIFF OF NOTTINGHAM!
I HAVE BEEN MADE AN OUTLAW SIMPLY BECAUSE I TRIED TO RETURN HOME.
MY STORY IS A FAMILIAR ONE, FOR YOU HAVE ALSO BEEN MADE OUTLAWS AND OUTCASTS FOR EQUALLY UNJUST THINGS! WHETHER YOU WERE UNABLE TO PAY AN UNFAIR TAX, UNABLE TO LIVE UP TO FAMILY EXPECTATIONS, OR JUST WANTING TO LIVE AROUND A BUNCH OF PLANTS...
...YOU HAVE HAD YOUR RIGHT TO LIVE AS PART OF BRITISH SOCIETY STRIPPED AWAY FROM YOU!

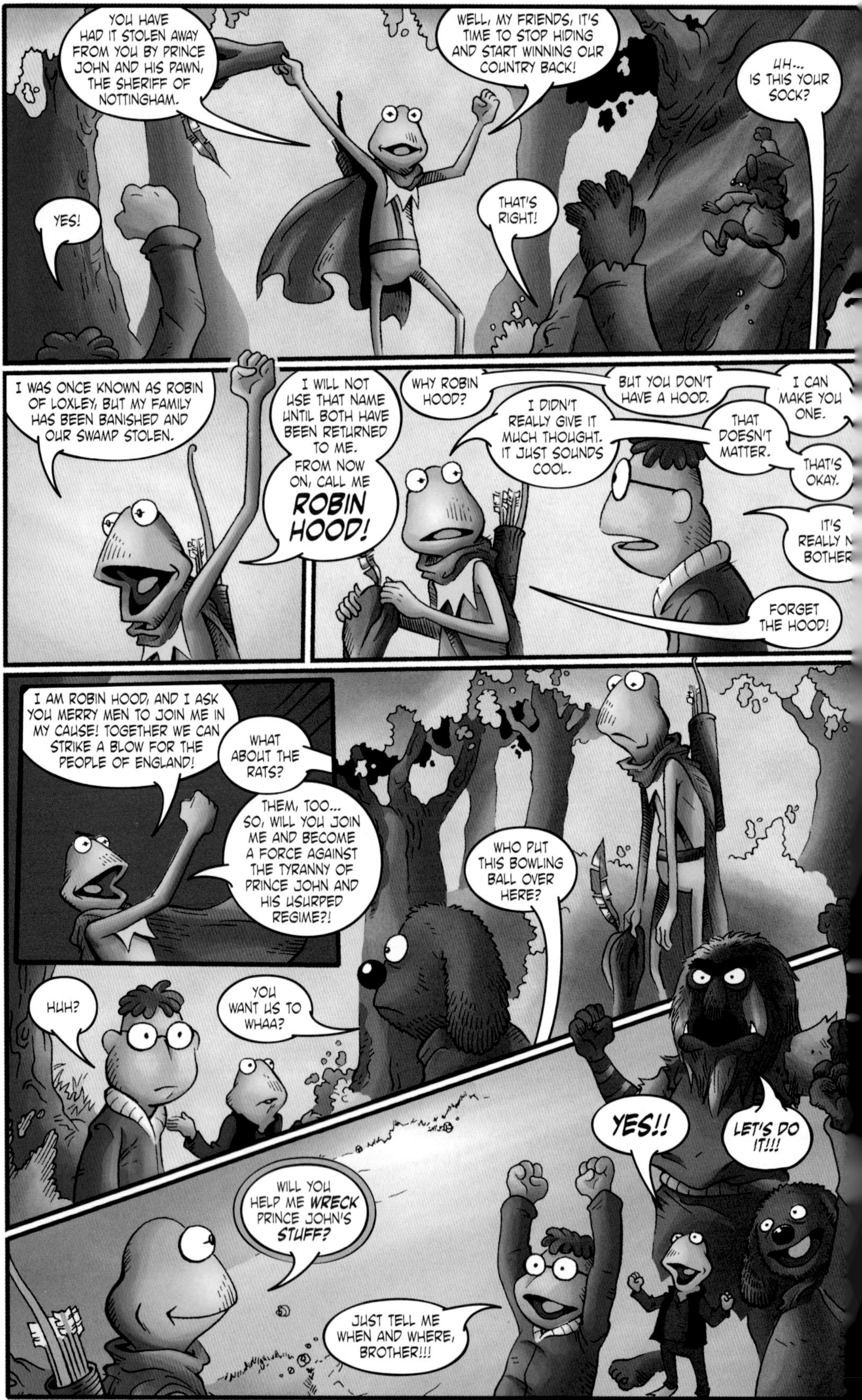
YOU HAVE HAD IT STOLEN AWAY FROM YOU BY PRINCE JOHN AND HIS PAWN, THE SHERIFF OF NOTTINGHAM.
WELL, MY FRIENDS, IT'S TIME TO STOP HIDING AND START WINNING OUR COUNTRY BACK!
UH... IS THIS YOUR SOCK?
YES!
THAT'S RIGHT!
I WAS ONCE KNOWN AS ROBIN OF LOXLEY, BUT MY FAMILY HAS BEEN BANISHED AND OUR SWAMP STOLEN.
I WILL NOT USE THAT NAME UNTIL BOTH HAVE BEEN RETURNED TO ME. FROM NOW ON, CALL ME ROBIN HOOD!
WHY ROBIN HOOD?
BUT YOU DON'T HAVE A HOOD.
I CAN MAKE YOU ONE.
I DIDN'T REALLY GIVE IT MUCH THOUGHT. IT JUST SOUNDS COOL.
THAT DOESN'T MATTER.
THAT'S OKAY.
IT'S REALLY N BOTHER
FORGET THE HOOD!
I AM ROBIN HOOD, AND I ASK YOU MERRY MEN TO JOIN ME IN MY CAUSE! TOGETHER WE CAN STRIKE A BLOW FOR THE PEOPLE OF ENGLAND!
WHAT ABOUT THE RATS?
THEM, TOO... SO, WILL YOU JOIN ME AND BECOME A FORCE AGAINST THE TYRANNY OF PRINCE JOHN AND HIS USURPED REGIME?!
WHO PUT THIS BOWLING BALL OVER HERE?
HUH?
YOU WANT US TO WHAA?
WILL YOU HELP ME WRECK PRINCE JOHN'S STUFF?
YES!!
LET'S DO IT!!!
JUST TELL ME WHEN AND WHERE, BROTHER!!!

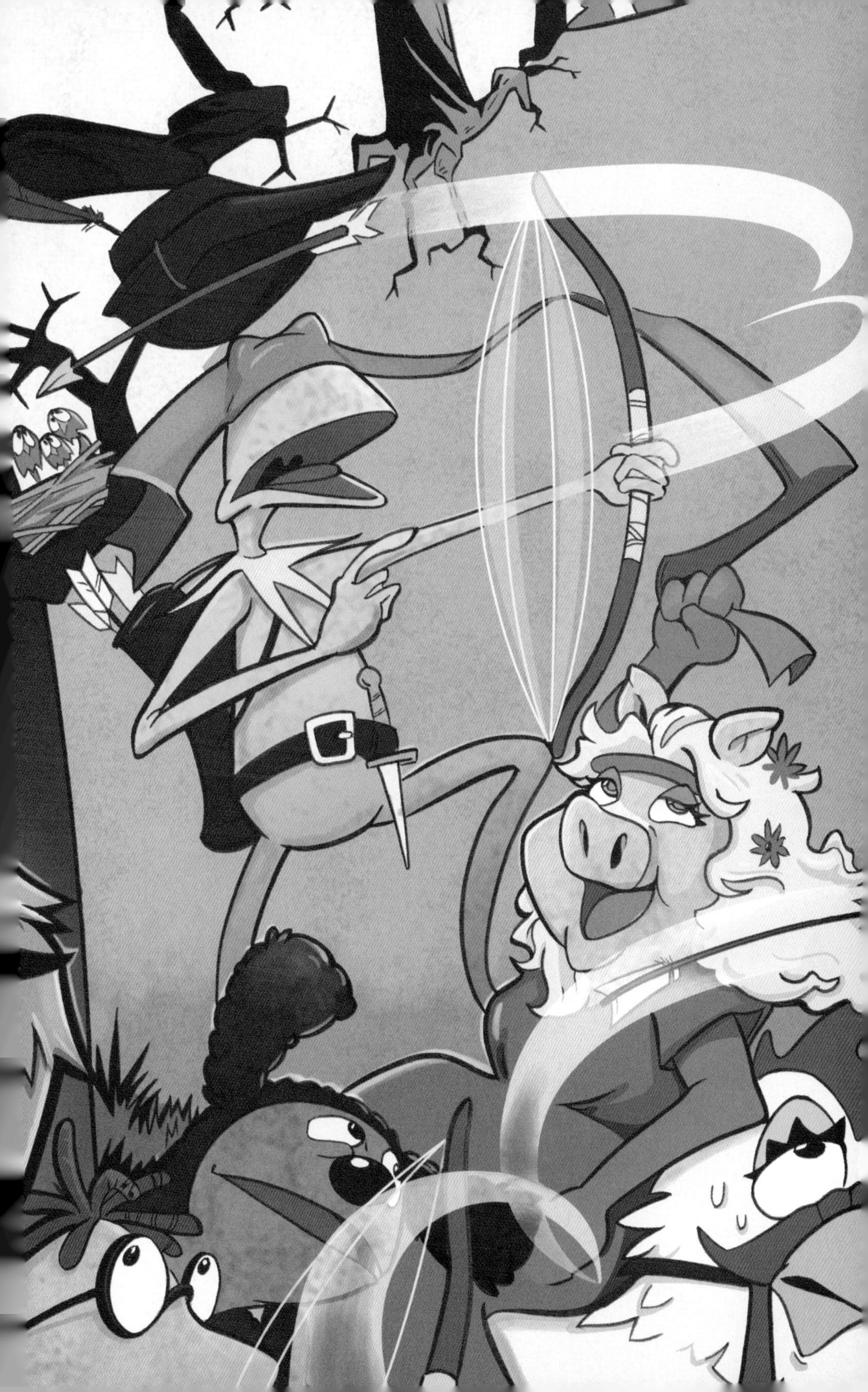

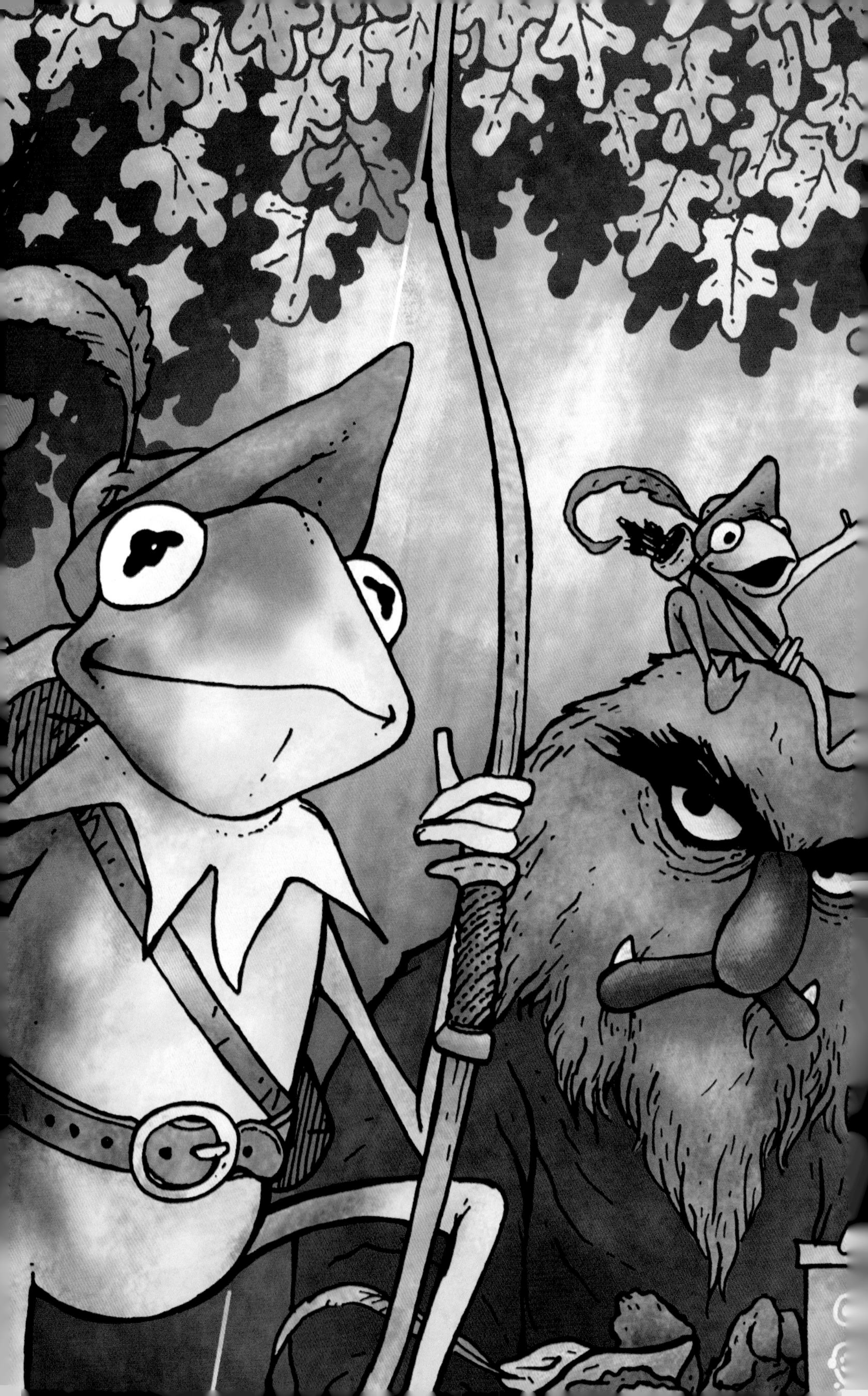

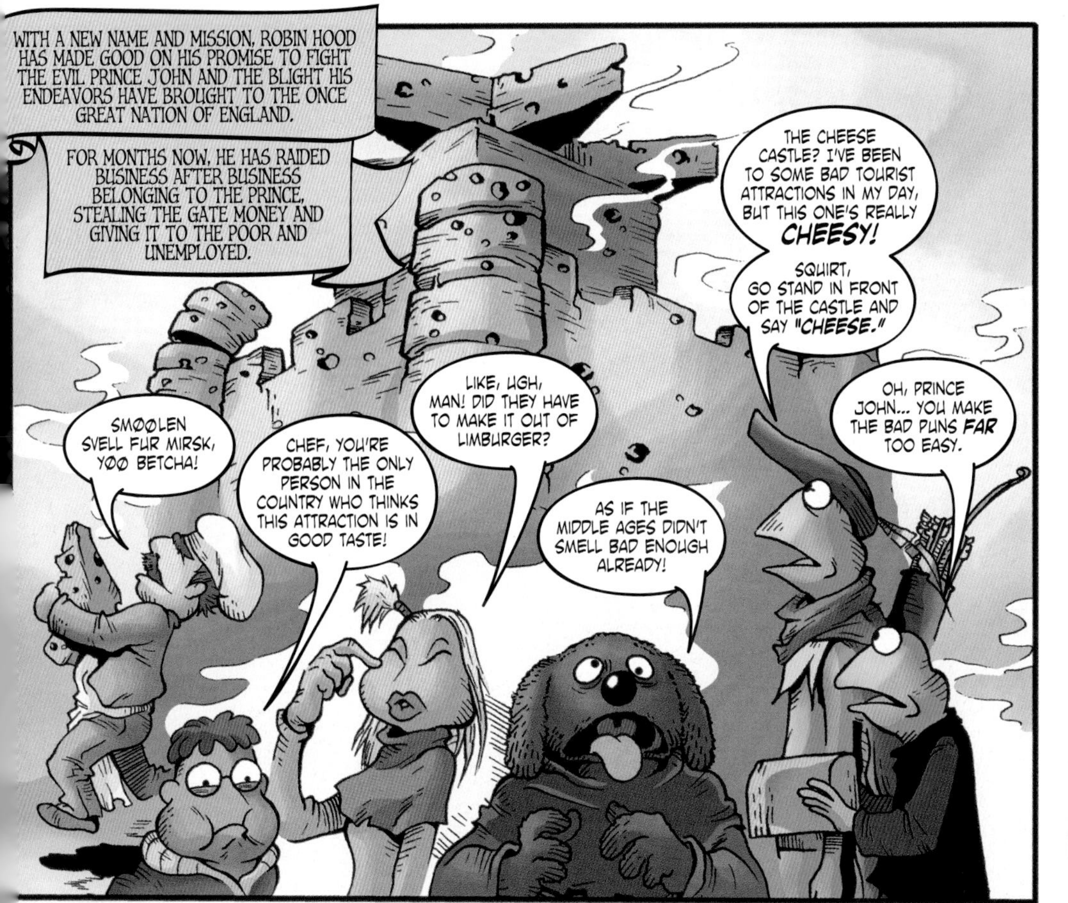
WITH A NEW NAME AND MISSION, ROBIN HOOD HAS MADE GOOD ON HIS PROMISE TO FIGHT THE EVIL PRINCE JOHN AND THE BLIGHT HIS ENDEAVORS HAVE BROUGHT TO THE ONCE GREAT NATION OF ENGLAND.
FOR MONTHS NOW, HE HAS RAIDED BUSINESS AFTER BUSINESS BELONGING TO THE PRINCE, STEALING THE GATE MONEY AND GIVING IT TO THE POOR AND UNEMPLOYED.
THE CHEESE CASTLE? I'VE BEEN TO SOME BAD TOURIST ATTRACTIONS IN MY DAY, BUT THIS ONE'S REALLY CHEESY!
SQUIRT, GO STAND IN FRONT OF THE CASTLE AND SAY "CHEESE."
SMØØLEN SVELL FUR MIRSK, YØØ BETCHA!
CHEF, YOU'RE PROBABLY THE ONLY PERSON IN THE COUNTRY WHO THINKS THIS ATTRACTION IS IN GOOD TASTE!
LIKE, UGH, MAN! DID THEY HAVE TO MAKE IT OUT OF LIMBURGER?
AS IF THE MIDDLE AGES DIDN'T SMELL BAD ENOUGH ALREADY!
OH, PRINCE JOHN... YOU MAKE THE BAD PUNS FAR TOO EASY.
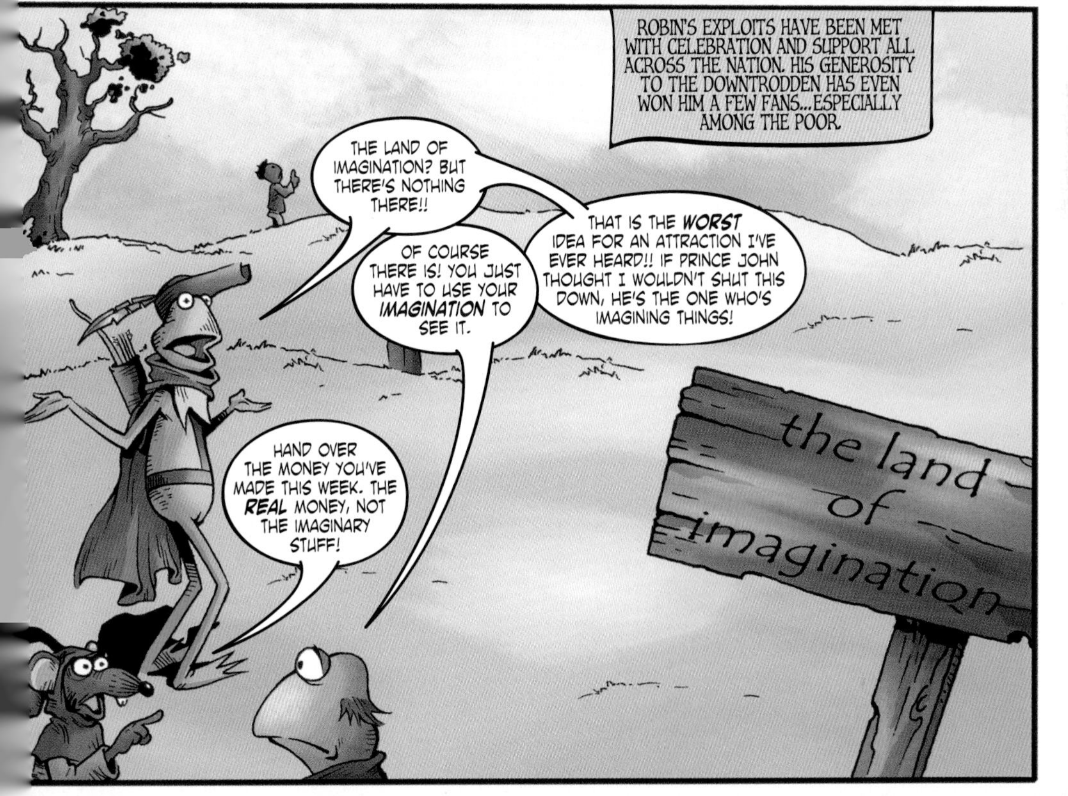
ROBIN'S EXPLOITS HAVE BEEN MET WITH CELEBRATION AND SUPPORT ALL ACROSS THE NATION. HIS GENEROSITY TO THE DOWNTRODDEN HAS EVEN WON HIM A FEW FANS...ESPECIALLY AMONG THE POOR.
THE LAND OF IMAGINATION? BUT THERE'S NOTHING THERE!!
OF COURSE THERE IS! YOU JUST HAVE TO USE YOUR IMAGINATION TO SEE IT.
THAT IS THE WORST IDEA FOR AN ATTRACTION I'VE EVER HEARD!! IF PRINCE JOHN THOUGHT I WOULDN'T SHUT THIS DOWN, HE'S THE ONE WHO'S IMAGINING THINGS!
HAND OVER THE MONEY YOU'VE MADE THIS WEEK. THE REAL MONEY, NOT THE IMAGINARY STUFF!
the land of imagination

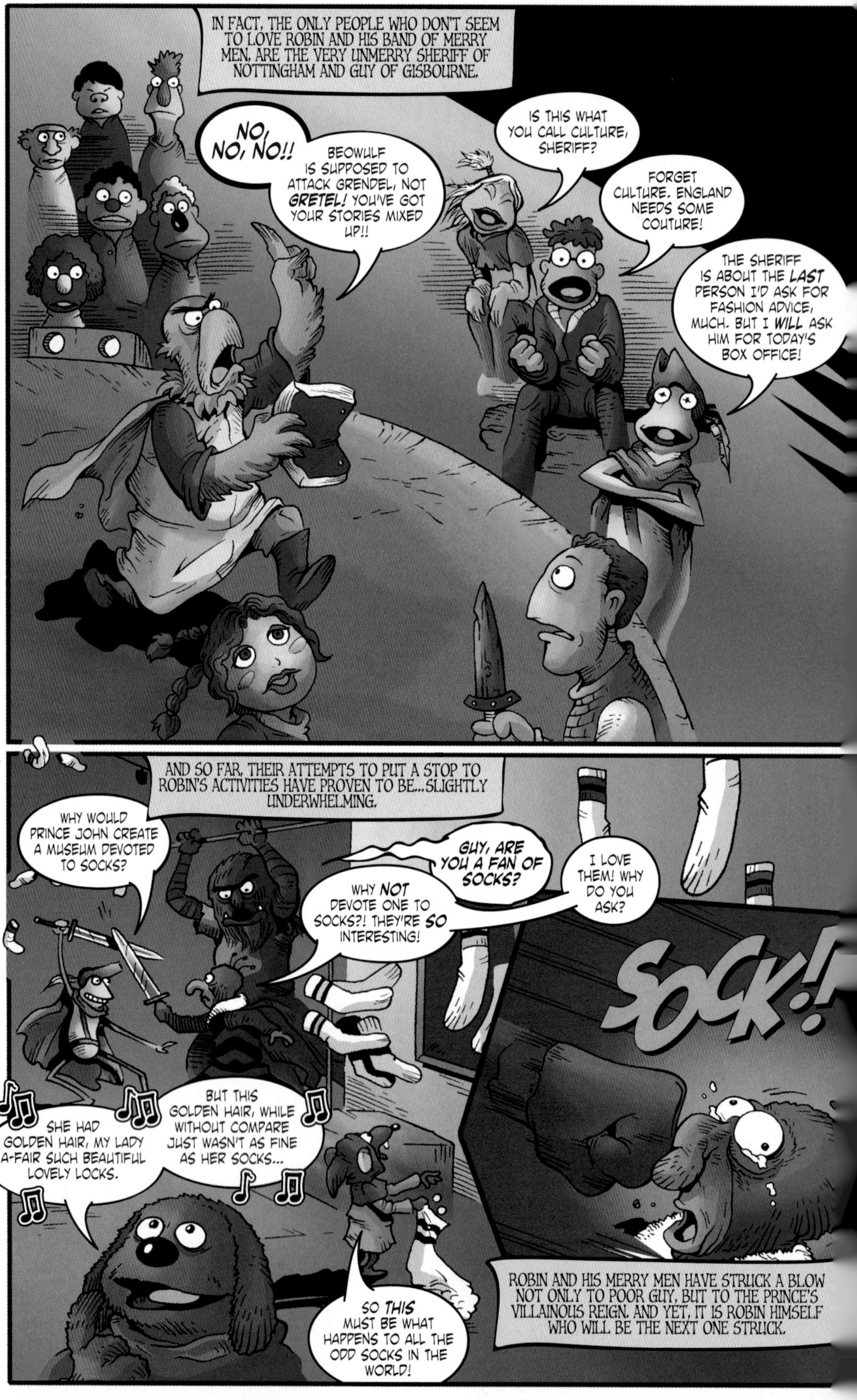
IN FACT, THE ONLY PEOPLE WHO DON'T SEEM TO LOVE ROBIN AND HIS BAND OF MERRY MEN, ARE THE VERY UNMERRY SHERIFF OF NOTTINGHAM AND GUY OF GISBOURNE.
NO, NO, NO!!
BEOWULF IS SUPPOSED TO ATTACK GRENDEL, NOT GRETEL! YOU'VE GOT YOUR STORIES MIXED UP!!
IS THIS WHAT YOU CALL CULTURE, SHERIFF?
FORGET CULTURE. ENGLAND NEEDS SOME COUTURE!
THE SHERIFF IS ABOUT THE LAST PERSON I'D ASK FOR FASHION ADVICE, MUCH. BUT I WILL ASK HIM FOR TODAY'S BOX OFFICE!
AND SO FAR, THEIR ATTEMPTS TO PUT A STOP TO ROBIN'S ACTIVITIES HAVE PROVEN TO BE...SLIGHTLY UNDERWHELMING.
WHY WOULD PRINCE JOHN CREATE A MUSEUM DEVOTED TO SOCKS?
WHY NOT DEVOTE ONE TO SOCKS?! THEY'RE SO INTERESTING!
GUY, ARE YOU A FAN OF SOCKS?
I LOVE THEM! WHY DO YOU ASK?
SOCK!!
SHE HAD GOLDEN HAIR, MY LADY A-FAIR SUCH BEAUTIFUL LOVELY LOCKS.
BUT THIS GOLDEN HAIR, WHILE WITHOUT COMPARE JUST WASN'T AS FINE AS HER SOCKS...
SO THIS MUST BE WHAT HAPPENS TO ALL THE ODD SOCKS IN THE WORLD!
ROBIN AND HIS MERRY MEN HAVE STRUCK A BLOW NOT ONLY TO POOR GUY, BUT TO THE PRINCE'S VILLAINOUS REIGN. AND YET, IT IS ROBIN HIMSELF WHO WILL BE THE NEXT ONE STRUCK.

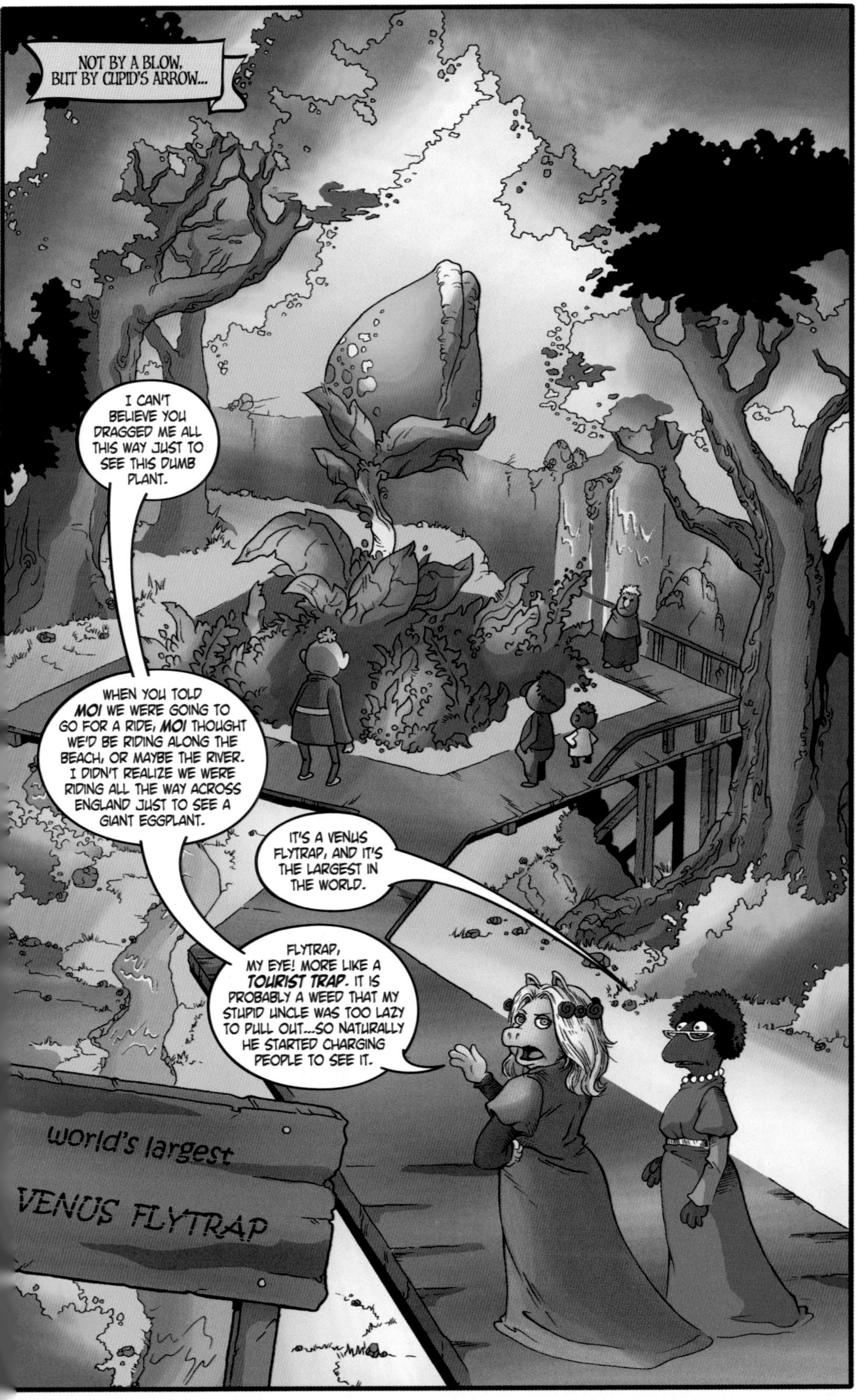
NOT BY A BLOW, BUT BY CUPID'S ARROW...
I CAN'T BELIEVE YOU DRAGGED ME ALL THIS WAY JUST TO SEE THIS DUMB PLANT.
WHEN YOU TOLD MOI WE WERE GOING TO GO FOR A RIDE, MOI THOUGHT WE'D BE RIDING ALONG THE BEACH, OR MAYBE THE RIVER. I DIDN'T REALIZE WE WERE RIDING ALL THE WAY ACROSS ENGLAND JUST TO SEE A GIANT EGGPLANT.
IT'S A VENUS FLYTRAP, AND IT'S THE LARGEST IN THE WORLD.
FLYTRAP, MY EYE! MORE LIKE A TOURIST TRAP. IT IS PROBABLY A WEED THAT MY STUPID UNCLE WAS TOO LAZY TO PULL OUT...SO NATURALLY HE STARTED CHARGING PEOPLE TO SEE IT.
world's largest
VENUS FLYTRAP

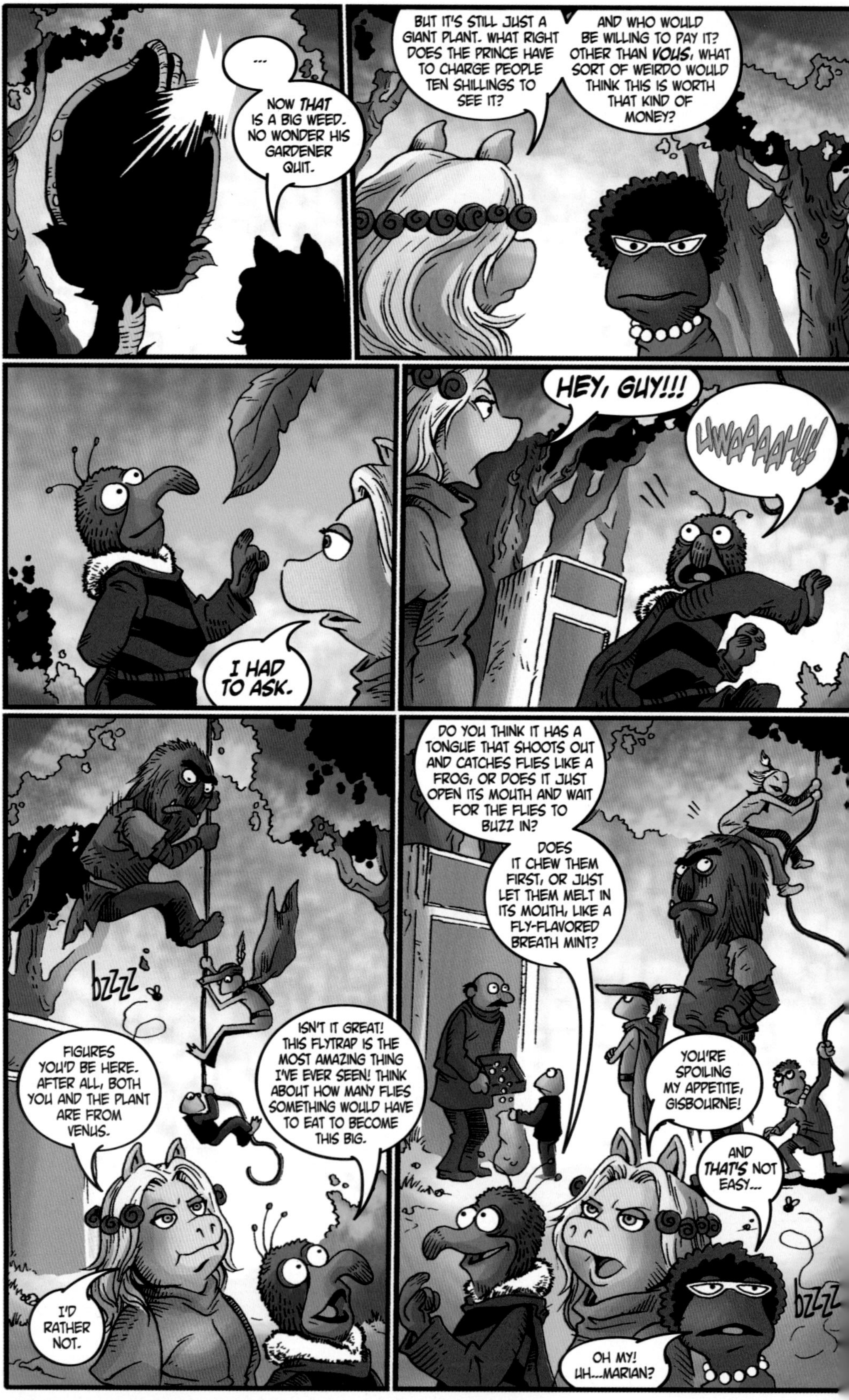
...
NOW THAT IS A BIG WEED. NO WONDER HIS GARDENER QUIT.
BUT IT'S STILL JUST A GIANT PLANT. WHAT RIGHT DOES THE PRINCE HAVE TO CHARGE PEOPLE TEN SHILLINGS TO SEE IT?
AND WHO WOULD BE WILLING TO PAY IT? OTHER THAN VOUS, WHAT SORT OF WEIRDO WOULD THINK THIS IS WORTH THAT KIND OF MONEY?
I HAD TO ASK.
HEY, GUY!!!
UWAAAAH!!!
bzzzz
FIGURES YOU'D BE HERE. AFTER ALL, BOTH YOU AND THE PLANT ARE FROM VENUS.
ISN'T IT GREAT! THIS FLYTRAP IS THE MOST AMAZING THING I'VE EVER SEEN! THINK ABOUT HOW MANY FLIES SOMETHING WOULD HAVE TO EAT TO BECOME THIS BIG.
I'D RATHER NOT.
DO YOU THINK IT HAS A TONGUE THAT SHOOTS OUT AND CATCHES FLIES LIKE A FROG, OR DOES IT JUST OPEN ITS MOUTH AND WAIT FOR THE FLIES TO BUZZ IN?
DOES IT CHEW THEM FIRST, OR JUST LET THEM MELT IN ITS MOUTH, LIKE A FLY-FLAVORED BREATH MINT?
YOU'RE SPOILING MY APPETITE, GISBOURNE!
AND THAT'S NOT EASY...
bzzzz
OH MY! UH...MARIAN?

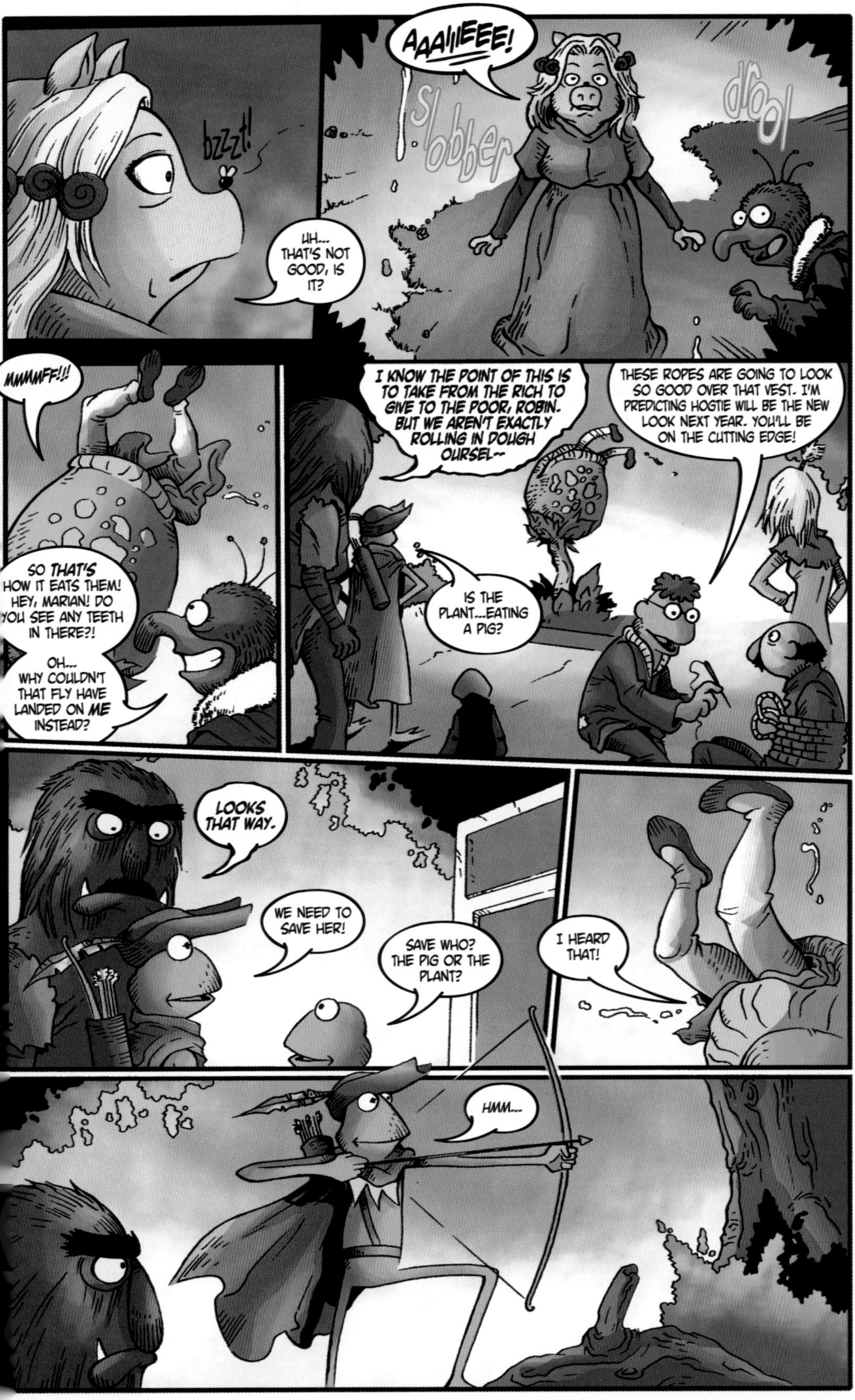

bzzzt!
UH... THAT'S NOT GOOD, IS IT?
AAAIIIEEE!
slobber
drool
MMMMFF!!!
SO THAT'S HOW IT EATS THEM! HEY, MARIAN! DO YOU SEE ANY TEETH IN THERE?!
OH... WHY COULDN'T THAT FLY HAVE LANDED ON ME INSTEAD?
I KNOW THE POINT OF THIS IS TO TAKE FROM THE RICH TO GIVE TO THE POOR, ROBIN. BUT WE AREN'T EXACTLY ROLLING IN DOUGH OURSEL--
THESE ROPES ARE GOING TO LOOK SO GOOD OVER THAT VEST. I'M PREDICTING HOGTIE WILL BE THE NEW LOOK NEXT YEAR. YOU'LL BE ON THE CUTTING EDGE!
IS THE PLANT...EATING A PIG?
LOOKS THAT WAY.
WE NEED TO SAVE HER!
SAVE WHO? THE PIG OR THE PLANT?
I HEARD THAT!
HMM...

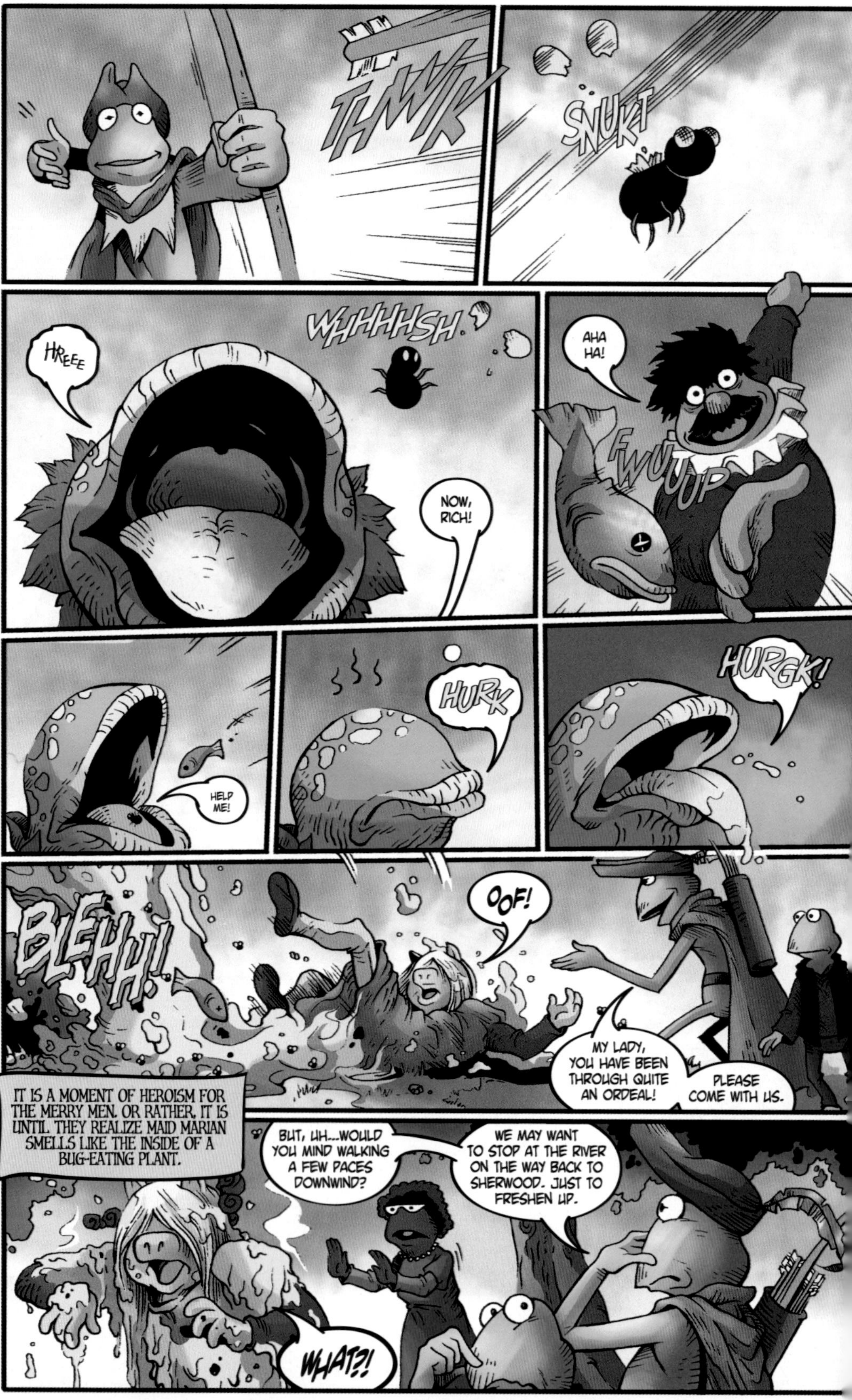
THWIK
SNUKT
HREEE
WHHHHSH
AHA HA!
NOW, RICH!
FWUUUP
HELP ME!
HURK
HURGK!
BLEHH!
OOF!
MY LADY, YOU HAVE BEEN THROUGH QUITE AN ORDEAL!
PLEASE COME WITH US.
IT IS A MOMENT OF HEROISM FOR THE MERRY MEN. OR RATHER, IT IS UNTIL THEY REALIZE MAID MARIAN SMELLS LIKE THE INSIDE OF A BUG-EATING PLANT.
BUT, UH...WOULD YOU MIND WALKING A FEW PACES DOWNWIND?
WE MAY WANT TO STOP AT THE RIVER ON THE WAY BACK TO SHERWOOD. JUST TO FRESHEN UP.
WHAT?!

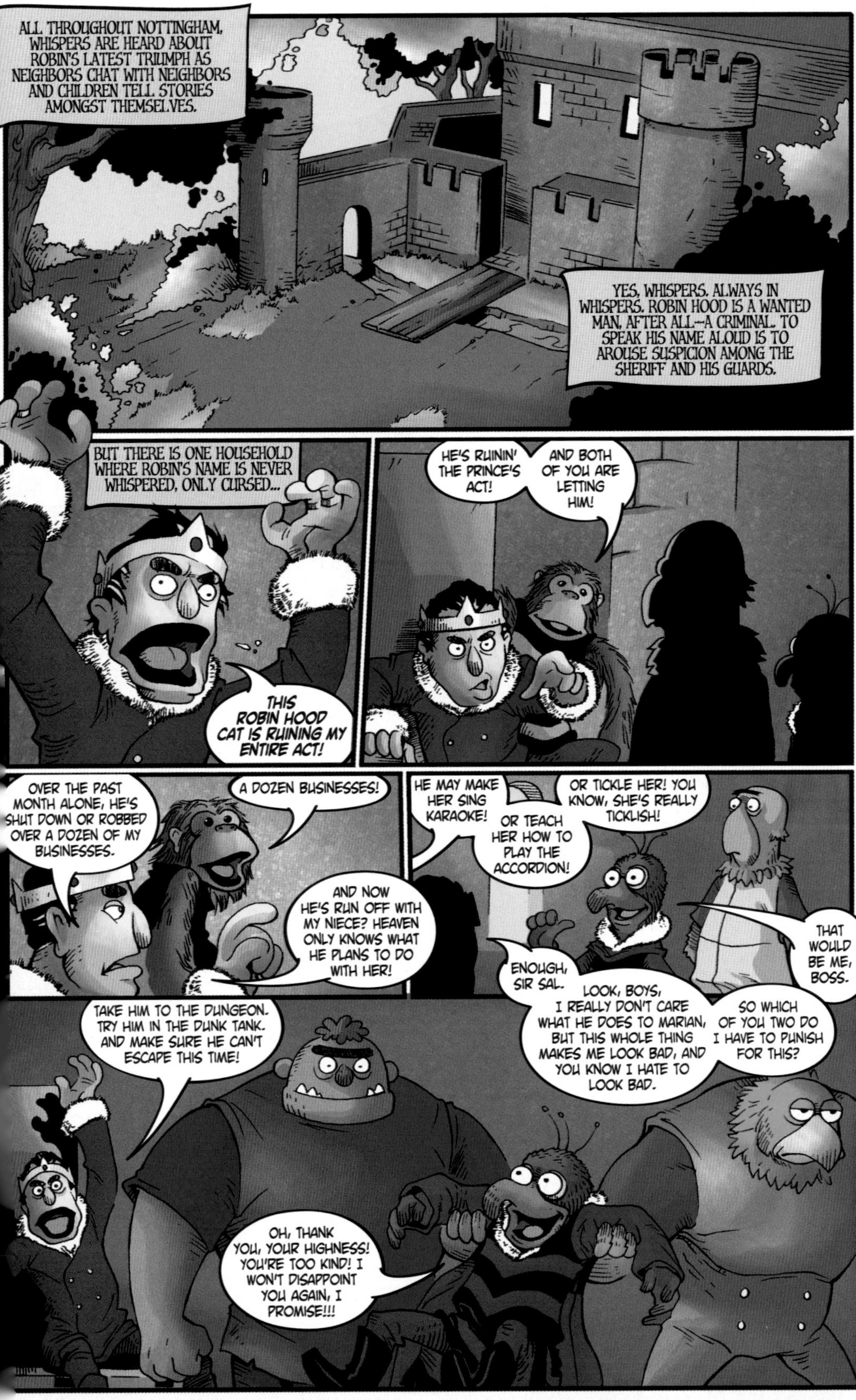
ALL THROUGHOUT NOTTINGHAM, WHISPERS ARE HEARD ABOUT ROBIN'S LATEST TRIUMPH AS NEIGHBORS CHAT WITH NEIGHBORS AND CHILDREN TELL STORIES AMONGST THEMSELVES.
YES, WHISPERS. ALWAYS IN WHISPERS. ROBIN HOOD IS A WANTED MAN, AFTER ALL--A CRIMINAL. TO SPEAK HIS NAME ALOUD IS TO AROUSE SUSPICION AMONG THE SHERIFF AND HIS GUARDS.
BUT THERE IS ONE HOUSEHOLD WHERE ROBIN'S NAME IS NEVER WHISPERED, ONLY CURSED...
THIS ROBIN HOOD CAT IS RUINING MY ENTIRE ACT!
HE'S RUININ' THE PRINCE'S ACT!
AND BOTH OF YOU ARE LETTING HIM!
OVER THE PAST MONTH ALONE, HE'S SHUT DOWN OR ROBBED OVER A DOZEN OF MY BUSINESSES.
A DOZEN BUSINESSES!
AND NOW HE'S RUN OFF WITH MY NIECE? HEAVEN ONLY KNOWS WHAT HE PLANS TO DO WITH HER!
HE MAY MAKE HER SING KARAOKE!
OR TEACH HER HOW TO PLAY THE ACCORDION!
OR TICKLE HER! YOU KNOW, SHE'S REALLY TICKLISH!
ENOUGH, SIR SAL.
THAT WOULD BE ME, BOSS.
LOOK, BOYS, I REALLY DON'T CARE WHAT HE DOES TO MARIAN, BUT THIS WHOLE THING MAKES ME LOOK BAD, AND YOU KNOW I HATE TO LOOK BAD.
SO WHICH OF YOU TWO DO I HAVE TO PUNISH FOR THIS?
TAKE HIM TO THE DUNGEON. TRY HIM IN THE DUNK TANK. AND MAKE SURE HE CAN'T ESCAPE THIS TIME!
OH, THANK YOU, YOUR HIGHNESS! YOU'RE TOO KIND! I WON'T DISAPPOINT YOU AGAIN, I PROMISE!!!

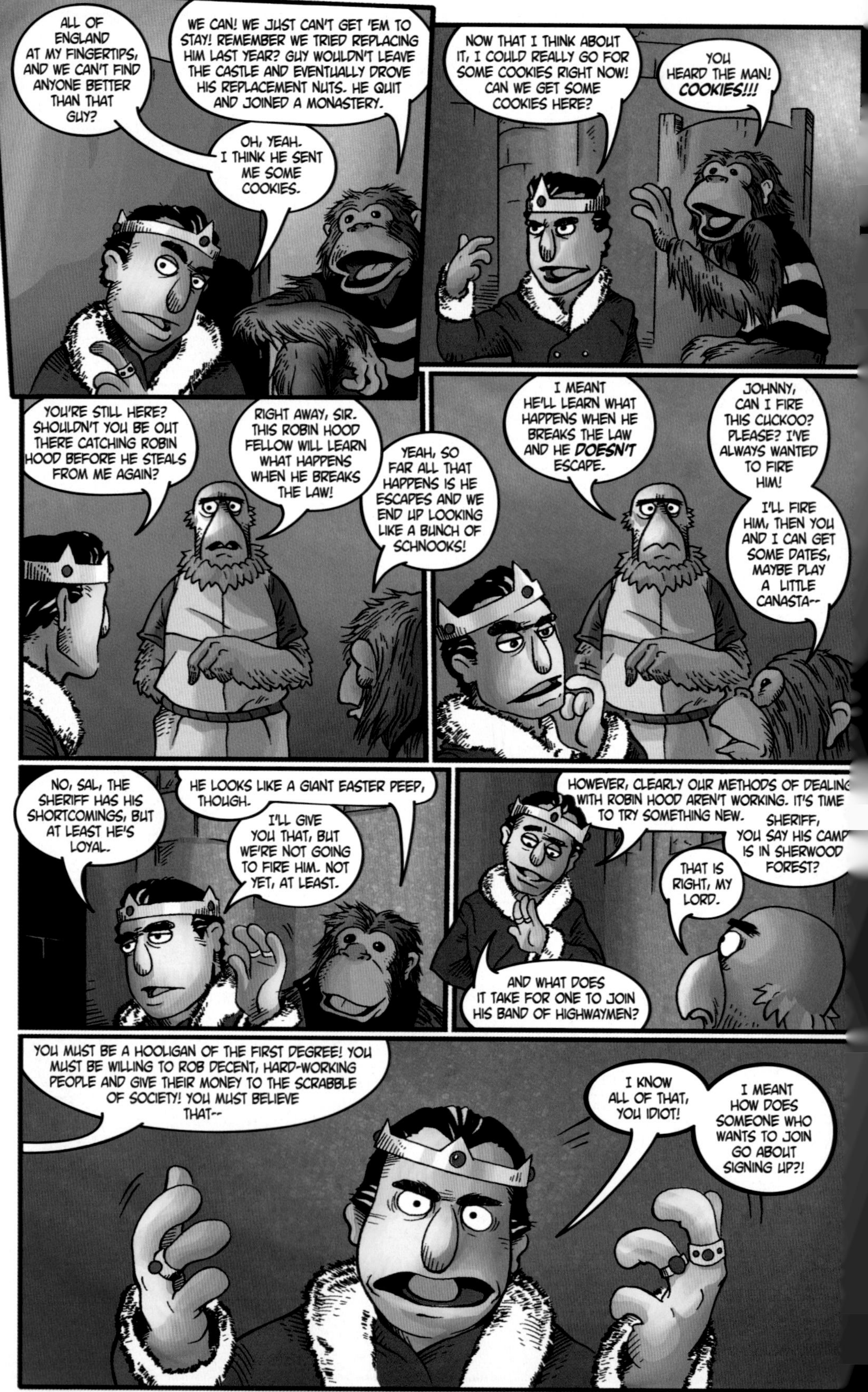
ALL OF ENGLAND AT MY FINGERTIPS, AND WE CAN'T FIND ANYONE BETTER THAN THAT GUY?
WE CAN! WE JUST CAN'T GET 'EM TO STAY! REMEMBER WE TRIED REPLACING HIM LAST YEAR? GUY WOULDN'T LEAVE THE CASTLE AND EVENTUALLY DROVE HIS REPLACEMENT NUTS. HE QUIT AND JOINED A MONASTERY.
OH, YEAH. I THINK HE SENT ME SOME COOKIES.
NOW THAT I THINK ABOUT IT, I COULD REALLY GO FOR SOME COOKIES RIGHT NOW! CAN WE GET SOME COOKIES HERE?
YOU HEARD THE MAN! COOKIES!!!
YOU'RE STILL HERE? SHOULDN'T YOU BE OUT THERE CATCHING ROBIN HOOD BEFORE HE STEALS FROM ME AGAIN?
RIGHT AWAY, SIR. THIS ROBIN HOOD FELLOW WILL LEARN WHAT HAPPENS WHEN HE BREAKS THE LAW!
YEAH, SO FAR ALL THAT HAPPENS IS HE ESCAPES AND WE END UP LOOKING LIKE A BUNCH OF SCHNOOKS!
I MEANT HE'LL LEARN WHAT HAPPENS WHEN HE BREAKS THE LAW AND HE DOESN'T ESCAPE.
JOHNNY, CAN I FIRE THIS CUCKOO? PLEASE? I'VE ALWAYS WANTED TO FIRE HIM!
I'LL FIRE HIM, THEN YOU AND I CAN GET SOME DATES, MAYBE PLAY A LITTLE CANASTA--
NO, SAL, THE SHERIFF HAS HIS SHORTCOMINGS, BUT AT LEAST HE'S LOYAL.
HE LOOKS LIKE A GIANT EASTER PEEP, THOUGH.
I'LL GIVE YOU THAT, BUT WE'RE NOT GOING TO FIRE HIM. NOT YET, AT LEAST.
HOWEVER, CLEARLY OUR METHODS OF DEALING WITH ROBIN HOOD AREN'T WORKING. IT'S TIME TO TRY SOMETHING NEW.
SHERIFF, YOU SAY HIS CAMP IS IN SHERWOOD FOREST?
THAT IS RIGHT, MY LORD.
AND WHAT DOES IT TAKE FOR ONE TO JOIN HIS BAND OF HIGHWAYMEN?
YOU MUST BE A HOOLIGAN OF THE FIRST DEGREE! YOU MUST BE WILLING TO ROB DECENT, HARD-WORKING PEOPLE AND GIVE THEIR MONEY TO THE SCRABBLE OF SOCIETY! YOU MUST BELIEVE THAT--
I KNOW ALL OF THAT, YOU IDIOT!
I MEANT HOW DOES SOMEONE WHO WANTS TO JOIN GO ABOUT SIGNING UP?!

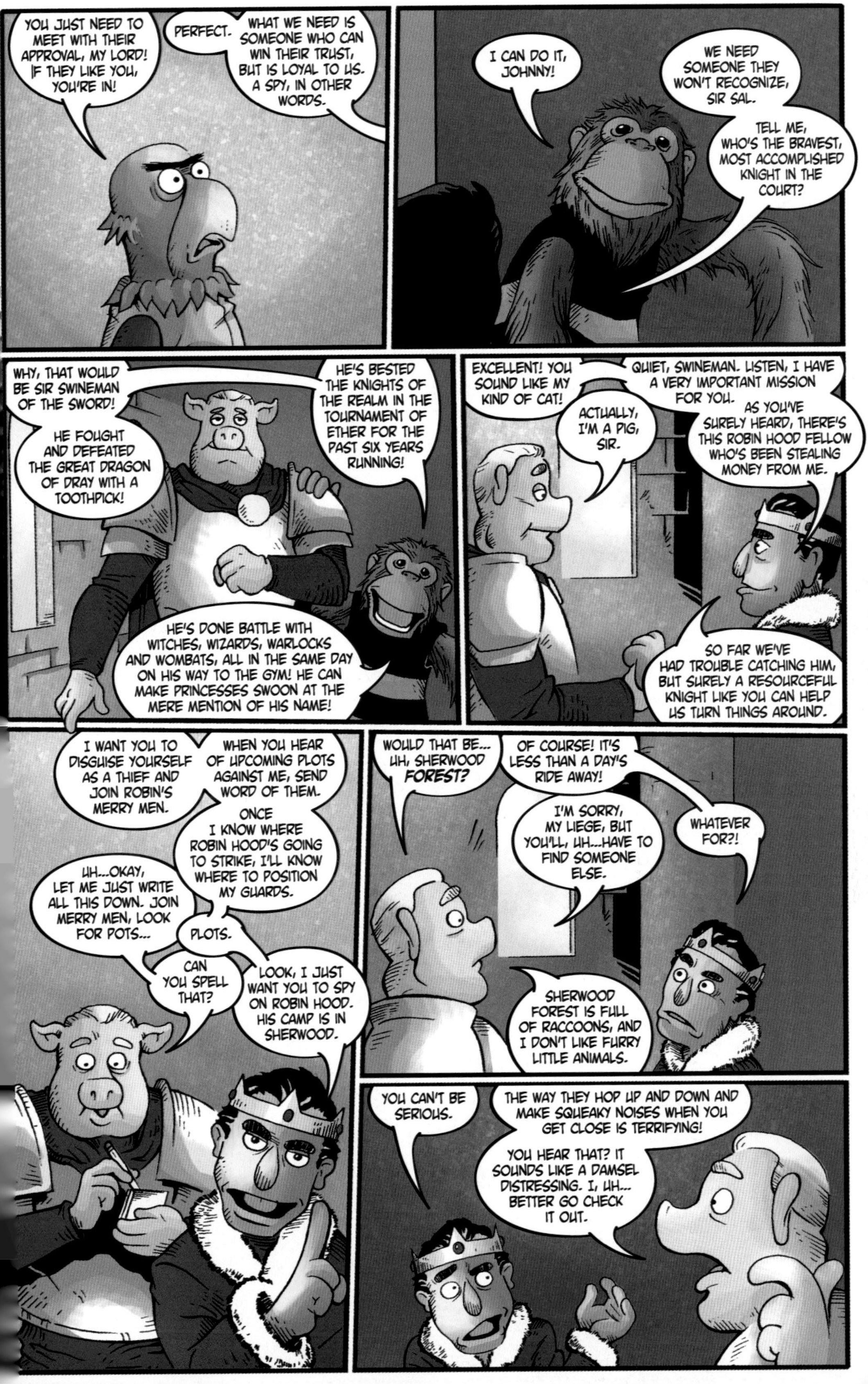
YOU JUST NEED TO MEET WITH THEIR APPROVAL, MY LORD! IF THEY LIKE YOU, YOU'RE IN!
PERFECT.
WHAT WE NEED IS SOMEONE WHO CAN WIN THEIR TRUST, BUT IS LOYAL TO US. A SPY, IN OTHER WORDS.
I CAN DO IT, JOHNNY!
WE NEED SOMEONE THEY WON'T RECOGNIZE, SIR SAL.
TELL ME, WHO'S THE BRAVEST, MOST ACCOMPLISHED KNIGHT IN THE COURT?
WHY, THAT WOULD BE SIR SWINEMAN OF THE SWORD!
HE FOUGHT AND DEFEATED THE GREAT DRAGON OF DRAY WITH A TOOTHPICK!
HE'S BESTED THE KNIGHTS OF THE REALM IN THE TOURNAMENT OF ETHER FOR THE PAST SIX YEARS RUNNING!
HE'S DONE BATTLE WITH WITCHES, WIZARDS, WARLOCKS AND WOMBATS, ALL IN THE SAME DAY ON HIS WAY TO THE GYM! HE CAN MAKE PRINCESSES SWOON AT THE MERE MENTION OF HIS NAME!
EXCELLENT! YOU SOUND LIKE MY KIND OF CAT!
ACTUALLY, I'M A PIG, SIR.
QUIET, SWINEMAN. LISTEN, I HAVE A VERY IMPORTANT MISSION FOR YOU.
AS YOU'VE SURELY HEARD, THERE'S THIS ROBIN HOOD FELLOW WHO'S BEEN STEALING MONEY FROM ME.
SO FAR WE'VE HAD TROUBLE CATCHING HIM, BUT SURELY A RESOURCEFUL KNIGHT LIKE YOU CAN HELP US TURN THINGS AROUND.
I WANT YOU TO DISGUISE YOURSELF AS A THIEF AND JOIN ROBIN'S MERRY MEN.
WHEN YOU HEAR OF UPCOMING PLOTS AGAINST ME, SEND WORD OF THEM.
ONCE I KNOW WHERE ROBIN HOOD'S GOING TO STRIKE, I'LL KNOW WHERE TO POSITION MY GUARDS.
UH...OKAY, LET ME JUST WRITE ALL THIS DOWN. JOIN MERRY MEN, LOOK FOR POTS...
PLOTS.
CAN YOU SPELL THAT?
LOOK, I JUST WANT YOU TO SPY ON ROBIN HOOD. HIS CAMP IS IN SHERWOOD.
WOULD THAT BE... UH, SHERWOOD ***FOREST?***
OF COURSE! IT'S LESS THAN A DAY'S RIDE AWAY!
I'M SORRY, MY LIEGE, BUT YOU'LL, UH...HAVE TO FIND SOMEONE ELSE.
WHATEVER FOR?!
SHERWOOD FOREST IS FULL OF RACCOONS, AND I DON'T LIKE FURRY LITTLE ANIMALS.
YOU CAN'T BE SERIOUS.
THE WAY THEY HOP UP AND DOWN AND MAKE SQUEAKY NOISES WHEN YOU GET CLOSE IS TERRIFYING!
YOU HEAR THAT? IT SOUNDS LIKE A DAMSEL DISTRESSING. I, UH... BETTER GO CHECK IT OUT.

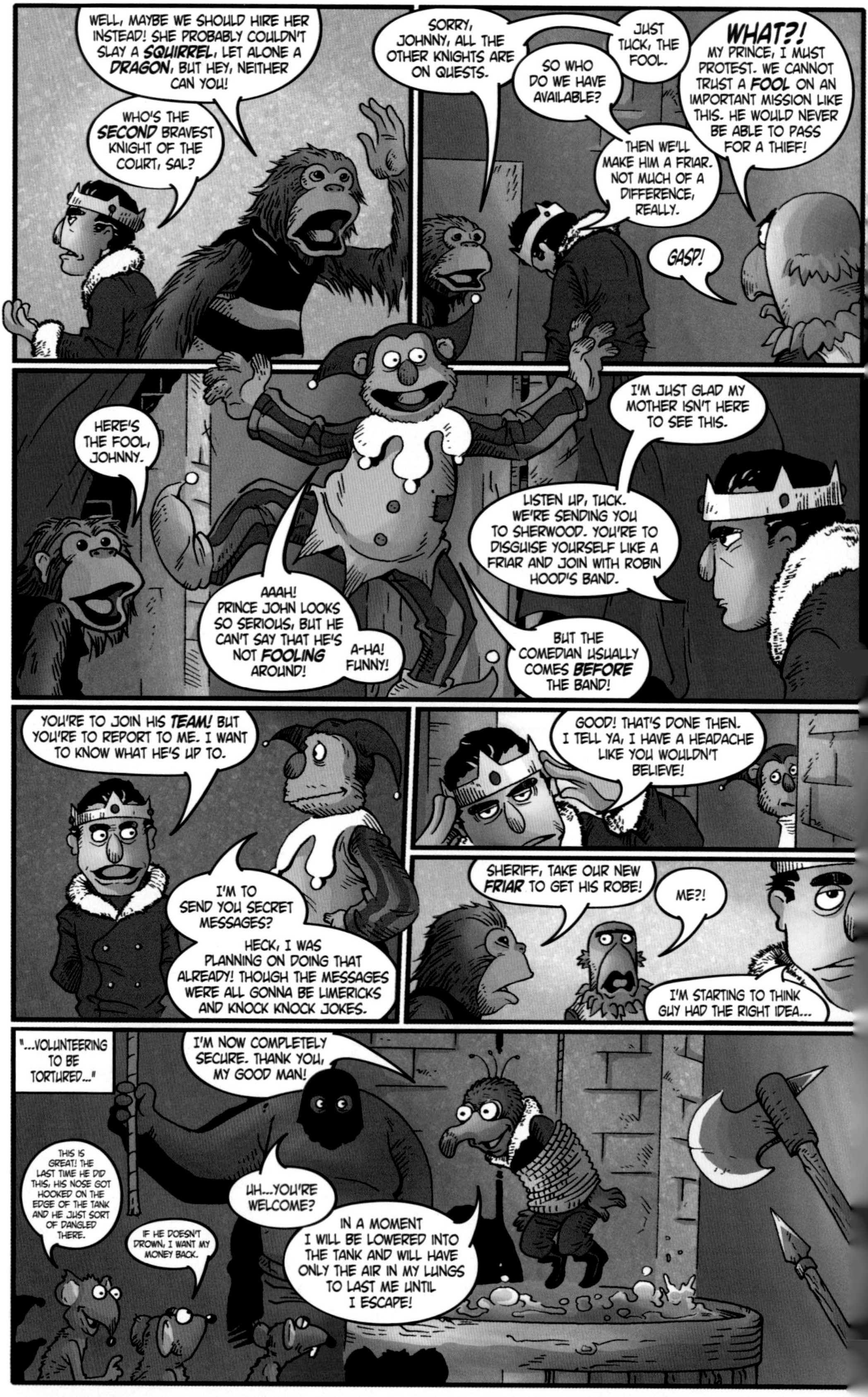
WELL, MAYBE WE SHOULD HIRE HER INSTEAD! SHE PROBABLY COULDN'T SLAY A SQUIRREL, LET ALONE A DRAGON, BUT HEY, NEITHER CAN YOU!
WHO'S THE SECOND BRAVEST KNIGHT OF THE COURT, SAL?
SORRY, JOHNNY, ALL THE OTHER KNIGHTS ARE ON QUESTS.
SO WHO DO WE HAVE AVAILABLE?
JUST TUCK, THE FOOL.
THEN WE'LL MAKE HIM A FRIAR. NOT MUCH OF A DIFFERENCE, REALLY.
WHAT?! MY PRINCE, I MUST PROTEST. WE CANNOT TRUST A FOOL ON AN IMPORTANT MISSION LIKE THIS. HE WOULD NEVER BE ABLE TO PASS FOR A THIEF!
GASP!
HERE'S THE FOOL, JOHNNY.
I'M JUST GLAD MY MOTHER ISN'T HERE TO SEE THIS.
LISTEN UP, TUCK. WE'RE SENDING YOU TO SHERWOOD. YOU'RE TO DISGUISE YOURSELF LIKE A FRIAR AND JOIN WITH ROBIN HOOD'S BAND.
AAAH! PRINCE JOHN LOOKS SO SERIOUS, BUT HE CAN'T SAY THAT HE'S NOT FOOLING AROUND!
A-HA! FUNNY!
BUT THE COMEDIAN USUALLY COMES BEFORE THE BAND!
YOU'RE TO JOIN HIS TEAM! BUT YOU'RE TO REPORT TO ME. I WANT TO KNOW WHAT HE'S UP TO.
I'M TO SEND YOU SECRET MESSAGES?
HECK, I WAS PLANNING ON DOING THAT ALREADY! THOUGH THE MESSAGES WERE ALL GONNA BE LIMERICKS AND KNOCK KNOCK JOKES.
GOOD! THAT'S DONE THEN. I TELL YA, I HAVE A HEADACHE LIKE YOU WOULDN'T BELIEVE!
SHERIFF, TAKE OUR NEW FRIAR TO GET HIS ROBE!
ME?!
I'M STARTING TO THINK GUY HAD THE RIGHT IDEA...
"...VOLUNTEERING TO BE TORTURED..."
I'M NOW COMPLETELY SECURE. THANK YOU, MY GOOD MAN!
UH...YOU'RE WELCOME?
IN A MOMENT I WILL BE LOWERED INTO THE TANK AND WILL HAVE ONLY THE AIR IN MY LUNGS TO LAST ME UNTIL I ESCAPE!
THIS IS GREAT! THE LAST TIME HE DID THIS, HIS NOSE GOT HOOKED ON THE EDGE OF THE TANK AND HE JUST SORT OF DANGLED THERE.
IF HE DOESN'T DROWN, I WANT MY MONEY BACK.

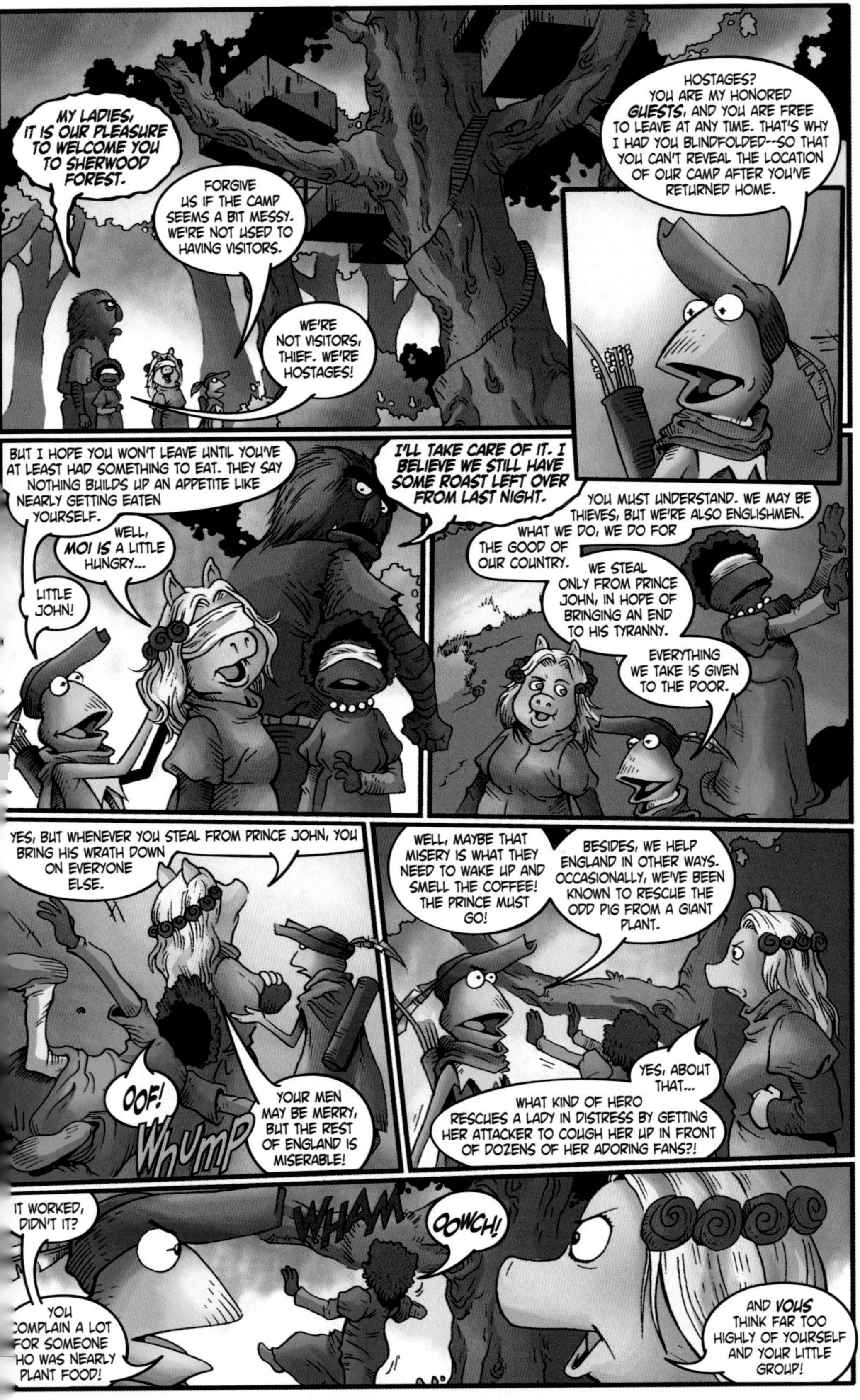
MY LADIES, IT IS OUR PLEASURE TO WELCOME YOU TO SHERWOOD FOREST.
FORGIVE US IF THE CAMP SEEMS A BIT MESSY. WE'RE NOT USED TO HAVING VISITORS.
WE'RE NOT VISITORS, THIEF. WE'RE HOSTAGES!
HOSTAGES? YOU ARE MY HONORED GUESTS, AND YOU ARE FREE TO LEAVE AT ANY TIME. THAT'S WHY I HAD YOU BLINDFOLDED--SO THAT YOU CAN'T REVEAL THE LOCATION OF OUR CAMP AFTER YOU'VE RETURNED HOME.
BUT I HOPE YOU WON'T LEAVE UNTIL YOU'VE AT LEAST HAD SOMETHING TO EAT. THEY SAY NOTHING BUILDS UP AN APPETITE LIKE NEARLY GETTING EATEN YOURSELF.
WELL, MOI IS A LITTLE HUNGRY...
LITTLE JOHN!
I'LL TAKE CARE OF IT. I BELIEVE WE STILL HAVE SOME ROAST LEFT OVER FROM LAST NIGHT.
YOU MUST UNDERSTAND. WE MAY BE THIEVES, BUT WE'RE ALSO ENGLISHMEN.
WHAT WE DO, WE DO FOR THE GOOD OF OUR COUNTRY.
WE STEAL ONLY FROM PRINCE JOHN, IN HOPE OF BRINGING AN END TO HIS TYRANNY.
EVERYTHING WE TAKE IS GIVEN TO THE POOR.
YES, BUT WHENEVER YOU STEAL FROM PRINCE JOHN, YOU BRING HIS WRATH DOWN ON EVERYONE ELSE.
OOF!
WHUMP
YOUR MEN MAY BE MERRY, BUT THE REST OF ENGLAND IS MISERABLE!
WELL, MAYBE THAT MISERY IS WHAT THEY NEED TO WAKE UP AND SMELL THE COFFEE! THE PRINCE MUST GO!
BESIDES, WE HELP ENGLAND IN OTHER WAYS. OCCASIONALLY, WE'VE BEEN KNOWN TO RESCUE THE ODD PIG FROM A GIANT PLANT.
YES, ABOUT THAT...
WHAT KIND OF HERO RESCUES A LADY IN DISTRESS BY GETTING HER ATTACKER TO COUGH HER UP IN FRONT OF DOZENS OF HER ADORING FANS?!
IT WORKED, DIDN'T IT?
WHAM
OOWCH!
YOU COMPLAIN A LOT FOR SOMEONE WHO WAS NEARLY PLANT FOOD!
AND VOUS THINK FAR TOO HIGHLY OF YOURSELF AND YOUR LITTLE GROUP!

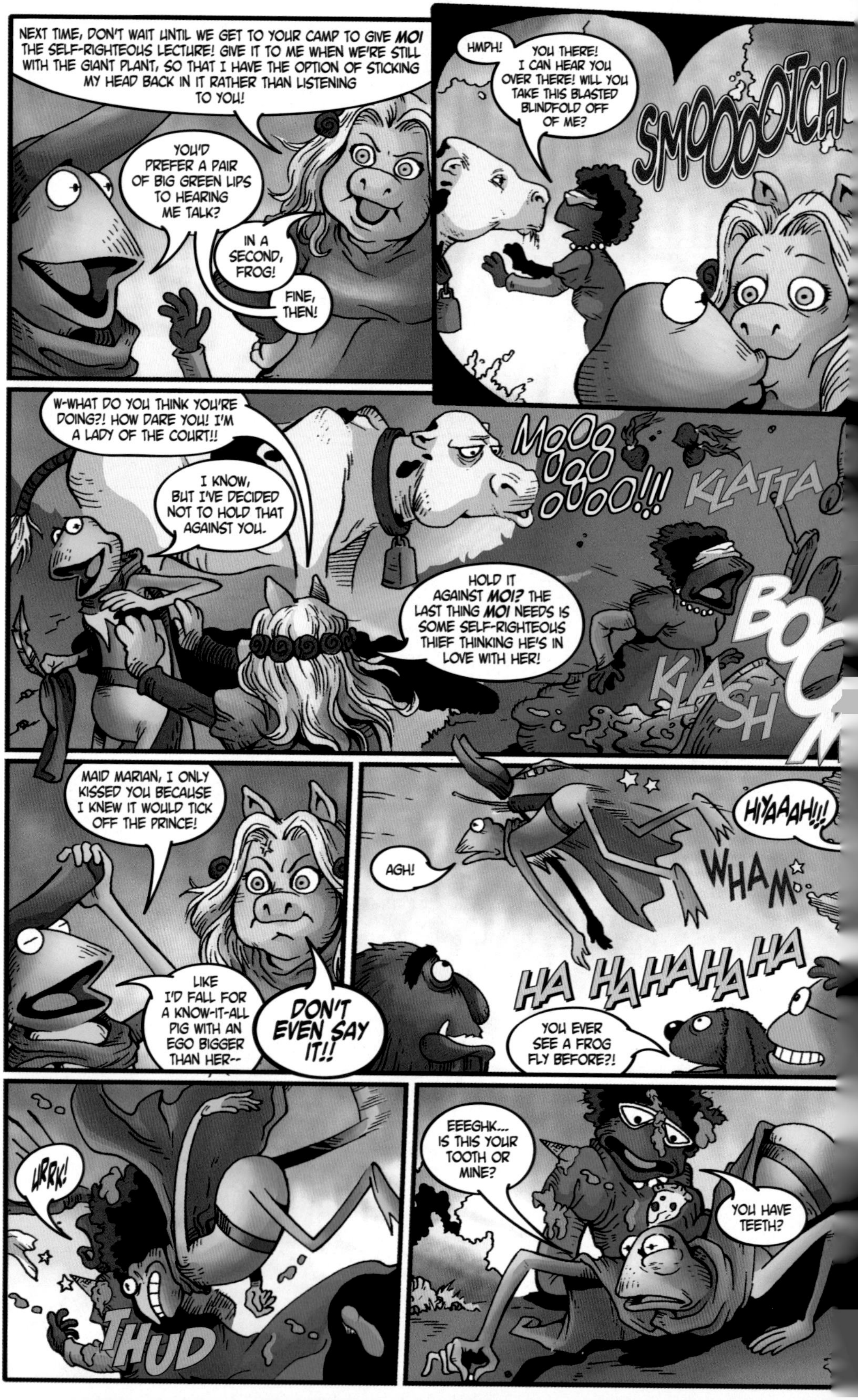
NEXT TIME, DON'T WAIT UNTIL WE GET TO YOUR CAMP TO GIVE MOI THE SELF-RIGHTEOUS LECTURE! GIVE IT TO ME WHEN WE'RE STILL WITH THE GIANT PLANT, SO THAT I HAVE THE OPTION OF STICKING MY HEAD BACK IN IT RATHER THAN LISTENING TO YOU!
YOU'D PREFER A PAIR OF BIG GREEN LIPS TO HEARING ME TALK?
IN A SECOND, FROG!
FINE, THEN!
HMPH!
YOU THERE! I CAN HEAR YOU OVER THERE! WILL YOU TAKE THIS BLASTED BLINDFOLD OFF OF ME?
SMOOOOOTCH
W-WHAT DO YOU THINK YOU'RE DOING?! HOW DARE YOU! I'M A LADY OF THE COURT!!
I KNOW, BUT I'VE DECIDED NOT TO HOLD THAT AGAINST YOU.
MOOOOOOOOOOOO!!!
KLATTA
HOLD IT AGAINST MOI? THE LAST THING MOI NEEDS IS SOME SELF-RIGHTEOUS THIEF THINKING HE'S IN LOVE WITH HER!
BOOM
KLASH
MAID MARIAN, I ONLY KISSED YOU BECAUSE I KNEW IT WOULD TICK OFF THE PRINCE!
LIKE I'D FALL FOR A KNOW-IT-ALL PIG WITH AN EGO BIGGER THAN HER--
DON'T EVEN SAY IT!!
HIYAAAH!!!
AGH!
WHAM
HA HAHAHAHAHA
YOU EVER SEE A FROG FLY BEFORE?!
URRK!
THUD
EEEGHK... IS THIS YOUR TOOTH OR MINE?
YOU HAVE TEETH?

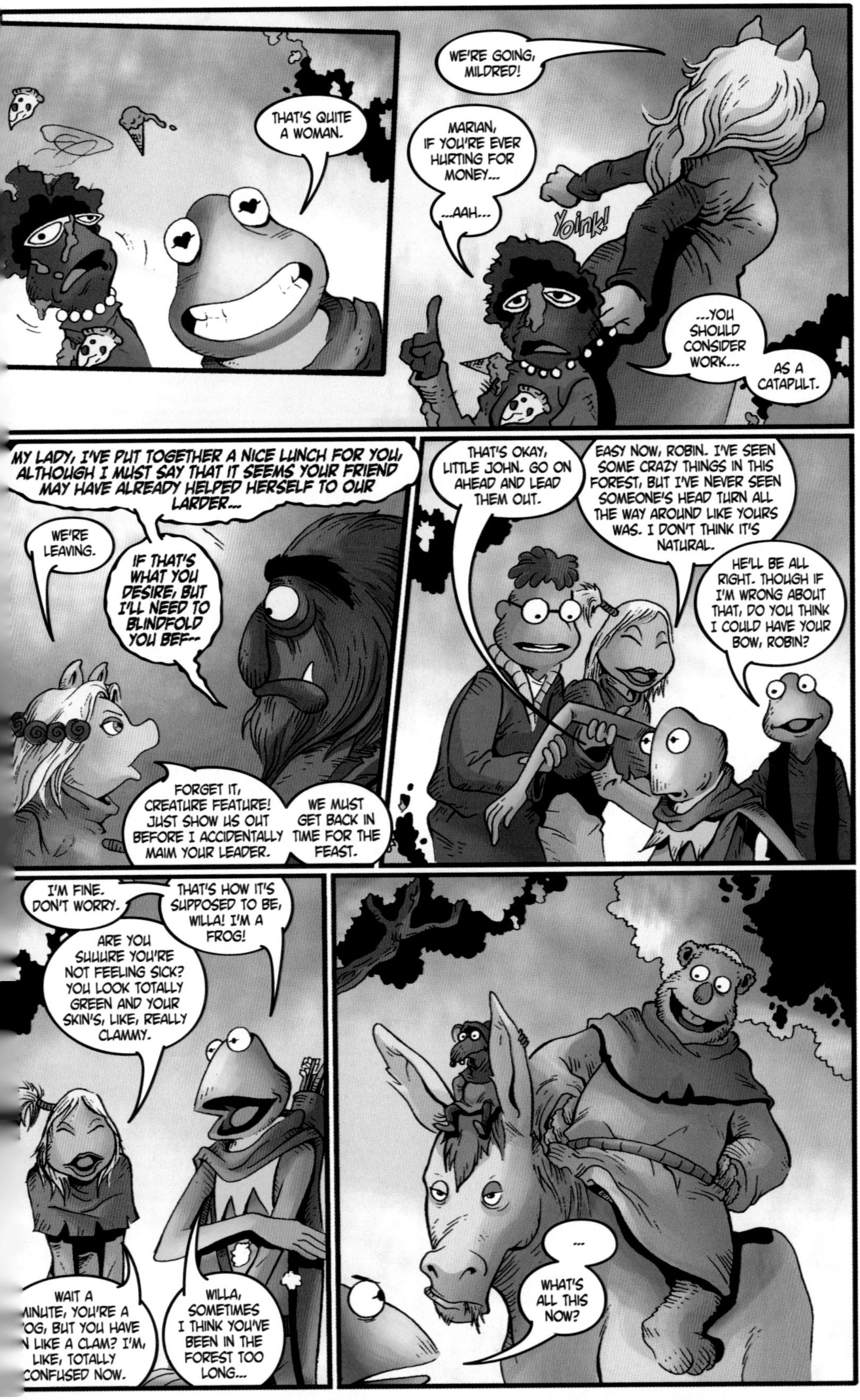
THAT'S QUITE A WOMAN.
WE'RE GOING, MILDRED!
MARIAN, IF YOU'RE EVER HURTING FOR MONEY...
...AAH...
YOINK!
...YOU SHOULD CONSIDER WORK...
AS A CATAPULT.
MY LADY, I'VE PUT TOGETHER A NICE LUNCH FOR YOU, ALTHOUGH I MUST SAY THAT IT SEEMS YOUR FRIEND MAY HAVE ALREADY HELPED HERSELF TO OUR LARDER...
WE'RE LEAVING.
IF THAT'S WHAT YOU DESIRE, BUT I'LL NEED TO BLINDFOLD YOU BEF--
FORGET IT, CREATURE FEATURE! JUST SHOW US OUT BEFORE I ACCIDENTALLY MAIM YOUR LEADER.
WE MUST GET BACK IN TIME FOR THE FEAST.
THAT'S OKAY, LITTLE JOHN. GO ON AHEAD AND LEAD THEM OUT.
EASY NOW, ROBIN. I'VE SEEN SOME CRAZY THINGS IN THIS FOREST, BUT I'VE NEVER SEEN SOMEONE'S HEAD TURN ALL THE WAY AROUND LIKE YOURS WAS. I DON'T THINK IT'S NATURAL.
HE'LL BE ALL RIGHT. THOUGH IF I'M WRONG ABOUT THAT, DO YOU THINK I COULD HAVE YOUR BOW, ROBIN?
I'M FINE. DON'T WORRY.
THAT'S HOW IT'S SUPPOSED TO BE, WILLA! I'M A FROG!
ARE YOU SUUURE YOU'RE NOT FEELING SICK? YOU LOOK TOTALLY GREEN AND YOUR SKIN'S, LIKE, REALLY CLAMMY.
WAIT A MINUTE, YOU'RE A ROG, BUT YOU HAVE N LIKE A CLAM? I'M, LIKE, TOTALLY CONFUSED NOW.
WILLA, SOMETIMES I THINK YOU'VE BEEN IN THE FOREST TOO LONG...
...
WHAT'S ALL THIS NOW?

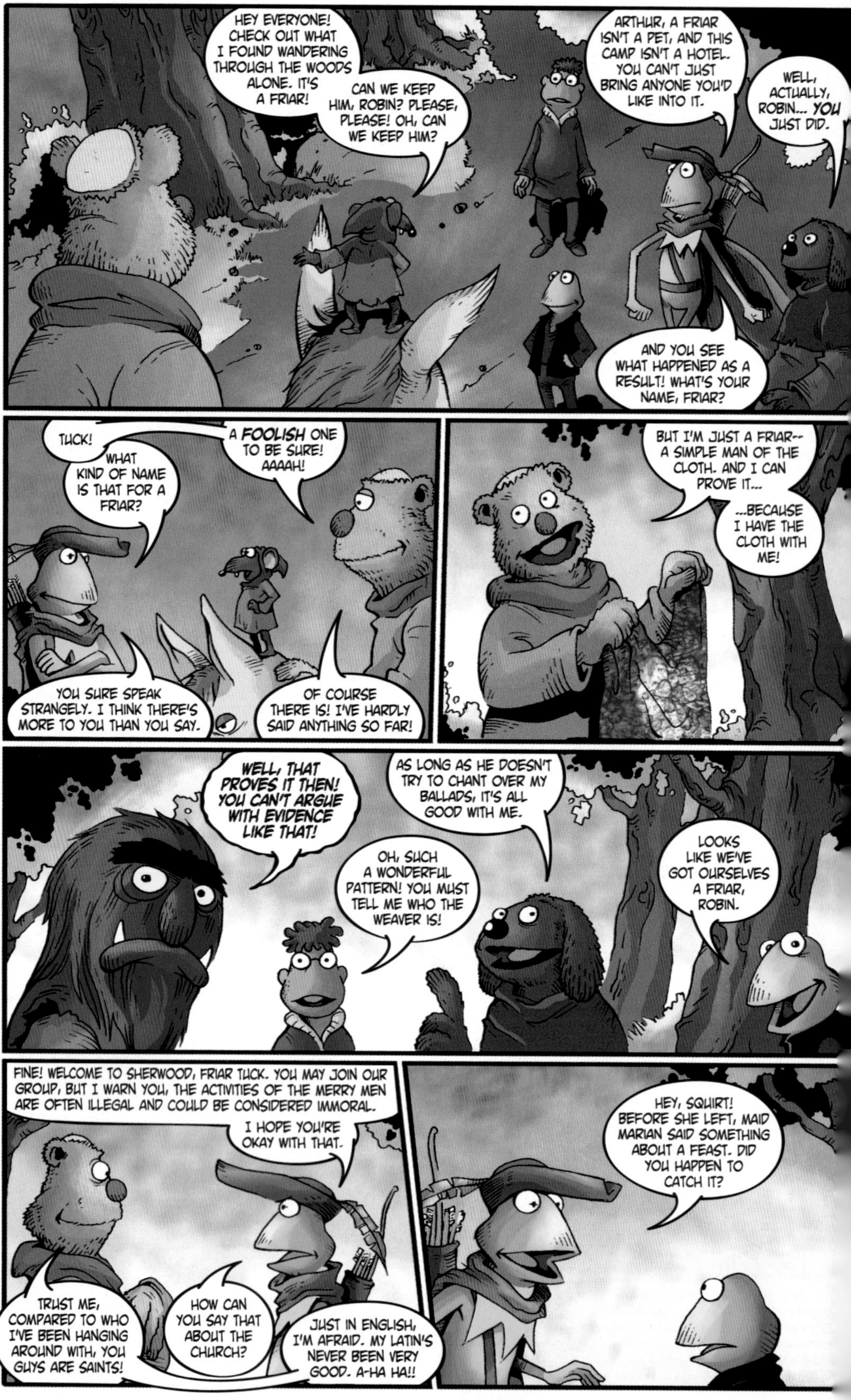
HEY EVERYONE! CHECK OUT WHAT I FOUND WANDERING THROUGH THE WOODS ALONE. IT'S A FRIAR!
CAN WE KEEP HIM, ROBIN? PLEASE, PLEASE! OH, CAN WE KEEP HIM?
ARTHUR, A FRIAR ISN'T A PET, AND THIS CAMP ISN'T A HOTEL. YOU CAN'T JUST BRING ANYONE YOU'D LIKE INTO IT.
WELL, ACTUALLY, ROBIN... YOU JUST DID.
AND YOU SEE WHAT HAPPENED AS A RESULT! WHAT'S YOUR NAME, FRIAR?
TUCK!
WHAT KIND OF NAME IS THAT FOR A FRIAR?
A FOOLISH ONE TO BE SURE! AAAAH!
YOU SURE SPEAK STRANGELY. I THINK THERE'S MORE TO YOU THAN YOU SAY.
OF COURSE THERE IS! I'VE HARDLY SAID ANYTHING SO FAR!
BUT I'M JUST A FRIAR-- A SIMPLE MAN OF THE CLOTH. AND I CAN PROVE IT...
...BECAUSE I HAVE THE CLOTH WITH ME!
WELL, THAT PROVES IT THEN! YOU CAN'T ARGUE WITH EVIDENCE LIKE THAT!
AS LONG AS HE DOESN'T TRY TO CHANT OVER MY BALLADS, IT'S ALL GOOD WITH ME.
OH, SUCH A WONDERFUL PATTERN! YOU MUST TELL ME WHO THE WEAVER IS!
LOOKS LIKE WE'VE GOT OURSELVES A FRIAR, ROBIN.
FINE! WELCOME TO SHERWOOD, FRIAR TUCK. YOU MAY JOIN OUR GROUP, BUT I WARN YOU, THE ACTIVITIES OF THE MERRY MEN ARE OFTEN ILLEGAL AND COULD BE CONSIDERED IMMORAL.
I HOPE YOU'RE OKAY WITH THAT.
TRUST ME, COMPARED TO WHO I'VE BEEN HANGING AROUND WITH, YOU GUYS ARE SAINTS!
HOW CAN YOU SAY THAT ABOUT THE CHURCH?
JUST IN ENGLISH, I'M AFRAID. MY LATIN'S NEVER BEEN VERY GOOD. A-HA HA!!
HEY, SQUIRT! BEFORE SHE LEFT, MAID MARIAN SAID SOMETHING ABOUT A FEAST. DID YOU HAPPEN TO CATCH IT?

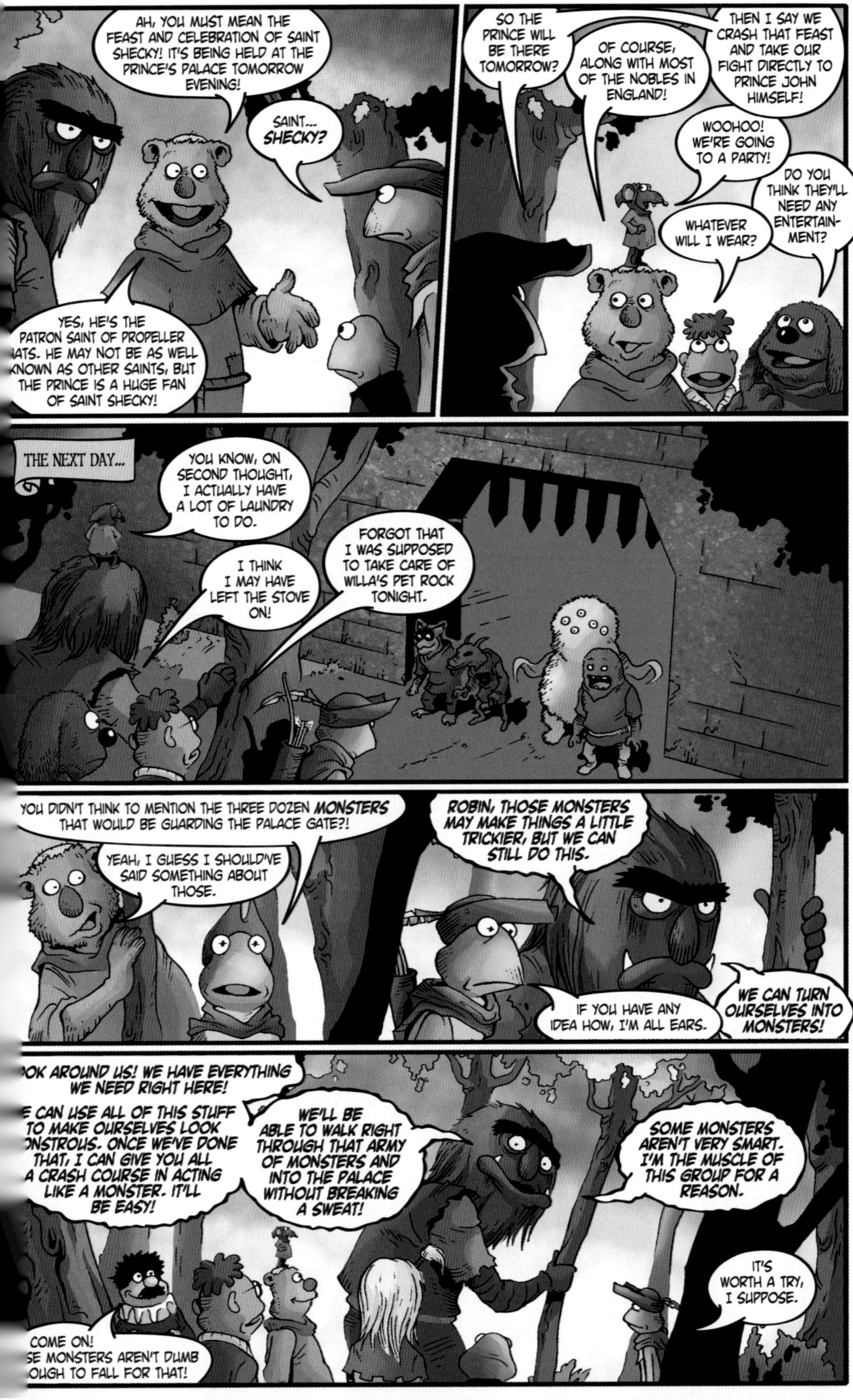
AH, YOU MUST MEAN THE FEAST AND CELEBRATION OF SAINT SHECKY! IT'S BEING HELD AT THE PRINCE'S PALACE TOMORROW EVENING!
SAINT... SHECKY?
YES, HE'S THE PATRON SAINT OF PROPELLER HATS. HE MAY NOT BE AS WELL KNOWN AS OTHER SAINTS, BUT THE PRINCE IS A HUGE FAN OF SAINT SHECKY!
SO THE PRINCE WILL BE THERE TOMORROW?
OF COURSE, ALONG WITH MOST OF THE NOBLES IN ENGLAND!
THEN I SAY WE CRASH THAT FEAST AND TAKE OUR FIGHT DIRECTLY TO PRINCE JOHN HIMSELF!
WOOHOO! WE'RE GOING TO A PARTY!
WHATEVER WILL I WEAR?
DO YOU THINK THEY'LL NEED ANY ENTERTAIN-MENT?
THE NEXT DAY...
YOU KNOW, ON SECOND THOUGHT, I ACTUALLY HAVE A LOT OF LAUNDRY TO DO.
I THINK I MAY HAVE LEFT THE STOVE ON!
FORGOT THAT I WAS SUPPOSED TO TAKE CARE OF WILLA'S PET ROCK TONIGHT.
YOU DIDN'T THINK TO MENTION THE THREE DOZEN MONSTERS THAT WOULD BE GUARDING THE PALACE GATE?!
YEAH, I GUESS I SHOULD'VE SAID SOMETHING ABOUT THOSE.
ROBIN, THOSE MONSTERS MAY MAKE THINGS A LITTLE TRICKIER, BUT WE CAN STILL DO THIS.
IF YOU HAVE ANY IDEA HOW, I'M ALL EARS.
WE CAN TURN OURSELVES INTO MONSTERS!
OOK AROUND US! WE HAVE EVERYTHING WE NEED RIGHT HERE!
E CAN USE ALL OF THIS STUFF TO MAKE OURSELVES LOOK ONSTROUS. ONCE WE'VE DONE THAT, I CAN GIVE YOU ALL A CRASH COURSE IN ACTING LIKE A MONSTER. IT'LL BE EASY!
WE'LL BE ABLE TO WALK RIGHT THROUGH THAT ARMY OF MONSTERS AND INTO THE PALACE WITHOUT BREAKING A SWEAT!
COME ON! SE MONSTERS AREN'T DUMB OUGH TO FALL FOR THAT!
SOME MONSTERS AREN'T VERY SMART. I'M THE MUSCLE OF THIS GROUP FOR A REASON.
IT'S WORTH A TRY, I SUPPOSE.

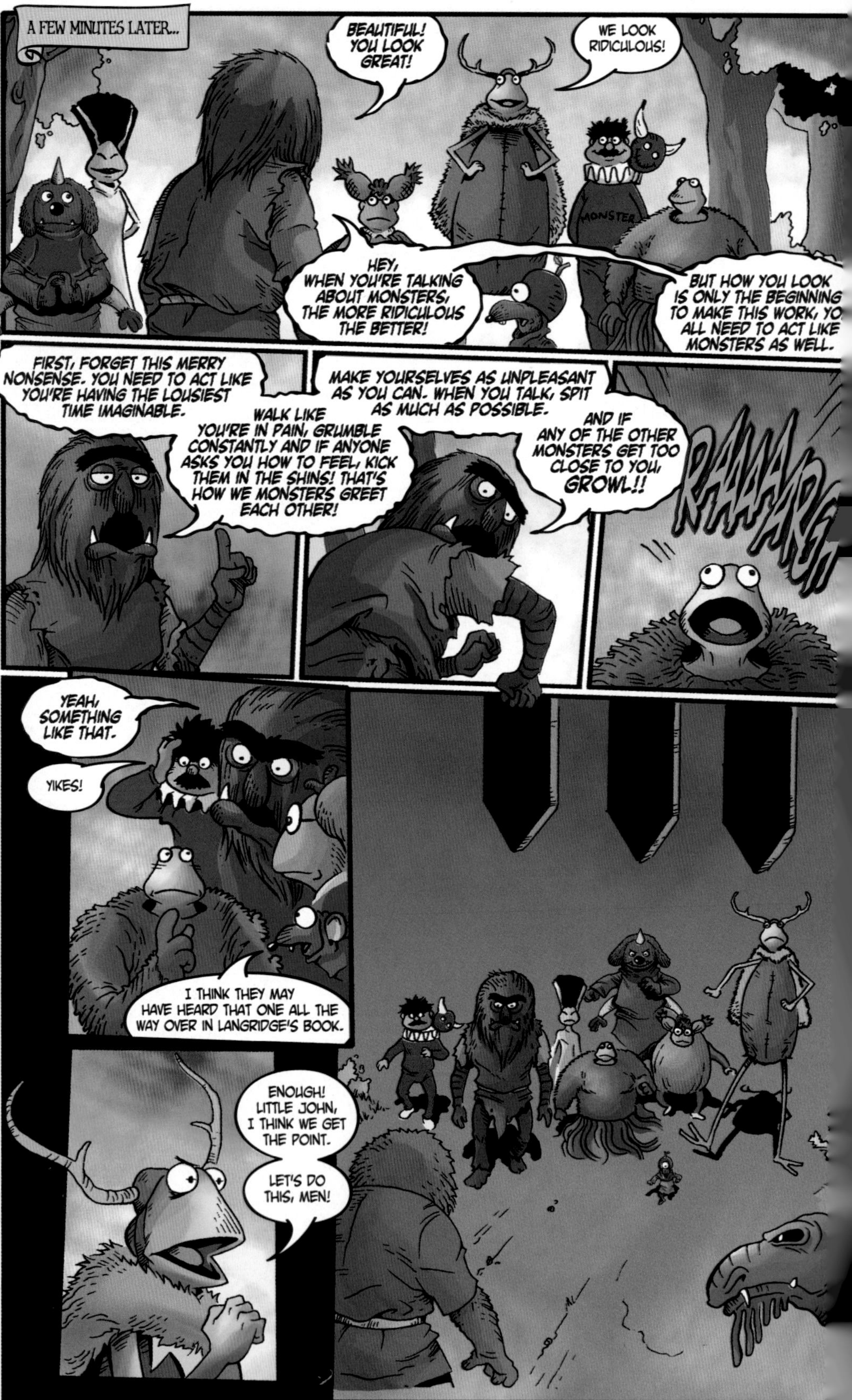
A FEW MINUTES LATER...
BEAUTIFUL! YOU LOOK GREAT!
WE LOOK RIDICULOUS!
HEY, WHEN YOU'RE TALKING ABOUT MONSTERS, THE MORE RIDICULOUS THE BETTER!
BUT HOW YOU LOOK IS ONLY THE BEGINNING TO MAKE THIS WORK, YO ALL NEED TO ACT LIKE MONSTERS AS WELL.
FIRST, FORGET THIS MERRY NONSENSE. YOU NEED TO ACT LIKE YOU'RE HAVING THE LOUSIEST TIME IMAGINABLE.
WALK LIKE YOU'RE IN PAIN, GRUMBLE CONSTANTLY AND IF ANYONE ASKS YOU HOW TO FEEL, KICK THEM IN THE SHINS! THAT'S HOW WE MONSTERS GREET EACH OTHER!
MAKE YOURSELVES AS UNPLEASANT AS YOU CAN. WHEN YOU TALK, SPIT AS MUCH AS POSSIBLE.
AND IF ANY OF THE OTHER MONSTERS GET TOO CLOSE TO YOU, GROWL!!
RAAARG
YEAH, SOMETHING LIKE THAT.
YIKES!
I THINK THEY MAY HAVE HEARD THAT ONE ALL THE WAY OVER IN LANGRIDGE'S BOOK.
ENOUGH! LITTLE JOHN, I THINK WE GET THE POINT.
LET'S DO THIS, MEN!

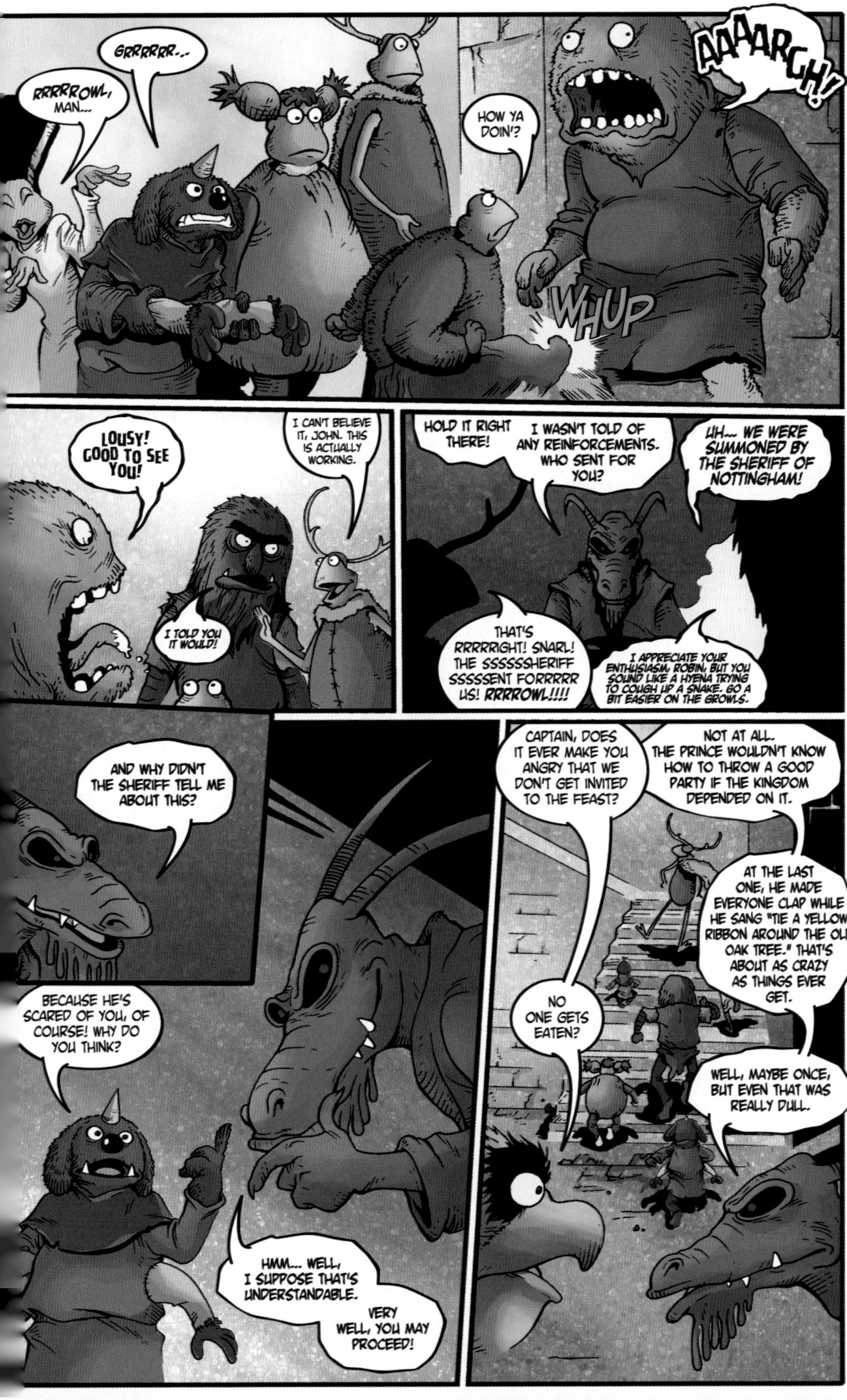
RRRRROWL, MAN...
GRRRRRR...
HOW YA DOIN'?
AAAARGH!
WHUP
LOUSY! GOOD TO SEE YOU!
I CAN'T BELIEVE IT, JOHN. THIS IS ACTUALLY WORKING.
I TOLD YOU IT WOULD!
HOLD IT RIGHT THERE!
I WASN'T TOLD OF ANY REINFORCEMENTS. WHO SENT FOR YOU?
UH... WE WERE SUMMONED BY THE SHERIFF OF NOTTINGHAM!
THAT'S RRRRRIGHT! SNARL! THE SSSSSSHERIFF SSSSSENT FORRRRR US! RRRROWL!!!!
I APPRECIATE YOUR ENTHUSIASM, ROBIN, BUT YOU SOUND LIKE A HYENA TRYING TO COUGH UP A SNAKE. GO A BIT EASIER ON THE GROWLS.
AND WHY DIDN'T THE SHERIFF TELL ME ABOUT THIS?
BECAUSE HE'S SCARED OF YOU, OF COURSE! WHY DO YOU THINK?
HMM... WELL, I SUPPOSE THAT'S UNDERSTANDABLE.
VERY WELL, YOU MAY PROCEED!
CAPTAIN, DOES IT EVER MAKE YOU ANGRY THAT WE DON'T GET INVITED TO THE FEAST?
NOT AT ALL. THE PRINCE WOULDN'T KNOW HOW TO THROW A GOOD PARTY IF THE KINGDOM DEPENDED ON IT.
AT THE LAST ONE, HE MADE EVERYONE CLAP WHILE HE SANG "TIE A YELLOW RIBBON AROUND THE OLD OAK TREE." THAT'S ABOUT AS CRAZY AS THINGS EVER GET.
NO ONE GETS EATEN?
WELL, MAYBE ONCE, BUT EVEN THAT WAS REALLY DULL.

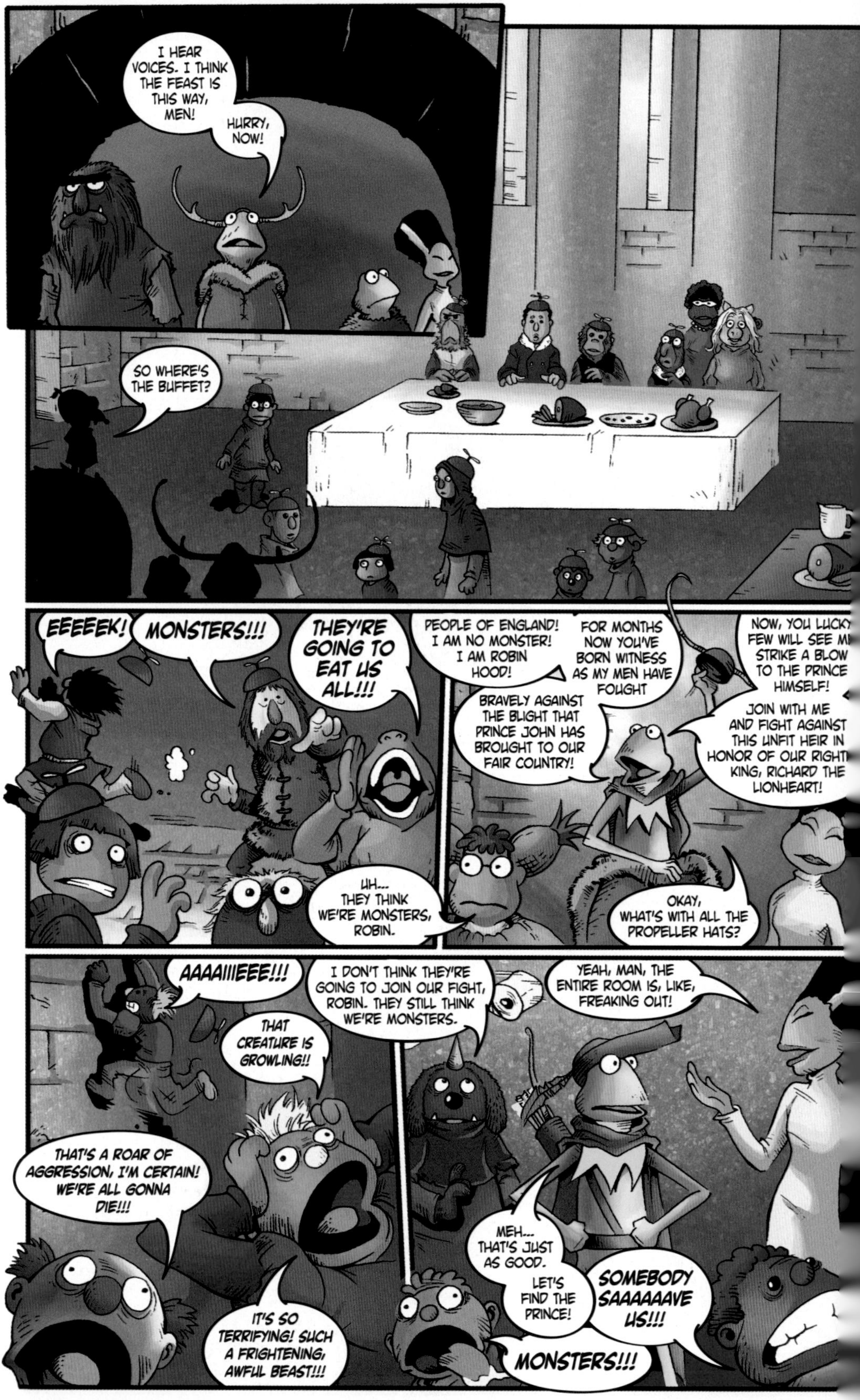
I HEAR VOICES. I THINK THE FEAST IS THIS WAY, MEN!
HURRY, NOW!
SO WHERE'S THE BUFFET?
EEEEEK!
MONSTERS!!!
THEY'RE GOING TO EAT US ALL!!!
UH... THEY THINK WE'RE MONSTERS, ROBIN.
PEOPLE OF ENGLAND! I AM NO MONSTER! I AM ROBIN HOOD!
FOR MONTHS NOW YOU'VE BORN WITNESS AS MY MEN HAVE FOUGHT
BRAVELY AGAINST THE BLIGHT THAT PRINCE JOHN HAS BROUGHT TO OUR FAIR COUNTRY!
NOW, YOU LUCKY FEW WILL SEE ME STRIKE A BLOW TO THE PRINCE HIMSELF!
JOIN WITH ME AND FIGHT AGAINST THIS UNFIT HEIR IN HONOR OF OUR RIGHTFUL KING, RICHARD THE LIONHEART!
OKAY, WHAT'S WITH ALL THE PROPELLER HATS?
AAAAIIIEEE!!!
THAT CREATURE IS GROWLING!!
THAT'S A ROAR OF AGGRESSION, I'M CERTAIN! WE'RE ALL GONNA DIE!!!
IT'S SO TERRIFYING! SUCH A FRIGHTENING, AWFUL BEAST!!!
I DON'T THINK THEY'RE GOING TO JOIN OUR FIGHT, ROBIN. THEY STILL THINK WE'RE MONSTERS.
YEAH, MAN, THE ENTIRE ROOM IS, LIKE, FREAKING OUT!
MEH... THAT'S JUST AS GOOD.
LET'S FIND THE PRINCE!
SOMEBODY SAAAAAAVE US!!!
MONSTERS!!!

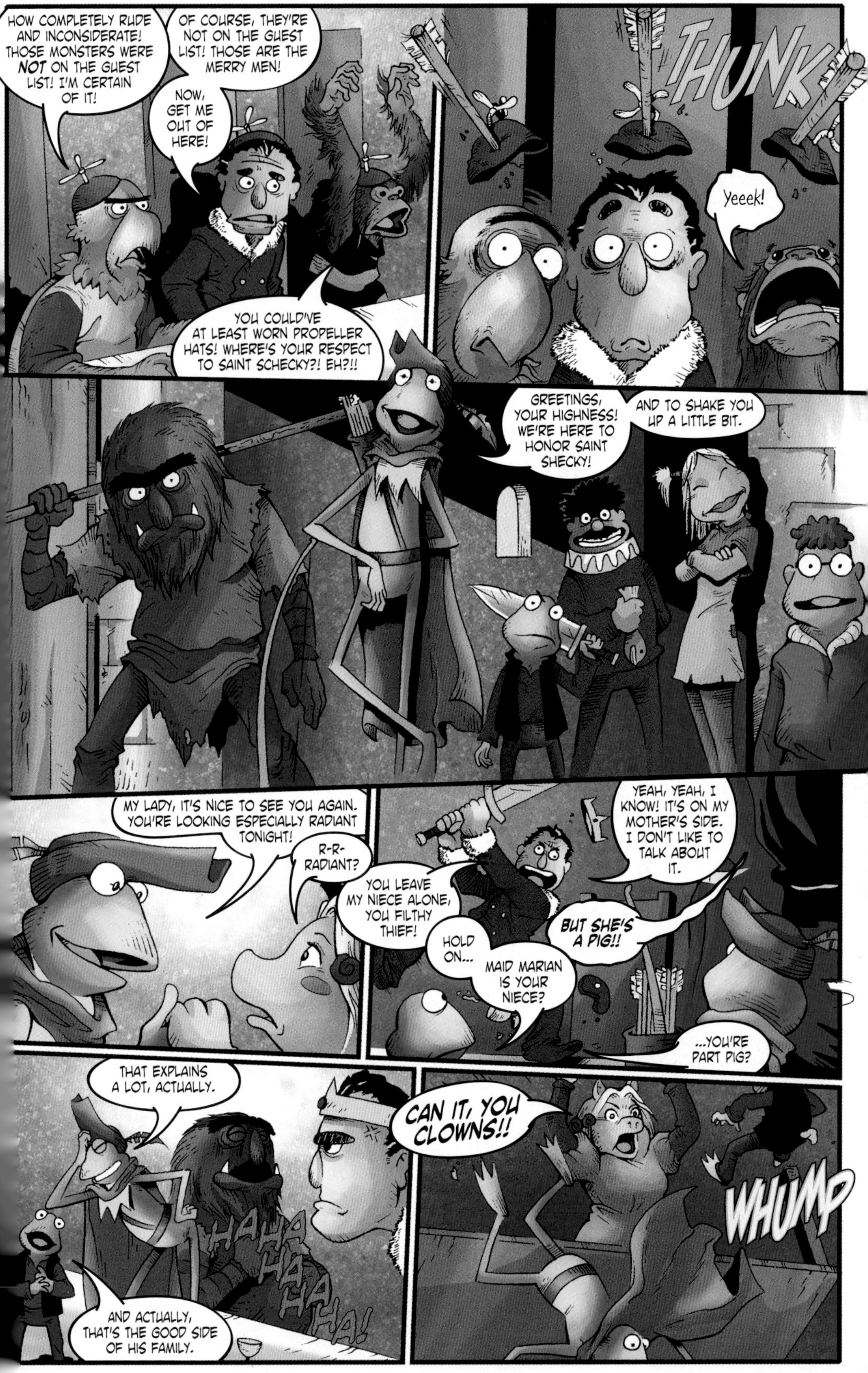
HOW COMPLETELY RUDE AND INCONSIDERATE! THOSE MONSTERS WERE NOT ON THE GUEST LIST! I'M CERTAIN OF IT!
OF COURSE, THEY'RE NOT ON THE GUEST LIST! THOSE ARE THE MERRY MEN!
NOW, GET ME OUT OF HERE!
YOU COULD'VE AT LEAST WORN PROPELLER HATS! WHERE'S YOUR RESPECT TO SAINT SCHECKY?! EH?!!
THUNK
Yeeek!
GREETINGS, YOUR HIGHNESS! WE'RE HERE TO HONOR SAINT SHECKY!
AND TO SHAKE YOU UP A LITTLE BIT.
MY LADY, IT'S NICE TO SEE YOU AGAIN. YOU'RE LOOKING ESPECIALLY RADIANT TONIGHT!
R-R-RADIANT?
YOU LEAVE MY NIECE ALONE, YOU FILTHY THIEF!
HOLD ON...
MAID MARIAN IS YOUR NIECE?
BUT SHE'S A PIG!!
YEAH, YEAH, I KNOW! IT'S ON MY MOTHER'S SIDE. I DON'T LIKE TO TALK ABOUT IT.
...YOU'RE PART PIG?
THAT EXPLAINS A LOT, ACTUALLY.
HAHA HA HA HA!
AND ACTUALLY, THAT'S THE GOOD SIDE OF HIS FAMILY.
CAN IT, YOU CLOWNS!!
WHUMP

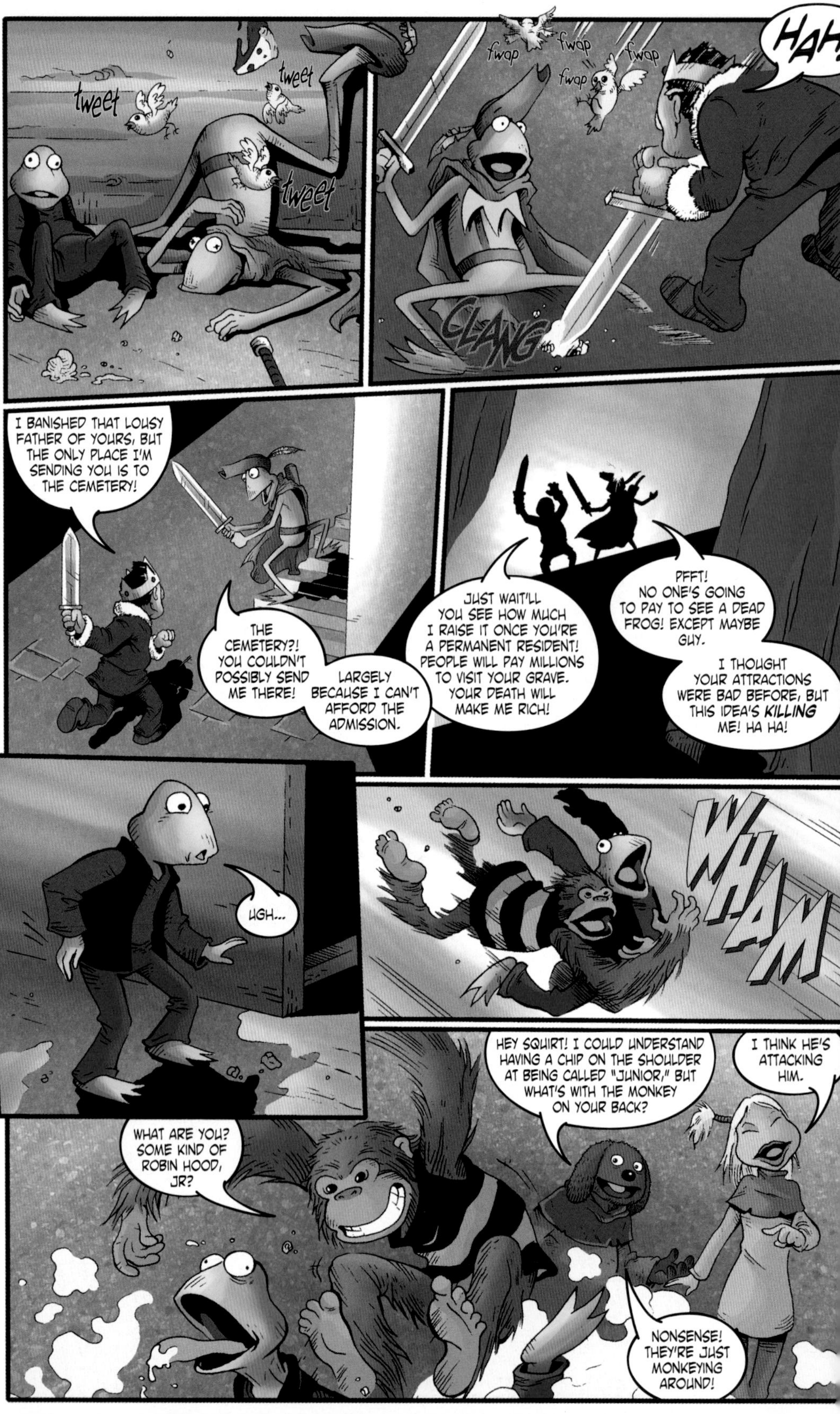
tweet
tweet
tweet
fwap
fwap
fwap
fwap
HAH!
CLANG
I BANISHED THAT LOUSY FATHER OF YOURS, BUT THE ONLY PLACE I'M SENDING YOU IS TO THE CEMETERY!
THE CEMETERY?! YOU COULDN'T POSSIBLY SEND ME THERE!
LARGELY BECAUSE I CAN'T AFFORD THE ADMISSION.
JUST WAIT'LL YOU SEE HOW MUCH I RAISE IT ONCE YOU'RE A PERMANENT RESIDENT! PEOPLE WILL PAY MILLIONS TO VISIT YOUR GRAVE. YOUR DEATH WILL MAKE ME RICH!
PFFT! NO ONE'S GOING TO PAY TO SEE A DEAD FROG! EXCEPT MAYBE GUY.
I THOUGHT YOUR ATTRACTIONS WERE BAD BEFORE, BUT THIS IDEA'S KILLING ME! HA HA!
UGH...
WHAM
WHAT ARE YOU? SOME KIND OF ROBIN HOOD, JR?
HEY SQUIRT! I COULD UNDERSTAND HAVING A CHIP ON THE SHOULDER AT BEING CALLED "JUNIOR," BUT WHAT'S WITH THE MONKEY ON YOUR BACK?
I THINK HE'S ATTACKING HIM.
NONSENSE! THEY'RE JUST MONKEYING AROUND!

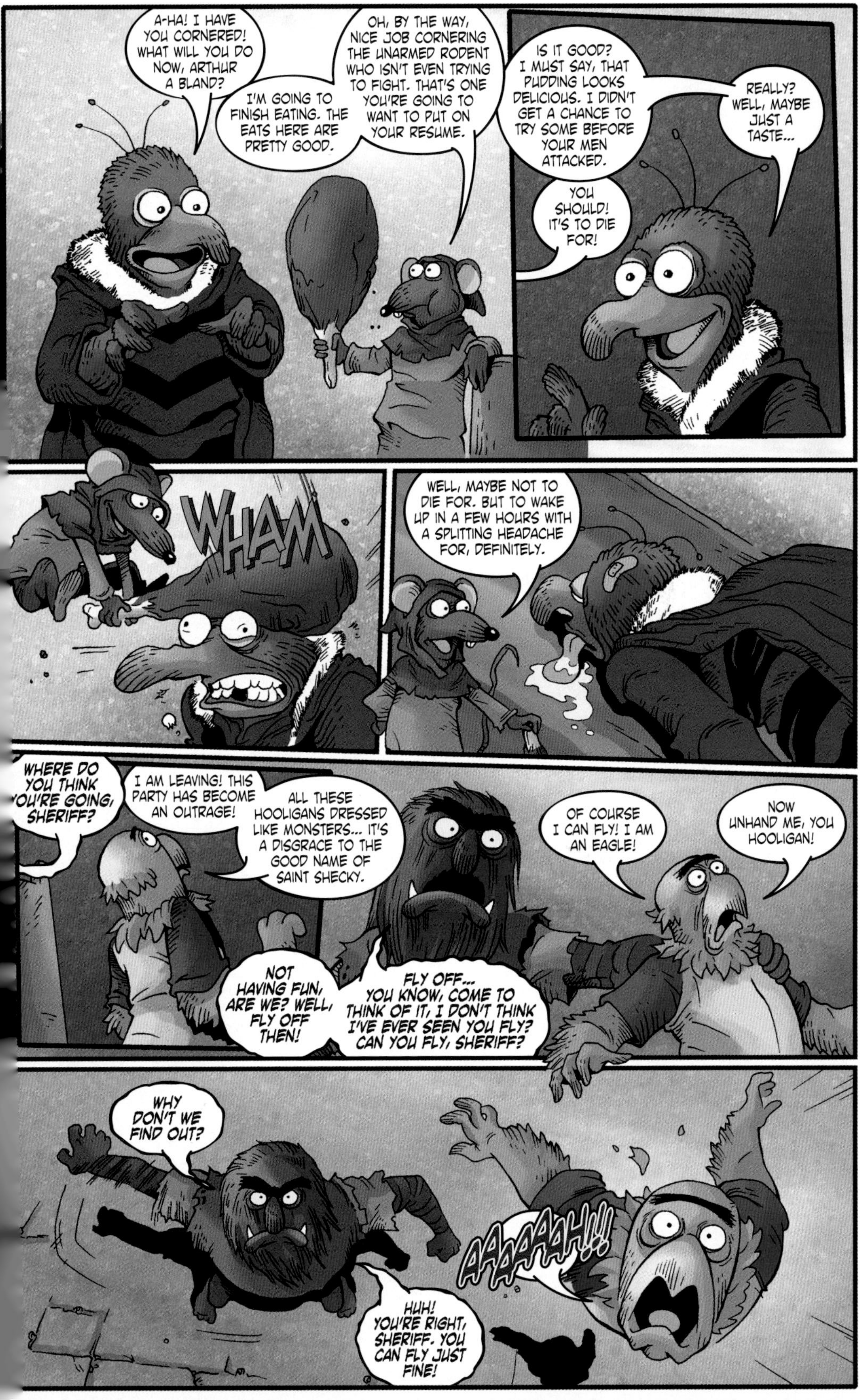

A-HA! I HAVE YOU CORNERED! WHAT WILL YOU DO NOW, ARTHUR A BLAND?
I'M GOING TO FINISH EATING. THE EATS HERE ARE PRETTY GOOD.
OH, BY THE WAY, NICE JOB CORNERING THE UNARMED RODENT WHO ISN'T EVEN TRYING TO FIGHT. THAT'S ONE YOU'RE GOING TO WANT TO PUT ON YOUR RESUME.
IS IT GOOD? I MUST SAY, THAT PUDDING LOOKS DELICIOUS. I DIDN'T GET A CHANCE TO TRY SOME BEFORE YOUR MEN ATTACKED.
YOU SHOULD! IT'S TO DIE FOR!
REALLY? WELL, MAYBE JUST A TASTE...
WHAM
WELL, MAYBE NOT TO DIE FOR. BUT TO WAKE UP IN A FEW HOURS WITH A SPLITTING HEADACHE FOR, DEFINITELY.
WHERE DO YOU THINK YOU'RE GOING, SHERIFF?
I AM LEAVING! THIS PARTY HAS BECOME AN OUTRAGE!
ALL THESE HOOLIGANS DRESSED LIKE MONSTERS... IT'S A DISGRACE TO THE GOOD NAME OF SAINT SHECKY.
NOT HAVING FUN, ARE WE? WELL, FLY OFF THEN!
FLY OFF... YOU KNOW, COME TO THINK OF IT, I DON'T THINK I'VE EVER SEEN YOU FLY? CAN YOU FLY, SHERIFF?
OF COURSE I CAN FLY! I AM AN EAGLE!
NOW UNHAND ME, YOU HOOLIGAN!
WHY DON'T WE FIND OUT?
AAAAAAH!!!
HUH! YOU'RE RIGHT, SHERIFF. YOU CAN FLY JUST FINE!

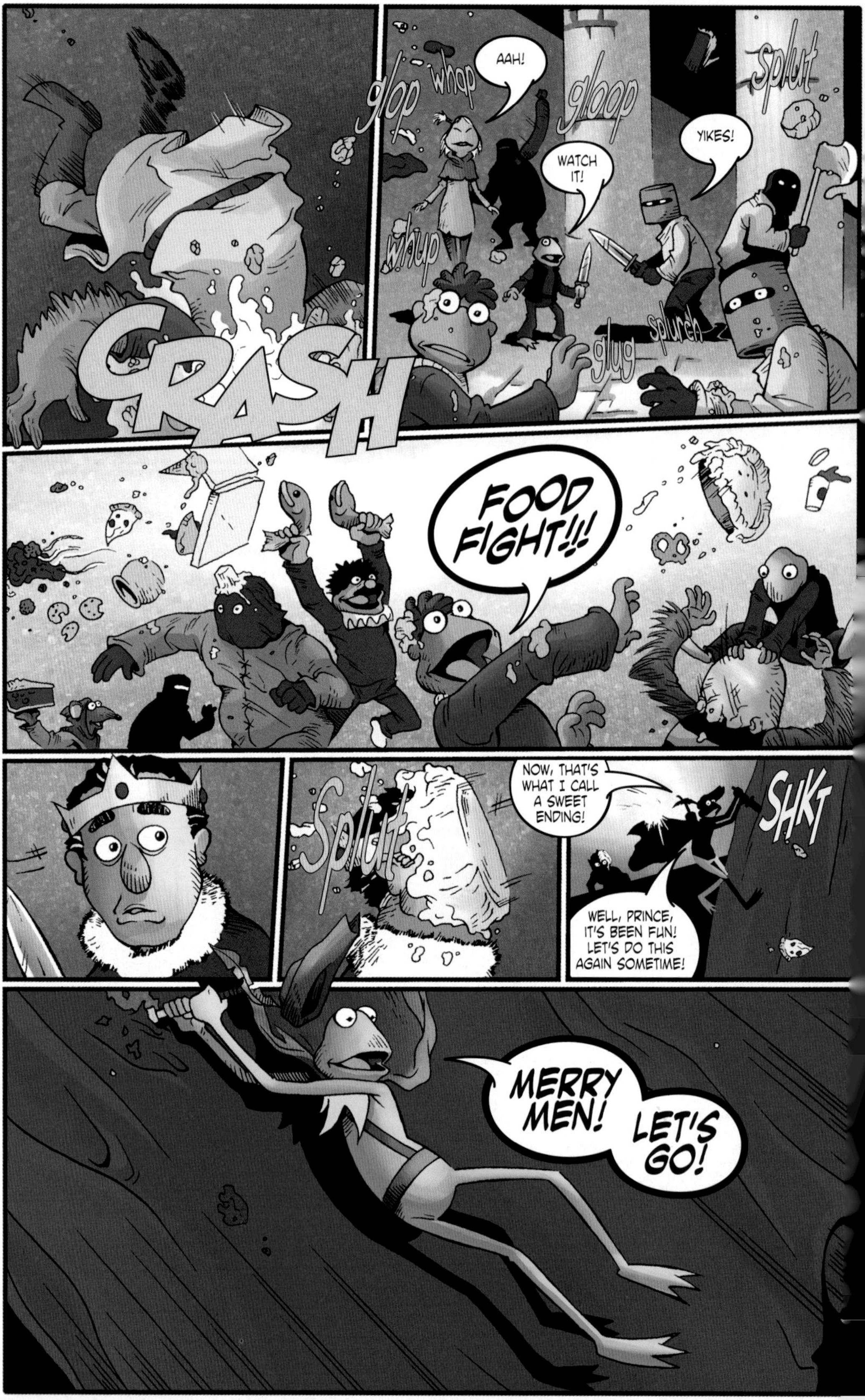
CRASH
glop
whap
AAH!
gloop
splut
WATCH IT!
YIKES!
whup
glug
splurch
FOOD FIGHT!!!
Splut
NOW, THAT'S WHAT I CALL A SWEET ENDING!
SHKT
WELL, PRINCE, IT'S BEEN FUN! LET'S DO THIS AGAIN SOMETIME!
MERRY MEN!
LET'S GO!

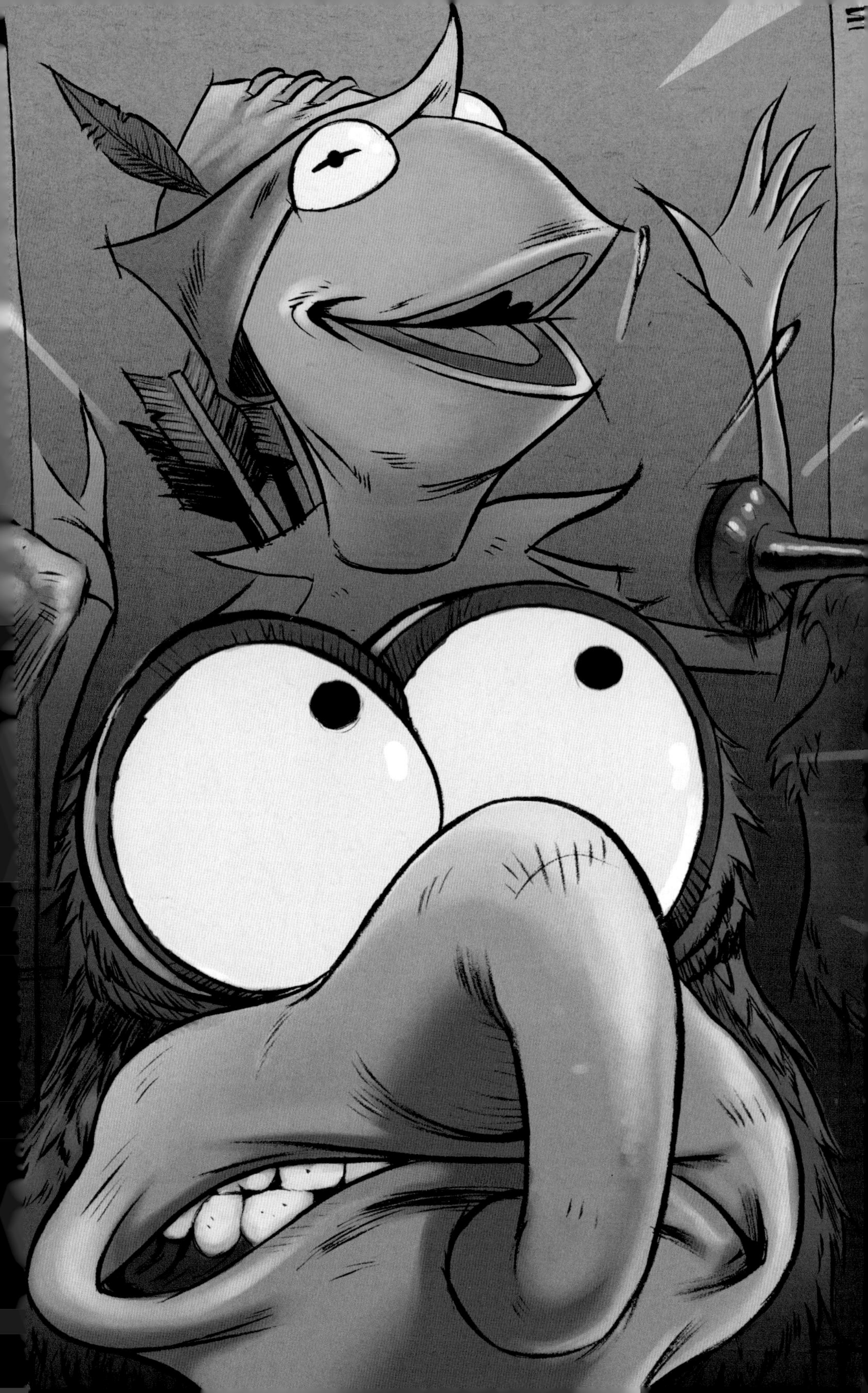

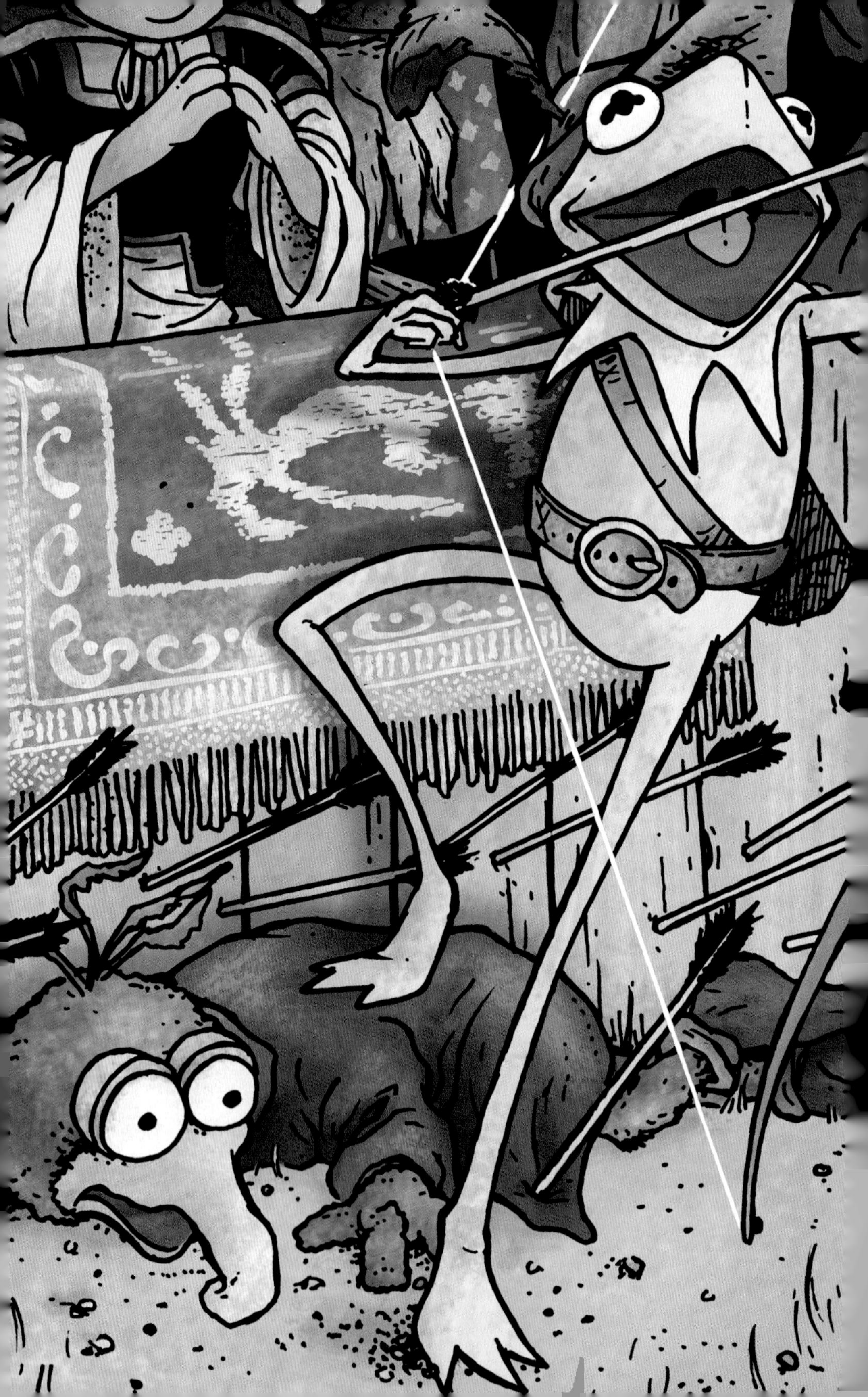

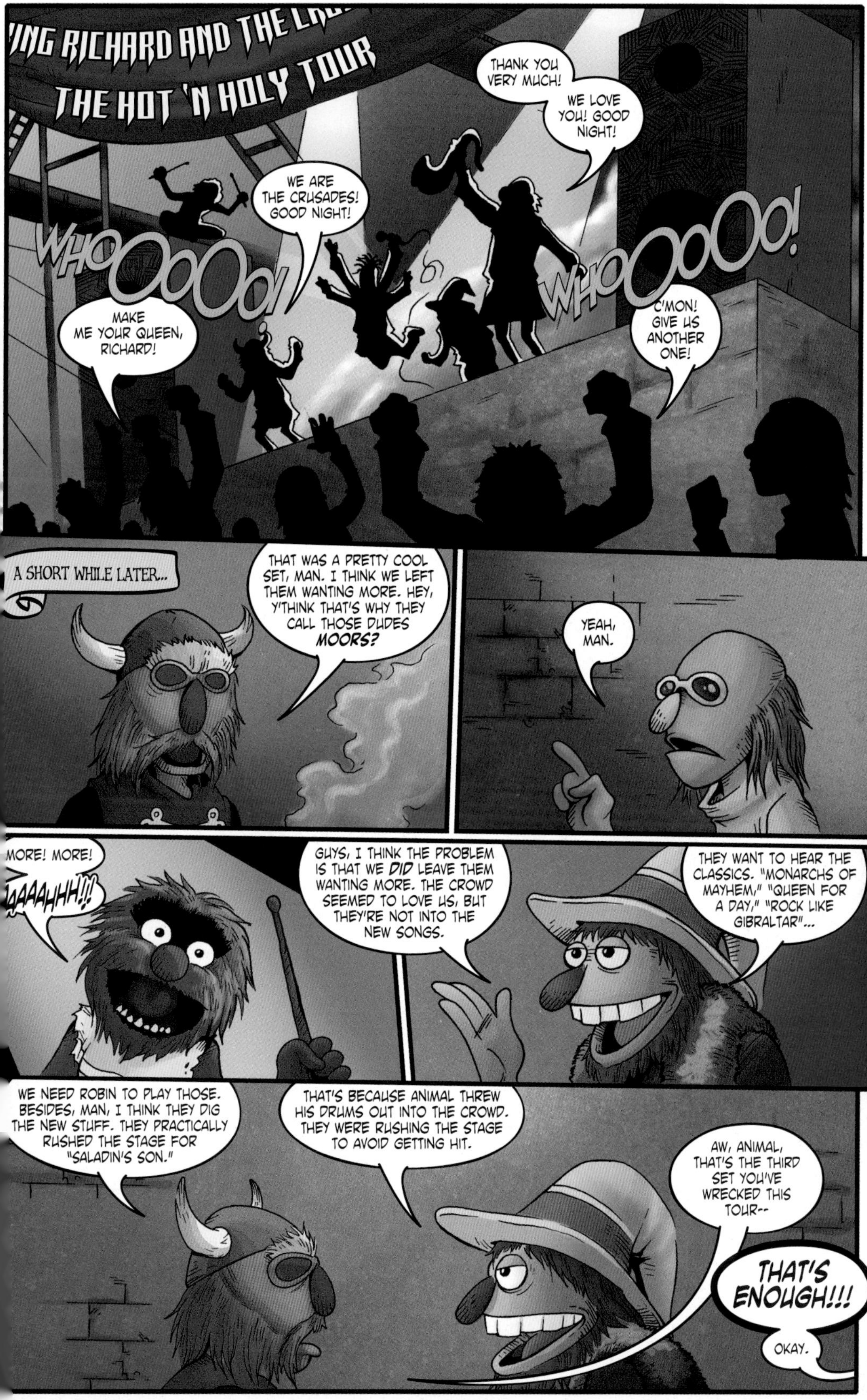

…ING RICHARD AND THE CR…
THE HOT 'N HOLY TOUR
THANK YOU VERY MUCH!
WE LOVE YOU! GOOD NIGHT!
WE ARE THE CRUSADES! GOOD NIGHT!
WHOOOOO!
WHOOOOOO!
MAKE ME YOUR QUEEN, RICHARD!
C'MON! GIVE US ANOTHER ONE!
A SHORT WHILE LATER...
THAT WAS A PRETTY COOL SET, MAN. I THINK WE LEFT THEM WANTING MORE. HEY, Y'THINK THAT'S WHY THEY CALL THOSE DUDES ***MOORS?***
YEAH, MAN.
MORE! MORE!
…AAAAHHH!!!
GUYS, I THINK THE PROBLEM IS THAT WE ***DID*** LEAVE THEM WANTING MORE. THE CROWD SEEMED TO LOVE US, BUT THEY'RE NOT INTO THE NEW SONGS.
THEY WANT TO HEAR THE CLASSICS. "MONARCHS OF MAYHEM," "QUEEN FOR A DAY," "ROCK LIKE GIBRALTAR"...
WE NEED ROBIN TO PLAY THOSE. BESIDES, MAN, I THINK THEY DIG THE NEW STUFF. THEY PRACTICALLY RUSHED THE STAGE FOR "SALADIN'S SON."
THAT'S BECAUSE ANIMAL THREW HIS DRUMS OUT INTO THE CROWD. THEY WERE RUSHING THE STAGE TO AVOID GETTING HIT.
AW, ANIMAL, THAT'S THE THIRD SET YOU'VE WRECKED THIS TOUR--
THAT'S ENOUGH!!!
OKAY.

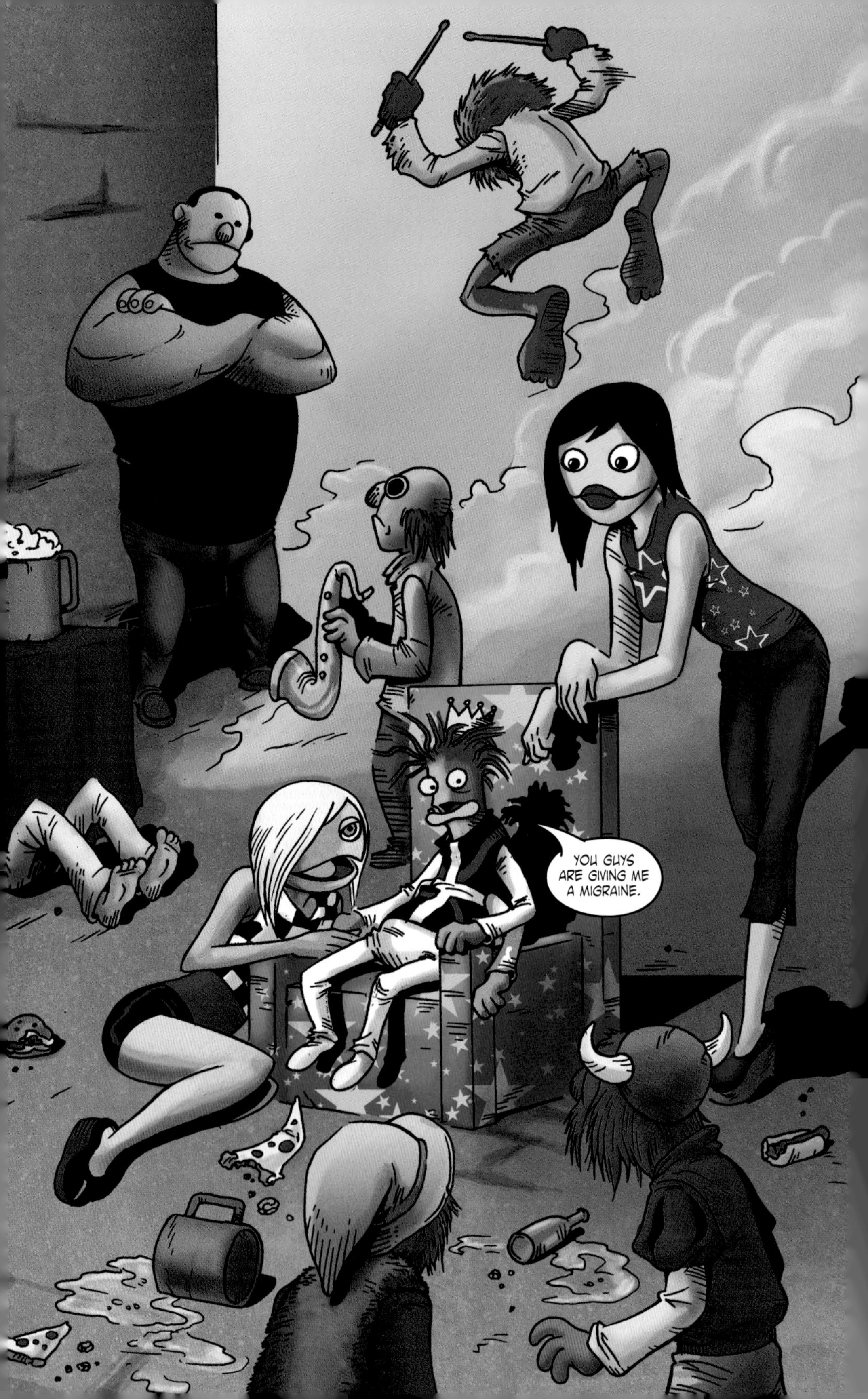
YOU GUYS
ARE GIVING ME
A MIGRAINE.

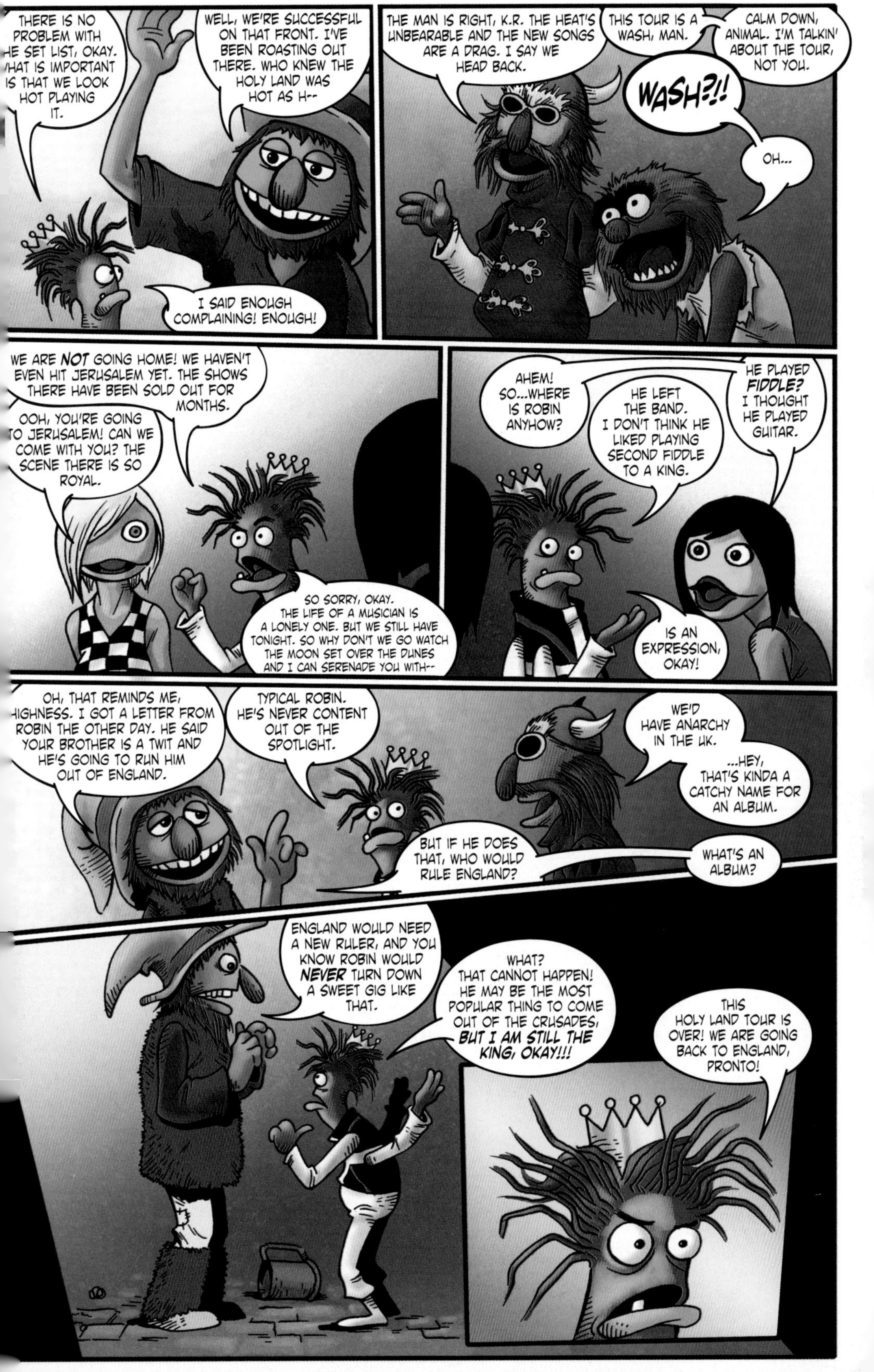
THERE IS NO PROBLEM WITH HE SET LIST, OKAY. WHAT IS IMPORTANT IS THAT WE LOOK HOT PLAYING IT.
WELL, WE'RE SUCCESSFUL ON THAT FRONT. I'VE BEEN ROASTING OUT THERE. WHO KNEW THE HOLY LAND WAS HOT AS H--
I SAID ENOUGH COMPLAINING! ENOUGH!
THE MAN IS RIGHT, K.R. THE HEAT'S UNBEARABLE AND THE NEW SONGS ARE A DRAG. I SAY WE HEAD BACK.
THIS TOUR IS A WASH, MAN.
CALM DOWN, ANIMAL. I'M TALKIN' ABOUT THE TOUR, NOT YOU.
WASH?!!
OH...
WE ARE NOT GOING HOME! WE HAVEN'T EVEN HIT JERUSALEM YET. THE SHOWS THERE HAVE BEEN SOLD OUT FOR MONTHS.
OOH, YOU'RE GOING TO JERUSALEM! CAN WE COME WITH YOU? THE SCENE THERE IS SO ROYAL.
SO SORRY, OKAY. THE LIFE OF A MUSICIAN IS A LONELY ONE. BUT WE STILL HAVE TONIGHT. SO WHY DON'T WE GO WATCH THE MOON SET OVER THE DUNES AND I CAN SERENADE YOU WITH--
AHEM! SO...WHERE IS ROBIN ANYHOW?
HE LEFT THE BAND. I DON'T THINK HE LIKED PLAYING SECOND FIDDLE TO A KING.
HE PLAYED FIDDLE? I THOUGHT HE PLAYED GUITAR.
IS AN EXPRESSION, OKAY!
OH, THAT REMINDS ME, HIGHNESS. I GOT A LETTER FROM ROBIN THE OTHER DAY. HE SAID YOUR BROTHER IS A TWIT AND HE'S GOING TO RUN HIM OUT OF ENGLAND.
TYPICAL ROBIN. HE'S NEVER CONTENT OUT OF THE SPOTLIGHT.
BUT IF HE DOES THAT, WHO WOULD RULE ENGLAND?
WE'D HAVE ANARCHY IN THE UK.
...HEY, THAT'S KINDA A CATCHY NAME FOR AN ALBUM.
WHAT'S AN ALBUM?
ENGLAND WOULD NEED A NEW RULER, AND YOU KNOW ROBIN WOULD NEVER TURN DOWN A SWEET GIG LIKE THAT.
WHAT? THAT CANNOT HAPPEN! HE MAY BE THE MOST POPULAR THING TO COME OUT OF THE CRUSADES, BUT I AM STILL THE KING, OKAY!!!
THIS HOLY LAND TOUR IS OVER! WE ARE GOING BACK TO ENGLAND, PRONTO!

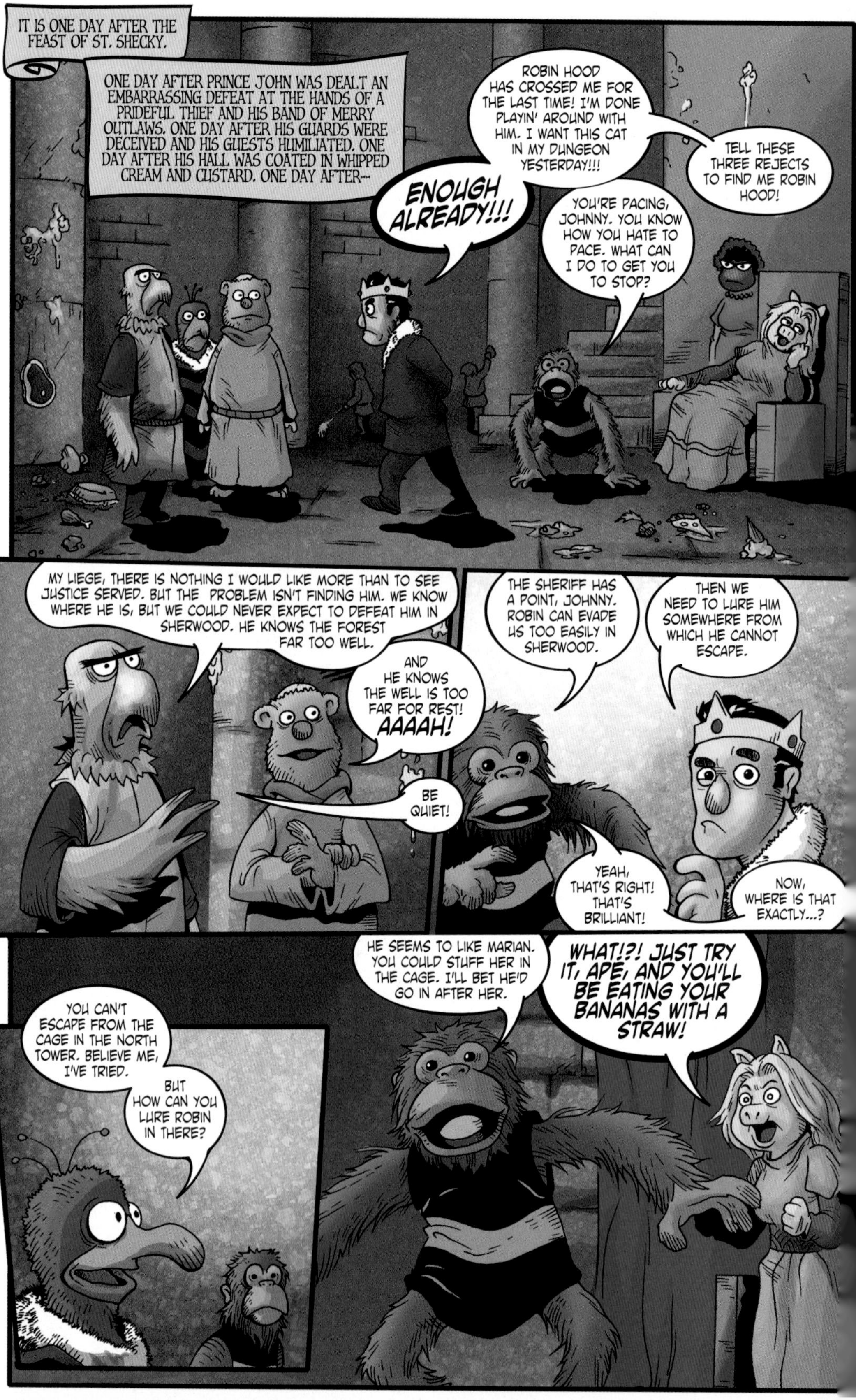
IT IS ONE DAY AFTER THE FEAST OF ST. SHECKY.
ONE DAY AFTER PRINCE JOHN WAS DEALT AN EMBARRASSING DEFEAT AT THE HANDS OF A PRIDEFUL THIEF AND HIS BAND OF MERRY OUTLAWS. ONE DAY AFTER HIS GUARDS WERE DECEIVED AND HIS GUESTS HUMILIATED. ONE DAY AFTER HIS HALL WAS COATED IN WHIPPED CREAM AND CUSTARD. ONE DAY AFTER--
ENOUGH ALREADY!!!
ROBIN HOOD HAS CROSSED ME FOR THE LAST TIME! I'M DONE PLAYIN' AROUND WITH HIM. I WANT THIS CAT IN MY DUNGEON YESTERDAY!!!
TELL THESE THREE REJECTS TO FIND ME ROBIN HOOD!
YOU'RE PACING, JOHNNY. YOU KNOW HOW YOU HATE TO PACE. WHAT CAN I DO TO GET YOU TO STOP?
MY LIEGE, THERE IS NOTHING I WOULD LIKE MORE THAN TO SEE JUSTICE SERVED. BUT THE PROBLEM ISN'T FINDING HIM. WE KNOW WHERE HE IS, BUT WE COULD NEVER EXPECT TO DEFEAT HIM IN SHERWOOD. HE KNOWS THE FOREST FAR TOO WELL.
AND HE KNOWS THE WELL IS TOO FAR FOR REST! AAAAH!
BE QUIET!
THE SHERIFF HAS A POINT, JOHNNY. ROBIN CAN EVADE US TOO EASILY IN SHERWOOD.
THEN WE NEED TO LURE HIM SOMEWHERE FROM WHICH HE CANNOT ESCAPE.
YEAH, THAT'S RIGHT! THAT'S BRILLIANT!
NOW, WHERE IS THAT EXACTLY...?
YOU CAN'T ESCAPE FROM THE CAGE IN THE NORTH TOWER. BELIEVE ME, I'VE TRIED.
BUT HOW CAN YOU LURE ROBIN IN THERE?
HE SEEMS TO LIKE MARIAN. YOU COULD STUFF HER IN THE CAGE. I'LL BET HE'D GO IN AFTER HER.
WHAT!?! JUST TRY IT, APE, AND YOU'LL BE EATING YOUR BANANAS WITH A STRAW!

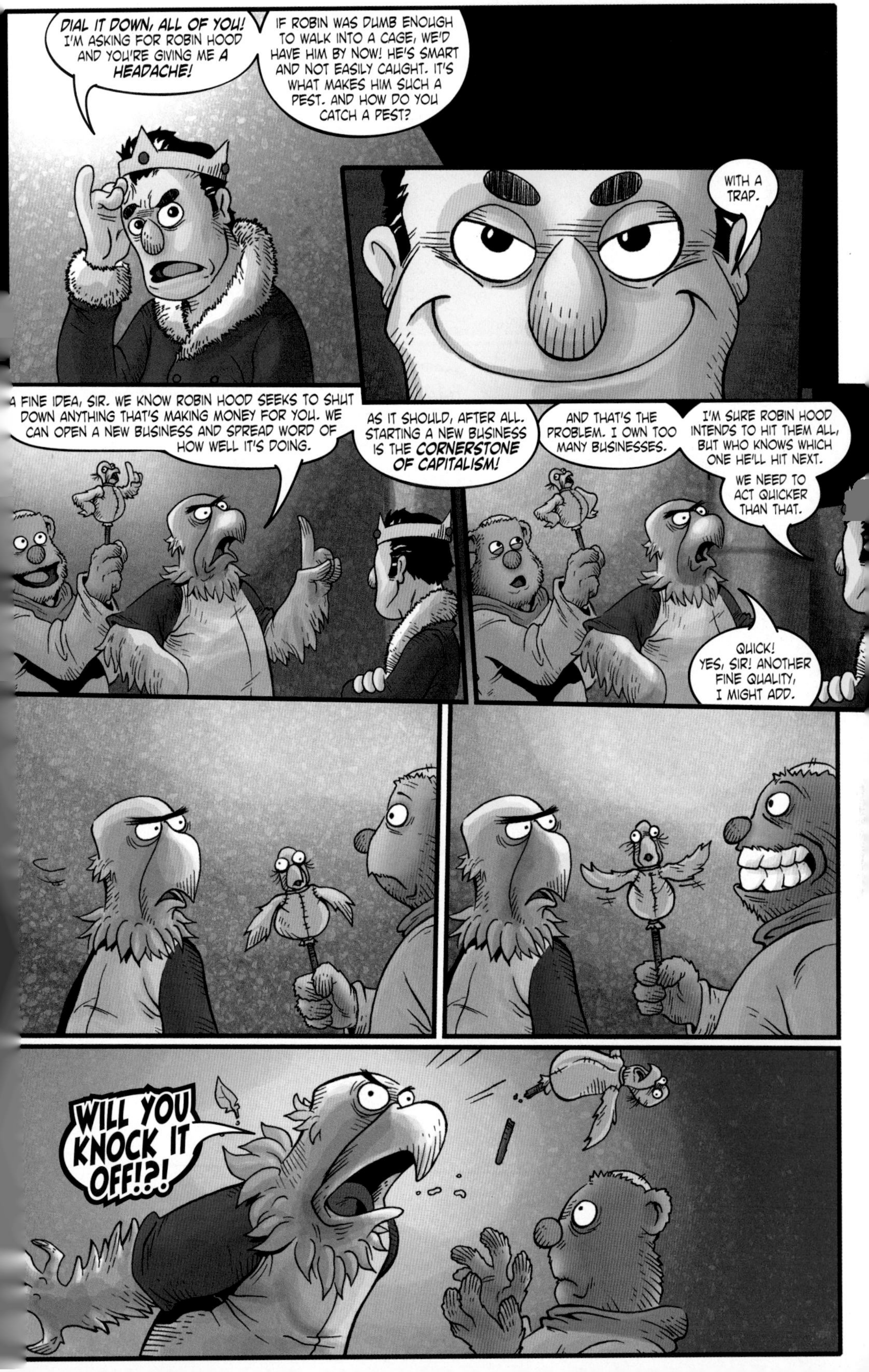
DIAL IT DOWN, ALL OF YOU! I'M ASKING FOR ROBIN HOOD AND YOU'RE GIVING ME A HEADACHE!
IF ROBIN WAS DUMB ENOUGH TO WALK INTO A CAGE, WE'D HAVE HIM BY NOW! HE'S SMART AND NOT EASILY CAUGHT. IT'S WHAT MAKES HIM SUCH A PEST. AND HOW DO YOU CATCH A PEST?
WITH A TRAP.
A FINE IDEA, SIR. WE KNOW ROBIN HOOD SEEKS TO SHUT DOWN ANYTHING THAT'S MAKING MONEY FOR YOU. WE CAN OPEN A NEW BUSINESS AND SPREAD WORD OF HOW WELL IT'S DOING.
AS IT SHOULD, AFTER ALL. STARTING A NEW BUSINESS IS THE CORNERSTONE OF CAPITALISM!
AND THAT'S THE PROBLEM. I OWN TOO MANY BUSINESSES.
I'M SURE ROBIN HOOD INTENDS TO HIT THEM ALL, BUT WHO KNOWS WHICH ONE HE'LL HIT NEXT.
WE NEED TO ACT QUICKER THAN THAT.
QUICK! YES, SIR! ANOTHER FINE QUALITY, I MIGHT ADD.
WILL YOU KNOCK IT OFF!?!

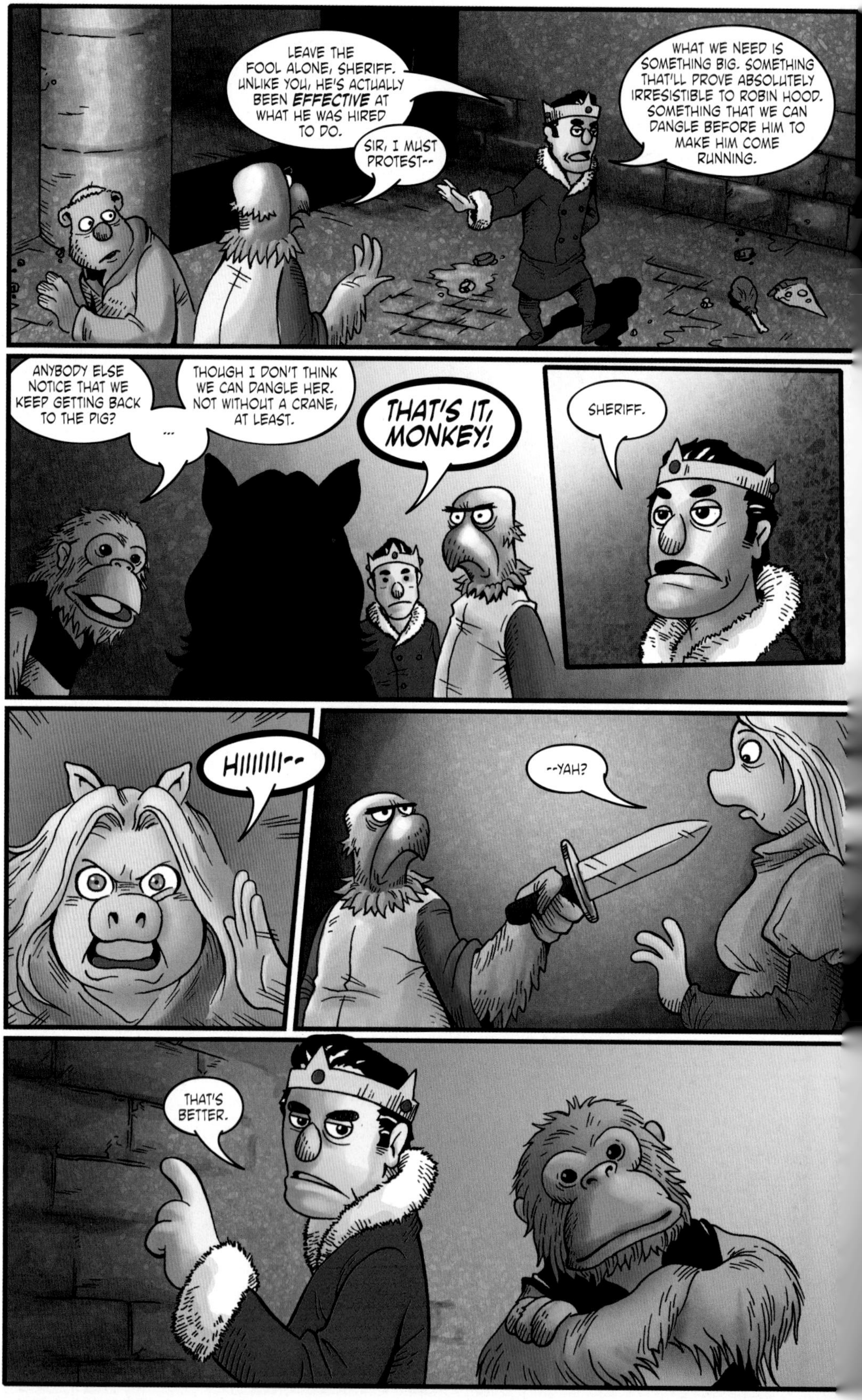
LEAVE THE FOOL ALONE, SHERIFF. UNLIKE YOU, HE'S ACTUALLY BEEN EFFECTIVE AT WHAT HE WAS HIRED TO DO.
WHAT WE NEED IS SOMETHING BIG. SOMETHING THAT'LL PROVE ABSOLUTELY IRRESISTIBLE TO ROBIN HOOD. SOMETHING THAT WE CAN DANGLE BEFORE HIM TO MAKE HIM COME RUNNING.
SIR, I MUST PROTEST--
ANYBODY ELSE NOTICE THAT WE KEEP GETTING BACK TO THE PIG?
...
THOUGH I DON'T THINK WE CAN DANGLE HER. NOT WITHOUT A CRANE, AT LEAST.
THAT'S IT, MONKEY!
SHERIFF.
HIIIIIII--
--YAH?
THAT'S BETTER.

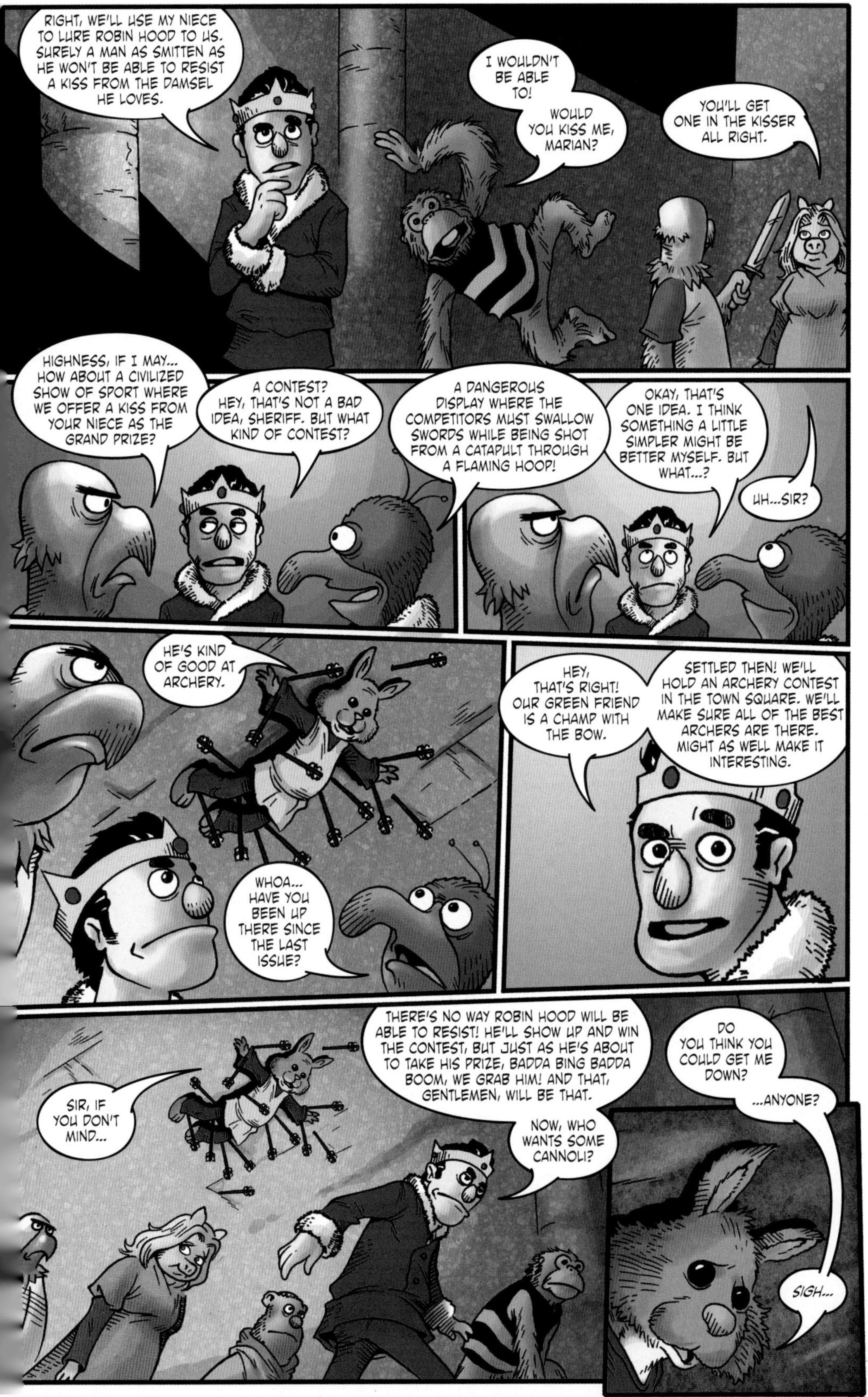
RIGHT, WE'LL USE MY NIECE TO LURE ROBIN HOOD TO US. SURELY A MAN AS SMITTEN AS HE WON'T BE ABLE TO RESIST A KISS FROM THE DAMSEL HE LOVES.
I WOULDN'T BE ABLE TO!
WOULD YOU KISS ME, MARIAN?
YOU'LL GET ONE IN THE KISSER ALL RIGHT.
HIGHNESS, IF I MAY... HOW ABOUT A CIVILIZED SHOW OF SPORT WHERE WE OFFER A KISS FROM YOUR NIECE AS THE GRAND PRIZE?
A CONTEST? HEY, THAT'S NOT A BAD IDEA, SHERIFF. BUT WHAT KIND OF CONTEST?
A DANGEROUS DISPLAY WHERE THE COMPETITORS MUST SWALLOW SWORDS WHILE BEING SHOT FROM A CATAPULT THROUGH A FLAMING HOOP!
OKAY, THAT'S ONE IDEA. I THINK SOMETHING A LITTLE SIMPLER MIGHT BE BETTER MYSELF. BUT WHAT...?
UH...SIR?
HE'S KIND OF GOOD AT ARCHERY.
WHOA... HAVE YOU BEEN UP THERE SINCE THE LAST ISSUE?
HEY, THAT'S RIGHT! OUR GREEN FRIEND IS A CHAMP WITH THE BOW.
SETTLED THEN! WE'LL HOLD AN ARCHERY CONTEST IN THE TOWN SQUARE. WE'LL MAKE SURE ALL OF THE BEST ARCHERS ARE THERE. MIGHT AS WELL MAKE IT INTERESTING.
THERE'S NO WAY ROBIN HOOD WILL BE ABLE TO RESIST! HE'LL SHOW UP AND WIN THE CONTEST, BUT JUST AS HE'S ABOUT TO TAKE HIS PRIZE, BADDA BING BADDA BOOM, WE GRAB HIM! AND THAT, GENTLEMEN, WILL BE THAT.
NOW, WHO WANTS SOME CANNOLI?
SIR, IF YOU DON'T MIND...
DO YOU THINK YOU COULD GET ME DOWN?
...ANYONE?
SIGH...

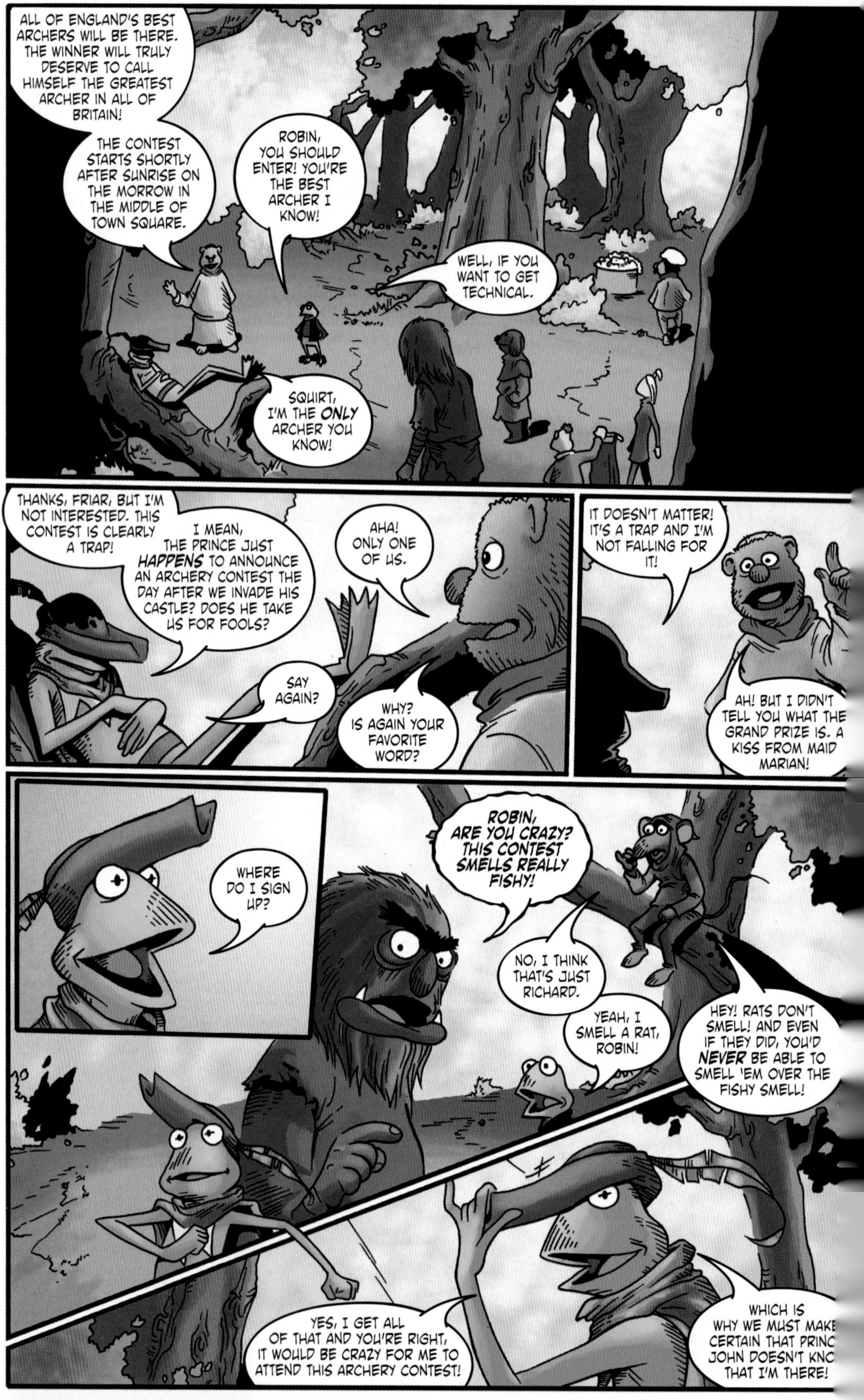
ALL OF ENGLAND'S BEST ARCHERS WILL BE THERE. THE WINNER WILL TRULY DESERVE TO CALL HIMSELF THE GREATEST ARCHER IN ALL OF BRITAIN!
THE CONTEST STARTS SHORTLY AFTER SUNRISE ON THE MORROW IN THE MIDDLE OF TOWN SQUARE.
ROBIN, YOU SHOULD ENTER! YOU'RE THE BEST ARCHER I KNOW!
WELL, IF YOU WANT TO GET TECHNICAL.
SQUIRT, I'M THE ONLY ARCHER YOU KNOW!
THANKS, FRIAR, BUT I'M NOT INTERESTED. THIS CONTEST IS CLEARLY A TRAP!
I MEAN, THE PRINCE JUST HAPPENS TO ANNOUNCE AN ARCHERY CONTEST THE DAY AFTER WE INVADE HIS CASTLE? DOES HE TAKE US FOR FOOLS?
AHA! ONLY ONE OF US.
SAY AGAIN?
WHY? IS AGAIN YOUR FAVORITE WORD?
IT DOESN'T MATTER! IT'S A TRAP AND I'M NOT FALLING FOR IT!
AH! BUT I DIDN'T TELL YOU WHAT THE GRAND PRIZE IS. A KISS FROM MAID MARIAN!
WHERE DO I SIGN UP?
ROBIN, ARE YOU CRAZY? THIS CONTEST SMELLS REALLY FISHY!
NO, I THINK THAT'S JUST RICHARD.
YEAH, I SMELL A RAT, ROBIN!
HEY! RATS DON'T SMELL! AND EVEN IF THEY DID, YOU'D NEVER BE ABLE TO SMELL 'EM OVER THE FISHY SMELL!
YES, I GET ALL OF THAT AND YOU'RE RIGHT, IT WOULD BE CRAZY FOR ME TO ATTEND THIS ARCHERY CONTEST!
WHICH IS WHY WE MUST MAKE CERTAIN THAT PRINC JOHN DOESN'T KNO THAT I'M THERE!

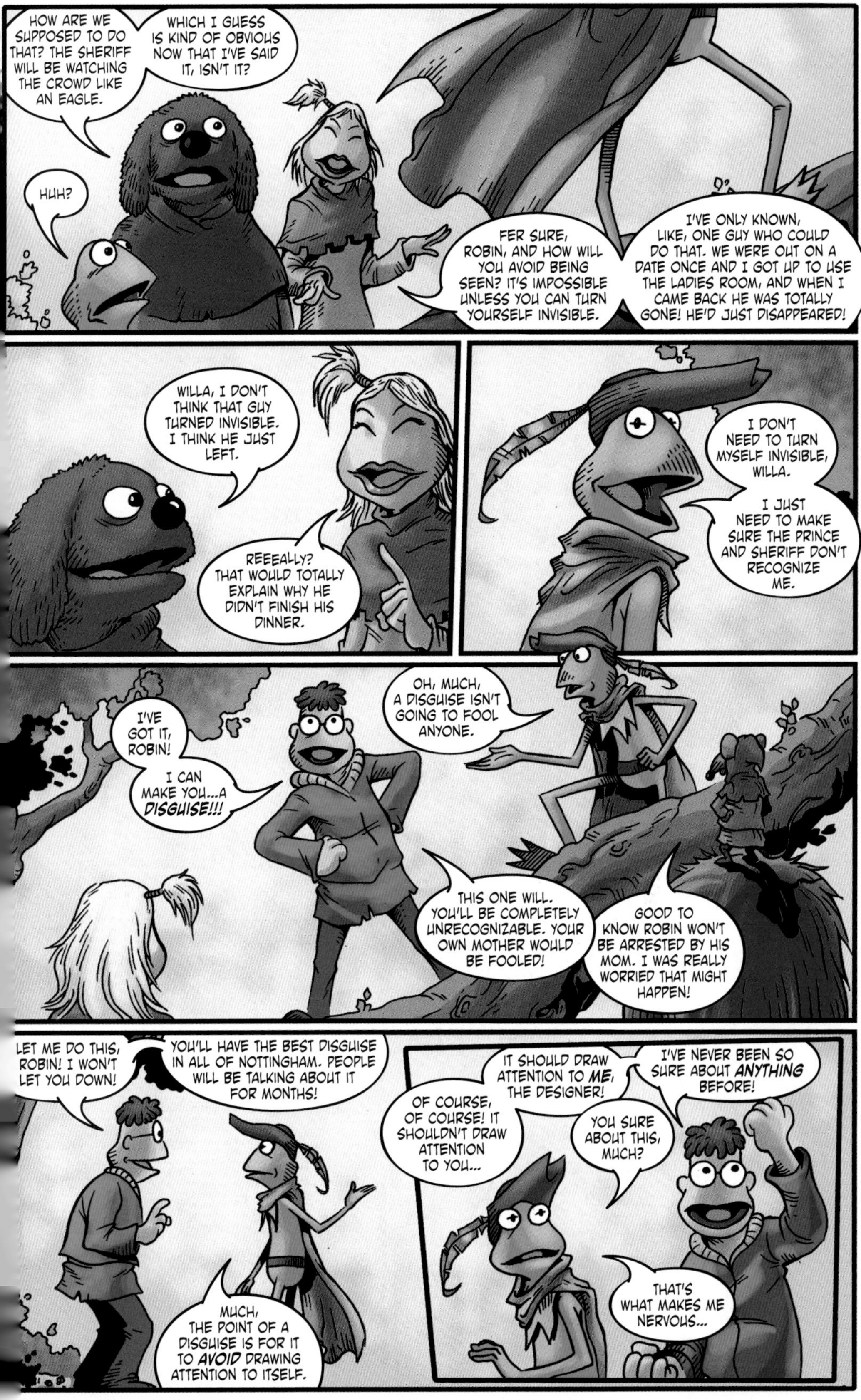

HOW ARE WE SUPPOSED TO DO THAT? THE SHERIFF WILL BE WATCHING THE CROWD LIKE AN EAGLE.
WHICH I GUESS IS KIND OF OBVIOUS NOW THAT I'VE SAID IT, ISN'T IT?
HUH?
FER SURE, ROBIN, AND HOW WILL YOU AVOID BEING SEEN? IT'S IMPOSSIBLE UNLESS YOU CAN TURN YOURSELF INVISIBLE.
I'VE ONLY KNOWN, LIKE, ONE GUY WHO COULD DO THAT. WE WERE OUT ON A DATE ONCE AND I GOT UP TO USE THE LADIES ROOM, AND WHEN I CAME BACK HE WAS TOTALLY GONE! HE'D JUST DISAPPEARED!
WILLA, I DON'T THINK THAT GUY TURNED INVISIBLE. I THINK HE JUST LEFT.
REEEALLY? THAT WOULD TOTALLY EXPLAIN WHY HE DIDN'T FINISH HIS DINNER.
I DON'T NEED TO TURN MYSELF INVISIBLE, WILLA.
I JUST NEED TO MAKE SURE THE PRINCE AND SHERIFF DON'T RECOGNIZE ME.
I'VE GOT IT, ROBIN!
I CAN MAKE YOU...A ***DISGUISE!!!***
OH, MUCH, A DISGUISE ISN'T GOING TO FOOL ANYONE.
THIS ONE WILL. YOU'LL BE COMPLETELY UNRECOGNIZABLE. YOUR OWN MOTHER WOULD BE FOOLED!
GOOD TO KNOW ROBIN WON'T BE ARRESTED BY HIS MOM. I WAS REALLY WORRIED THAT MIGHT HAPPEN!
LET ME DO THIS, ROBIN! I WON'T LET YOU DOWN!
YOU'LL HAVE THE BEST DISGUISE IN ALL OF NOTTINGHAM. PEOPLE WILL BE TALKING ABOUT IT FOR MONTHS!
MUCH, THE POINT OF A DISGUISE IS FOR IT TO ***AVOID*** DRAWING ATTENTION TO ITSELF.
OF COURSE, OF COURSE! IT SHOULDN'T DRAW ATTENTION TO YOU...
IT SHOULD DRAW ATTENTION TO ***ME***, THE DESIGNER!
YOU SURE ABOUT THIS, MUCH?
I'VE NEVER BEEN SO SURE ABOUT ***ANYTHING*** BEFORE!
THAT'S WHAT MAKES ME NERVOUS...

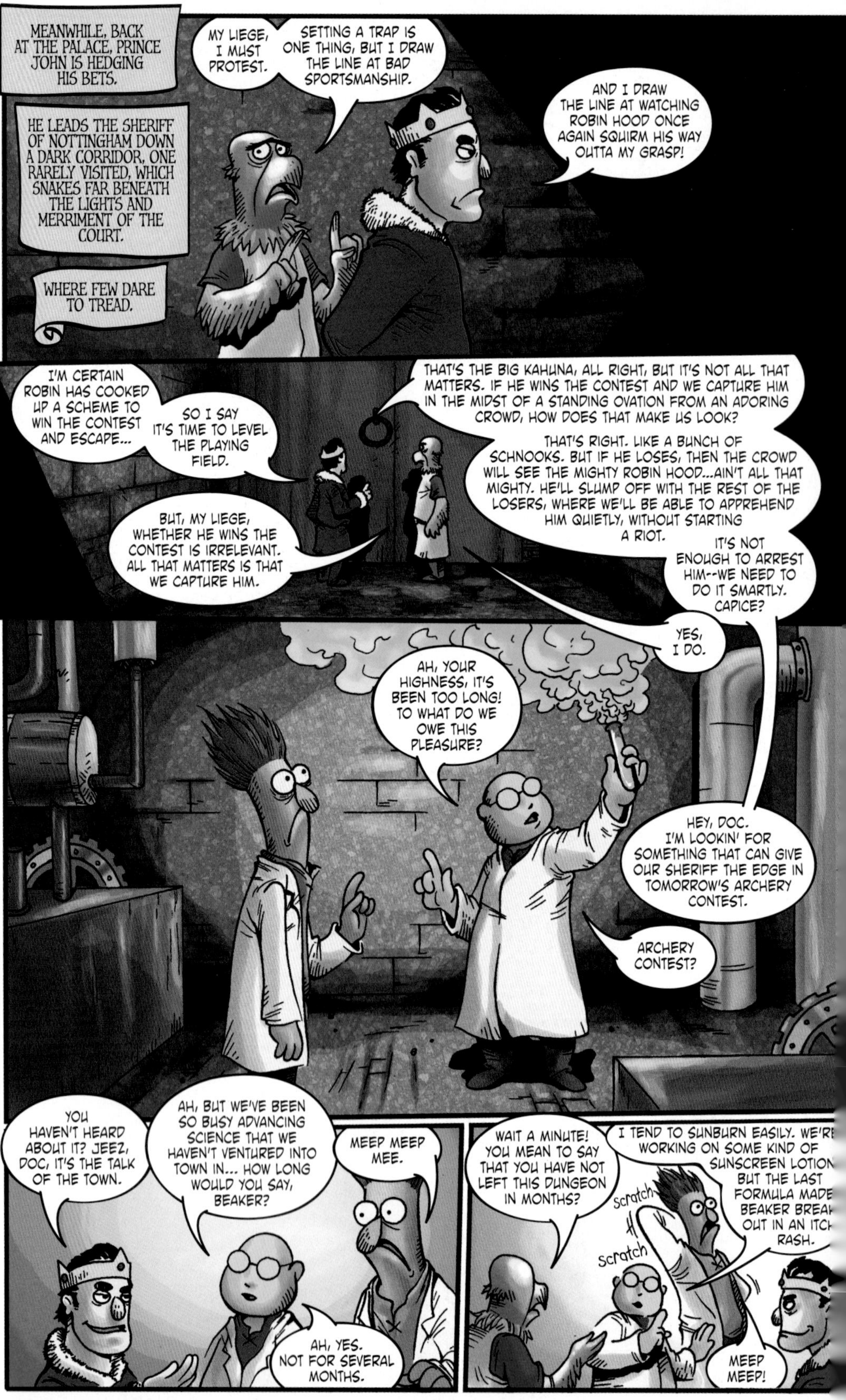

MEANWHILE, BACK AT THE PALACE, PRINCE JOHN IS HEDGING HIS BETS.
MY LIEGE, I MUST PROTEST.
SETTING A TRAP IS ONE THING, BUT I DRAW THE LINE AT BAD SPORTSMANSHIP.
AND I DRAW THE LINE AT WATCHING ROBIN HOOD ONCE AGAIN SQUIRM HIS WAY OUTTA MY GRASP!
HE LEADS THE SHERIFF OF NOTTINGHAM DOWN A DARK CORRIDOR, ONE RARELY VISITED, WHICH SNAKES FAR BENEATH THE LIGHTS AND MERRIMENT OF THE COURT.
WHERE FEW DARE TO TREAD.
I'M CERTAIN ROBIN HAS COOKED UP A SCHEME TO WIN THE CONTEST AND ESCAPE...
SO I SAY IT'S TIME TO LEVEL THE PLAYING FIELD.
BUT, MY LIEGE, WHETHER HE WINS THE CONTEST IS IRRELEVANT. ALL THAT MATTERS IS THAT WE CAPTURE HIM.
THAT'S THE BIG KAHUNA, ALL RIGHT, BUT IT'S NOT ALL THAT MATTERS. IF HE WINS THE CONTEST AND WE CAPTURE HIM IN THE MIDST OF A STANDING OVATION FROM AN ADORING CROWD, HOW DOES THAT MAKE US LOOK?
THAT'S RIGHT. LIKE A BUNCH OF SCHNOOKS. BUT IF HE LOSES, THEN THE CROWD WILL SEE THE MIGHTY ROBIN HOOD...AIN'T ALL THAT MIGHTY. HE'LL SLUMP OFF WITH THE REST OF THE LOSERS, WHERE WE'LL BE ABLE TO APPREHEND HIM QUIETLY, WITHOUT STARTING A RIOT.
IT'S NOT ENOUGH TO ARREST HIM--WE NEED TO DO IT SMARTLY. CAPICE?
YES, I DO.
AH, YOUR HIGHNESS, IT'S BEEN TOO LONG! TO WHAT DO WE OWE THIS PLEASURE?
HEY, DOC. I'M LOOKIN' FOR SOMETHING THAT CAN GIVE OUR SHERIFF THE EDGE IN TOMORROW'S ARCHERY CONTEST.
ARCHERY CONTEST?
YOU HAVEN'T HEARD ABOUT IT? JEEZ, DOC, IT'S THE TALK OF THE TOWN.
AH, BUT WE'VE BEEN SO BUSY ADVANCING SCIENCE THAT WE HAVEN'T VENTURED INTO TOWN IN... HOW LONG WOULD YOU SAY, BEAKER?
MEEP MEEP MEE.
AH, YES. NOT FOR SEVERAL MONTHS.
WAIT A MINUTE! YOU MEAN TO SAY THAT YOU HAVE NOT LEFT THIS DUNGEON IN MONTHS?
I TEND TO SUNBURN EASILY. WE'R WORKING ON SOME KIND OF SUNSCREEN LOTION BUT THE LAST FORMULA MADE BEAKER BREAK OUT IN AN ITCH RASH.
Scratch
Scratch
MEEP MEEP!

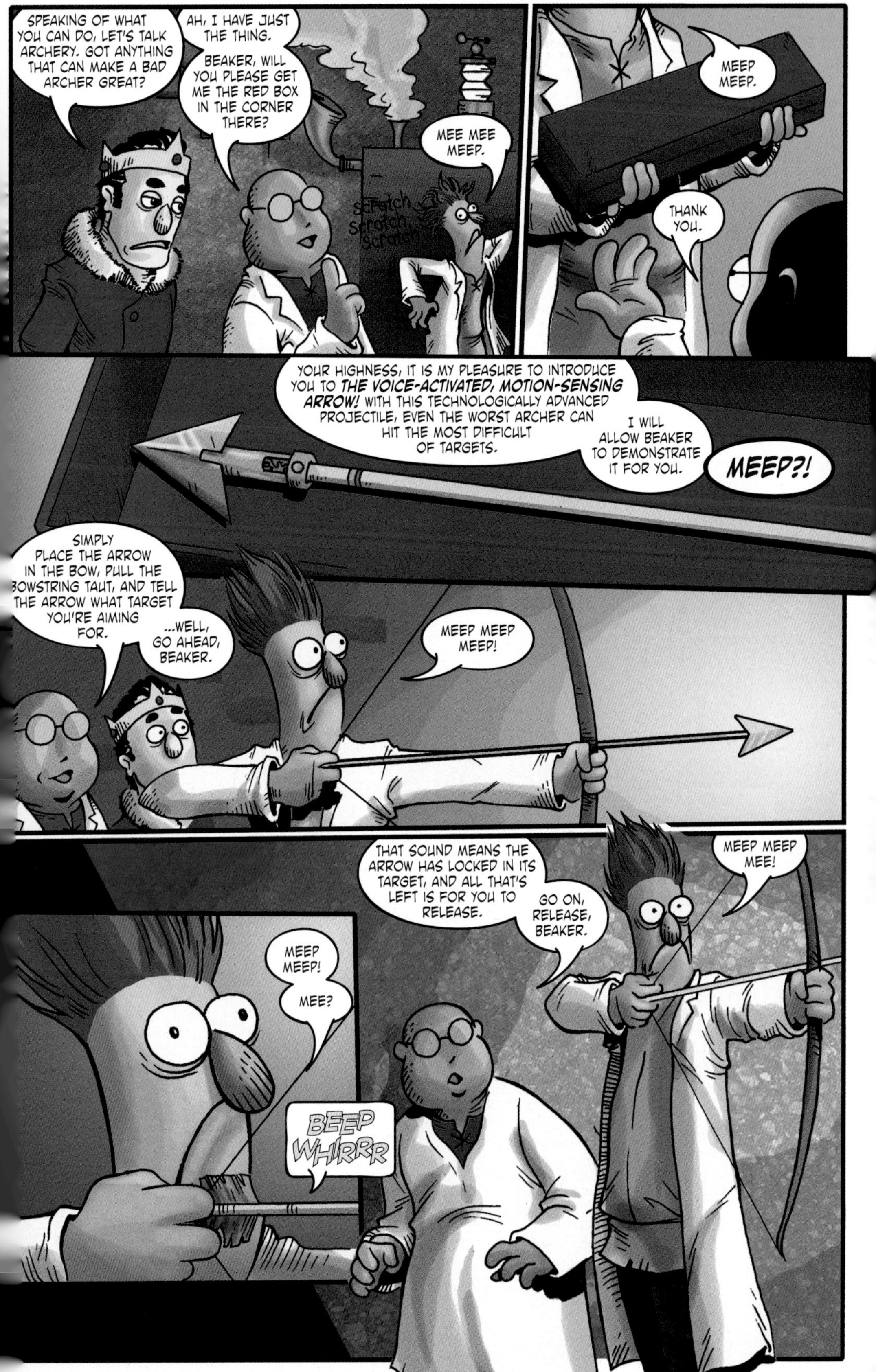
SPEAKING OF WHAT YOU CAN DO, LET'S TALK ARCHERY. GOT ANYTHING THAT CAN MAKE A BAD ARCHER GREAT?
AH, I HAVE JUST THE THING.
BEAKER, WILL YOU PLEASE GET ME THE RED BOX IN THE CORNER THERE?
MEE MEE MEEP.
SCRATCH SCRATCH SCRATCH
MEEP MEEP.
THANK YOU.
YOUR HIGHNESS, IT IS MY PLEASURE TO INTRODUCE YOU TO ***THE VOICE-ACTIVATED, MOTION-SENSING ARROW!*** WITH THIS TECHNOLOGICALLY ADVANCED PROJECTILE, EVEN THE WORST ARCHER CAN HIT THE MOST DIFFICULT OF TARGETS.
I WILL ALLOW BEAKER TO DEMONSTRATE IT FOR YOU.
MEEP?!
SIMPLY PLACE THE ARROW IN THE BOW, PULL THE BOWSTRING TAUT, AND TELL THE ARROW WHAT TARGET YOU'RE AIMING FOR.
...WELL, GO AHEAD, BEAKER.
MEEP MEEP MEEP!
MEEP MEEP!
MEE?
BEEP WHIRRR
THAT SOUND MEANS THE ARROW HAS LOCKED IN ITS TARGET, AND ALL THAT'S LEFT IS FOR YOU TO RELEASE.
GO ON, RELEASE, BEAKER.
MEEP MEEP MEE!

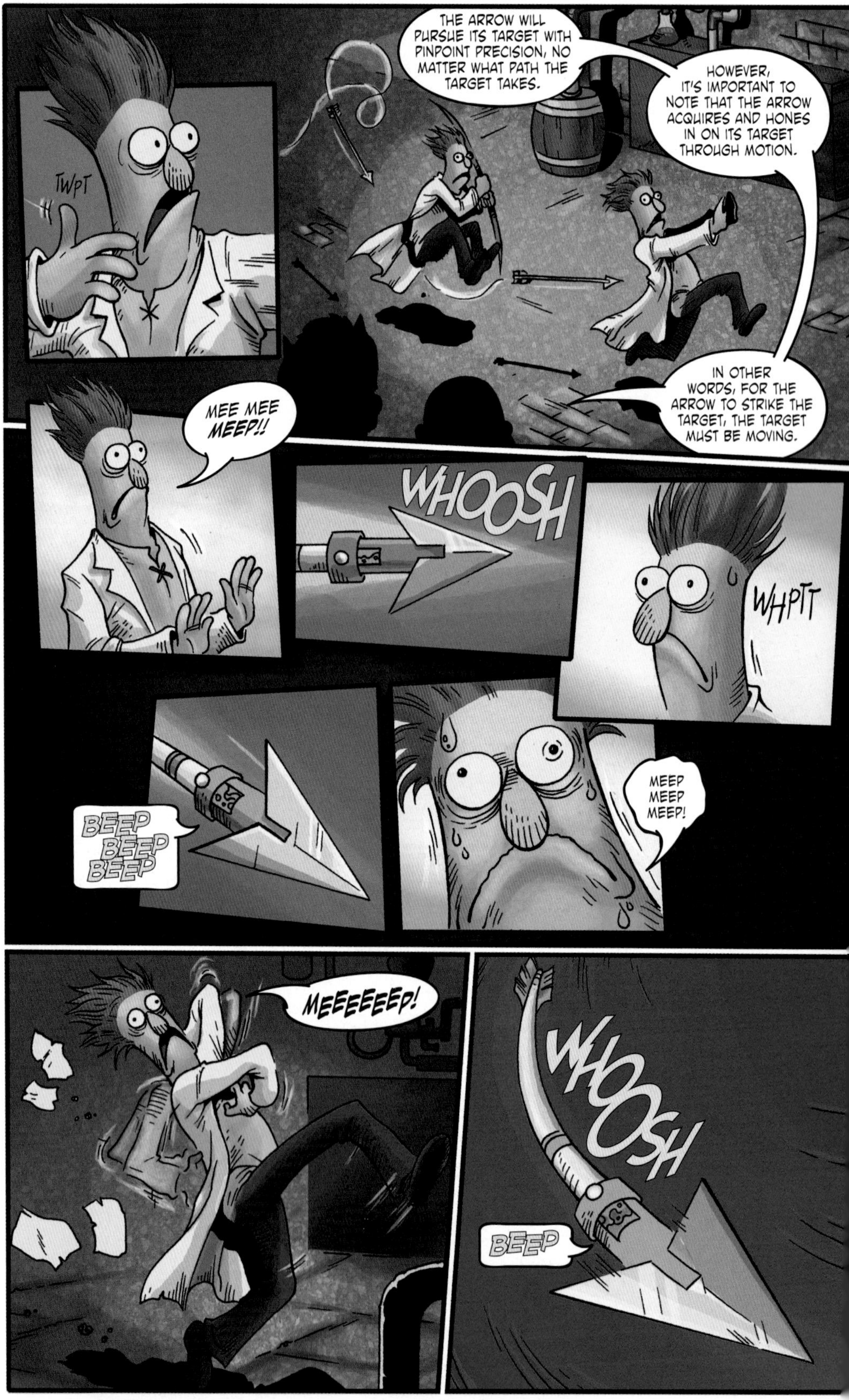
TWPT
THE ARROW WILL PURSUE ITS TARGET WITH PINPOINT PRECISION, NO MATTER WHAT PATH THE TARGET TAKES.
HOWEVER, IT'S IMPORTANT TO NOTE THAT THE ARROW ACQUIRES AND HONES IN ON ITS TARGET THROUGH MOTION.
IN OTHER WORDS, FOR THE ARROW TO STRIKE THE TARGET, THE TARGET MUST BE MOVING.
MEE MEE MEEP!!
WHOOSH
WHPTT
BEEP BEEP BEEP
MEEP MEEP MEEP!
MEEEEEEP!
WHOOSH
BEEP

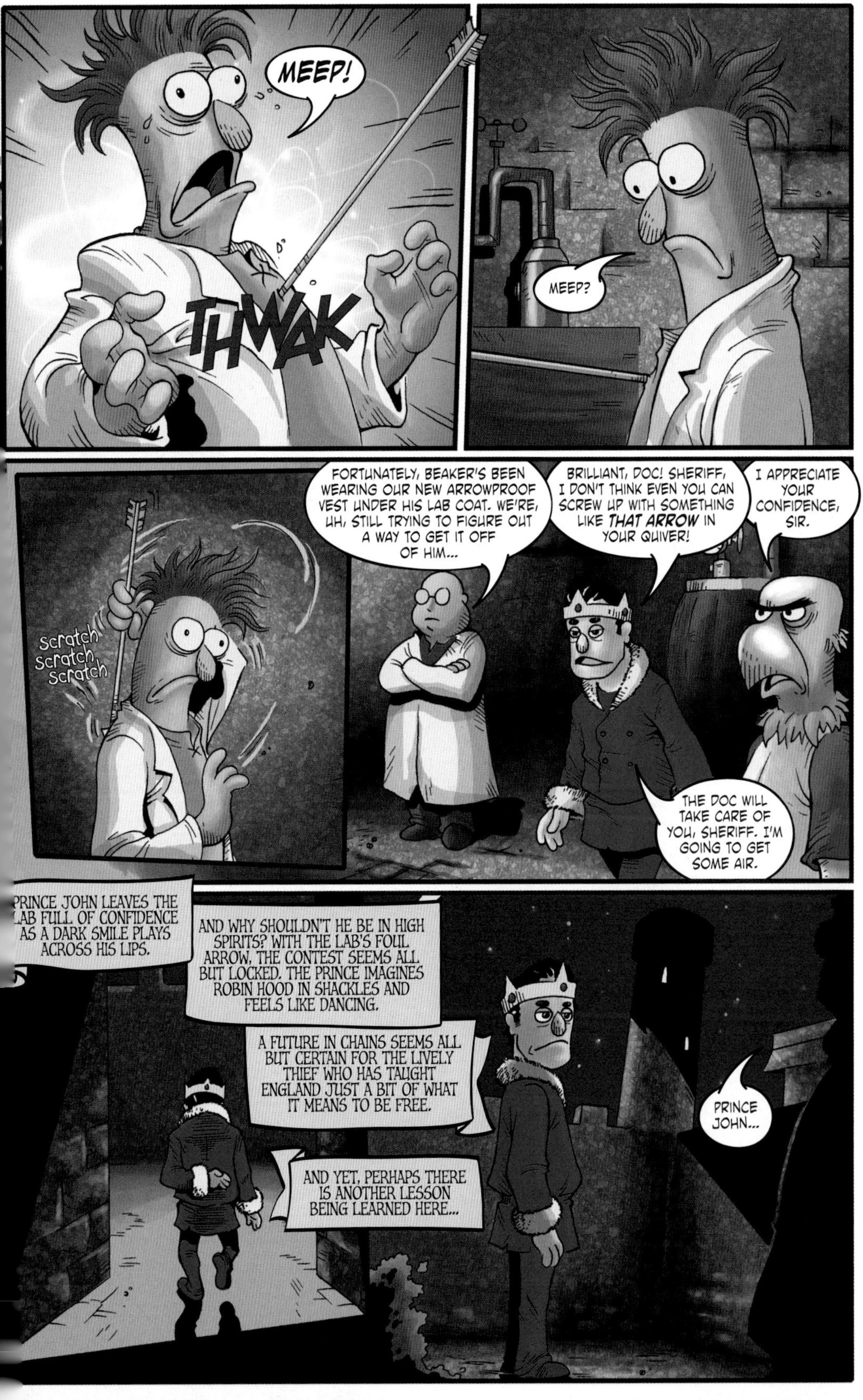
MEEP!
THWAK
MEEP?
scratch scratch scratch
FORTUNATELY, BEAKER'S BEEN WEARING OUR NEW ARROWPROOF VEST UNDER HIS LAB COAT. WE'RE, UH, STILL TRYING TO FIGURE OUT A WAY TO GET IT OFF OF HIM...
BRILLIANT, DOC! SHERIFF, I DON'T THINK EVEN YOU CAN SCREW UP WITH SOMETHING LIKE THAT ARROW IN YOUR QUIVER!
I APPRECIATE YOUR CONFIDENCE, SIR.
THE DOC WILL TAKE CARE OF YOU, SHERIFF. I'M GOING TO GET SOME AIR.
PRINCE JOHN LEAVES THE LAB FULL OF CONFIDENCE AS A DARK SMILE PLAYS ACROSS HIS LIPS.
AND WHY SHOULDN'T HE BE IN HIGH SPIRITS? WITH THE LAB'S FOUL ARROW, THE CONTEST SEEMS ALL BUT LOCKED. THE PRINCE IMAGINES ROBIN HOOD IN SHACKLES AND FEELS LIKE DANCING.
A FUTURE IN CHAINS SEEMS ALL BUT CERTAIN FOR THE LIVELY THIEF WHO HAS TAUGHT ENGLAND JUST A BIT OF WHAT IT MEANS TO BE FREE.
AND YET, PERHAPS THERE IS ANOTHER LESSON BEING LEARNED HERE...
PRINCE JOHN...

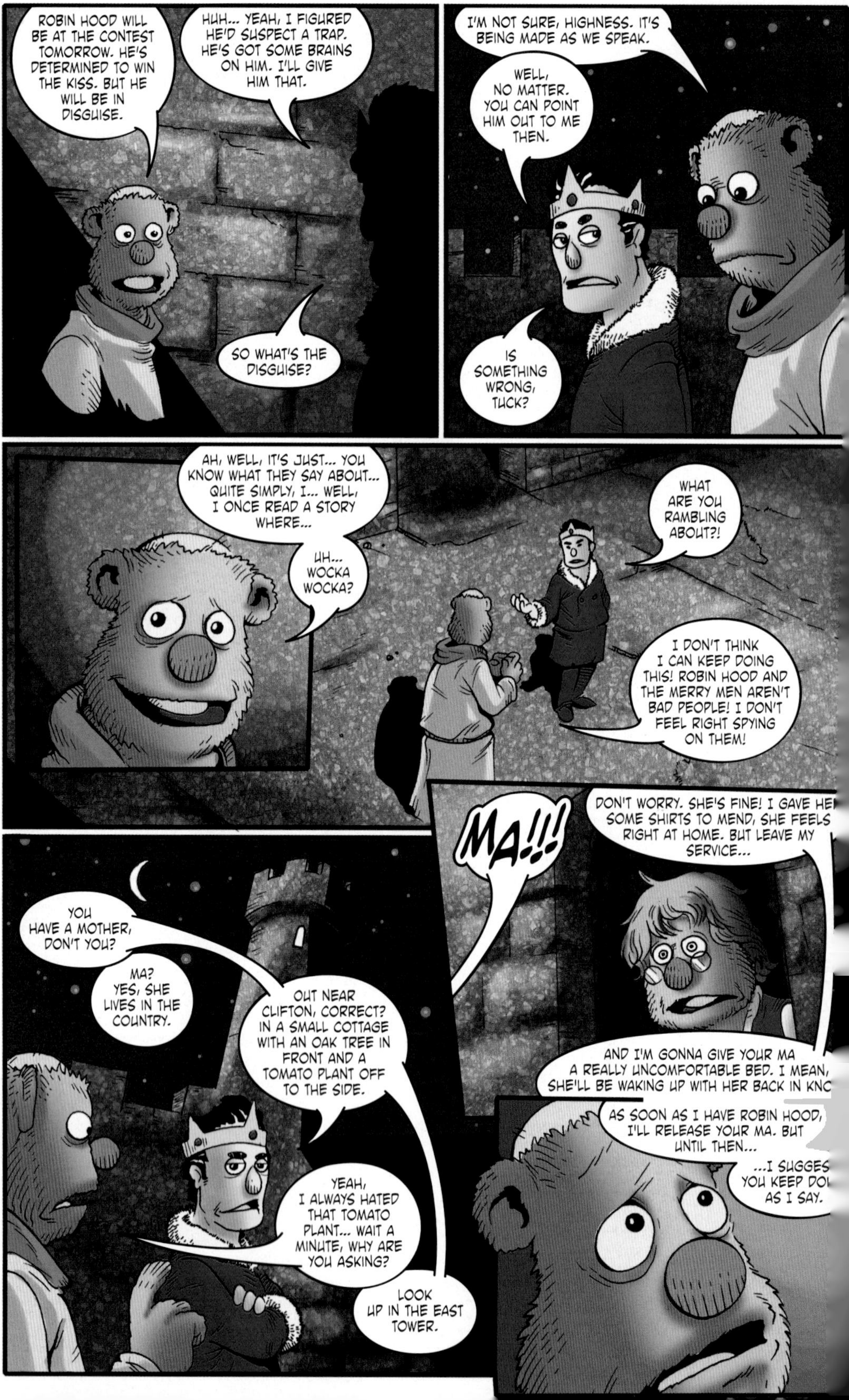
ROBIN HOOD WILL BE AT THE CONTEST TOMORROW. HE'S DETERMINED TO WIN THE KISS. BUT HE WILL BE IN DISGUISE.
HUH... YEAH, I FIGURED HE'D SUSPECT A TRAP. HE'S GOT SOME BRAINS ON HIM. I'LL GIVE HIM THAT.
SO WHAT'S THE DISGUISE?
I'M NOT SURE, HIGHNESS. IT'S BEING MADE AS WE SPEAK.
WELL, NO MATTER. YOU CAN POINT HIM OUT TO ME THEN.
IS SOMETHING WRONG, TUCK?
AH, WELL, IT'S JUST... YOU KNOW WHAT THEY SAY ABOUT... QUITE SIMPLY, I... WELL, I ONCE READ A STORY WHERE...
UH... WOCKA WOCKA?
WHAT ARE YOU RAMBLING ABOUT?!
I DON'T THINK I CAN KEEP DOING THIS! ROBIN HOOD AND THE MERRY MEN AREN'T BAD PEOPLE! I DON'T FEEL RIGHT SPYING ON THEM!
YOU HAVE A MOTHER, DON'T YOU?
MA? YES, SHE LIVES IN THE COUNTRY.
OUT NEAR CLIFTON, CORRECT? IN A SMALL COTTAGE WITH AN OAK TREE IN FRONT AND A TOMATO PLANT OFF TO THE SIDE.
YEAH, I ALWAYS HATED THAT TOMATO PLANT... WAIT A MINUTE, WHY ARE YOU ASKING?
LOOK UP IN THE EAST TOWER.
MA!!!
DON'T WORRY. SHE'S FINE! I GAVE HE SOME SHIRTS TO MEND, SHE FEELS RIGHT AT HOME. BUT LEAVE MY SERVICE...
AND I'M GONNA GIVE YOUR MA A REALLY UNCOMFORTABLE BED. I MEAN, SHE'LL BE WAKING UP WITH HER BACK IN KNO
AS SOON AS I HAVE ROBIN HOOD, I'LL RELEASE YOUR MA. BUT UNTIL THEN...
...I SUGGES YOU KEEP DO AS I SAY.

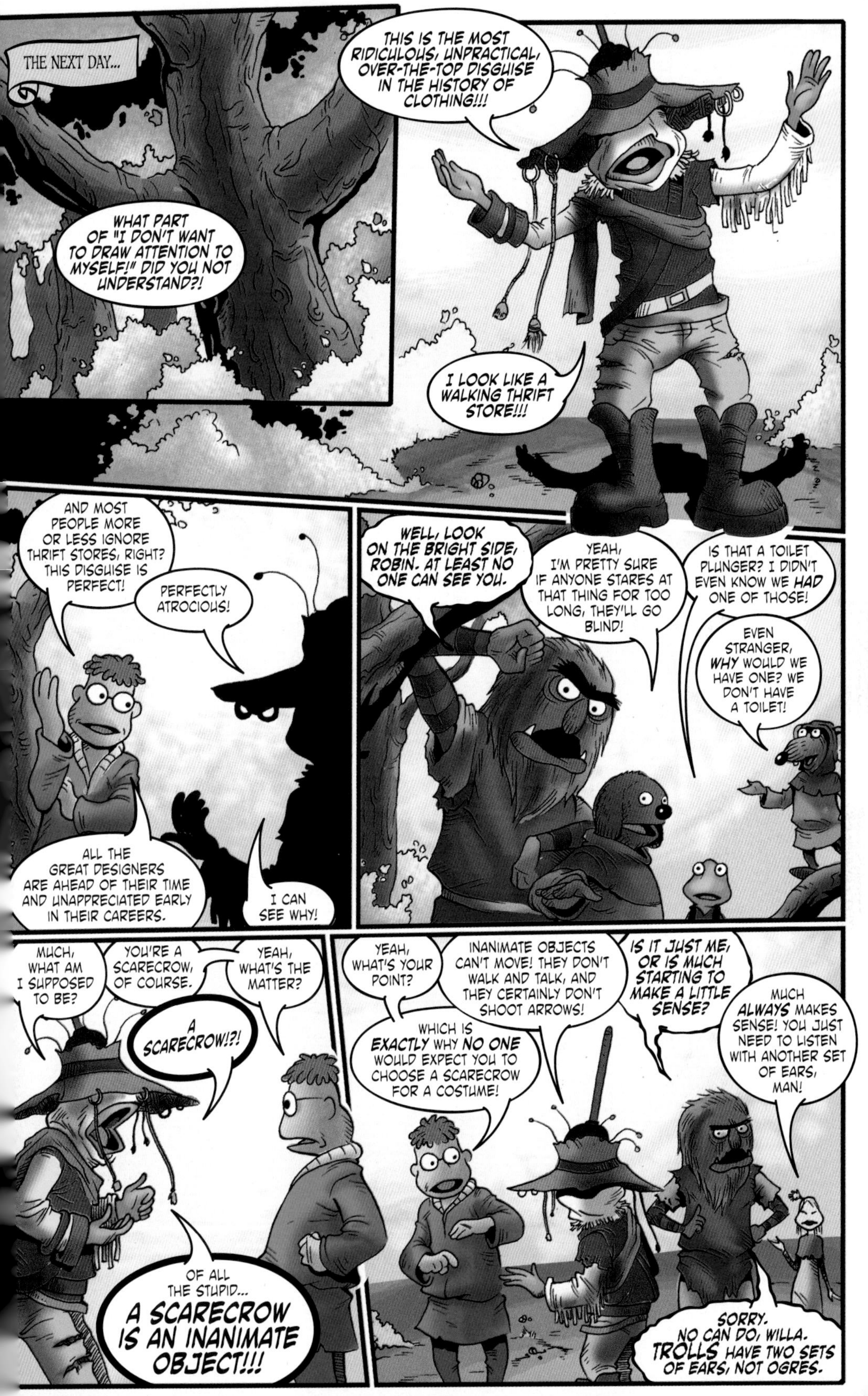
THE NEXT DAY...
THIS IS THE MOST RIDICULOUS, UNPRACTICAL, OVER-THE-TOP DISGUISE IN THE HISTORY OF CLOTHING!!!
WHAT PART OF "I DON'T WANT TO DRAW ATTENTION TO MYSELF!" DID YOU NOT UNDERSTAND?!
I LOOK LIKE A WALKING THRIFT STORE!!!
AND MOST PEOPLE MORE OR LESS IGNORE THRIFT STORES, RIGHT? THIS DISGUISE IS PERFECT!
PERFECTLY ATROCIOUS!
ALL THE GREAT DESIGNERS ARE AHEAD OF THEIR TIME AND UNAPPRECIATED EARLY IN THEIR CAREERS.
I CAN SEE WHY!
WELL, LOOK ON THE BRIGHT SIDE, ROBIN. AT LEAST NO ONE CAN SEE YOU.
YEAH, I'M PRETTY SURE IF ANYONE STARES AT THAT THING FOR TOO LONG, THEY'LL GO BLIND!
IS THAT A TOILET PLUNGER? I DIDN'T EVEN KNOW WE HAD ONE OF THOSE!
EVEN STRANGER, WHY WOULD WE HAVE ONE? WE DON'T HAVE A TOILET!
MUCH, WHAT AM I SUPPOSED TO BE?
YOU'RE A SCARECROW, OF COURSE.
YEAH, WHAT'S THE MATTER?
A SCARECROW!?!
OF ALL THE STUPID... A SCARECROW IS AN INANIMATE OBJECT!!!
YEAH, WHAT'S YOUR POINT?
INANIMATE OBJECTS CAN'T MOVE! THEY DON'T WALK AND TALK, AND THEY CERTAINLY DON'T SHOOT ARROWS!
WHICH IS EXACTLY WHY NO ONE WOULD EXPECT YOU TO CHOOSE A SCARECROW FOR A COSTUME!
IS IT JUST ME, OR IS MUCH STARTING TO MAKE A LITTLE SENSE?
MUCH ALWAYS MAKES SENSE! YOU JUST NEED TO LISTEN WITH ANOTHER SET OF EARS, MAN!
SORRY. NO CAN DO, WILLA. TROLLS HAVE TWO SETS OF EARS, NOT OGRES.

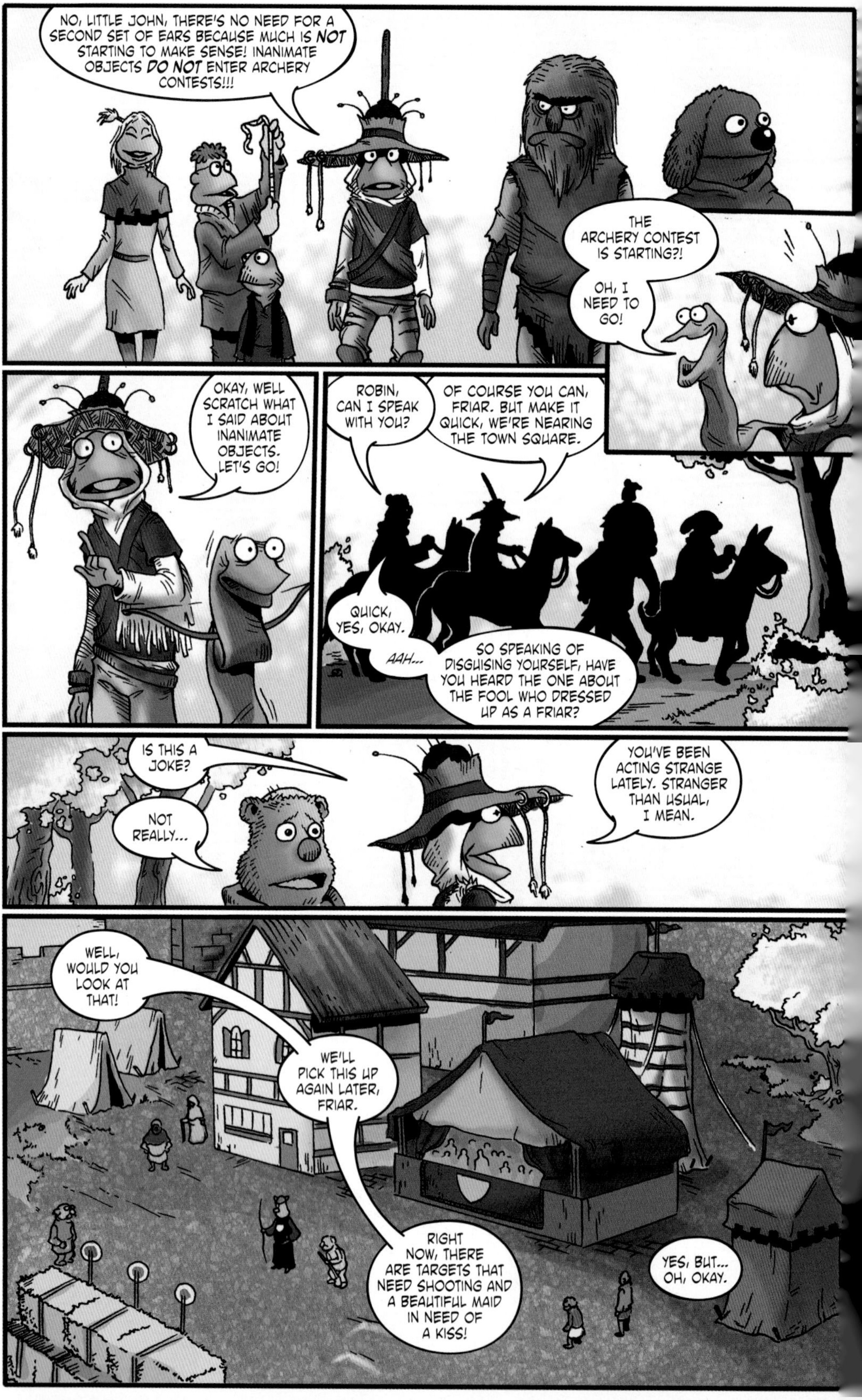
NO, LITTLE JOHN, THERE'S NO NEED FOR A SECOND SET OF EARS BECAUSE MUCH IS NOT STARTING TO MAKE SENSE! INANIMATE OBJECTS DO NOT ENTER ARCHERY CONTESTS!!!
THE ARCHERY CONTEST IS STARTING?!
OH, I NEED TO GO!
OKAY, WELL SCRATCH WHAT I SAID ABOUT INANIMATE OBJECTS. LET'S GO!
ROBIN, CAN I SPEAK WITH YOU?
OF COURSE YOU CAN, FRIAR. BUT MAKE IT QUICK, WE'RE NEARING THE TOWN SQUARE.
QUICK, YES, OKAY.
AAH...
SO SPEAKING OF DISGUISING YOURSELF, HAVE YOU HEARD THE ONE ABOUT THE FOOL WHO DRESSED UP AS A FRIAR?
IS THIS A JOKE?
NOT REALLY...
YOU'VE BEEN ACTING STRANGE LATELY. STRANGER THAN USUAL, I MEAN.
WELL, WOULD YOU LOOK AT THAT!
WE'LL PICK THIS UP AGAIN LATER, FRIAR.
RIGHT NOW, THERE ARE TARGETS THAT NEED SHOOTING AND A BEAUTIFUL MAID IN NEED OF A KISS!
YES, BUT... OH, OKAY.

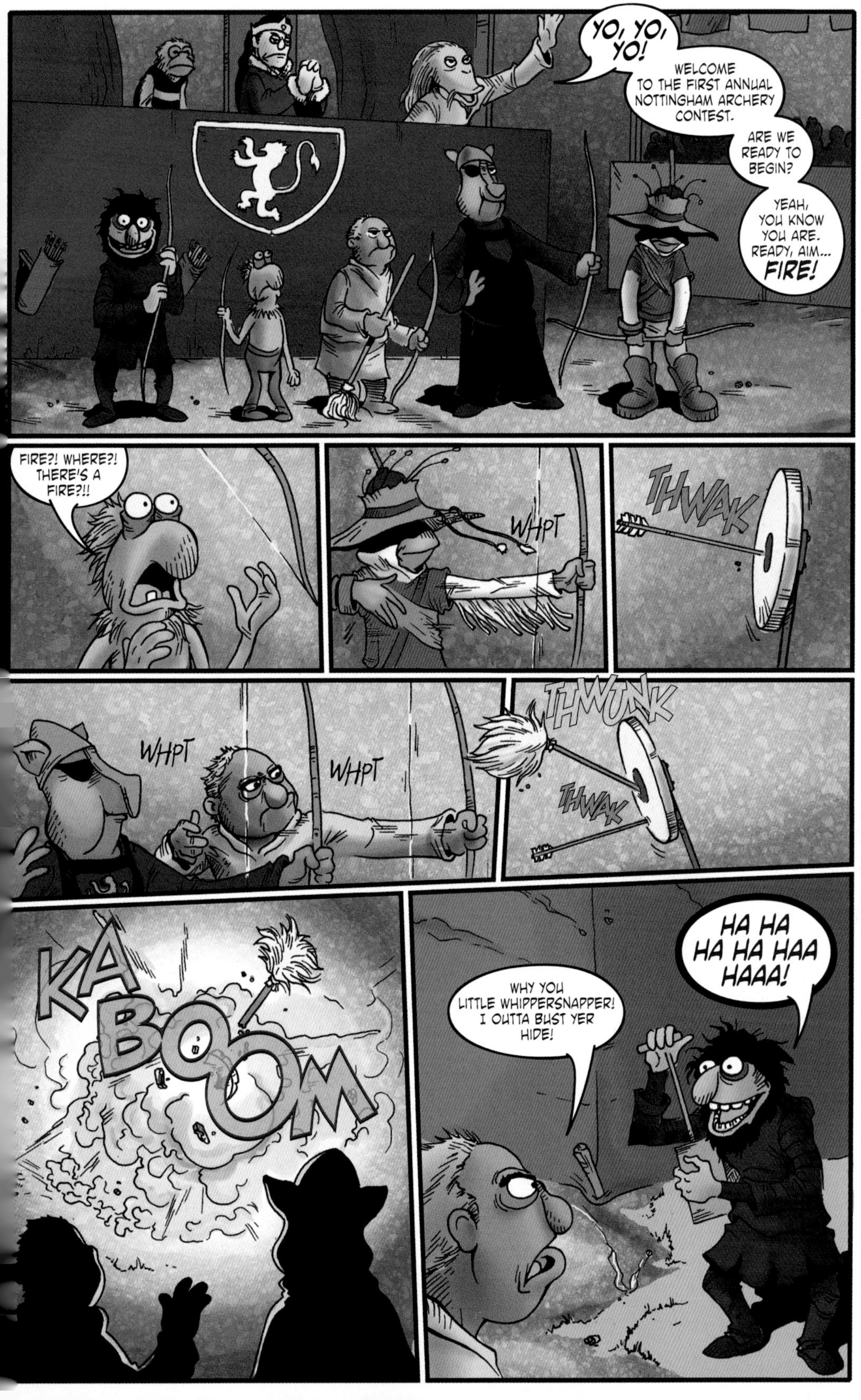
YO, YO, YO!
WELCOME TO THE FIRST ANNUAL NOTTINGHAM ARCHERY CONTEST.
ARE WE READY TO BEGIN?
YEAH, YOU KNOW YOU ARE. READY, AIM... FIRE!
FIRE?! WHERE?! THERE'S A FIRE?!!
WHPT
THWAK
WHPT
WHPT
THWUNK
THWAK
KA BOOM
WHY YOU LITTLE WHIPPERSNAPPER! I OUTTA BUST YER HIDE!
HA HA HA HA HAA HAAA!

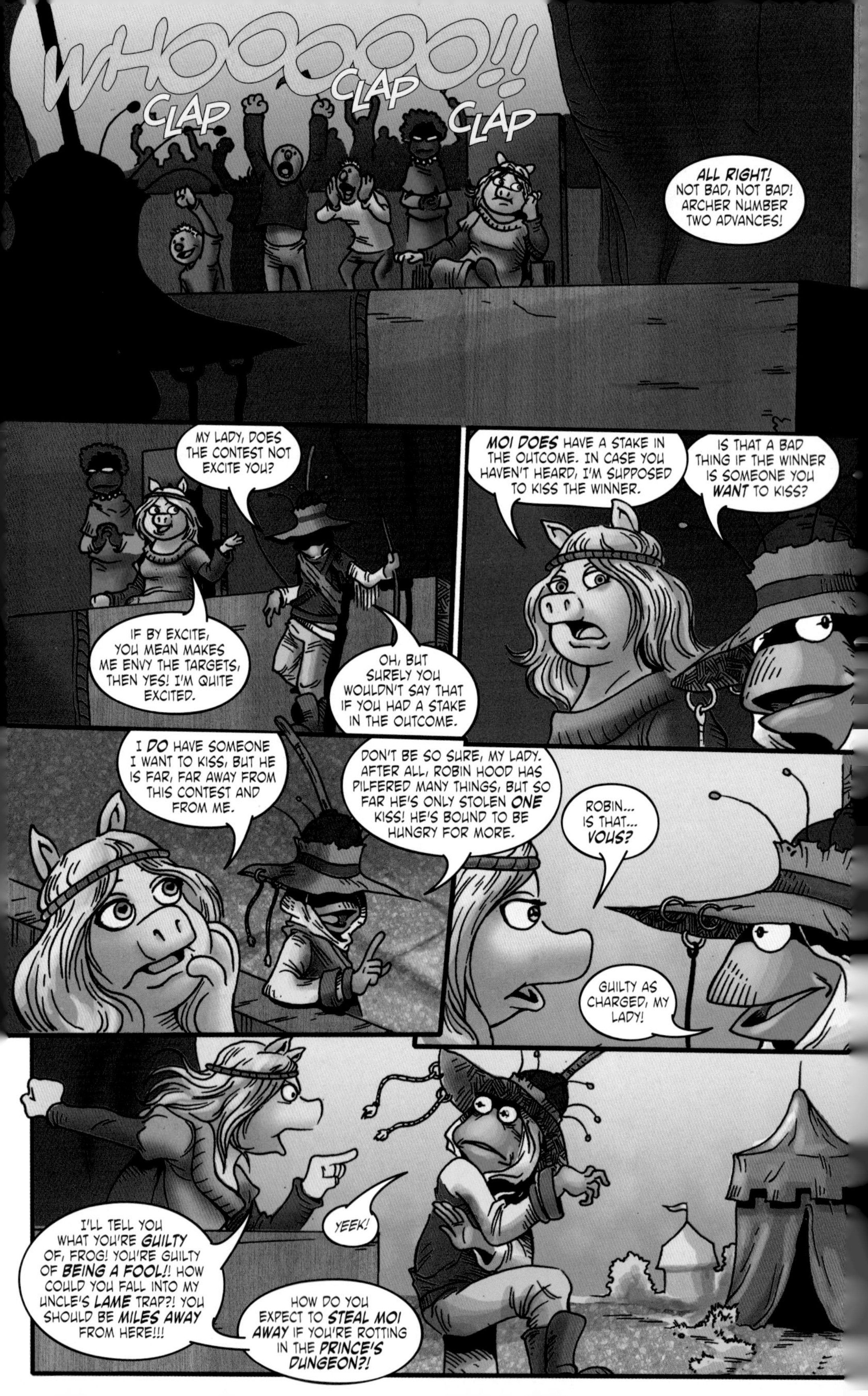
WHOOOOOO!!
CLAP
CLAP
CLAP
ALL RIGHT! NOT BAD, NOT BAD! ARCHER NUMBER TWO ADVANCES!
MY LADY, DOES THE CONTEST NOT EXCITE YOU?
IF BY EXCITE, YOU MEAN MAKES ME ENVY THE TARGETS, THEN YES! I'M QUITE EXCITED.
OH, BUT SURELY YOU WOULDN'T SAY THAT IF YOU HAD A STAKE IN THE OUTCOME.
MOI DOES HAVE A STAKE IN THE OUTCOME. IN CASE YOU HAVEN'T HEARD, I'M SUPPOSED TO KISS THE WINNER.
IS THAT A BAD THING IF THE WINNER IS SOMEONE YOU WANT TO KISS?
I DO HAVE SOMEONE I WANT TO KISS, BUT HE IS FAR, FAR AWAY FROM THIS CONTEST AND FROM ME.
DON'T BE SO SURE, MY LADY. AFTER ALL, ROBIN HOOD HAS PILFERED MANY THINGS, BUT SO FAR HE'S ONLY STOLEN ONE KISS! HE'S BOUND TO BE HUNGRY FOR MORE.
ROBIN... IS THAT... VOUS?
GUILTY AS CHARGED, MY LADY!
I'LL TELL YOU WHAT YOU'RE GUILTY OF, FROG! YOU'RE GUILTY OF BEING A FOOL!! HOW COULD YOU FALL INTO MY UNCLE'S LAME TRAP?! YOU SHOULD BE MILES AWAY FROM HERE!!!
YEEK!
HOW DO YOU EXPECT TO STEAL MOI AWAY IF YOU'RE ROTTING IN THE PRINCE'S DUNGEON?!

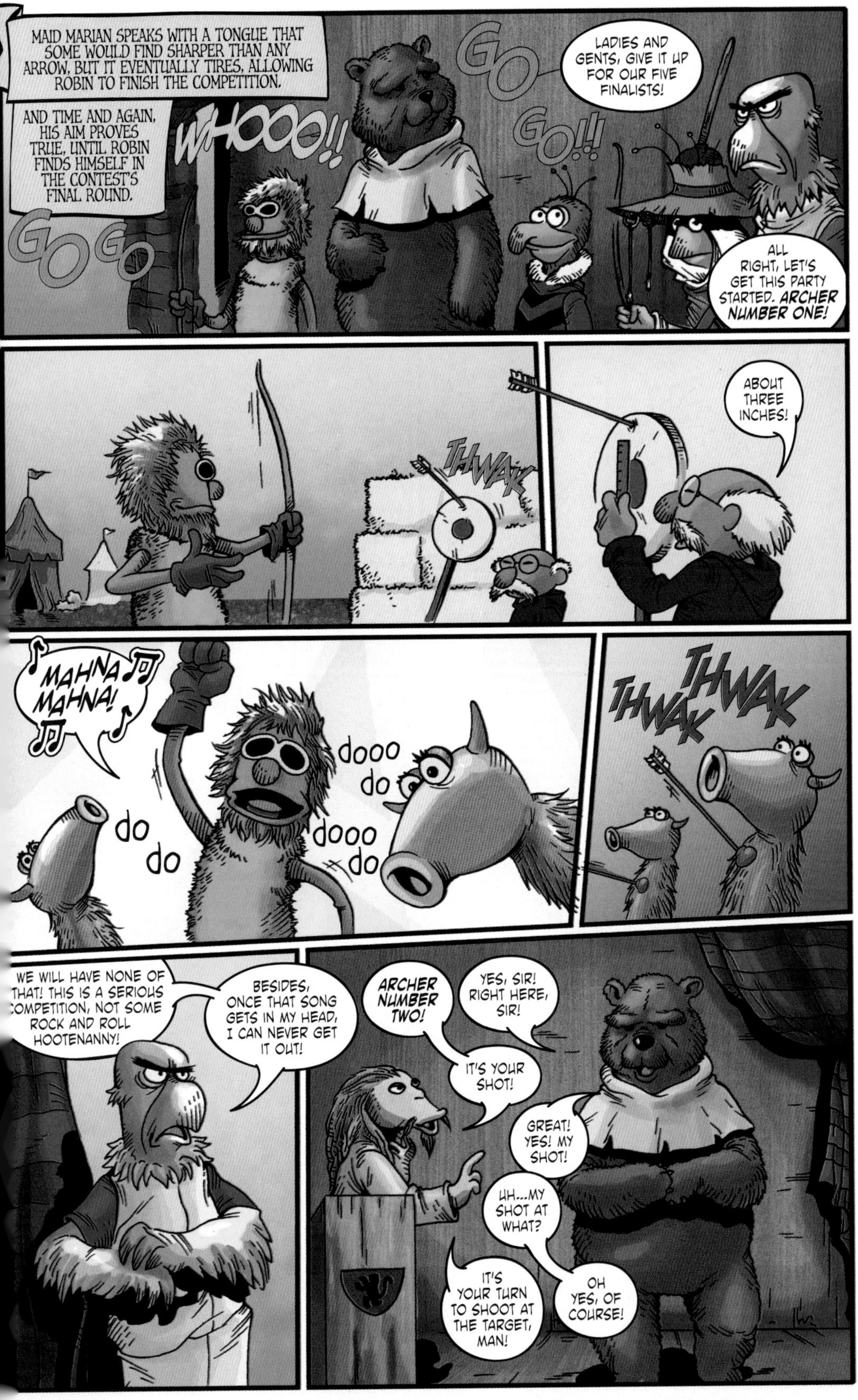
MAID MARIAN SPEAKS WITH A TONGUE THAT SOME WOULD FIND SHARPER THAN ANY ARROW, BUT IT EVENTUALLY TIRES, ALLOWING ROBIN TO FINISH THE COMPETITION.
AND TIME AND AGAIN, HIS AIM PROVES TRUE, UNTIL ROBIN FINDS HIMSELF IN THE CONTEST'S FINAL ROUND.
WHOOOO!!
GO GO
GO
GO!!
LADIES AND GENTS, GIVE IT UP FOR OUR FIVE FINALISTS!
ALL RIGHT, LET'S GET THIS PARTY STARTED. ARCHER NUMBER ONE!
THWAK
ABOUT THREE INCHES!
MAHNA MAHNA!
do do
dooo do
dooo do
THWAK THWAK
WE WILL HAVE NONE OF THAT! THIS IS A SERIOUS COMPETITION, NOT SOME ROCK AND ROLL HOOTENANNY!
BESIDES, ONCE THAT SONG GETS IN MY HEAD, I CAN NEVER GET IT OUT!
ARCHER NUMBER TWO!
YES, SIR! RIGHT HERE, SIR!
IT'S YOUR SHOT!
GREAT! YES! MY SHOT!
UH...MY SHOT AT WHAT?
IT'S YOUR TURN TO SHOOT AT THE TARGET, MAN!
OH YES, OF COURSE!

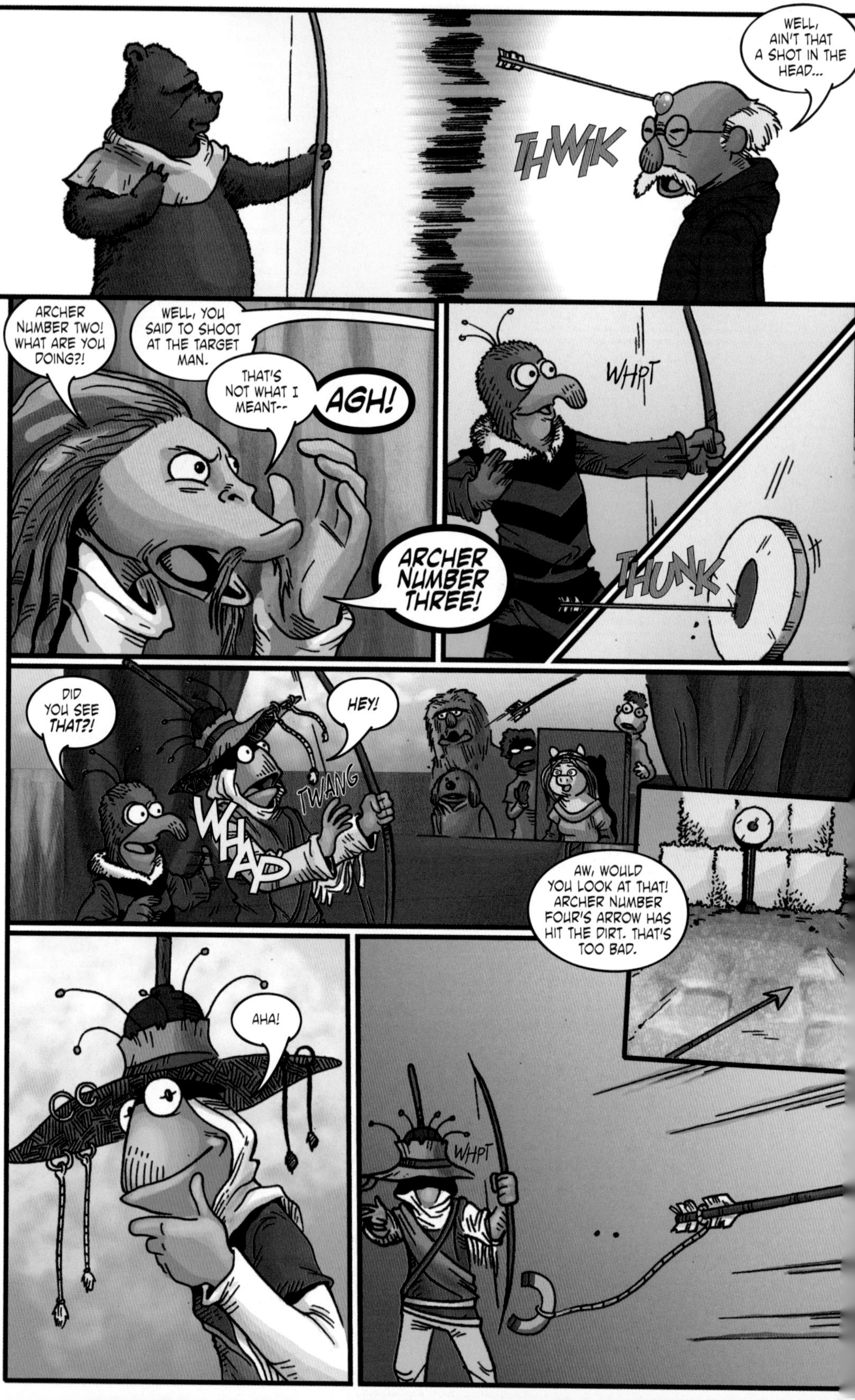
WELL, AIN'T THAT A SHOT IN THE HEAD...
THWIK
ARCHER NUMBER TWO! WHAT ARE YOU DOING?!
WELL, YOU SAID TO SHOOT AT THE TARGET MAN.
THAT'S NOT WHAT I MEANT--
AGH!
ARCHER NUMBER THREE!
WHPT
THUNK
DID YOU SEE THAT?!
HEY!
TWANG
WHAP
AW, WOULD YOU LOOK AT THAT! ARCHER NUMBER FOUR'S ARROW HAS HIT THE DIRT. THAT'S TOO BAD.
AHA!
WHPT
. .

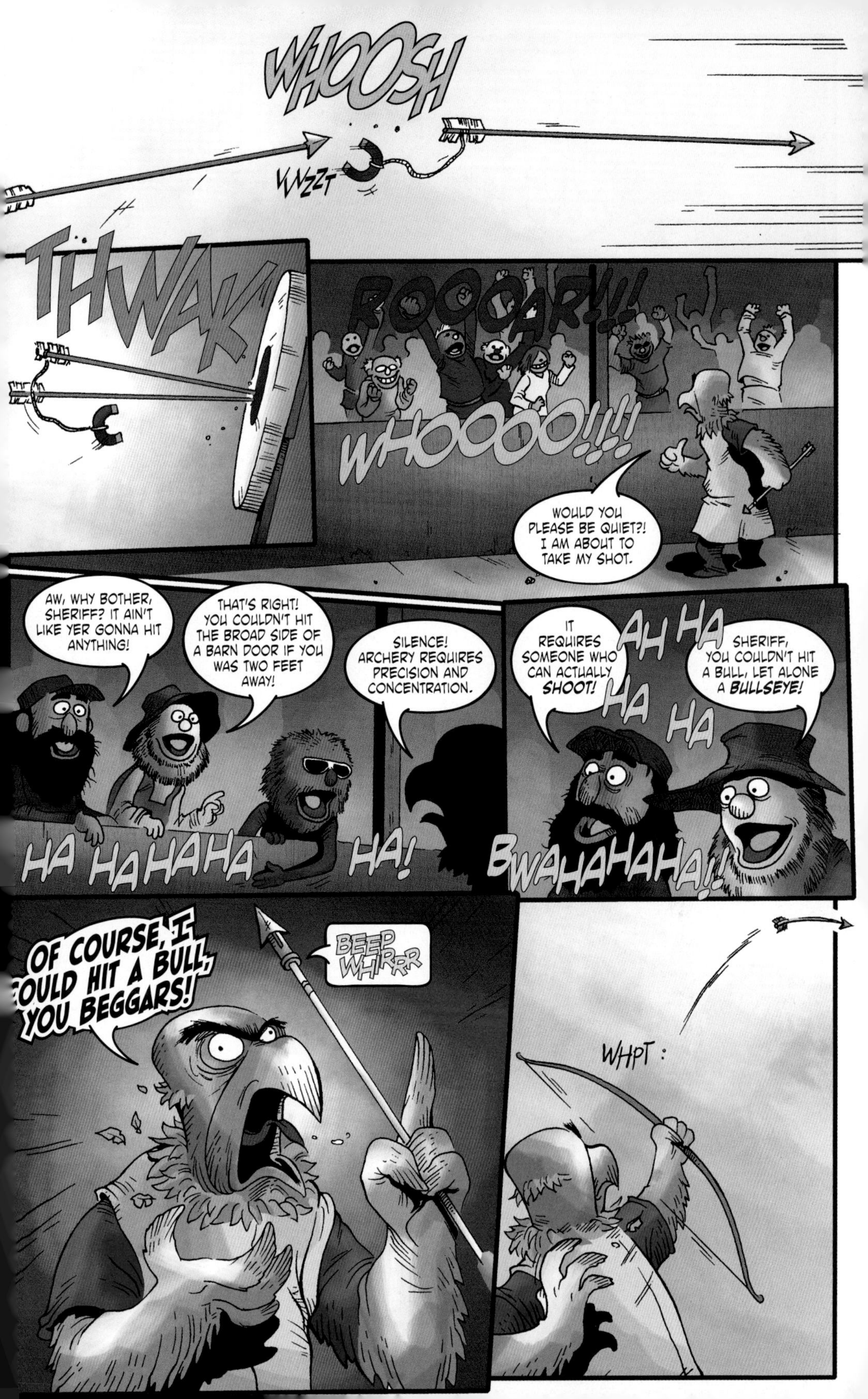
WHOOSH
VVVZZZT
THWAK
ROOOAR!!!
WHOOOO!!!!
WOULD YOU PLEASE BE QUIET?! I AM ABOUT TO TAKE MY SHOT.
AW, WHY BOTHER, SHERIFF? IT AIN'T LIKE YER GONNA HIT ANYTHING!
THAT'S RIGHT! YOU COULDN'T HIT THE BROAD SIDE OF A BARN DOOR IF YOU WAS TWO FEET AWAY!
HA HAHAHAHA HA!
SILENCE! ARCHERY REQUIRES PRECISION AND CONCENTRATION.
IT REQUIRES SOMEONE WHO CAN ACTUALLY SHOOT!
AH HA HA HA
SHERIFF, YOU COULDN'T HIT A BULL, LET ALONE A BULLSEYE!
BWAHAHAHAHA!!
OF COURSE, I COULD HIT A BULL, YOU BEGGARS!
BEEP WHIRRR
WHPT

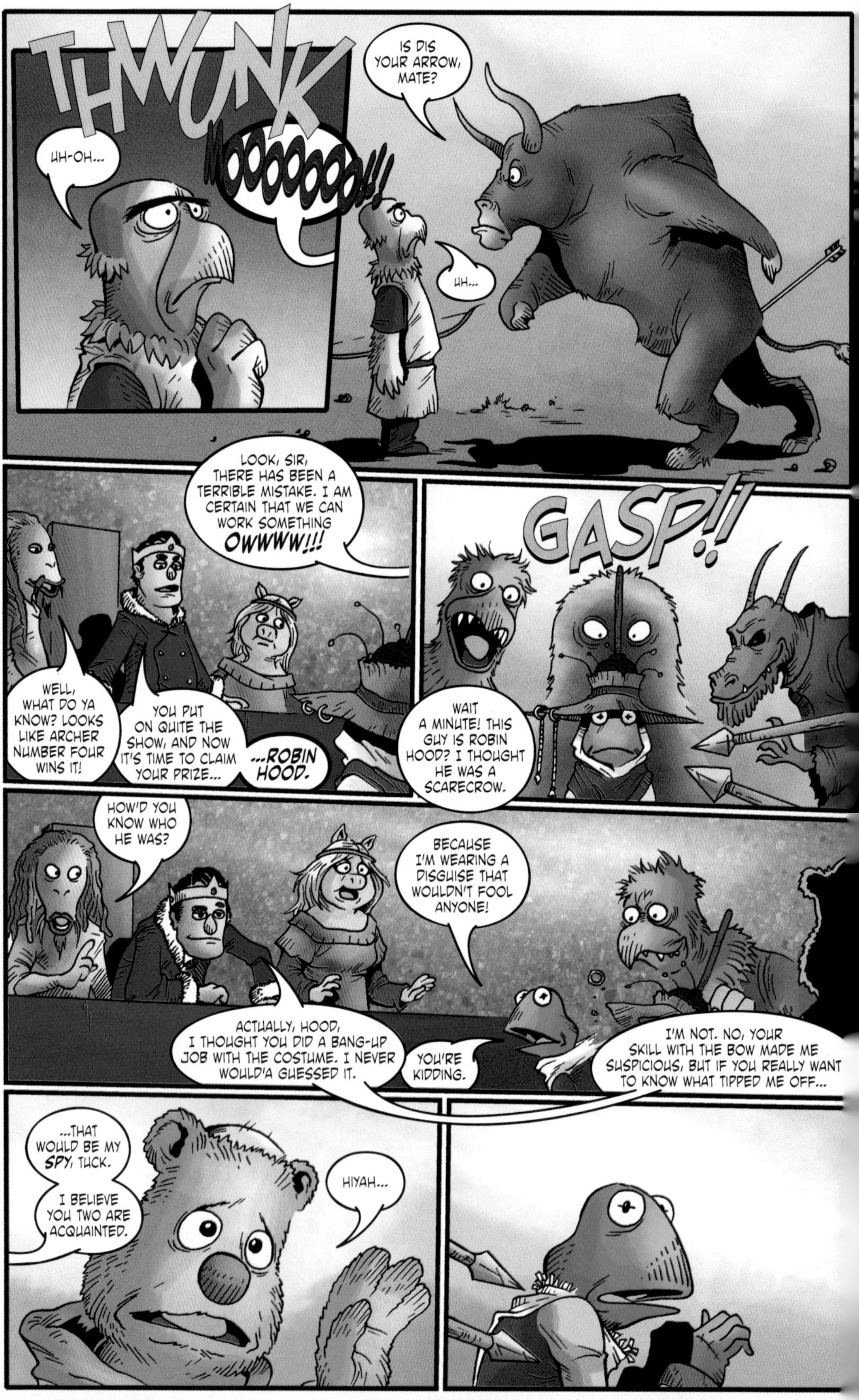
THWUNK!
UH-OH...
MOOOOOOO!!
IS DIS YOUR ARROW, MATE?
UH...
LOOK, SIR, THERE HAS BEEN A TERRIBLE MISTAKE. I AM CERTAIN THAT WE CAN WORK SOMETHING OWWWW!!!
WELL, WHAT DO YA KNOW? LOOKS LIKE ARCHER NUMBER FOUR WINS IT!
YOU PUT ON QUITE THE SHOW, AND NOW IT'S TIME TO CLAIM YOUR PRIZE...
...ROBIN HOOD.
GASP!!
WAIT A MINUTE! THIS GUY IS ROBIN HOOD? I THOUGHT HE WAS A SCARECROW.
HOW'D YOU KNOW WHO HE WAS?
BECAUSE I'M WEARING A DISGUISE THAT WOULDN'T FOOL ANYONE!
ACTUALLY, HOOD, I THOUGHT YOU DID A BANG-UP JOB WITH THE COSTUME. I NEVER WOULD'A GUESSED IT.
YOU'RE KIDDING.
I'M NOT. NO, YOUR SKILL WITH THE BOW MADE ME SUSPICIOUS, BUT IF YOU REALLY WANT TO KNOW WHAT TIPPED ME OFF...
...THAT WOULD BE MY SPY, TUCK.
I BELIEVE YOU TWO ARE ACQUAINTED.
HIYAH...

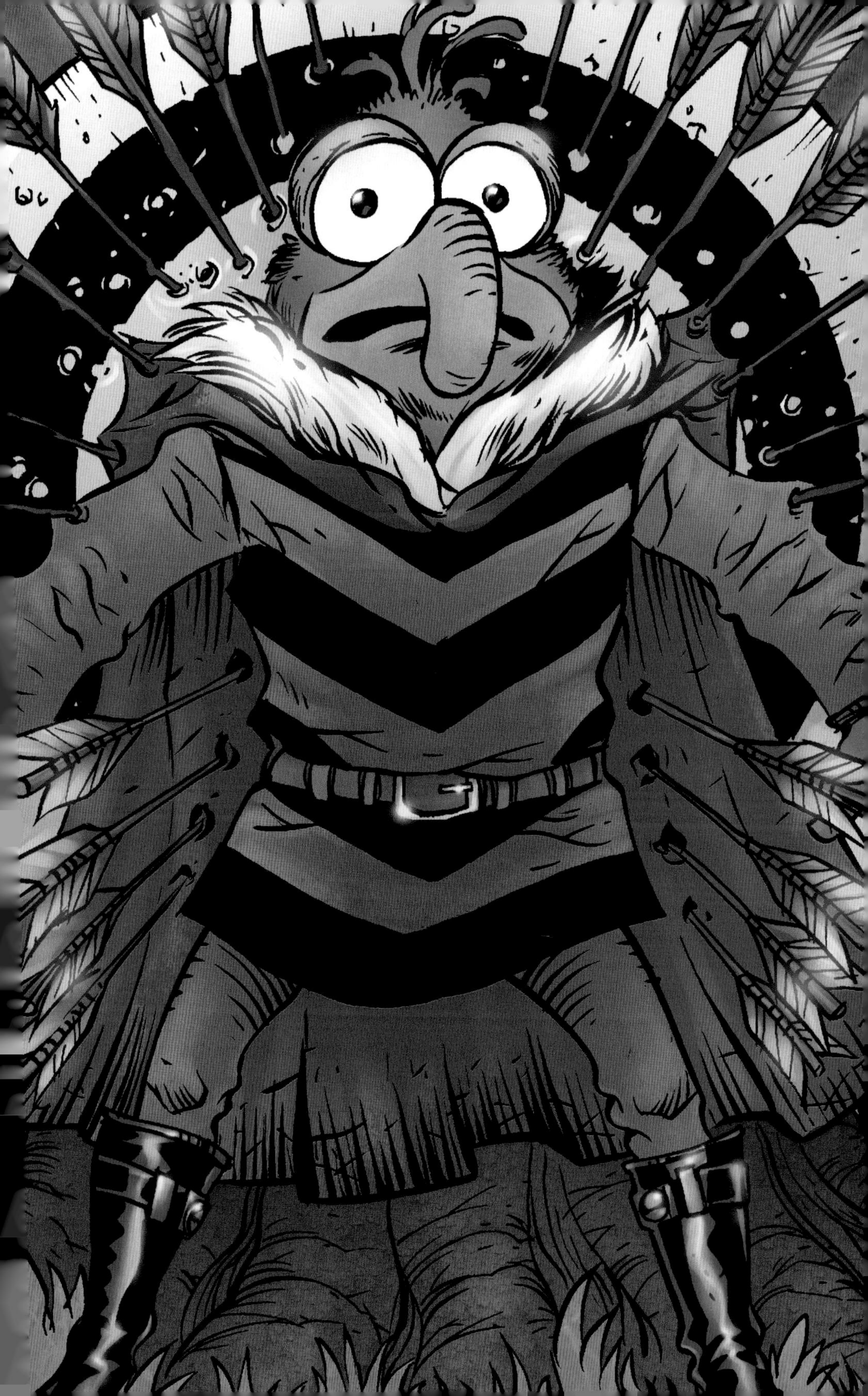

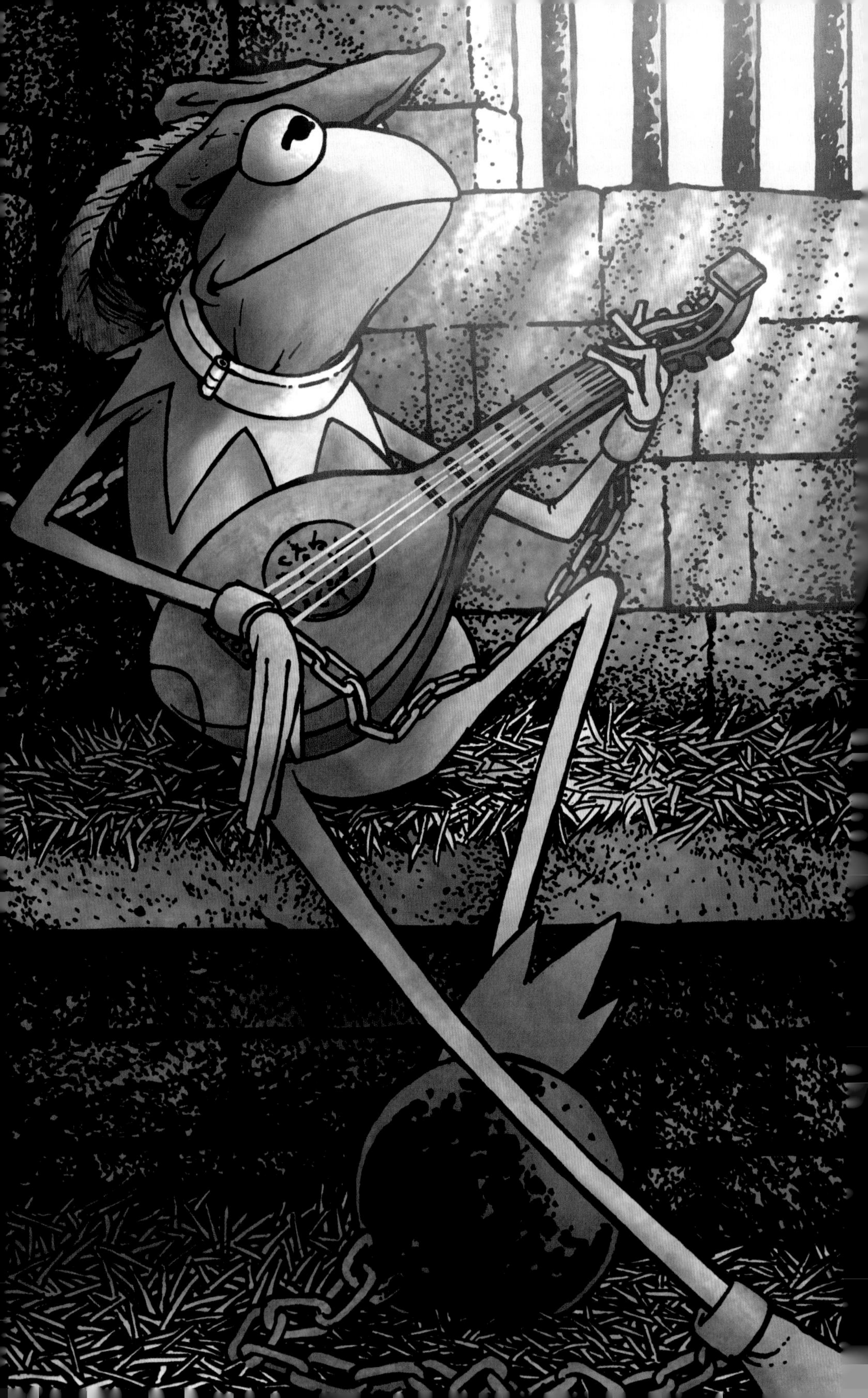

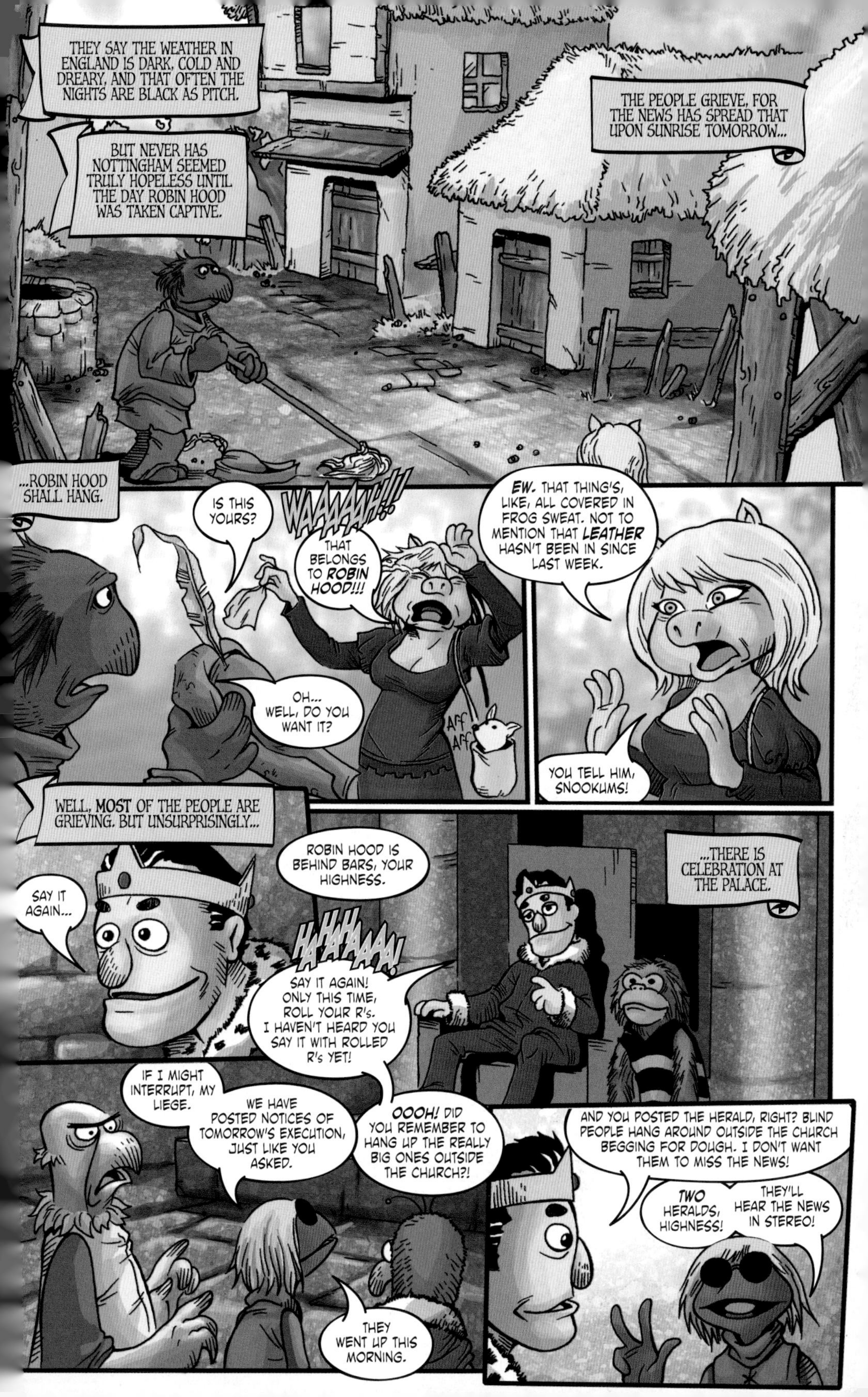
THEY SAY THE WEATHER IN ENGLAND IS DARK, COLD AND DREARY, AND THAT OFTEN THE NIGHTS ARE BLACK AS PITCH.
BUT NEVER HAS NOTTINGHAM SEEMED TRULY HOPELESS UNTIL THE DAY ROBIN HOOD WAS TAKEN CAPTIVE.
THE PEOPLE GRIEVE, FOR THE NEWS HAS SPREAD THAT UPON SUNRISE TOMORROW...
...ROBIN HOOD SHALL HANG.
IS THIS YOURS?
WAAAAAH!!!
THAT BELONGS TO ROBIN HOOD!!!
OH... WELL, DO YOU WANT IT?
AFF AFF
EW. THAT THING'S, LIKE, ALL COVERED IN FROG SWEAT. NOT TO MENTION THAT LEATHER HASN'T BEEN IN SINCE LAST WEEK.
YOU TELL HIM, SNOOKUMS!
WELL, MOST OF THE PEOPLE ARE GRIEVING. BUT UNSURPRISINGLY...
ROBIN HOOD IS BEHIND BARS, YOUR HIGHNESS.
...THERE IS CELEBRATION AT THE PALACE.
SAY IT AGAIN...
HAHAHAAAA!
SAY IT AGAIN! ONLY THIS TIME, ROLL YOUR R's. I HAVEN'T HEARD YOU SAY IT WITH ROLLED R's YET!
IF I MIGHT INTERRUPT, MY LIEGE.
WE HAVE POSTED NOTICES OF TOMORROW'S EXECUTION, JUST LIKE YOU ASKED.
OOOH! DID YOU REMEMBER TO HANG UP THE REALLY BIG ONES OUTSIDE THE CHURCH?!
THEY WENT UP THIS MORNING.
AND YOU POSTED THE HERALD, RIGHT? BLIND PEOPLE HANG AROUND OUTSIDE THE CHURCH BEGGING FOR DOUGH. I DON'T WANT THEM TO MISS THE NEWS!
TWO HERALDS, HIGHNESS!
THEY'LL HEAR THE NEWS IN STEREO!

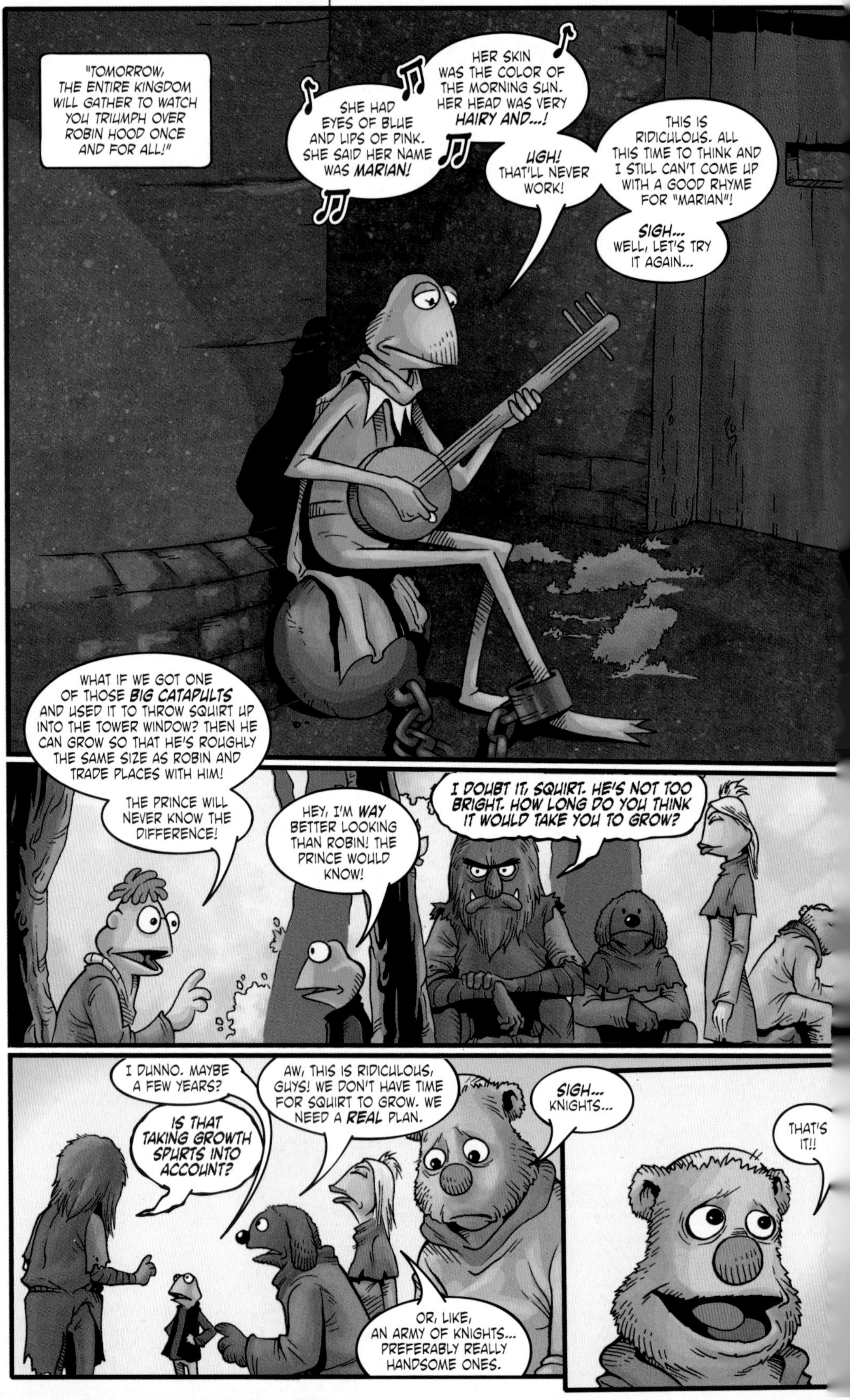
"TOMORROW, THE ENTIRE KINGDOM WILL GATHER TO WATCH YOU TRIUMPH OVER ROBIN HOOD ONCE AND FOR ALL!"
SHE HAD EYES OF BLUE AND LIPS OF PINK. SHE SAID HER NAME WAS MARIAN!
HER SKIN WAS THE COLOR OF THE MORNING SUN. HER HEAD WAS VERY HAIRY AND...!
UGH! THAT'LL NEVER WORK!
THIS IS RIDICULOUS. ALL THIS TIME TO THINK AND I STILL CAN'T COME UP WITH A GOOD RHYME FOR "MARIAN"!
SIGH... WELL, LET'S TRY IT AGAIN...
WHAT IF WE GOT ONE OF THOSE BIG CATAPULTS AND USED IT TO THROW SQUIRT UP INTO THE TOWER WINDOW? THEN HE CAN GROW SO THAT HE'S ROUGHLY THE SAME SIZE AS ROBIN AND TRADE PLACES WITH HIM!
THE PRINCE WILL NEVER KNOW THE DIFFERENCE!
HEY, I'M WAY BETTER LOOKING THAN ROBIN! THE PRINCE WOULD KNOW!
I DOUBT IT, SQUIRT. HE'S NOT TOO BRIGHT. HOW LONG DO YOU THINK IT WOULD TAKE YOU TO GROW?
I DUNNO. MAYBE A FEW YEARS?
IS THAT TAKING GROWTH SPURTS INTO ACCOUNT?
AW, THIS IS RIDICULOUS, GUYS! WE DON'T HAVE TIME FOR SQUIRT TO GROW. WE NEED A REAL PLAN.
SIGH... KNIGHTS...
OR, LIKE, AN ARMY OF KNIGHTS... PREFERABLY REALLY HANDSOME ONES.
THAT'S IT!!

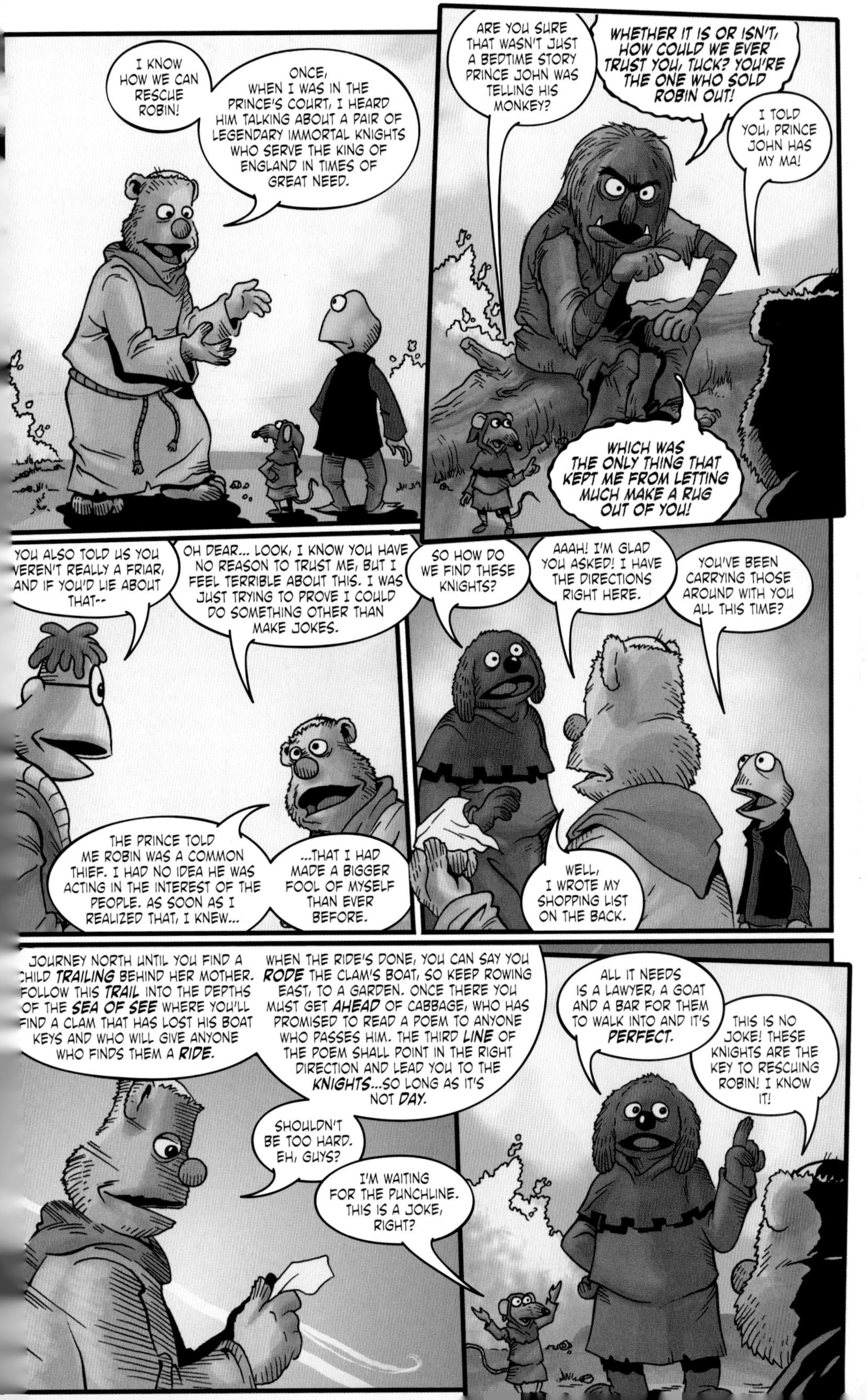
I KNOW HOW WE CAN RESCUE ROBIN!
ONCE, WHEN I WAS IN THE PRINCE'S COURT, I HEARD HIM TALKING ABOUT A PAIR OF LEGENDARY IMMORTAL KNIGHTS WHO SERVE THE KING OF ENGLAND IN TIMES OF GREAT NEED.
ARE YOU SURE THAT WASN'T JUST A BEDTIME STORY PRINCE JOHN WAS TELLING HIS MONKEY?
WHETHER IT IS OR ISN'T, HOW COULD WE EVER TRUST YOU, TUCK? YOU'RE THE ONE WHO SOLD ROBIN OUT!
I TOLD YOU, PRINCE JOHN HAS MY MA!
WHICH WAS THE ONLY THING THAT KEPT ME FROM LETTING MUCH MAKE A RUG OUT OF YOU!
YOU ALSO TOLD US YOU WEREN'T REALLY A FRIAR, AND IF YOU'D LIE ABOUT THAT--
OH DEAR... LOOK, I KNOW YOU HAVE NO REASON TO TRUST ME, BUT I FEEL TERRIBLE ABOUT THIS. I WAS JUST TRYING TO PROVE I COULD DO SOMETHING OTHER THAN MAKE JOKES.
THE PRINCE TOLD ME ROBIN WAS A COMMON THIEF. I HAD NO IDEA HE WAS ACTING IN THE INTEREST OF THE PEOPLE. AS SOON AS I REALIZED THAT, I KNEW...
...THAT I HAD MADE A BIGGER FOOL OF MYSELF THAN EVER BEFORE.
SO HOW DO WE FIND THESE KNIGHTS?
AAAH! I'M GLAD YOU ASKED! I HAVE THE DIRECTIONS RIGHT HERE.
YOU'VE BEEN CARRYING THOSE AROUND WITH YOU ALL THIS TIME?
WELL, I WROTE MY SHOPPING LIST ON THE BACK.
JOURNEY NORTH UNTIL YOU FIND A CHILD TRAILING BEHIND HER MOTHER. FOLLOW THIS TRAIL INTO THE DEPTHS OF THE SEA OF SEE WHERE YOU'LL FIND A CLAM THAT HAS LOST HIS BOAT KEYS AND WHO WILL GIVE ANYONE WHO FINDS THEM A RIDE.
WHEN THE RIDE'S DONE, YOU CAN SAY YOU RODE THE CLAM'S BOAT, SO KEEP ROWING EAST, TO A GARDEN. ONCE THERE YOU MUST GET AHEAD OF CABBAGE, WHO HAS PROMISED TO READ A POEM TO ANYONE WHO PASSES HIM. THE THIRD LINE OF THE POEM SHALL POINT IN THE RIGHT DIRECTION AND LEAD YOU TO THE KNIGHTS...SO LONG AS IT'S NOT DAY.
SHOULDN'T BE TOO HARD. EH, GUYS?
I'M WAITING FOR THE PUNCHLINE. THIS IS A JOKE, RIGHT?
ALL IT NEEDS IS A LAWYER, A GOAT AND A BAR FOR THEM TO WALK INTO AND IT'S PERFECT.
THIS IS NO JOKE! THESE KNIGHTS ARE THE KEY TO RESCUING ROBIN! I KNOW IT!

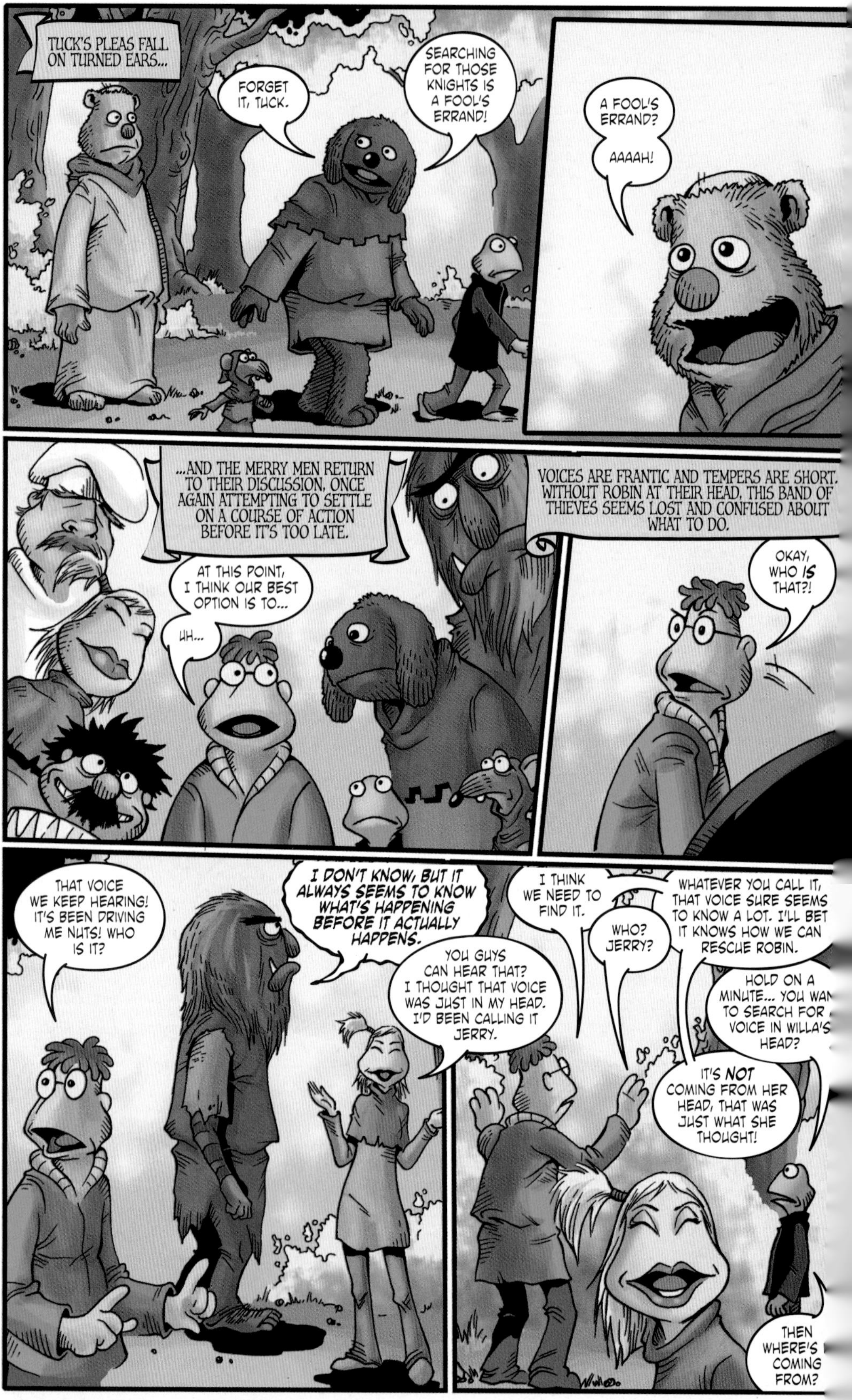

TUCK'S PLEAS FALL ON TURNED EARS...
FORGET IT, TUCK.
SEARCHING FOR THOSE KNIGHTS IS A FOOL'S ERRAND!
A FOOL'S ERRAND?
AAAAH!
...AND THE MERRY MEN RETURN TO THEIR DISCUSSION, ONCE AGAIN ATTEMPTING TO SETTLE ON A COURSE OF ACTION BEFORE IT'S TOO LATE.
AT THIS POINT, I THINK OUR BEST OPTION IS TO...
UH...
VOICES ARE FRANTIC AND TEMPERS ARE SHORT. WITHOUT ROBIN AT THEIR HEAD, THIS BAND OF THIEVES SEEMS LOST AND CONFUSED ABOUT WHAT TO DO.
OKAY, WHO *IS* THAT?!
THAT VOICE WE KEEP HEARING! IT'S BEEN DRIVING ME NUTS! WHO IS IT?
I DON'T KNOW, BUT IT ALWAYS SEEMS TO KNOW WHAT'S HAPPENING BEFORE IT ACTUALLY HAPPENS.
YOU GUYS CAN HEAR THAT? I THOUGHT THAT VOICE WAS JUST IN MY HEAD. I'D BEEN CALLING IT JERRY.
I THINK WE NEED TO FIND IT.
WHO? JERRY?
WHATEVER YOU CALL IT, THAT VOICE SURE SEEMS TO KNOW A LOT. I'LL BET IT KNOWS HOW WE CAN RESCUE ROBIN.
HOLD ON A MINUTE... YOU WAN TO SEARCH FOR VOICE IN WILLA'S HEAD?
IT'S *NOT* COMING FROM HER HEAD, THAT WAS JUST WHAT SHE THOUGHT!
THEN WHERE'S COMING FROM?

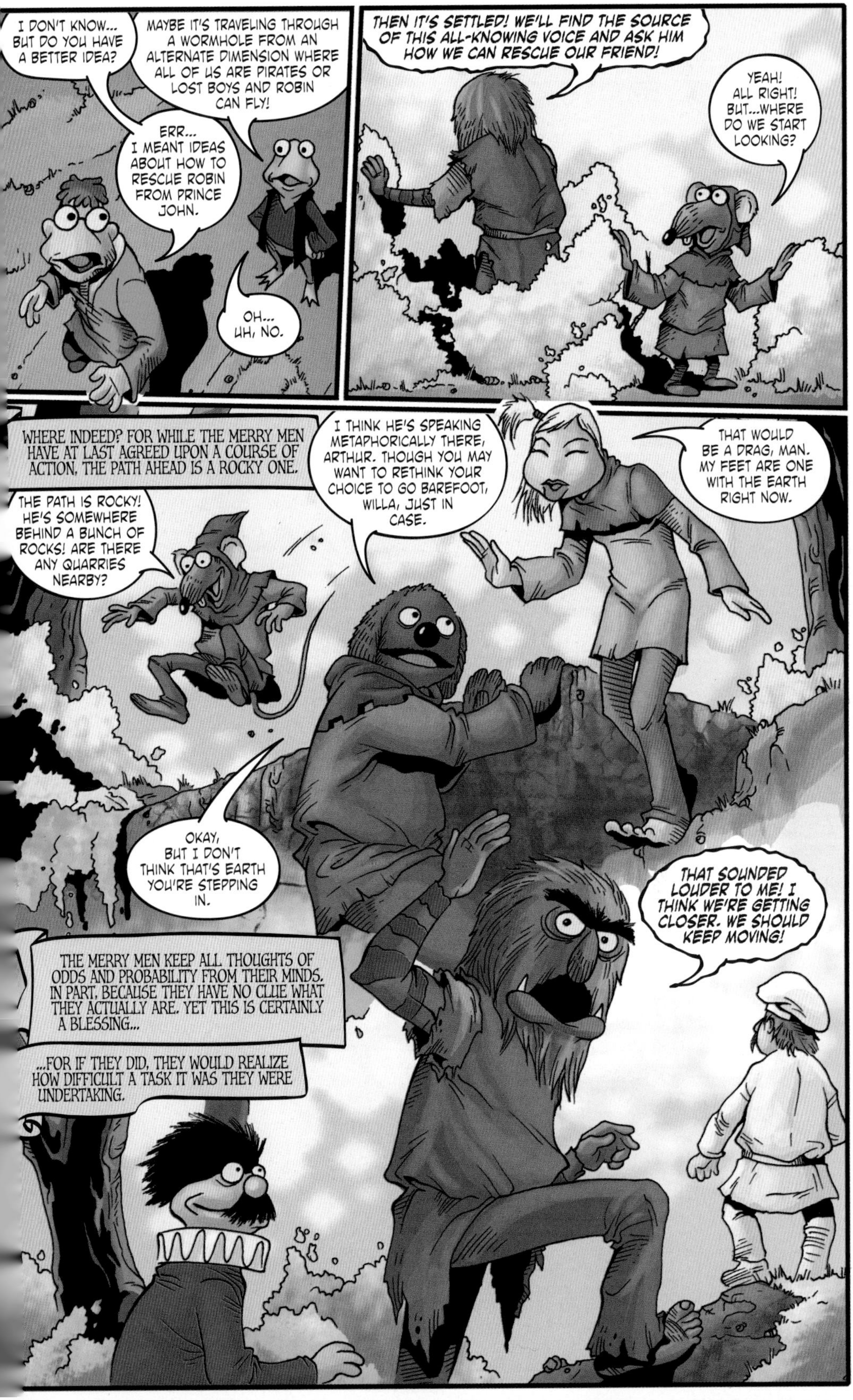
I DON'T KNOW... BUT DO YOU HAVE A BETTER IDEA?
MAYBE IT'S TRAVELING THROUGH A WORMHOLE FROM AN ALTERNATE DIMENSION WHERE ALL OF US ARE PIRATES OR LOST BOYS AND ROBIN CAN FLY!
ERR... I MEANT IDEAS ABOUT HOW TO RESCUE ROBIN FROM PRINCE JOHN.
OH... UH, NO.
THEN IT'S SETTLED! WE'LL FIND THE SOURCE OF THIS ALL-KNOWING VOICE AND ASK HIM HOW WE CAN RESCUE OUR FRIEND!
YEAH! ALL RIGHT! BUT...WHERE DO WE START LOOKING?
WHERE INDEED? FOR WHILE THE MERRY MEN HAVE AT LAST AGREED UPON A COURSE OF ACTION, THE PATH AHEAD IS A ROCKY ONE.
THE PATH IS ROCKY! HE'S SOMEWHERE BEHIND A BUNCH OF ROCKS! ARE THERE ANY QUARRIES NEARBY?
I THINK HE'S SPEAKING METAPHORICALLY THERE, ARTHUR. THOUGH YOU MAY WANT TO RETHINK YOUR CHOICE TO GO BAREFOOT, WILLA, JUST IN CASE.
THAT WOULD BE A DRAG, MAN. MY FEET ARE ONE WITH THE EARTH RIGHT NOW.
OKAY, BUT I DON'T THINK THAT'S EARTH YOU'RE STEPPING IN.
THAT SOUNDED LOUDER TO ME! I THINK WE'RE GETTING CLOSER. WE SHOULD KEEP MOVING!
THE MERRY MEN KEEP ALL THOUGHTS OF ODDS AND PROBABILITY FROM THEIR MINDS. IN PART, BECAUSE THEY HAVE NO CLUE WHAT THEY ACTUALLY ARE. YET THIS IS CERTAINLY A BLESSING...
...FOR IF THEY DID, THEY WOULD REALIZE HOW DIFFICULT A TASK IT WAS THEY WERE UNDERTAKING.

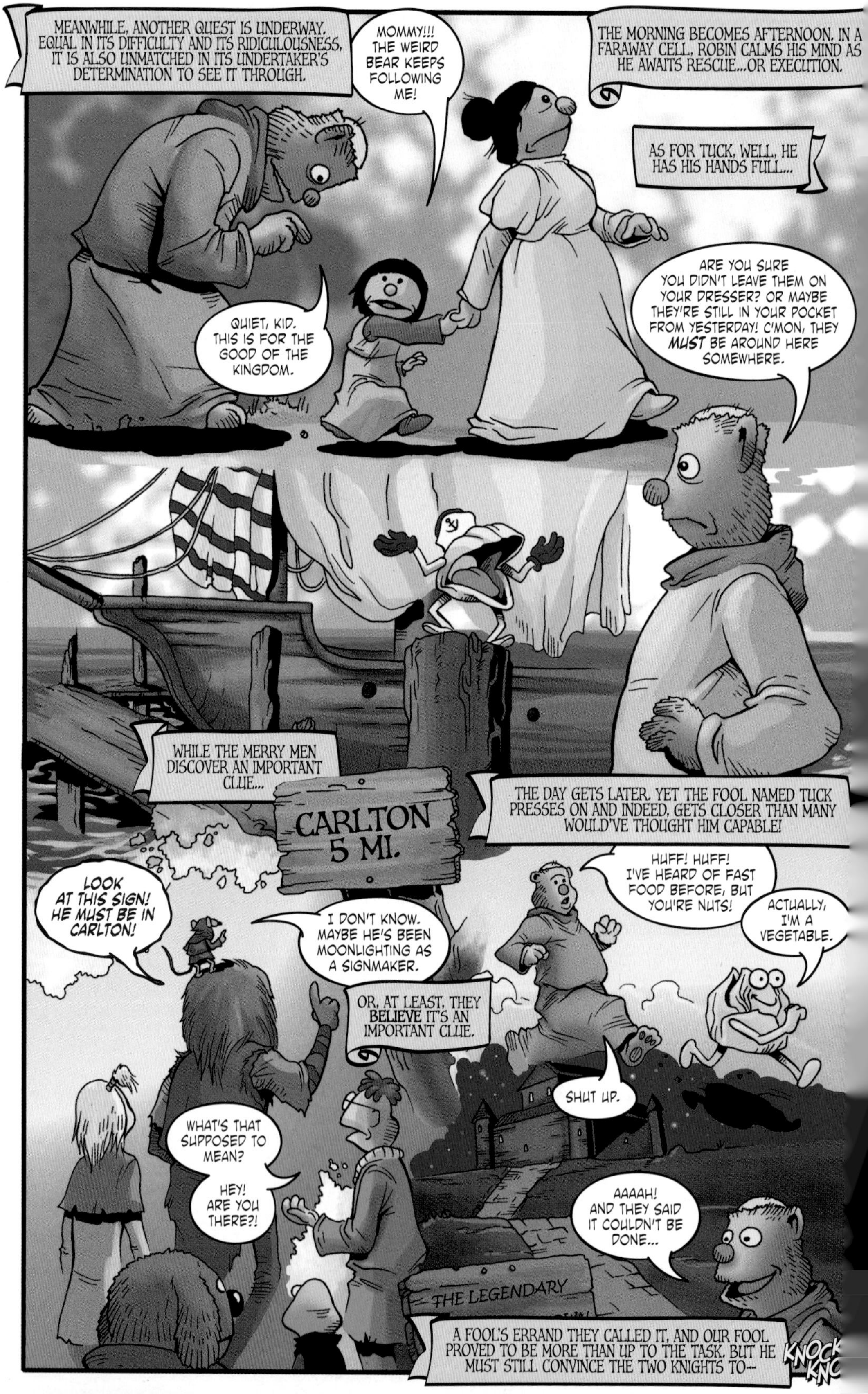
MEANWHILE, ANOTHER QUEST IS UNDERWAY. EQUAL IN ITS DIFFICULTY AND ITS RIDICULOUSNESS, IT IS ALSO UNMATCHED IN ITS UNDERTAKER'S DETERMINATION TO SEE IT THROUGH.
MOMMY!!! THE WEIRD BEAR KEEPS FOLLOWING ME!
QUIET, KID. THIS IS FOR THE GOOD OF THE KINGDOM.
THE MORNING BECOMES AFTERNOON. IN A FARAWAY CELL, ROBIN CALMS HIS MIND AS HE AWAITS RESCUE...OR EXECUTION.
AS FOR TUCK, WELL, HE HAS HIS HANDS FULL...
ARE YOU SURE YOU DIDN'T LEAVE THEM ON YOUR DRESSER? OR MAYBE THEY'RE STILL IN YOUR POCKET FROM YESTERDAY! C'MON, THEY MUST BE AROUND HERE SOMEWHERE.
WHILE THE MERRY MEN DISCOVER AN IMPORTANT CLUE...
CARLTON 5 MI.
LOOK AT THIS SIGN! HE MUST BE IN CARLTON!
I DON'T KNOW. MAYBE HE'S BEEN MOONLIGHTING AS A SIGNMAKER.
OR, AT LEAST, THEY BELIEVE IT'S AN IMPORTANT CLUE.
WHAT'S THAT SUPPOSED TO MEAN?
HEY! ARE YOU THERE?!
THE DAY GETS LATER. YET THE FOOL NAMED TUCK PRESSES ON AND INDEED, GETS CLOSER THAN MANY WOULD'VE THOUGHT HIM CAPABLE!
HUFF! HUFF! I'VE HEARD OF FAST FOOD BEFORE, BUT YOU'RE NUTS!
ACTUALLY, I'M A VEGETABLE.
SHUT UP.
AAAAH! AND THEY SAID IT COULDN'T BE DONE...
THE LEGENDARY
A FOOL'S ERRAND THEY CALLED IT, AND OUR FOOL PROVED TO BE MORE THAN UP TO THE TASK. BUT HE MUST STILL CONVINCE THE TWO KNIGHTS TO--
KNOCK KNO

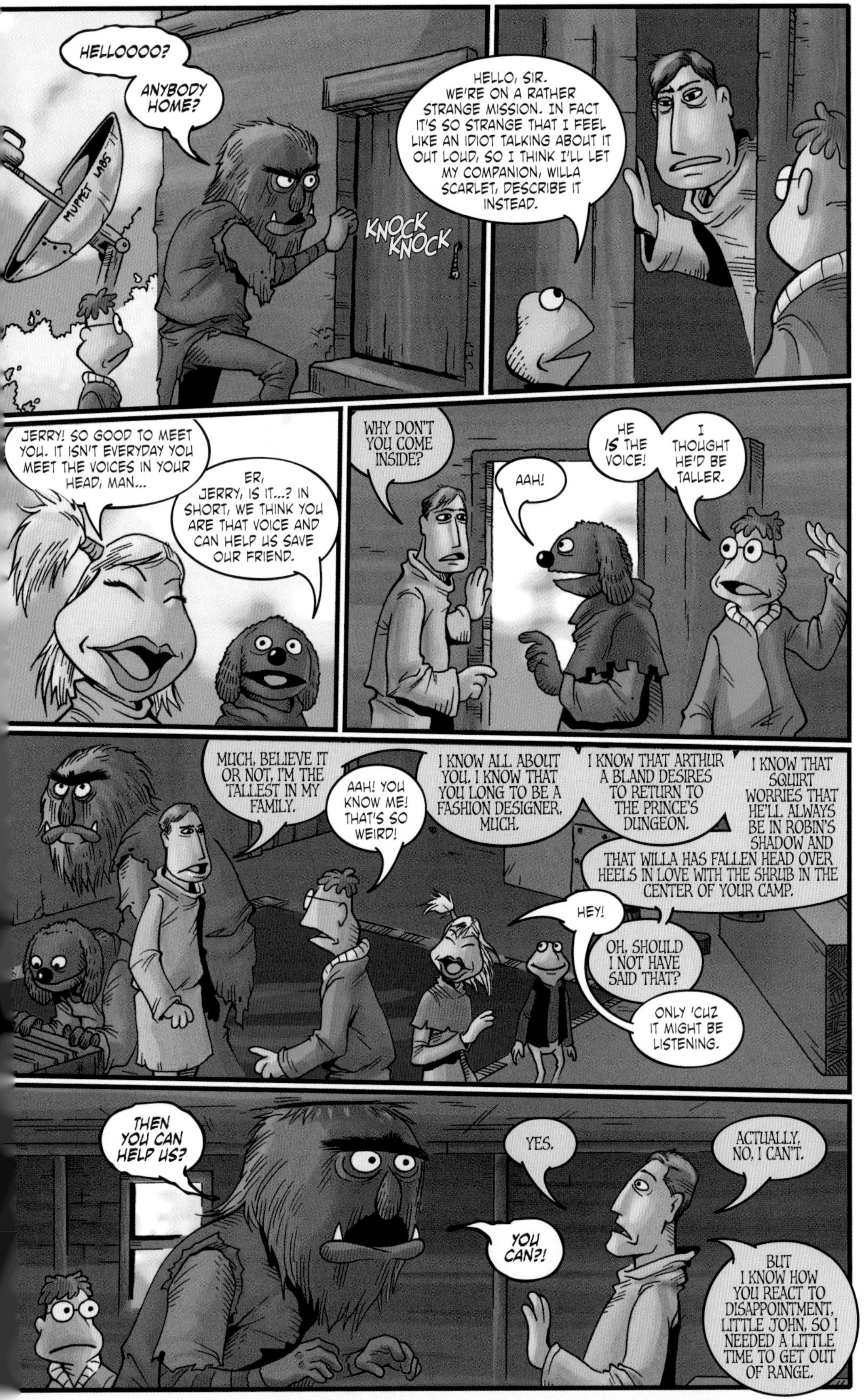
HELLOOOO?
ANYBODY HOME?
MUPPET LABS
KNOCK KNOCK
HELLO, SIR. WE'RE ON A RATHER STRANGE MISSION. IN FACT IT'S SO STRANGE THAT I FEEL LIKE AN IDIOT TALKING ABOUT IT OUT LOUD, SO I THINK I'LL LET MY COMPANION, WILLA SCARLET, DESCRIBE IT INSTEAD.
JERRY! SO GOOD TO MEET YOU. IT ISN'T EVERYDAY YOU MEET THE VOICES IN YOUR HEAD, MAN...
ER, JERRY, IS IT...? IN SHORT, WE THINK YOU ARE THAT VOICE AND CAN HELP US SAVE OUR FRIEND.
WHY DON'T YOU COME INSIDE?
AAH!
HE *IS* THE VOICE!
I THOUGHT HE'D BE TALLER.
MUCH, BELIEVE IT OR NOT, I'M THE TALLEST IN MY FAMILY.
AAH! YOU KNOW ME! THAT'S SO WEIRD!
I KNOW ALL ABOUT YOU. I KNOW THAT YOU LONG TO BE A FASHION DESIGNER, MUCH.
I KNOW THAT ARTHUR A BLAND DESIRES TO RETURN TO THE PRINCE'S DUNGEON.
I KNOW THAT SQUIRT WORRIES THAT HE'LL ALWAYS BE IN ROBIN'S SHADOW AND THAT WILLA HAS FALLEN HEAD OVER HEELS IN LOVE WITH THE SHRUB IN THE CENTER OF YOUR CAMP.
HEY!
OH, SHOULD I NOT HAVE SAID THAT?
ONLY 'CUZ IT MIGHT BE LISTENING.
THEN YOU CAN HELP US?
YES.
YOU CAN?!
ACTUALLY, NO, I CAN'T.
BUT I KNOW HOW YOU REACT TO DISAPPOINTMENT, LITTLE JOHN, SO I NEEDED A LITTLE TIME TO GET OUT OF RANGE.

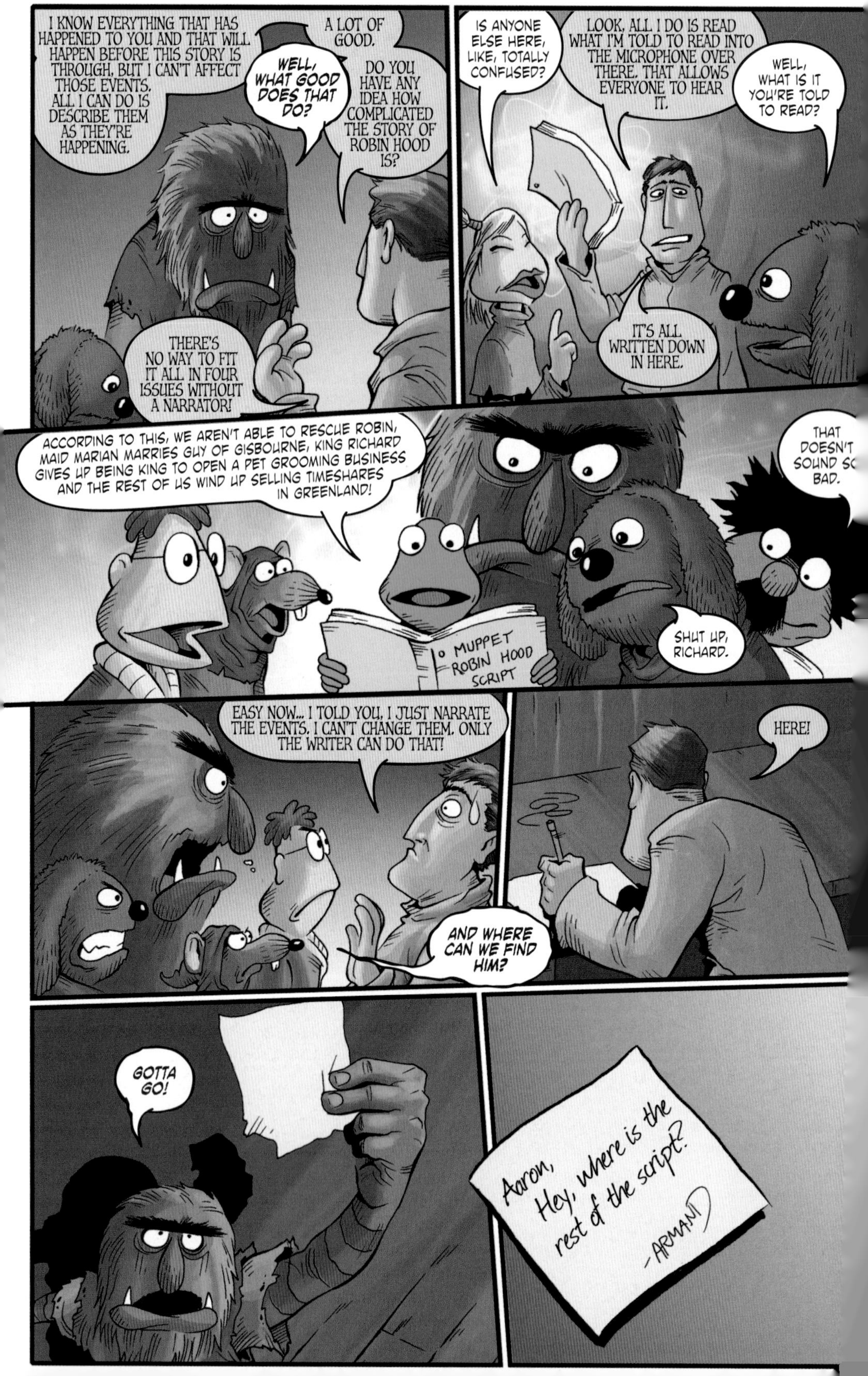

I KNOW EVERYTHING THAT HAS HAPPENED TO YOU AND THAT WILL HAPPEN BEFORE THIS STORY IS THROUGH, BUT I CAN'T AFFECT THOSE EVENTS. ALL I CAN DO IS DESCRIBE THEM AS THEY'RE HAPPENING.
WELL, WHAT GOOD DOES THAT DO?
A LOT OF GOOD.
DO YOU HAVE ANY IDEA HOW COMPLICATED THE STORY OF ROBIN HOOD IS?
THERE'S NO WAY TO FIT IT ALL IN FOUR ISSUES WITHOUT A NARRATOR!
IS ANYONE ELSE HERE, LIKE, TOTALLY CONFUSED?
LOOK, ALL I DO IS READ WHAT I'M TOLD TO READ INTO THE MICROPHONE OVER THERE. THAT ALLOWS EVERYONE TO HEAR IT.
WELL, WHAT IS IT YOU'RE TOLD TO READ?
IT'S ALL WRITTEN DOWN IN HERE.
ACCORDING TO THIS, WE AREN'T ABLE TO RESCUE ROBIN, MAID MARIAN MARRIES GUY OF GISBOURNE, KING RICHARD GIVES UP BEING KING TO OPEN A PET GROOMING BUSINESS AND THE REST OF US WIND UP SELLING TIMESHARES IN GREENLAND!
THAT DOESN'T SOUND SO BAD.
SHUT UP, RICHARD.
MUPPET ROBIN HOOD SCRIPT
EASY NOW... I TOLD YOU, I JUST NARRATE THE EVENTS. I CAN'T CHANGE THEM. ONLY THE WRITER CAN DO THAT!
AND WHERE CAN WE FIND HIM?
HERE!
GOTTA GO!
Aaron,
Hey, where is the rest of the script?
-ARMAND

Dear reader:

We here at BOOM! Studios regret to inform you that the writer of **Muppet Robin Hood** has unexpectedly and inexplicably gone missing, leaving the remainder of the series unwritten. After expending what we feel is a more than adequate amount of time and company resources to finding him, we have no choice but to replace him with another writer.

Unfortunately, the only writer we have available at this time doesn't speak English, and can only write in a rare dialect of Aboriginal Jingulu. Also, he seems to have a strange obsession with the Swedish Chef.

It is our hope that the following pages will be virtually indistinguishable from the pages leading up to them. Yet, with readers as discerning as ours, it's only to be expected that a few minor differences will be observed. We thank you for your understanding, and if you happen to see our missing writer, tell him to call us as soon as he's come to his senses.

Most sincerely,

The **Muppet Robin Hood** Editorial Team

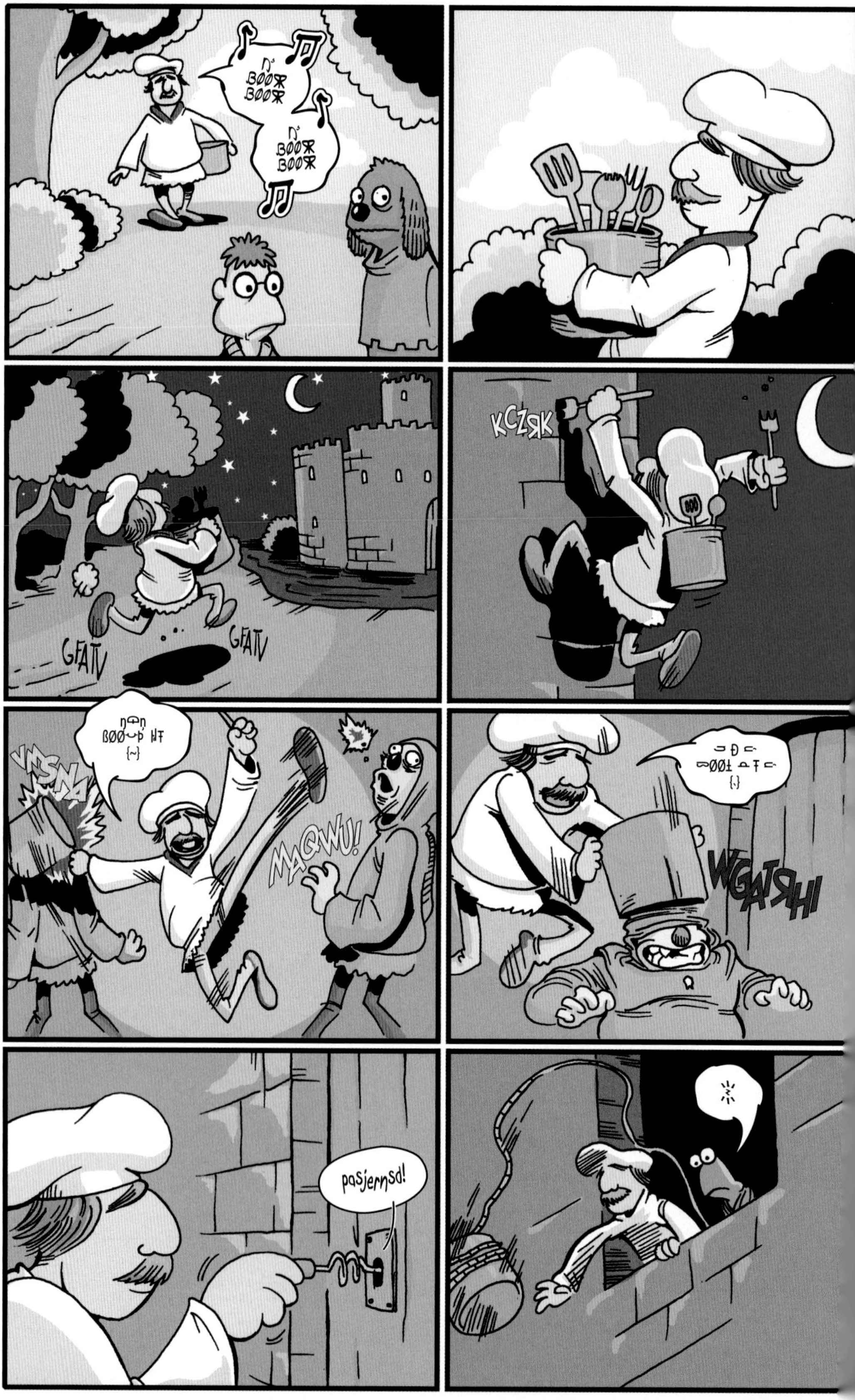

GFATV
GFATV
KCZЯK
MAQWU!
WGATЯHI
pasjernsd!

It's our great pleasure to inform you that our previous writer has been found safe and in possession of a new draft of the **Muppet Robin Hood** script. While it's unclear where he has been or what motivated him to write a new ending for **Muppet Robin Hood**, we will be immediately restoring him as our writer and will be using his revised ending at his (rather forceful) insistence.

Our Jingulu writer, meanwhile, has just accepted a writing position in Hollywood, where his inability to write in a manner that makes sense to anyone doesn't seem to be considered a flaw.

We thank you for your continued patronage and for all your letters inquiring about our mental health.

-The **Muppet Robin Hood** Editorial Team

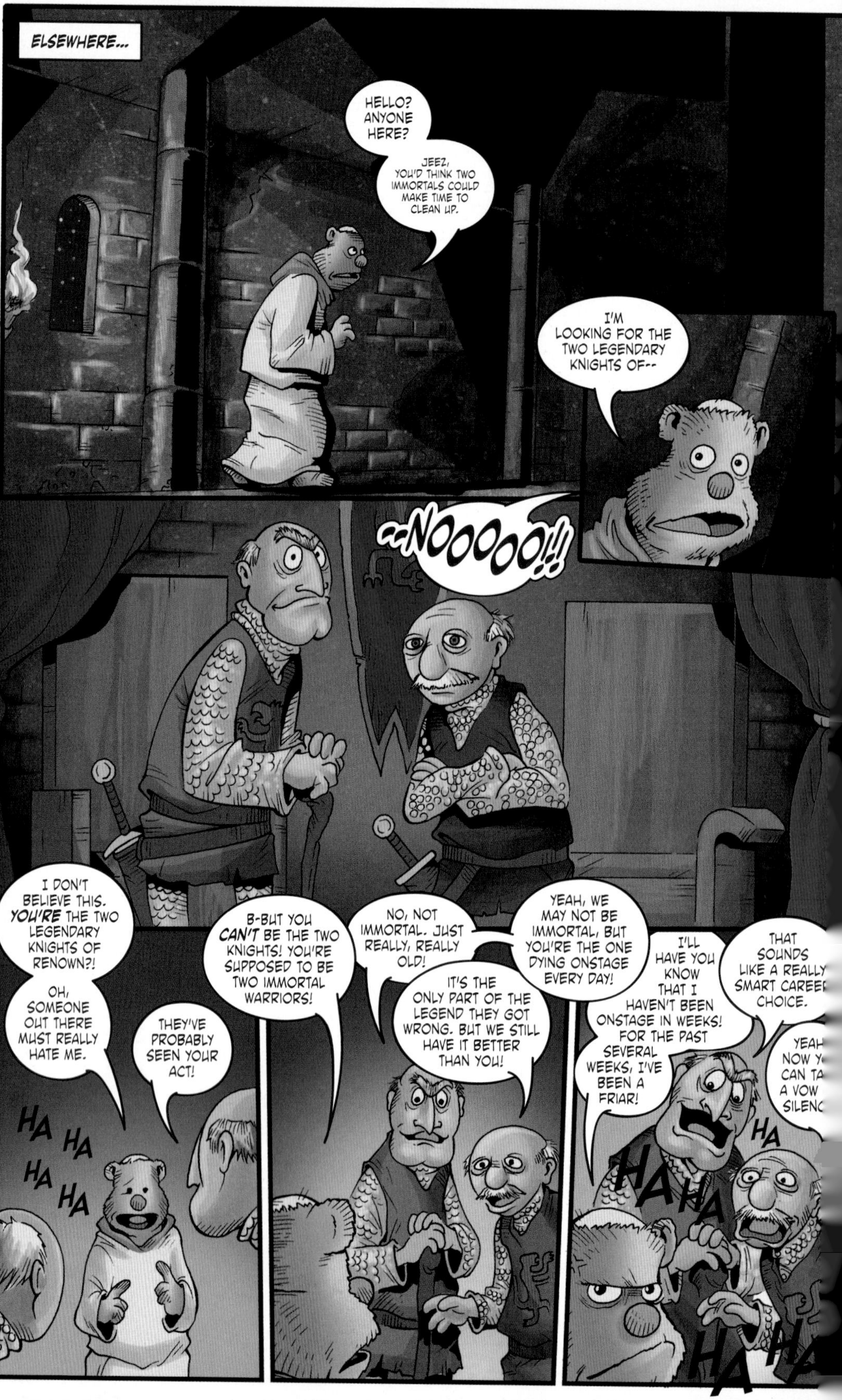

ELSEWHERE...
HELLO? ANYONE HERE?
JEEZ, YOU'D THINK TWO IMMORTALS COULD MAKE TIME TO CLEAN UP.
I'M LOOKING FOR THE TWO LEGENDARY KNIGHTS OF--
--NOOOOO!!!
I DON'T BELIEVE THIS. YOU'RE THE TWO LEGENDARY KNIGHTS OF RENOWN?!
OH, SOMEONE OUT THERE MUST REALLY HATE ME.
THEY'VE PROBABLY SEEN YOUR ACT!
HA HA HA HA
B-BUT YOU CAN'T BE THE TWO KNIGHTS! YOU'RE SUPPOSED TO BE TWO IMMORTAL WARRIORS!
NO, NOT IMMORTAL. JUST REALLY, REALLY OLD!
IT'S THE ONLY PART OF THE LEGEND THEY GOT WRONG. BUT WE STILL HAVE IT BETTER THAN YOU!
YEAH, WE MAY NOT BE IMMORTAL, BUT YOU'RE THE ONE DYING ONSTAGE EVERY DAY!
I'LL HAVE YOU KNOW THAT I HAVEN'T BEEN ONSTAGE IN WEEKS! FOR THE PAST SEVERAL WEEKS, I'VE BEEN A FRIAR!
THAT SOUNDS LIKE A REALLY SMART CAREE CHOICE.
YEAH NOW Y CAN TA A VOW SILENC
HA HAHA HA HA HA

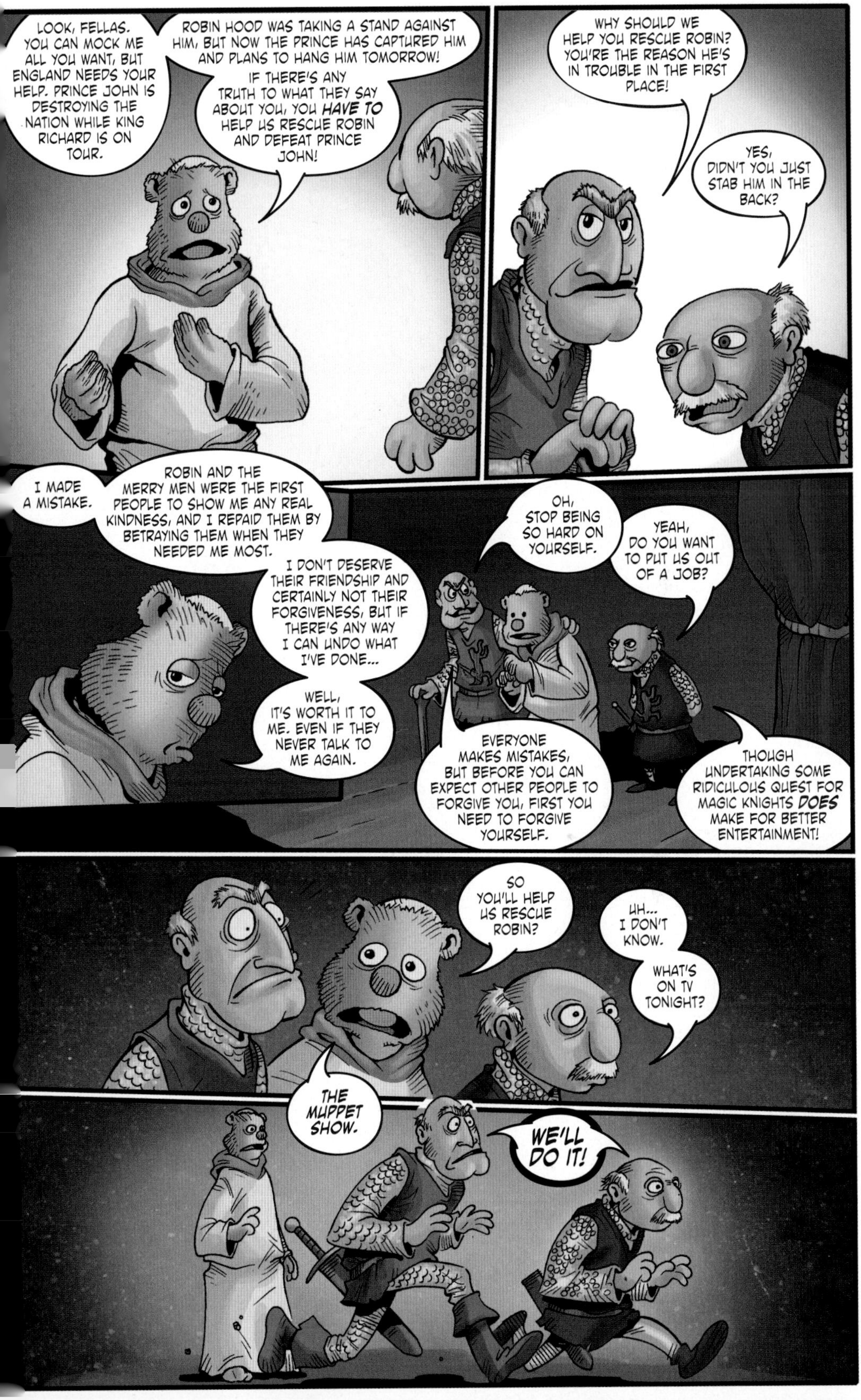
LOOK, FELLAS. YOU CAN MOCK ME ALL YOU WANT, BUT ENGLAND NEEDS YOUR HELP. PRINCE JOHN IS DESTROYING THE NATION WHILE KING RICHARD IS ON TOUR.
ROBIN HOOD WAS TAKING A STAND AGAINST HIM, BUT NOW THE PRINCE HAS CAPTURED HIM AND PLANS TO HANG HIM TOMORROW!
IF THERE'S ANY TRUTH TO WHAT THEY SAY ABOUT YOU, YOU ***HAVE TO*** HELP US RESCUE ROBIN AND DEFEAT PRINCE JOHN!
WHY SHOULD WE HELP YOU RESCUE ROBIN? YOU'RE THE REASON HE'S IN TROUBLE IN THE FIRST PLACE!
YES, DIDN'T YOU JUST STAB HIM IN THE BACK?
I MADE A MISTAKE.
ROBIN AND THE MERRY MEN WERE THE FIRST PEOPLE TO SHOW ME ANY REAL KINDNESS, AND I REPAID THEM BY BETRAYING THEM WHEN THEY NEEDED ME MOST.
I DON'T DESERVE THEIR FRIENDSHIP AND CERTAINLY NOT THEIR FORGIVENESS, BUT IF THERE'S ANY WAY I CAN UNDO WHAT I'VE DONE...
WELL, IT'S WORTH IT TO ME. EVEN IF THEY NEVER TALK TO ME AGAIN.
OH, STOP BEING SO HARD ON YOURSELF.
YEAH, DO YOU WANT TO PUT US OUT OF A JOB?
EVERYONE MAKES MISTAKES, BUT BEFORE YOU CAN EXPECT OTHER PEOPLE TO FORGIVE YOU, FIRST YOU NEED TO FORGIVE YOURSELF.
THOUGH UNDERTAKING SOME RIDICULOUS QUEST FOR MAGIC KNIGHTS ***DOES*** MAKE FOR BETTER ENTERTAINMENT!
SO YOU'LL HELP US RESCUE ROBIN?
UH... I DON'T KNOW.
WHAT'S ON TV TONIGHT?
THE MUPPET SHOW.
WE'LL DO IT!

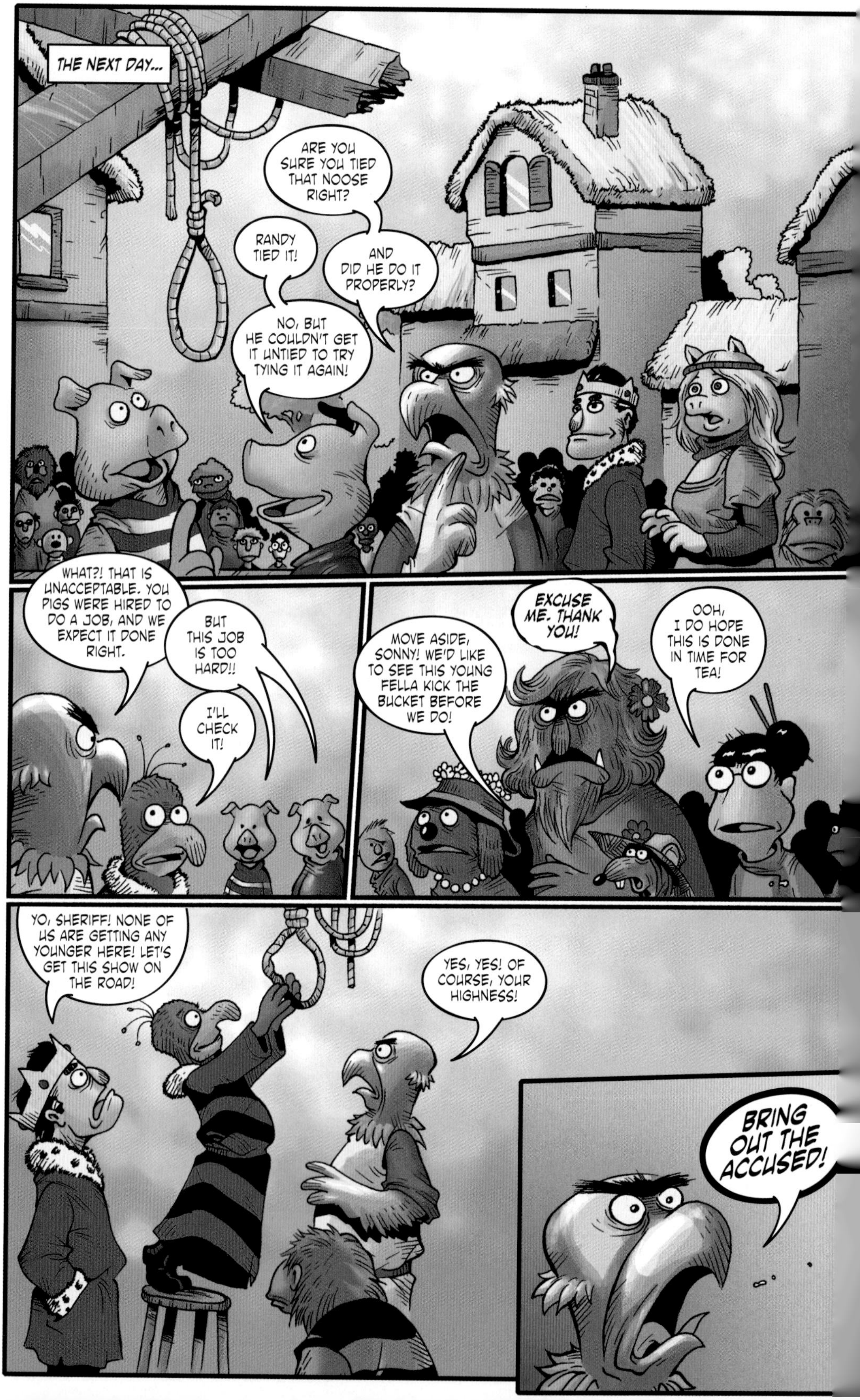
THE NEXT DAY...
ARE YOU SURE YOU TIED THAT NOOSE RIGHT?
RANDY TIED IT!
AND DID HE DO IT PROPERLY?
NO, BUT HE COULDN'T GET IT UNTIED TO TRY TYING IT AGAIN!
WHAT?! THAT IS UNACCEPTABLE. YOU PIGS WERE HIRED TO DO A JOB, AND WE EXPECT IT DONE RIGHT.
BUT THIS JOB IS TOO HARD!!
I'LL CHECK IT!
MOVE ASIDE, SONNY! WE'D LIKE TO SEE THIS YOUNG FELLA KICK THE BUCKET BEFORE WE DO!
EXCUSE ME. THANK YOU!
OOH, I DO HOPE THIS IS DONE IN TIME FOR TEA!
YO, SHERIFF! NONE OF US ARE GETTING ANY YOUNGER HERE! LET'S GET THIS SHOW ON THE ROAD!
YES, YES! OF COURSE, YOUR HIGHNESS!
BRING OUT THE ACCUSED!

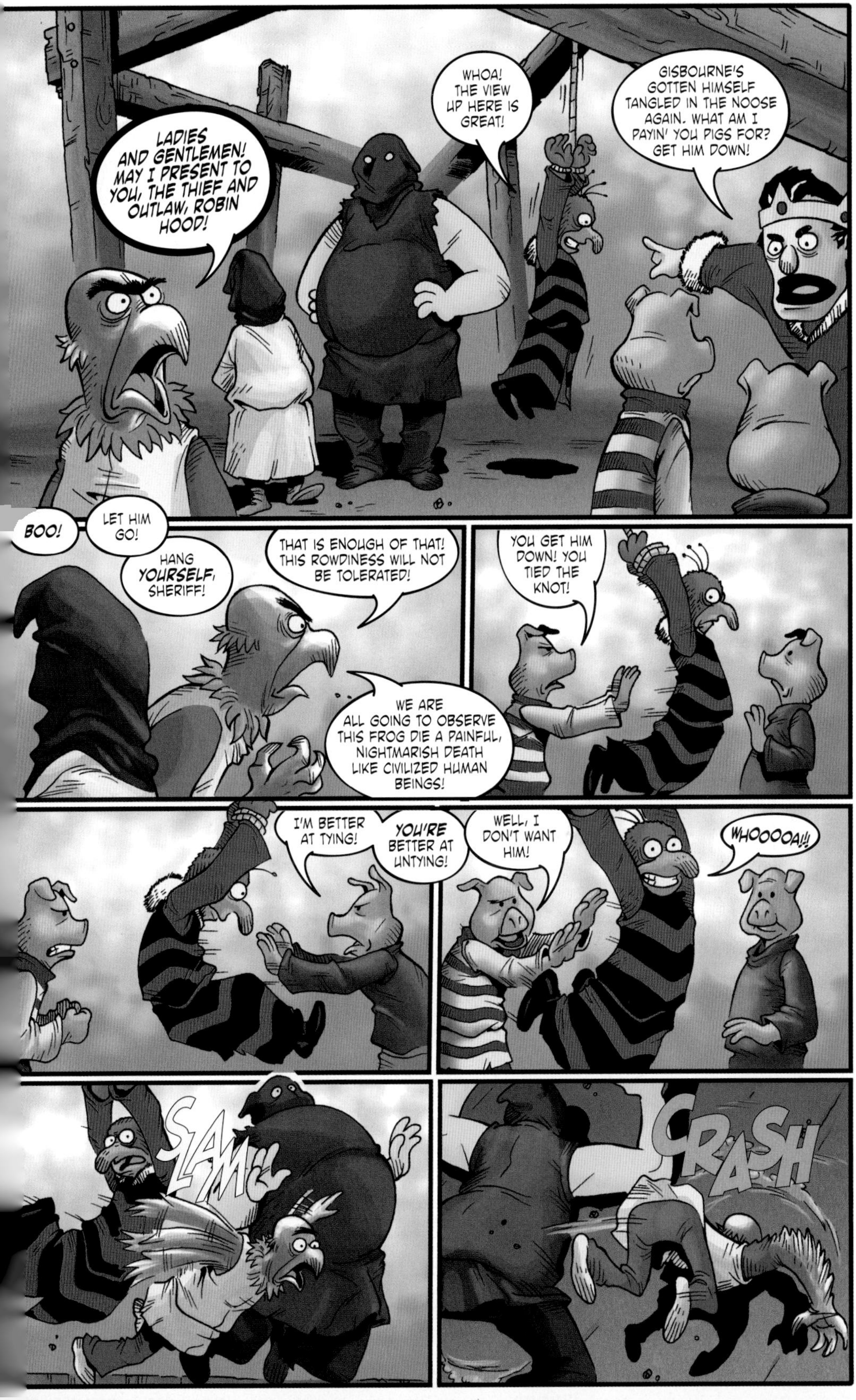
LADIES AND GENTLEMEN! MAY I PRESENT TO YOU, THE THIEF AND OUTLAW, ROBIN HOOD!
WHOA! THE VIEW UP HERE IS GREAT!
GISBOURNE'S GOTTEN HIMSELF TANGLED IN THE NOOSE AGAIN. WHAT AM I PAYIN' YOU PIGS FOR? GET HIM DOWN!
BOO!
LET HIM GO!
HANG YOURSELF, SHERIFF!
THAT IS ENOUGH OF THAT! THIS ROWDINESS WILL NOT BE TOLERATED!
WE ARE ALL GOING TO OBSERVE THIS FROG DIE A PAINFUL, NIGHTMARISH DEATH LIKE CIVILIZED HUMAN BEINGS!
YOU GET HIM DOWN! YOU TIED THE KNOT!
I'M BETTER AT TYING!
YOU'RE BETTER AT UNTYING!
WELL, I DON'T WANT HIM!
WHOOOOA!!!
SLAM
CRASH

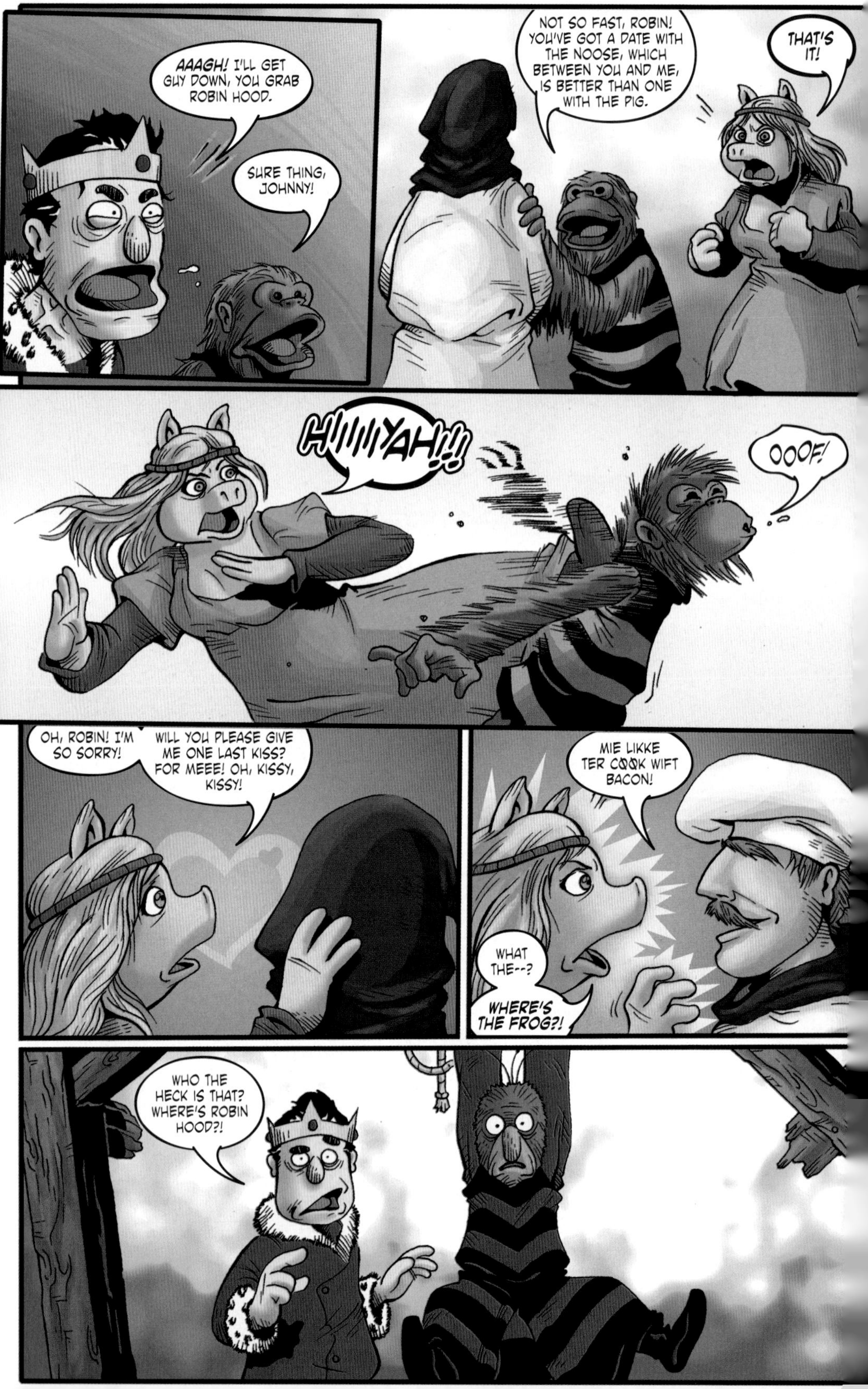
AAAGH! I'LL GET GUY DOWN, YOU GRAB ROBIN HOOD.
SURE THING, JOHNNY!
NOT SO FAST, ROBIN! YOU'VE GOT A DATE WITH THE NOOSE, WHICH BETWEEN YOU AND ME, IS BETTER THAN ONE WITH THE PIG.
THAT'S IT!
HIIIIIYAH!!!
OOOF!
OH, ROBIN! I'M SO SORRY!
WILL YOU PLEASE GIVE ME ONE LAST KISS? FOR MEEE! OH, KISSY, KISSY!
MIE LIKKE TER COOK WIFT BACON!
WHAT THE--?
WHERE'S THE FROG?!
WHO THE HECK IS THAT? WHERE'S ROBIN HOOD?!

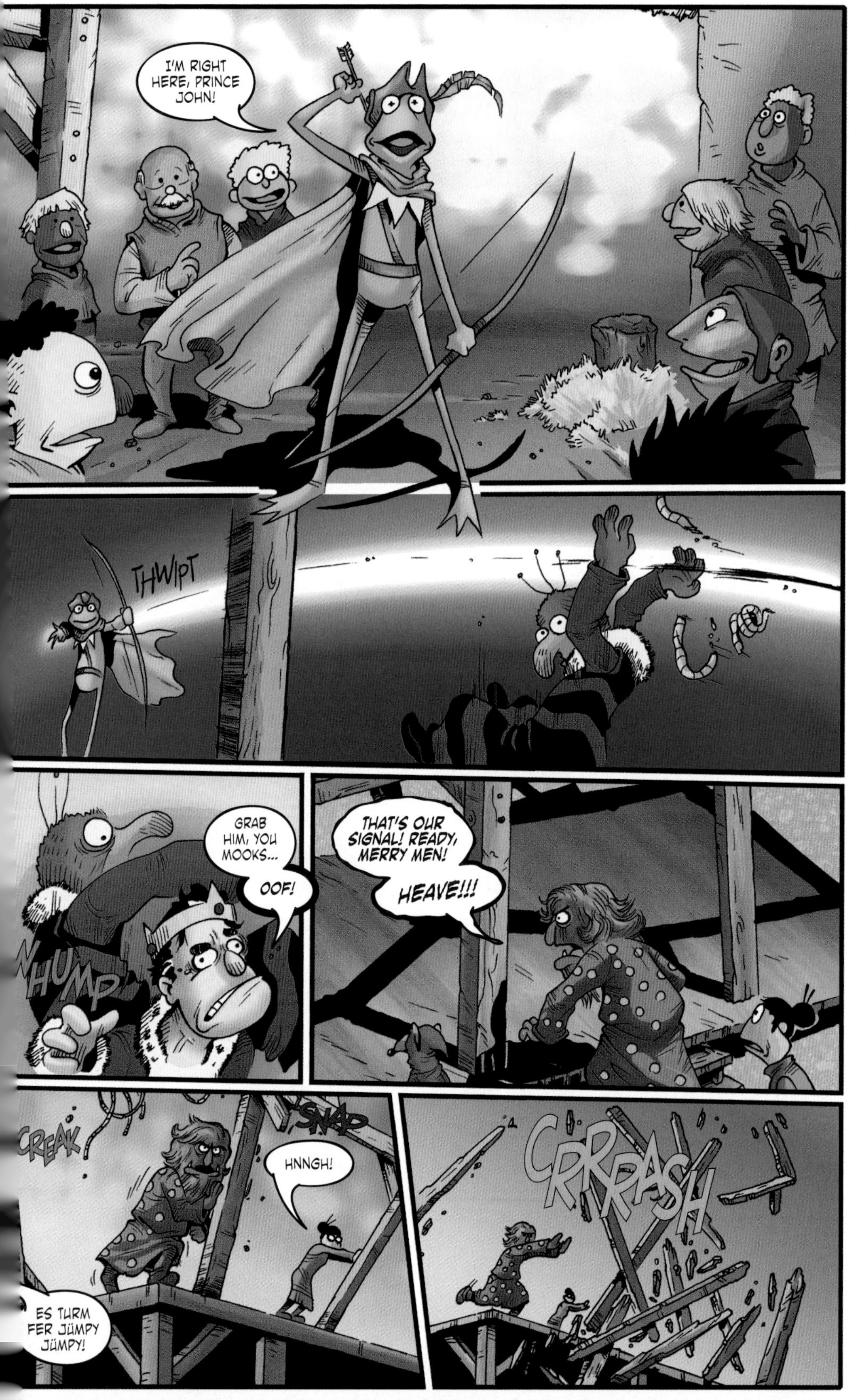
I'M RIGHT HERE, PRINCE JOHN!
THWIPT
GRAB HIM, YOU MOOKS...
OOF!
WHUMP
THAT'S OUR SIGNAL! READY, MERRY MEN!
HEAVE!!!
CREAK
SNAP
HNNGH!
ES TURM FER JÜMPY JÜMPY!
CRRRASH

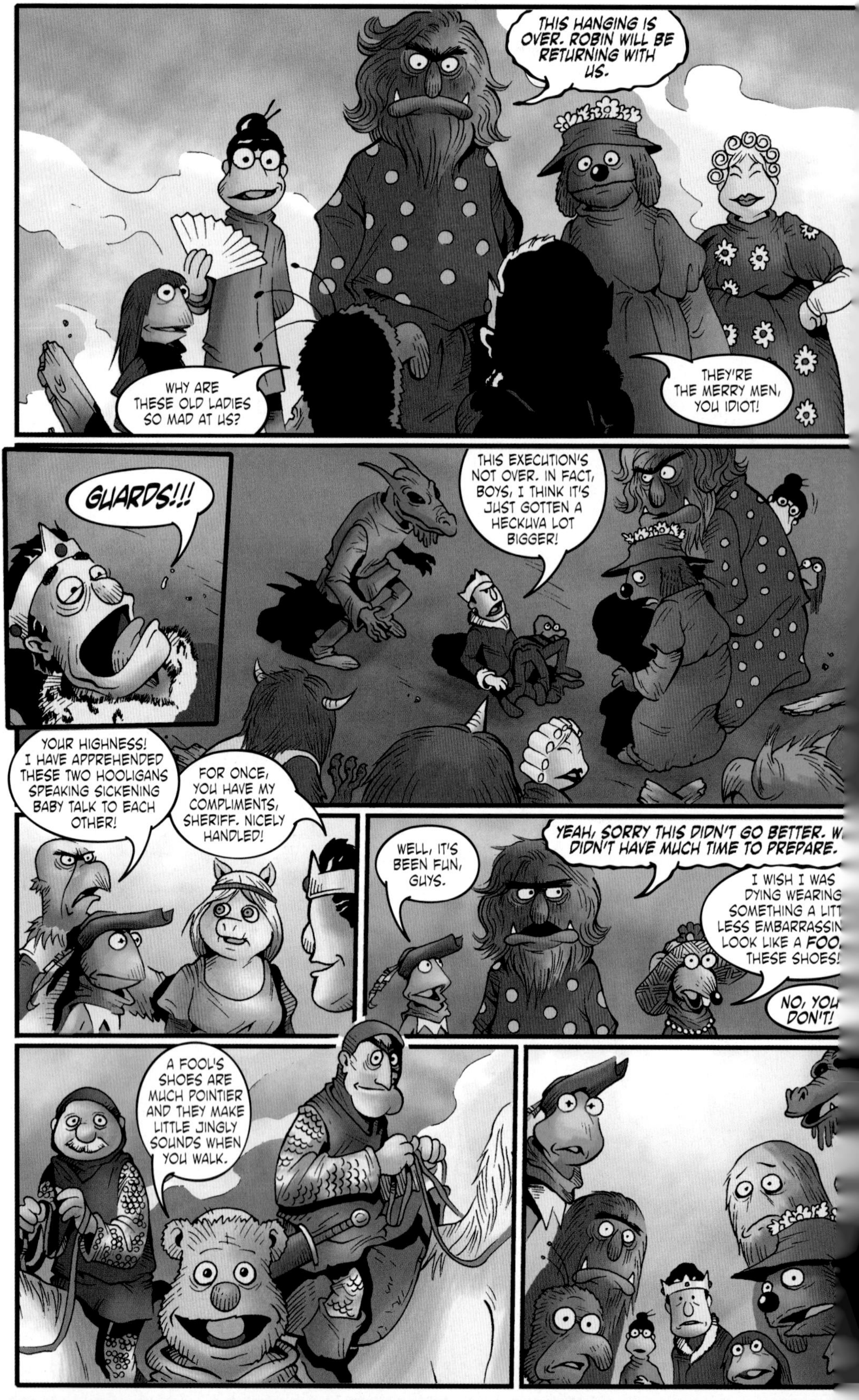
THIS HANGING IS OVER. ROBIN WILL BE RETURNING WITH US.
WHY ARE THESE OLD LADIES SO MAD AT US?
THEY'RE THE MERRY MEN, YOU IDIOT!
GUARDS!!!
THIS EXECUTION'S NOT OVER. IN FACT, BOYS, I THINK IT'S JUST GOTTEN A HECKUVA LOT BIGGER!
YOUR HIGHNESS! I HAVE APPREHENDED THESE TWO HOOLIGANS SPEAKING SICKENING BABY TALK TO EACH OTHER!
FOR ONCE, YOU HAVE MY COMPLIMENTS, SHERIFF. NICELY HANDLED!
WELL, IT'S BEEN FUN, GUYS.
YEAH, SORRY THIS DIDN'T GO BETTER. W DIDN'T HAVE MUCH TIME TO PREPARE.
I WISH I WAS DYING WEARING SOMETHING A LITT LESS EMBARRASSIN LOOK LIKE A FOO THESE SHOES!
NO, YOU DON'T!
A FOOL'S SHOES ARE MUCH POINTIER AND THEY MAKE LITTLE JINGLY SOUNDS WHEN YOU WALK.

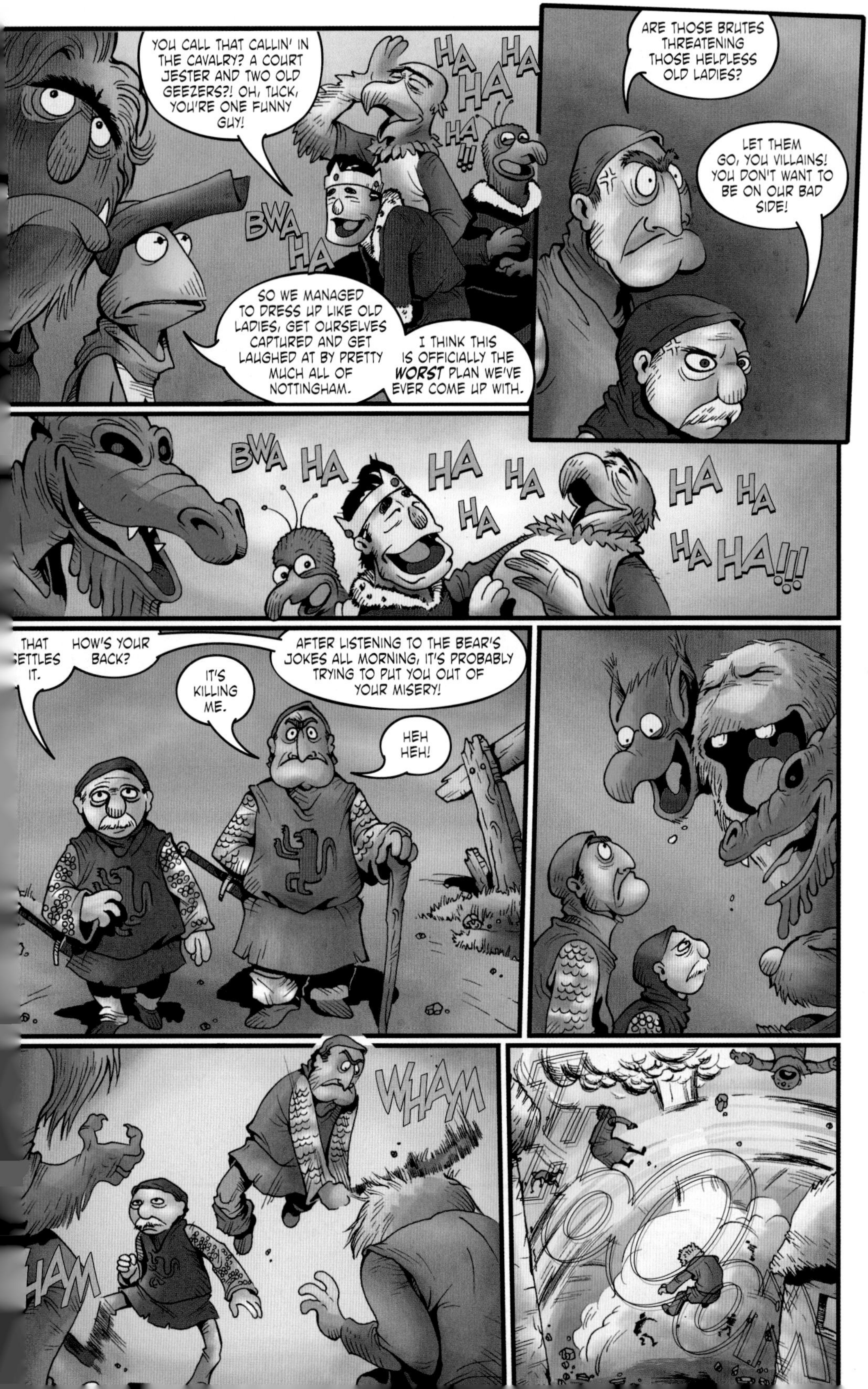
YOU CALL THAT CALLIN' IN THE CAVALRY? A COURT JESTER AND TWO OLD GEEZERS?! OH, TUCK, YOU'RE ONE FUNNY GUY!
HA HA HA HA!!!
BWA HA
SO WE MANAGED TO DRESS UP LIKE OLD LADIES, GET OURSELVES CAPTURED AND GET LAUGHED AT BY PRETTY MUCH ALL OF NOTTINGHAM.
I THINK THIS IS OFFICIALLY THE WORST PLAN WE'VE EVER COME UP WITH.
ARE THOSE BRUTES THREATENING THOSE HELPLESS OLD LADIES?
LET THEM GO, YOU VILLAINS! YOU DON'T WANT TO BE ON OUR BAD SIDE!
BWA HA HA HA HA HA HA HA HA HA!!!
THAT SETTLES IT.
HOW'S YOUR BACK?
IT'S KILLING ME.
AFTER LISTENING TO THE BEAR'S JOKES ALL MORNING, IT'S PROBABLY TRYING TO PUT YOU OUT OF YOUR MISERY!
HEH HEH!
WHAM
HAM

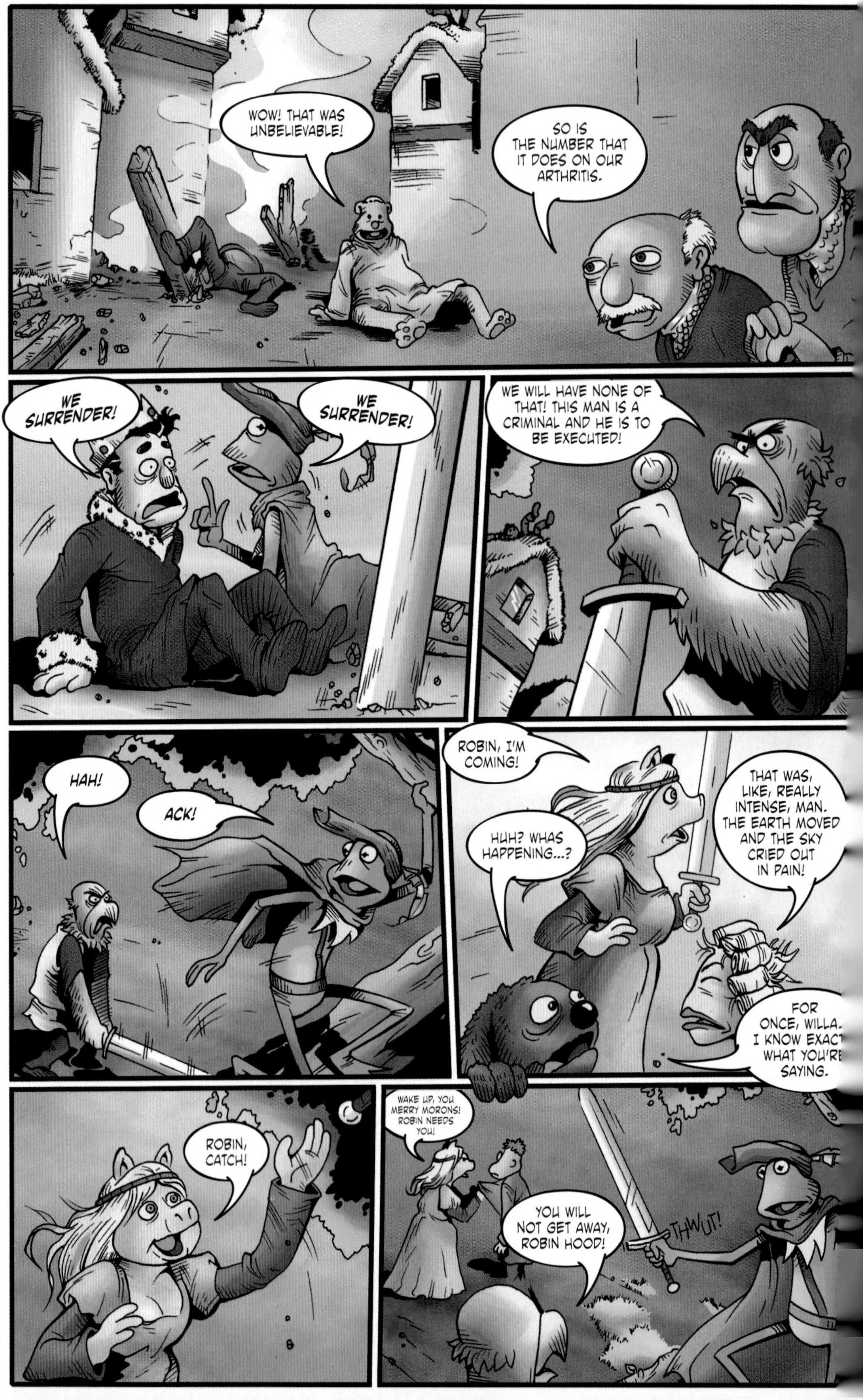
WOW! THAT WAS UNBELIEVABLE!
SO IS THE NUMBER THAT IT DOES ON OUR ARTHRITIS.
WE SURRENDER!
WE SURRENDER!
WE WILL HAVE NONE OF THAT! THIS MAN IS A CRIMINAL AND HE IS TO BE EXECUTED!
HAH!
ACK!
ROBIN, I'M COMING!
HUH? WHAS HAPPENING...?
THAT WAS, LIKE, REALLY INTENSE, MAN. THE EARTH MOVED AND THE SKY CRIED OUT IN PAIN!
FOR ONCE, WILLA. I KNOW EXAC WHAT YOU'R SAYING.
ROBIN, CATCH!
WAKE UP, YOU MERRY MORONS! ROBIN NEEDS YOU!
YOU WILL NOT GET AWAY, ROBIN HOOD!
THWUT!

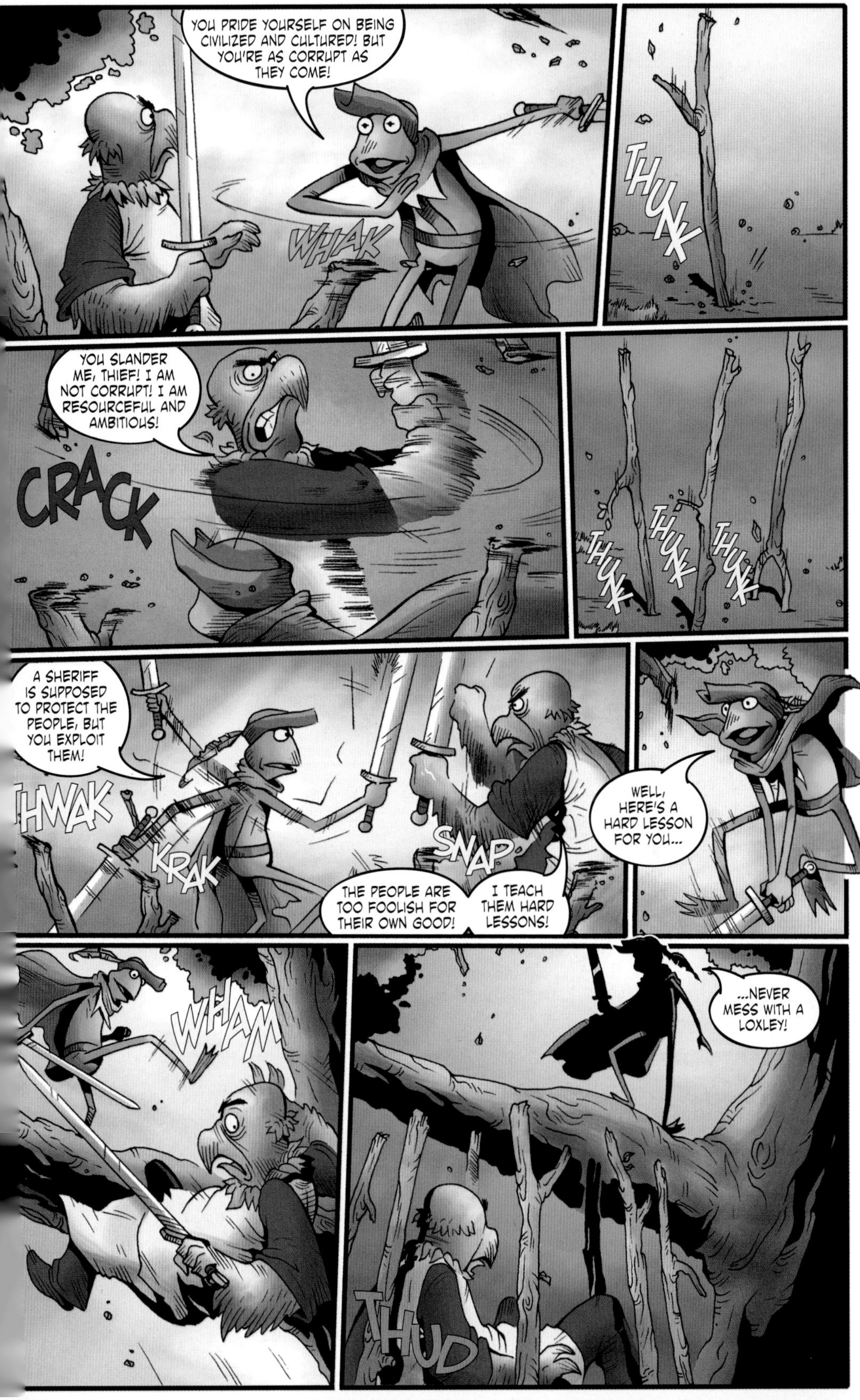
YOU PRIDE YOURSELF ON BEING CIVILIZED AND CULTURED! BUT YOU'RE AS CORRUPT AS THEY COME!
WHAK
THUNK
YOU SLANDER ME, THIEF! I AM NOT CORRUPT! I AM RESOURCEFUL AND AMBITIOUS!
CRACK
THUNK
THUNK
THUNK
A SHERIFF IS SUPPOSED TO PROTECT THE PEOPLE, BUT YOU EXPLOIT THEM!
THWAK
KRAK
SNAP
THE PEOPLE ARE TOO FOOLISH FOR THEIR OWN GOOD!
I TEACH THEM HARD LESSONS!
WELL, HERE'S A HARD LESSON FOR YOU...
WHAM
...NEVER MESS WITH A LOXLEY!
THUD

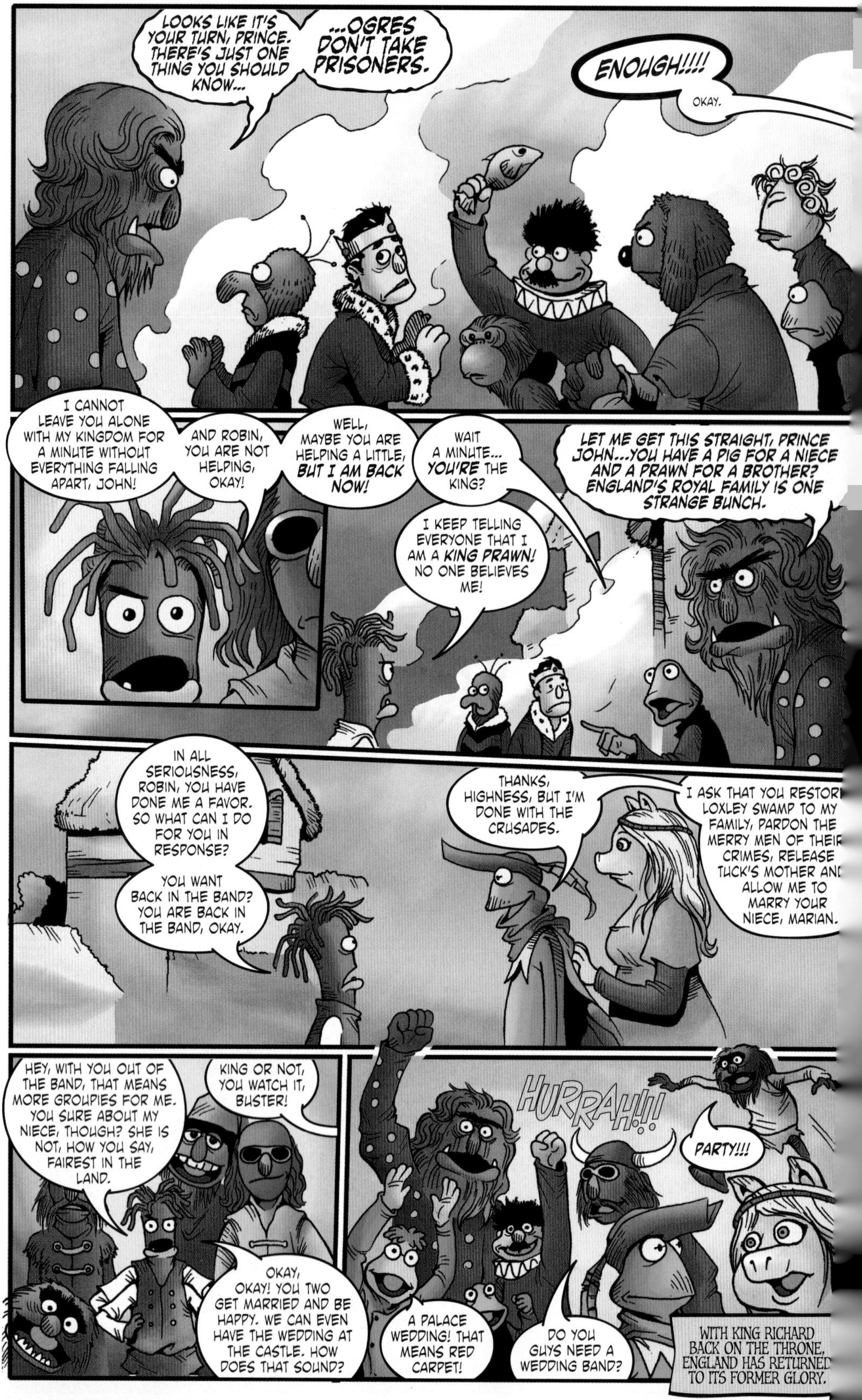
LOOKS LIKE IT'S YOUR TURN, PRINCE. THERE'S JUST ONE THING YOU SHOULD KNOW...
...OGRES DON'T TAKE PRISONERS.
ENOUGH!!!!
OKAY.
I CANNOT LEAVE YOU ALONE WITH MY KINGDOM FOR A MINUTE WITHOUT EVERYTHING FALLING APART, JOHN!
AND ROBIN, YOU ARE NOT HELPING, OKAY!
WELL, MAYBE YOU ARE HELPING A LITTLE, BUT I AM BACK NOW!
WAIT A MINUTE... YOU'RE THE KING?
I KEEP TELLING EVERYONE THAT I AM A KING PRAWN! NO ONE BELIEVES ME!
LET ME GET THIS STRAIGHT, PRINCE JOHN...YOU HAVE A PIG FOR A NIECE AND A PRAWN FOR A BROTHER? ENGLAND'S ROYAL FAMILY IS ONE STRANGE BUNCH.
IN ALL SERIOUSNESS, ROBIN, YOU HAVE DONE ME A FAVOR. SO WHAT CAN I DO FOR YOU IN RESPONSE?
YOU WANT BACK IN THE BAND? YOU ARE BACK IN THE BAND, OKAY.
THANKS, HIGHNESS, BUT I'M DONE WITH THE CRUSADES.
I ASK THAT YOU RESTOR LOXLEY SWAMP TO MY FAMILY, PARDON THE MERRY MEN OF THEI CRIMES, RELEASE TUCK'S MOTHER AND ALLOW ME TO MARRY YOUR NIECE, MARIAN.
HEY, WITH YOU OUT OF THE BAND, THAT MEANS MORE GROUPIES FOR ME. YOU SURE ABOUT MY NIECE, THOUGH? SHE IS NOT, HOW YOU SAY, FAIREST IN THE LAND.
KING OR NOT, YOU WATCH IT, BUSTER!
OKAY, OKAY! YOU TWO GET MARRIED AND BE HAPPY. WE CAN EVEN HAVE THE WEDDING AT THE CASTLE. HOW DOES THAT SOUND?
HURRAH!!!!
PARTY!!!
A PALACE WEDDING! THAT MEANS RED CARPET!
DO YOU GUYS NEED A WEDDING BAND?
WITH KING RICHARD BACK ON THE THRONE, ENGLAND HAS RETURNED TO ITS FORMER GLORY.

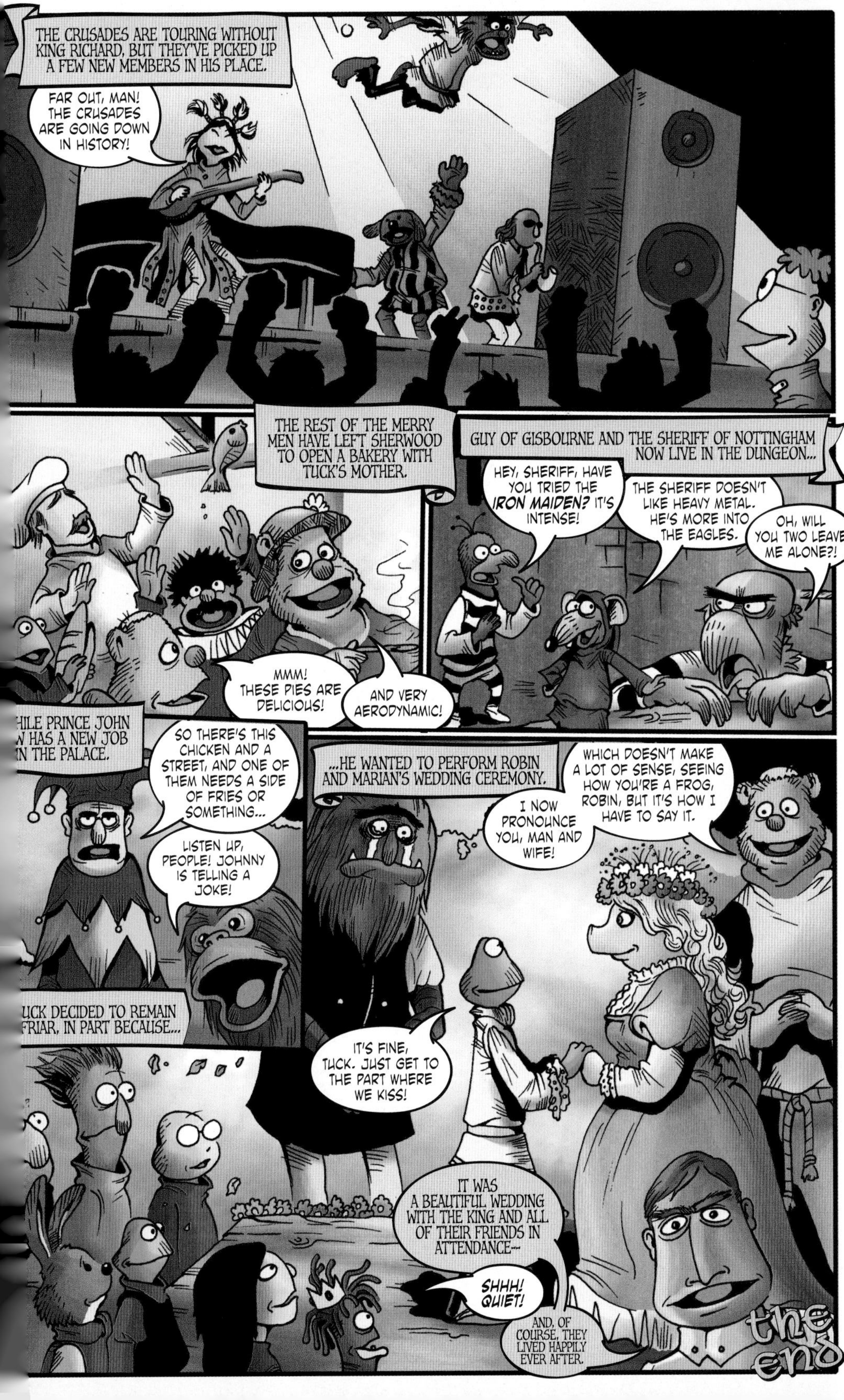
THE CRUSADES ARE TOURING WITHOUT KING RICHARD, BUT THEY'VE PICKED UP A FEW NEW MEMBERS IN HIS PLACE.
FAR OUT, MAN! THE CRUSADES ARE GOING DOWN IN HISTORY!
THE REST OF THE MERRY MEN HAVE LEFT SHERWOOD TO OPEN A BAKERY WITH TUCK'S MOTHER.
MMM! THESE PIES ARE DELICIOUS!
AND VERY AERODYNAMIC!
GUY OF GISBOURNE AND THE SHERIFF OF NOTTINGHAM NOW LIVE IN THE DUNGEON...
HEY, SHERIFF, HAVE YOU TRIED THE IRON MAIDEN? IT'S INTENSE!
THE SHERIFF DOESN'T LIKE HEAVY METAL. HE'S MORE INTO THE EAGLES.
OH, WILL YOU TWO LEAVE ME ALONE?!
HILE PRINCE JOHN W HAS A NEW JOB N THE PALACE.
SO THERE'S THIS CHICKEN AND A STREET, AND ONE OF THEM NEEDS A SIDE OF FRIES OR SOMETHING...
LISTEN UP, PEOPLE! JOHNNY IS TELLING A JOKE!
UCK DECIDED TO REMAIN FRIAR, IN PART BECAUSE...
...HE WANTED TO PERFORM ROBIN AND MARIAN'S WEDDING CEREMONY.
I NOW PRONOUNCE YOU, MAN AND WIFE!
WHICH DOESN'T MAKE A LOT OF SENSE, SEEING HOW YOU'RE A FROG, ROBIN, BUT IT'S HOW I HAVE TO SAY IT.
IT'S FINE, TUCK. JUST GET TO THE PART WHERE WE KISS!
IT WAS A BEAUTIFUL WEDDING WITH THE KING AND ALL OF THEIR FRIENDS IN ATTENDANCE--
SHHH! QUIET!
AND, OF COURSE, THEY LIVED HAPPILY EVER AFTER.
the end

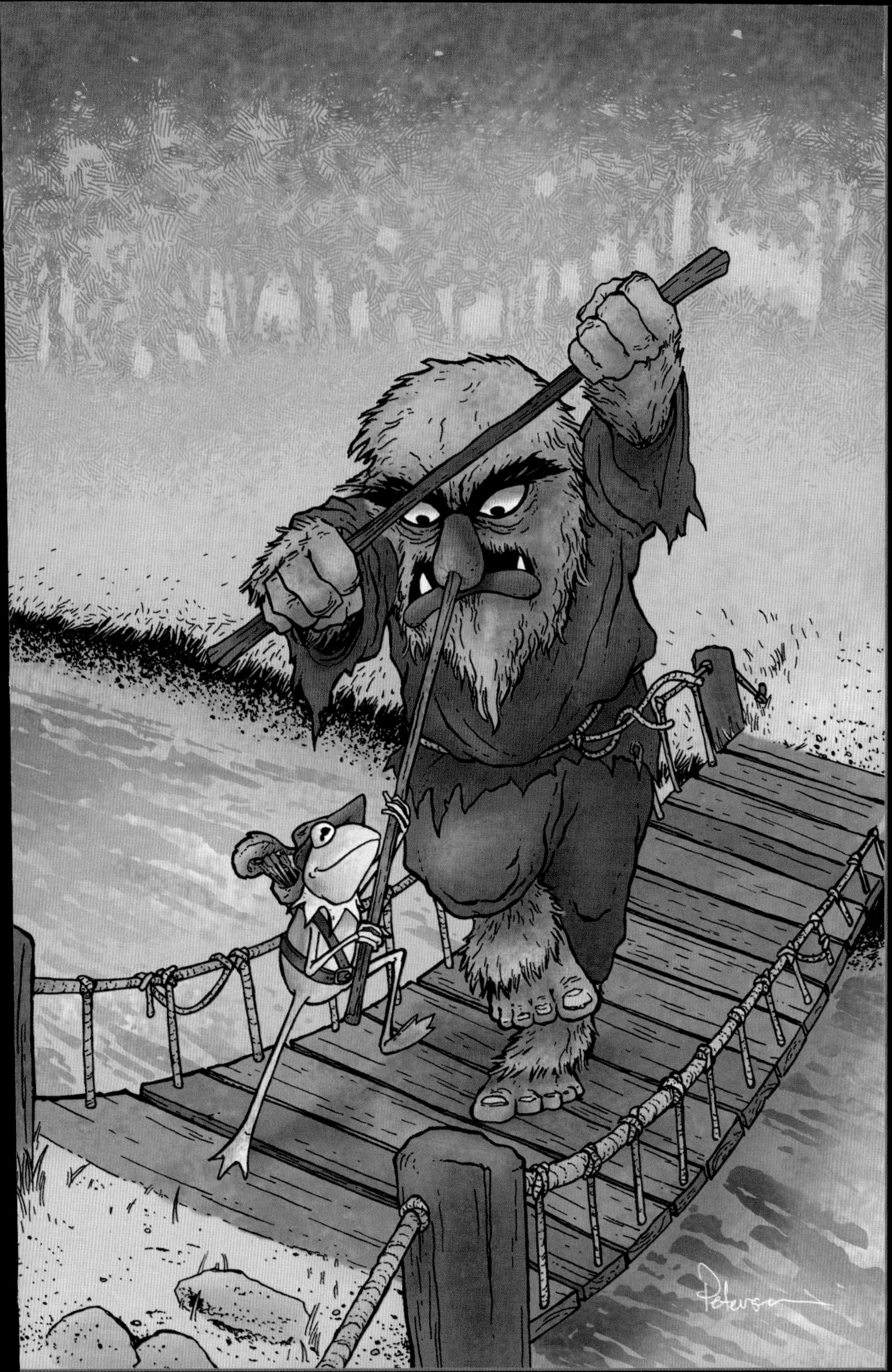
Peterson

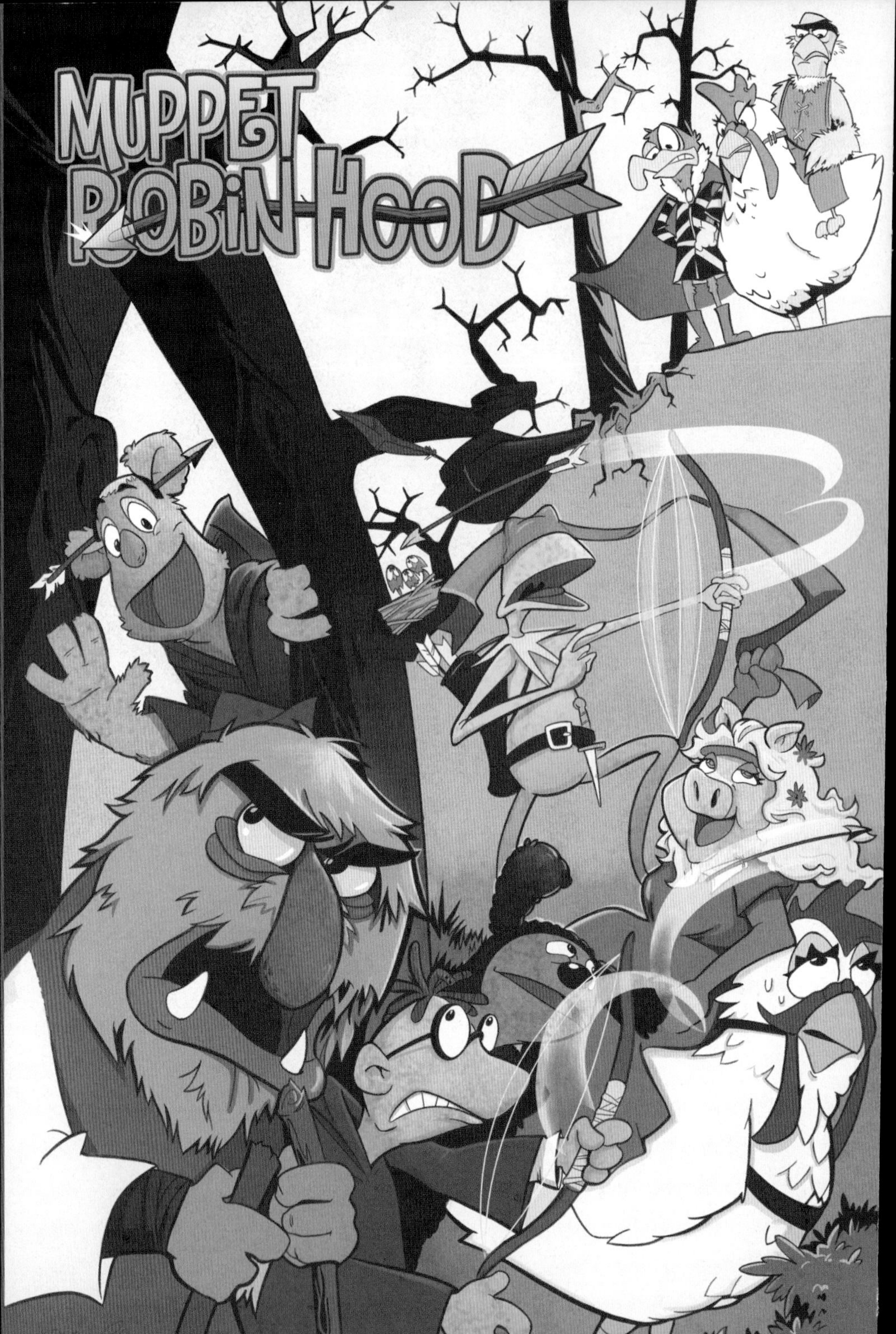
MUPPET ROBIN HOOD

COVER 1B: SHELLI PAROLINE

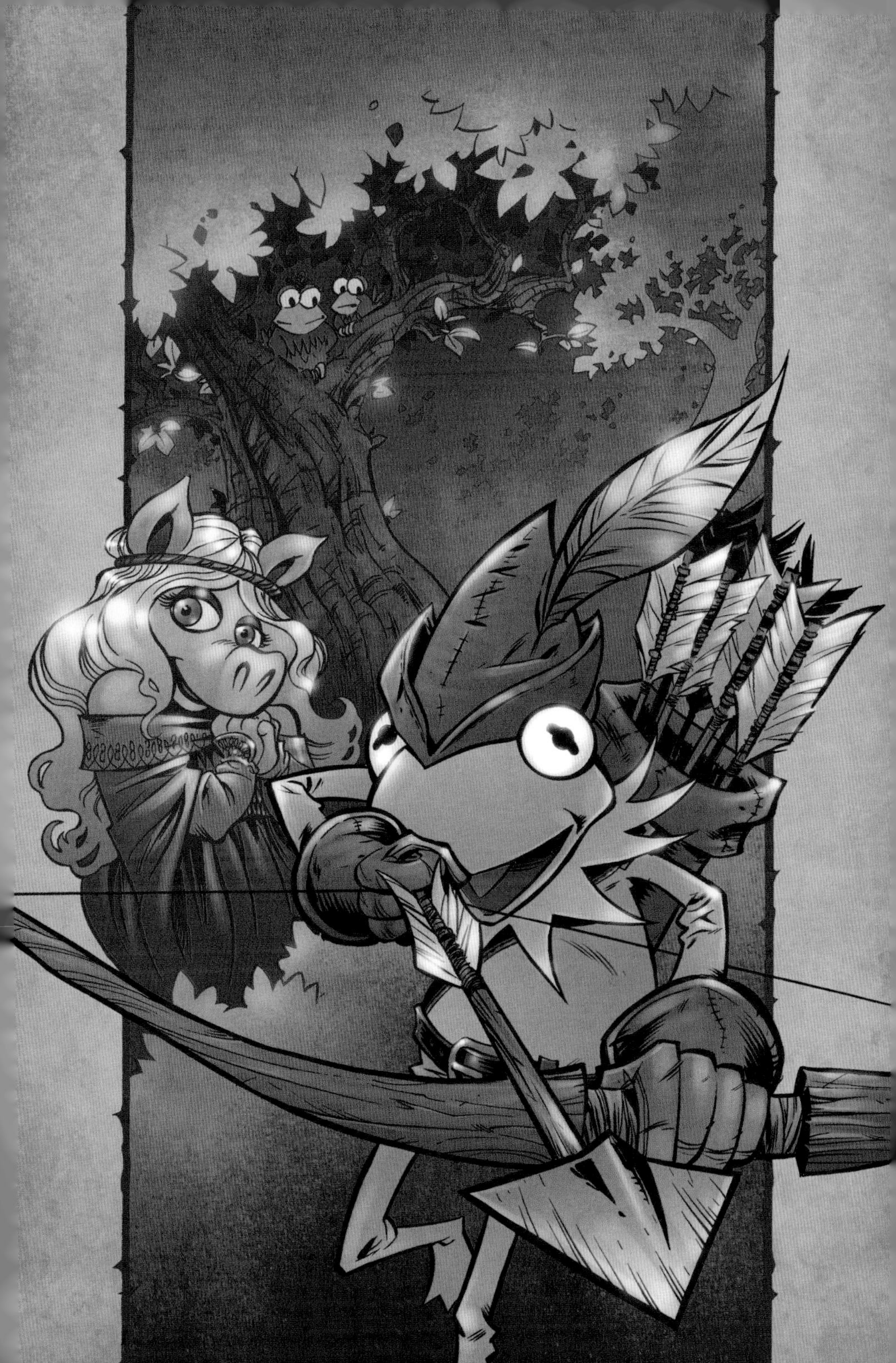

ISSUE 1, 2ND PRINT: CHRISTOPHER SCHONS

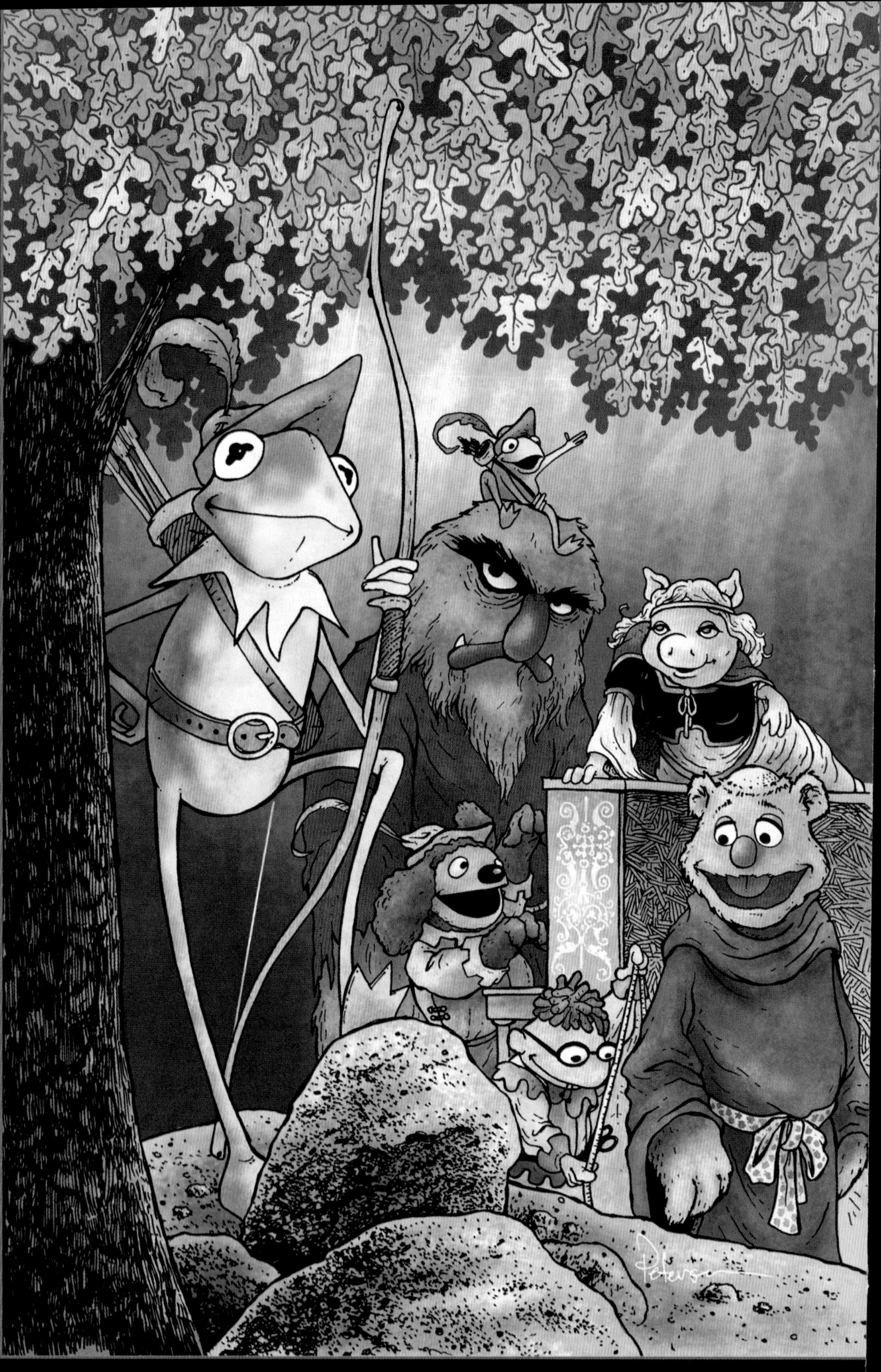

COVER 2A: DAVID PETERSEN

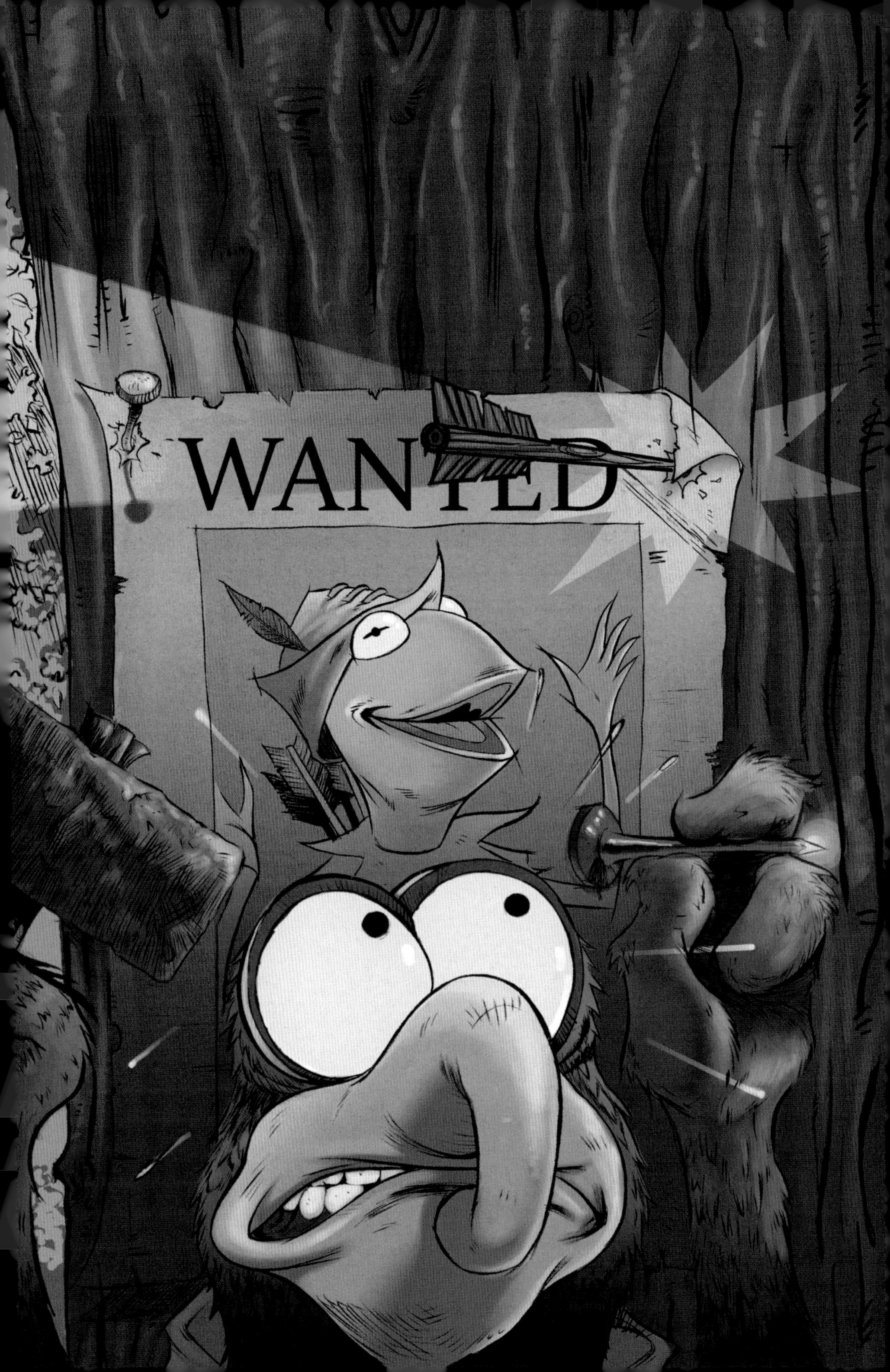
WANTED

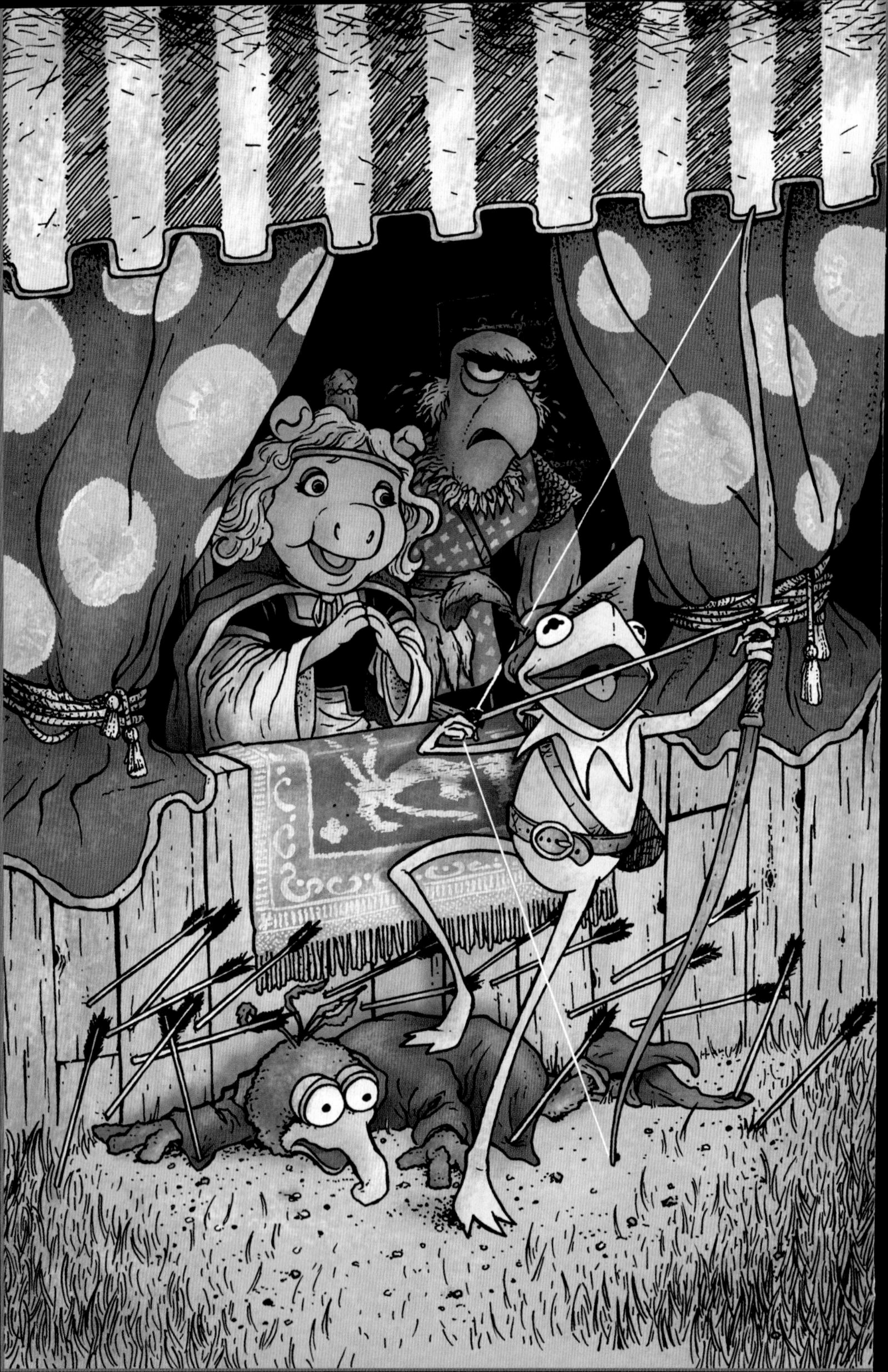

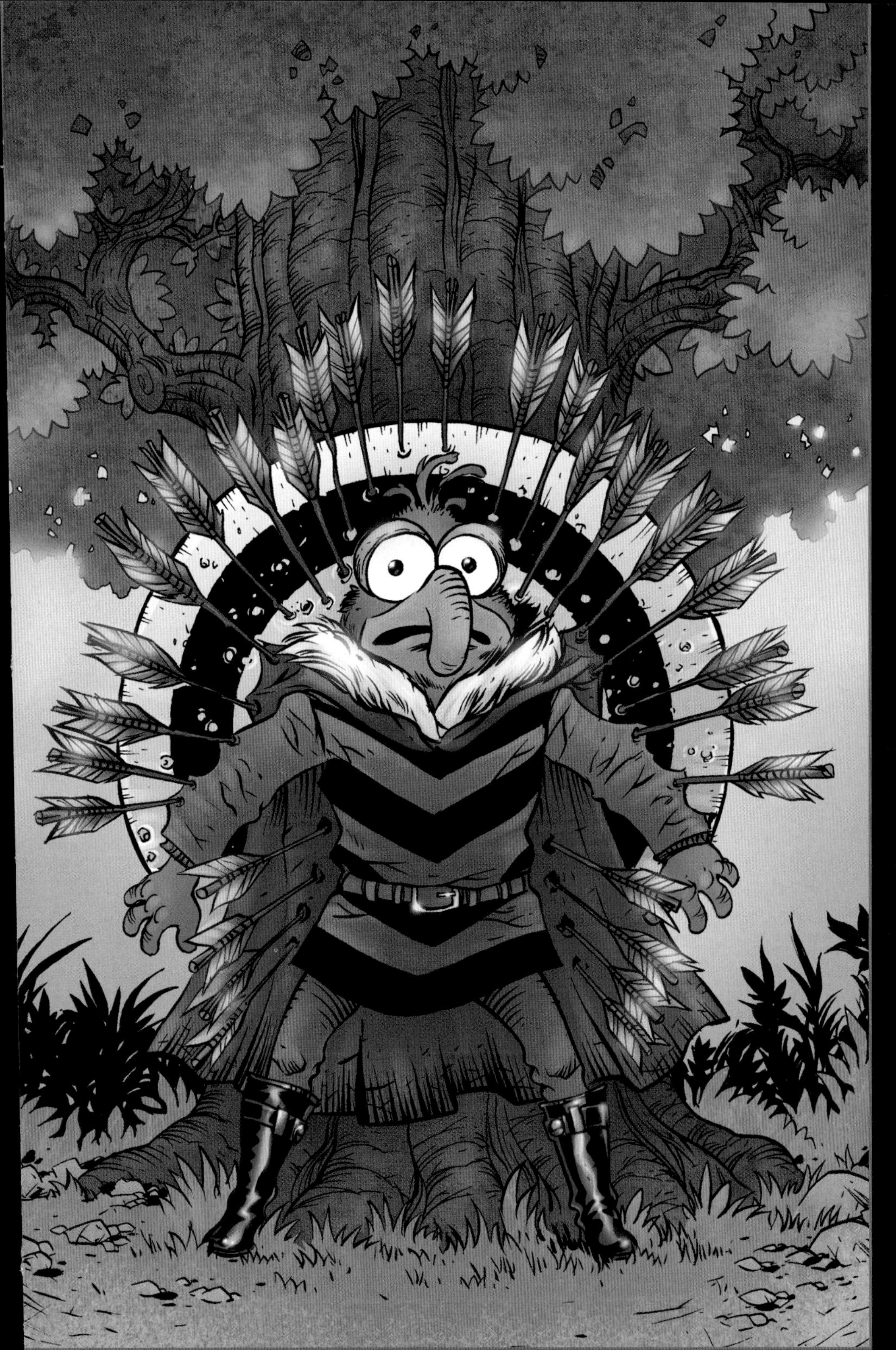

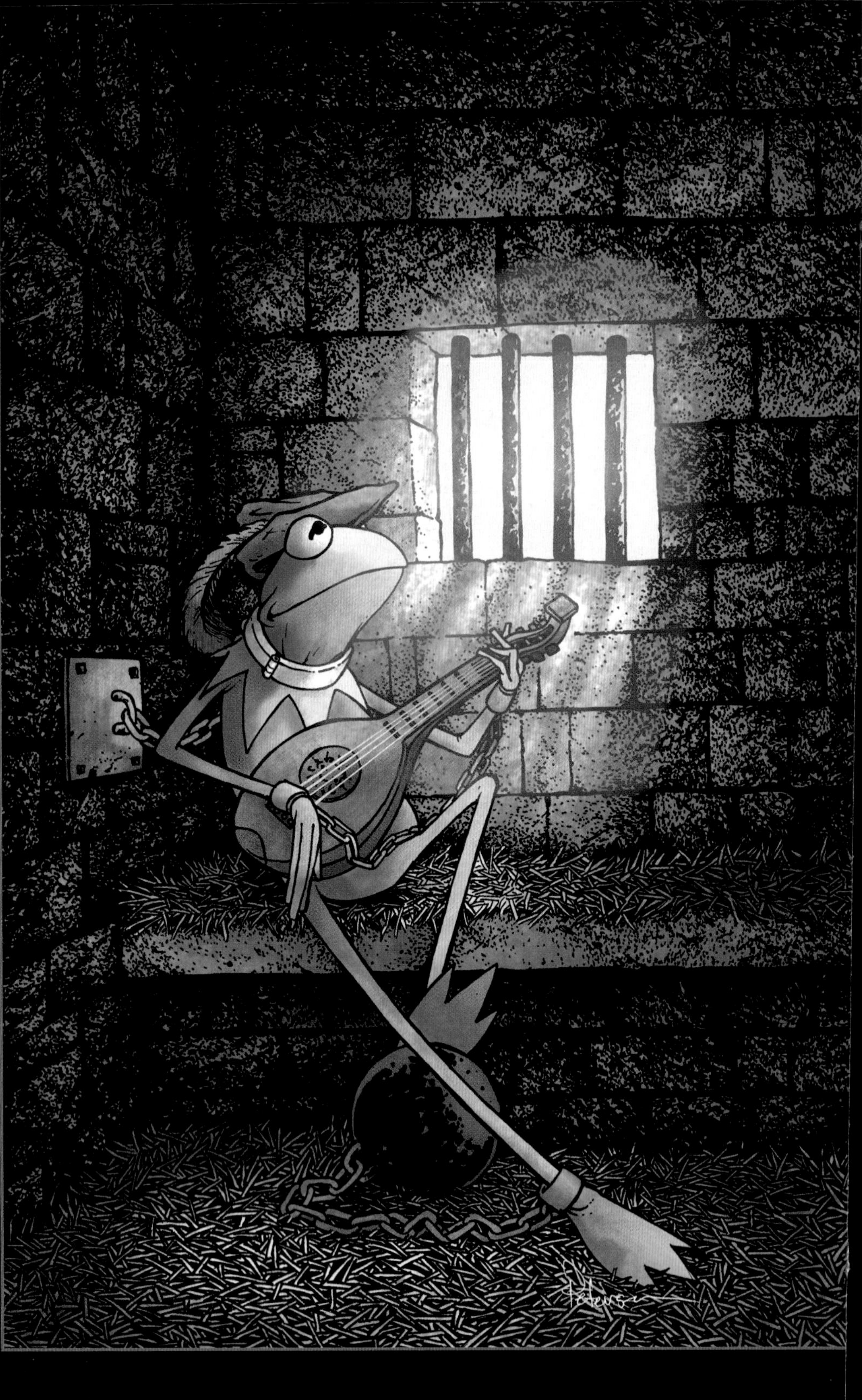

COVER 4A: DAVID PETERSEN

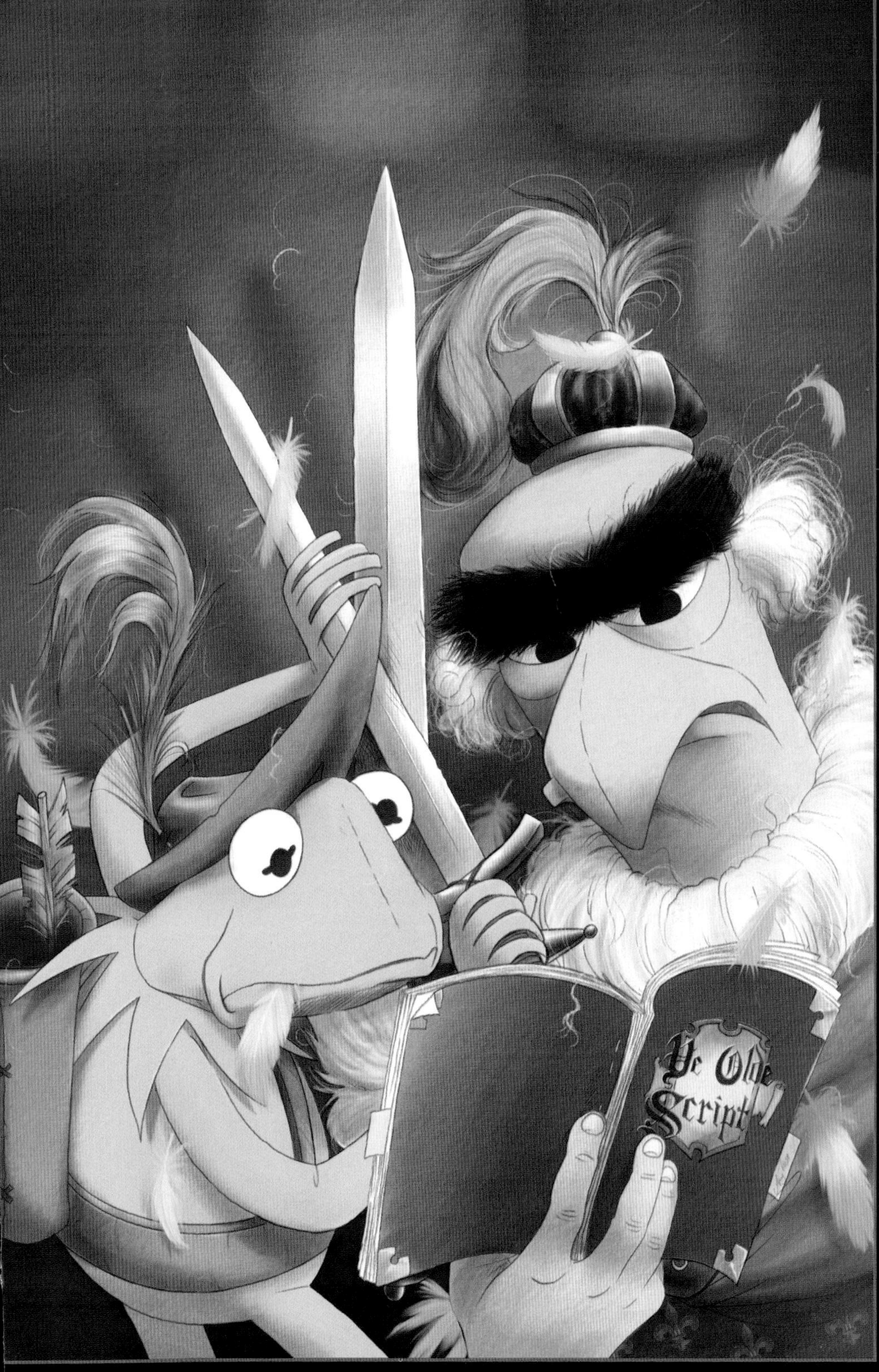
Ye Olde Script

COVER 4B: AMY MEBBERSON

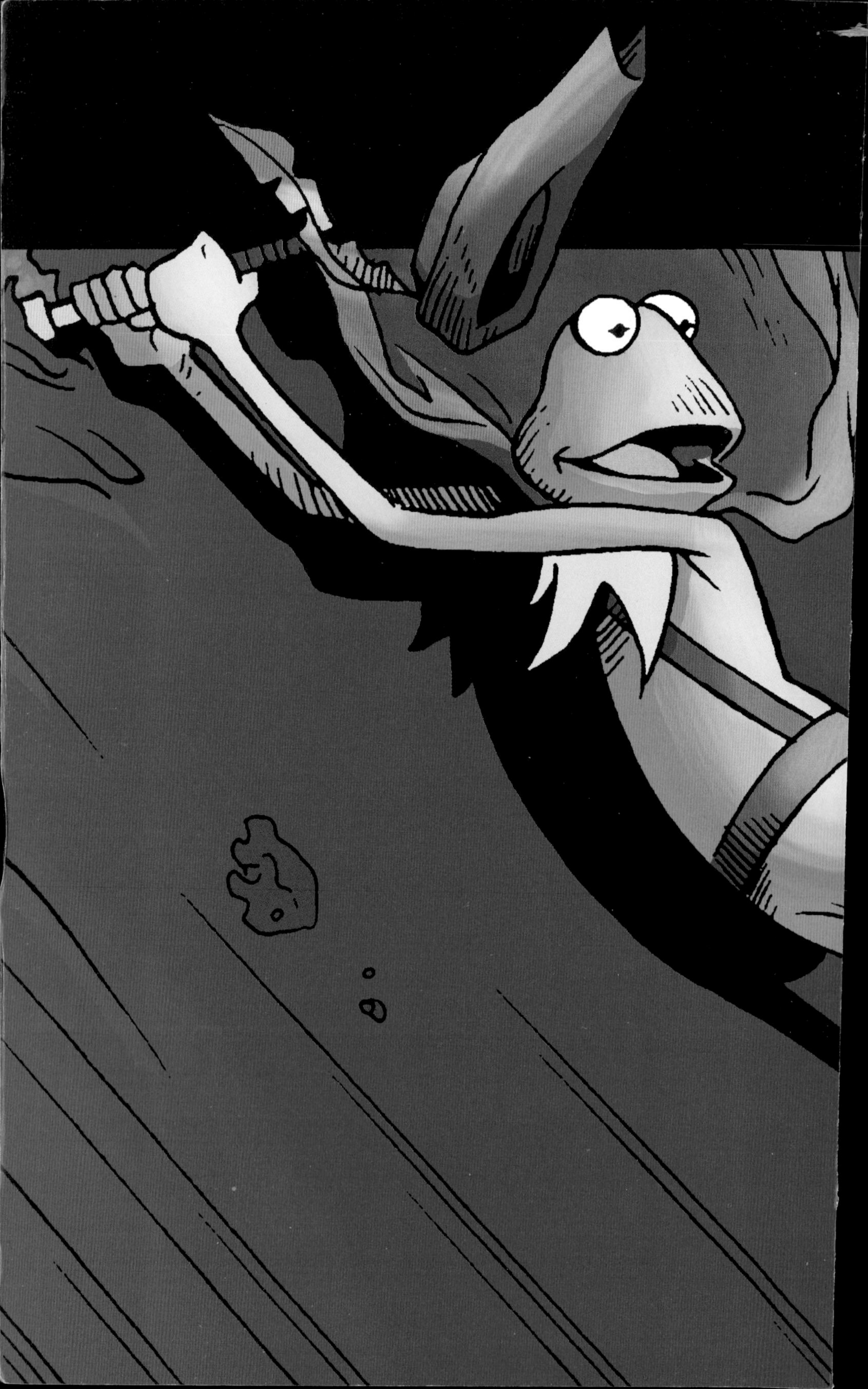